4-23-15

PRAISE FOR THE PRISCILLA HUTCHINS NOVELS BY JACK McDEVITT

STARHAWK

"Takes off like a shot . . . I was literally unable to put the book down . . . A fascinating story with exceptionally well-written characters and extremely believable world-building." —*Not Yet Read*

"All of the things one has come to expect from one of Jack Mc-Devitt's novels . . . Plenty of cool ideas." —*SF Site*

CAULDRON

One of *Library Journal*'s Best Books of 2007

"A superb writer . . . A more thoughtful book that gives readers a lot to ponder." —*The Florida Times-Union*

ODYSSEY

A *Kansas City Star* Noteworthy Book for 2006
One of *Library Journal*'s Best Books of 2006

"McDevitt's work is highly reminiscent of the best of Clarke, framed by what we've learned about the universe since then." —*SFRevu*

OMEGA

Winner of the John W. Campbell Award
A *Locus* Best Science Fiction Novel for 2003

"A satisfying answer to the mystery of the omegas that is appropriately cosmic without straining credulity." —*The New York Times Book Review*

continued . . .

CHINDI

TIME TRAVELERS NEVER DIE

Hugo and Nebula Award Nominee

"An entertaining romp through past and future, ringing in new changes in the genre . . . A good, fast read that leaves you thinking."
—Joe Haldeman, Hugo Award–winning author of *Work Done for Hire*

"[A] witty, charming, yearning novel that puts a new twist on time travel . . . A first-rate work by one of the true masters of the genre. Enjoy!"
—Robert J. Sawyer, Hugo Award–winning author of *Red Planet Blues*

"Believable and realistic . . . A powerful story full of mystery, romance, and surprises."
—Ben Bova, Hugo Award–winning author of *New Frontiers*

THE DEVIL'S EYE

"As usual with McDevitt, I recommend this one highly." —*Analog*

"A fast-paced novel . . . A book that has more ghost hunters than an Indiana Jones adventure, with twists that reveal secret after secret."
—*The Florida Times-Union*

SEEKER

Winner of the Nebula Award
A *Kansas City Star* Noteworthy Book for 2005
A *Locus* Recommended Book for 2005

"Ideas abound in McDevitt's classy riff on the familiar lost-colony theme. The novel delivers everything it promises with a gigantic wallop." —*Publishers Weekly* (starred review)

POLARIS

"An exemplary merger of mystery and science fiction . . . An intelligent, provocative entertainment by a man who brings energy, style, and a fresh perspective to everything he writes."
—*The Washington Post Book World*

STARHAWK

JACK McDEVITT

ACE BOOKS, NEW YORK

THE BERKLEY PUBLISHING GROUP
Published by the Penguin Group
Penguin Group (USA) LLC
375 Hudson Street, New York, New York 10014

USA • Canada • UK • Ireland • Australia • New Zealand • India • South Africa • China

penguin.com

A Penguin Random House Company

STARHAWK

An Ace Book / published by arrangement with Cryptic, Inc.

Ace Books are published by The Berkley Publishing Group.
ACE and the "A" design are trademarks of Penguin Group (USA) LLC.

For information, address: The Berkley Publishing Group,
a division of Penguin Group (USA) LLC,
375 Hudson Street, New York, New York 10014.

ISBN: 978-0-425-26086-9

PUBLISHING HISTORY
Ace hardcover edition / November 2013
Ace mass-market edition / November 2014

PRINTED IN THE UNITED STATES OF AMERICA

10 9 8 7 6 5 4 3 2 1

Cover art by Tony Mauro.
Cover design by Rita Frangie.

Chapter 1 was originally published in a slightly different version as the short story
"Waiting at the Altar" in *Asimov's Science Fiction*, June 2012.

*For Joyce Barrett
and the Freedom Riders*

Acknowledgments

Thanks to Les Johnson of NASA, to Rania Habib at Syracuse University, to David DeGraff of Alfred University, and to Walter Cuirle. Also my special appreciation to Frank Manning, formerly of NASA, and my son Christopher McDevitt for advice and technical assistance. Any blunders are on my plate. I'm also indebted to Ginjer Buchanan, my editor, and to Sara and Bob Schwager for their contributions. To my agent, Chris Lotts. And as always to my wife, Maureen, who continues to serve as in-house editor and general inspiration.

Prologue

Union Space Station ("The Wheel")
Wednesday, June 17, 2195

PRISCILLA WAS SITTING in the Skyview, enjoying a grilled cheese, her notebook propped up on the table. But she wasn't reading. The room-length portal had, as usual, stolen her attention. She was looking down at the Asian coast. Clusters of lights, like distant stars, sparkled in the night. Shanghai was down there somewhere, and Singapore and Calcutta.

"It's beautiful, isn't it?" said a familiar voice. She looked up. Leon Carlson, one of the engineers, was smiling at her. "Mind if I join you?"

"Sure." She glanced at the chair on the opposite side of the table, moved her notebook out of his way, and he sat down. "It's good to see you again, Leon."

The smile widened. "And you, Priscilla. How's the training going? You do your qualification flight yet?"

"No, I'm still a few months away."

"You must be looking forward to it."

"More or less. Actually, it's a little unnerving."

"You'll do fine." He glanced out at the lights. "I've never been able to get used to it."

"Me neither." He was tall and blond with blue eyes. And he looked pretty good. She took another bite out of her sandwich while he ordered. "How long have you been up here, Leon?" she asked.

"Two years. I'm getting near the end of my assignment. They'll be sending me back down to Toronto in a few weeks."

She was sorry to hear it. "That's home?"

"Yes. I—" His eyes locked on something behind her. He frowned, and a shadow crossed his face.

"Anything wrong?"

He shook his head. "No."

She looked around. Three people were being seated at a table. A trim, formal-looking woman, and two guys, one middle-aged and overweight, the other tall, gray, and bent, with a neatly trimmed beard.

"Who are they?" she asked, keeping her voice down.

He hesitated. "The guy with the beard is one of those Kosmik yo-yos. He's going out to Selika to help with killing everything off."

"Oh." She turned back to him. "You mean the terraforming operation."

"That's what I'm talking about. I was working on the *Sydney Thompson* yesterday. Getting it ready for the flight. There are seven of them going. I assume the other two are also part of the operation."

"I get the impression you don't approve of what they're doing."

"Priscilla, when they're finished turning the atmosphere over, they'll have killed everything on the planet." His voice was getting loud. "They talk about creating a special place for *us*, but they're taking down an entire *world* to do it."

Priscilla didn't like the idea very much either. But the experts were saying that Selika would be an ideal place for a colony. For a second Earth. The world was still undergoing severe problems with climate, global population was pushing its limits, and fanatics with bioweapons continued to leave a lot of people with a desire to retreat to somewhere else. Kosmik was denying the charges, insisting that the kill-off simply wasn't happening, but adding that even if it was, it would be a price well worth paying for a backup world.

A staring contest developed between Leon and the two men. "But that's okay," Leon said, getting still louder. "As long as *we* have a place to hang out. That's all that matters, right? If we have to butcher a lot of stuff, well, those things happen—"

She heard a chair move. (The chairs, of course were magnetized, to prevent their floating off the deck.) The fat guy had stood up. He was holding on to the table, but his eyes had narrowed, and he was showing teeth. He was bigger than she'd realized. A linebacker type.

"Don't," she told Leon, who was also getting to his feet. "Sit down."

He ignored her. "You got a problem?" he asked the fat man.

The restaurant was about half-full, but they had everyone's attention. The host was watching them nervously.

"You idiot," said the fat man. "Years from now, people will be thanking us for what we're doing." He was standing his ground, challenging Leon to act. Or sit back down.

Priscilla got up. Her inclination was to put both hands on Leon's chest to restrain him, but she'd have had to let go of the table to do that, not a good tactic in a near-zero-gee environment. "Please stop," she said, speaking to both.

The host hurried over and assured everyone, including the two potential combatants, that everything was all right and he hoped it wouldn't be necessary to call security.

Leon and the fat man continued to glare. The woman at the other table said something, and the man with the gray beard reached over, grabbed the fat man's sleeve, and tugged him back into his seat. Some of the tension dissipated, and Leon also dropped back into his chair.

"The problem," Leon said to her, still making no effort to keep his voice down, "is that people don't know what's going on." He reached for her notebook. "May I borrow this?"

"Sure," she said. "But go easy, okay?"

He brought up a forest scene. Trees were shrunken and desiccated. "This is Selika," he said. And they weren't really trees. Never had been. Not in the way Priscilla thought of trees. They were rather, or had been, an odd combination of animal and vegetable, large animated plants that had spread their leafy tendrils toward the sun when they were not swaying gently in the shifting winds. They weren't beautiful in the manner of a pine or a eucalyptus. They were a bit too unsettling for that. In fact, although she didn't like to admit it even to herself, they made her hair stand on end.

"They're not dangerous," Leon said. "There aren't any flytraps on Selika. Or pitcher plants or anything like that. As far as we know, there's no carnivorous vegetation of any kind."

"I'm glad to hear it," she said. But they were spooky all the same. She'd seen them before, of course. As virtuals. Their sheer animation was enough to rattle her.

"You should see Selika from orbit," Leon continued. "The vegetation has all turned gray. It used to be a lush, green place. Now what they have would make you sick. The skies, when we first went there, were filled with bags and birds and capos. They're now almost empty. Like the forest."

She heard a struggle beginning behind her. And a woman's frustrated voice: "For God's sake, Bernie, *sit*."

Then a male: "Let's just get out of here." Priscilla resisted the impulse to turn around.

Leon, of course, was watching them. "They're leaving," he said.

But there was a final round: The fat man, *Bernie*, took a step in their direction. "How the hell do *you* know anything, moron?" he said. "You ever been there? Or do you just watch HV?"

Leon stayed in his seat this time. "I've been there," he said. "I built your operational center. Which I will regret for the rest of my life."

Bernie's companions marched him away and left the host looking both annoyed and relieved. As they went out the door, two guys arrived and began talking with one of the waiters. Presumably security.

The host joined the conference, but they took it outside.

"You know," said Leon, "there were warnings. Kosmik knew in advance this would probably happen. There are several people doing research on an alternate method. But the corporates don't want to wait."

Priscilla nodded. "Too much money involved, I guess."

"Yeah. We wouldn't want Kosmik to lose its investment."

"So why *is* it happening? What's killing everything, do you know?"

"I'm not an expert, Priscilla. But, as I understand it, if you screw around with the atmosphere, change the oxygen-nitrogen balance even a little, you can expect consequences. They hired a lot of experts to explain how there'd be no problem, that the life-forms would be just fine." He couldn't restrain the bitterness. "And I helped them."

"What about the colonists? I wouldn't think they'll want to live in a place where everything's gone."

"Hell," he said, "they probably wouldn't have liked the native life anyhow. They'll bring their own German shepherds and house cats and oak trees and sycamores and hedges and never know the difference."

PRISCILLA'S JOURNAL

I couldn't help thinking about all those old science-fiction stories from the early years of the space age. There were always aliens showing up who wanted to kill everybody and take over the world. Turns out maybe, *we* are the aliens.

—June 17, 2195

Chapter 1

THE *COPPERHEAD* WAS floating through the fogs of transdimensional space, somewhere between Fomalhaut and Serenity
Station, which is to say it was well off the more traveled routes.
Priscilla Hutchins, the acting captain, was half-asleep in the
pilot's seat. The actual senior officer, Jake Loomis, had gone
back to the passenger cabin, where he might have drifted off, or
was maybe playing chess with Benny, the AI. Soft music drifted
through the ship. The Three Kings doing "Heartbreak."

Priscilla was vaguely aware of the humming and beeping
of the electronics and the quiet flow of air through the vents.
Then, suddenly, she wasn't. The lights had gone out. And the
ship bounced hard, as if it had been dropped into a storm-
tossed sea. The displays were off, and the warning klaxon
sounded. Power down.

"System failure," said Benny, using the slightly modified
tone that suggested he'd also suffered a cutback.

Emergency lights blinked on and cast an eerie glow across
the bridge. The ship rocked and slowed and accelerated and
rocked again. Then, within seconds, all sense of motion stopped.
"Did we jump back out, Benny?" she asked.

"Affirmative."

Jake's voice came loud and subtly amused from the cabin: "Priscilla, what happened?"

She knew exactly what had happened. This was one more test on her qualification flight. There was no danger to the *Copperhead*. Nobody was at risk other than herself.

"Engines have shut down," said Benny.

"Engines off," she told Jake. "Power outage."

The navigational display flickered back to life, and the stars blinked on. She couldn't see anything through the ports, of course. They were all blocked by the heavy shielding that protected the *Copperhead* against radiation. They'd used it for Priscilla's certification flight because the mission had included a visit to Palomus, which was located in the Wolf 359 system. Wolf 359 was a flare star. The shielding covered every piece of Plexiglas in the ship. The lander was also shielded.

Jake appeared at the hatch. "You okay, Priscilla?"

"I'm fine." The misty transdimensional universe that provided shortcuts across the cosmos had vanished, replaced by the vast sweep of the Milky Way. "We're back outside." That would have been automatic. During a power failure, the drive unit was designed to return the vehicle to normal space. Otherwise, the ship risked being lost forever, with no chance of rescue. "Benny, is there an imminent threat?"

"Negative, Priscilla. Ship is secure."

"Very good." She turned to Jake, who was buckling down beside her. He was middle-aged, low-key, competent. His voice never showed emotion. Forbearance sometimes. Tolerance. But that was all. "You want me to send out a distress call?"

"Where would you send it, Priscilla?"

"Serenity is closest." It would, of course, be a hyperspace transmission. The station would know within a few hours that they were in trouble.

"Good. No. Don't send. Let's assume you've done that. What's next?"

THERE WASN'T ACTUALLY that much else to do. She asked Benny for details on the damage and was told where the problems lay and what needed to be done before restarting the engines. The electronics had gone out because the main feeding line had ruptured. She went down into the cargo hold, opened the access hatch, and explained to Jake how she would have managed the repairs. He asked a few questions, seemed satisfied with her replies, and they started back topside.

They were just emerging from the connecting shaft when Benny came back on the circuit. "Priscilla, we're receiving a radio signal. Artificial."

She looked at Jake. And smiled.

"No," he said. "It's not part of the exercise."

That was hard to believe. But even though the ground rules allowed him to make stuff up, he was not permitted to lie about whether a given occurrence was a drill. "What's it say, Benny?"

"I have not been able to make a determination. The signal, I suspect, is greatly weakened."

It made no sense. There wouldn't be anybody out here. They were light-years from everything.

While she hesitated, Jake took over. "Benny, can you get a fix on it?"

"Within limits, yes."

"Where's it coming from?"

"The nearest star in that direction, Captain, is Capua. But Capua is more than two hundred light-years away. It certainly did not originate there. Moreover, I believe the transmission is a broadcast signal. Not directional."

"Okay," said Jake. "What do you make of it, Priscilla?"

"No way an artificial radio signal's going to travel two hundred light-years. Especially a broadcast."

"Therefore—?"

"It's a distress call. Somebody actually did what we've been rehearsing. Broke down and got thrown out into normal space."

"So what do we do?"

"If the signal's so deteriorated that we can't read it—"

"—Yes?—"

"They've been out here awhile and are probably beyond help."

"Very good, Priscilla. Shall we make that assumption?"

She straightened her shoulders. "No, sir."

"So what do you suggest?"

"Benny," said Priscilla, "is the signal still coming in?"

"Yes, it is."

"Any chance if we sit tight you'd be able to get a clear enough reading to tell us what it says?"

"Negative."

Jake looked at her. "What do we do?"

"Find the source."

TO DO THAT, they had to move. Get another angle. "Benny," she said, "start engines. Prep for a jump. We want a seventy-degree angle on the transmission. Set for eighty million kilometers."

"Starting engines, Priscilla."

The drive unit would require about forty minutes before they could actually do the transdimensional insertion. So she sat back to wait. "You ever run into anything like this before?" she asked Jake.

"Once," he said. "But it was an automated vehicle. No life-and-death issue. I've never seen one where there were actually people involved. I hope that's not the case here."

She brought up the signal. They could hear nothing but static. The routine racket produced by stars. With 1 or 2 percent left over from the Big Bang. That always blew her mind. "I wouldn't want to get stuck out here," she said.

"No, Priscilla, me neither."

There had been a few ships that had vanished over the years. Vehicles that simply went out somewhere and were never heard from again. It was, she supposed, inevitable. If you were going to travel to seriously remote places, you took your chances.

JUMP TECHNOLOGY WAS notoriously inexact. They jumped three more times to get readings on the signals.

Benny put a chart on the navigation display. He marked their initial position and drew a line from it indicating the direction from which the transmission had come. He showed their current location.

Jake brought some coffee back from the dispenser. "You want some?" he asked.

"No, thanks."

"Sorry it's taking so long," said Benny. "It's difficult to sort everything."

"It's okay, Benny. No hurry."

"I think we have it now."

Priscilla kept her eyes on the screen. They were able to establish the course and velocity of the radio source during a period of about six weeks during which it had been actively transmitting signals. After that, there was nothing. The system had shut down.

"Range," said Benny, "is slightly more than nine light-years. Continue the vector for the balance of the nine years, and the source should presently be—"

He showed them.

"MAYBE SOMEBODY GOT to them," said Jake. "Let's hope."

"So what do we do?"

"You're the captain, Priscilla. Call it."

She wondered momentarily if, despite Jake's denial, the signal was a plant. Part of the exercise. Maybe they were testing her judgment. "Benny," she said, "do we have a record of any lost ships nine years ago?"

"The *Forscher*," he said. "It was last reported at Talios in the spring of '86. Carrying an exobiologist and an actor. Started home and was never heard from again."

An actor? Priscilla's heart rate began to pick up. "Jake, that would be Dave Simmons." The ultimate action-hero vid star turned explorer. Simmons had turned out to be even bigger than the characters he portrayed. He'd financed scientific missions, founded schools in remote places, once famously challenged the African dictator Kali Anka to have it out man-to-man. Anka had declined and been driven from the country a year later.

"The exobiologist was Paul Trelawney," said Benny. Trelawney had won the Cassimir Award the year before. "And, of course, there would also have been a pilot."

The ship had sent a movement report when it left Talios. A

long search had yielded nothing. "Why would they send a radio transmission?" she asked, before answering her own question: "The hypercomm must have gone down."

Jake nodded.

It was hard to imagine the tall, lantern-jawed Simmons dead. The guy had been the epitome of the leading man, in charge, indestructible, always one step ahead of events. One entertainment commentator had remarked that his loss had "reminded us all of our mortality."

"So what are we going to do?" she asked.

"Make the call, Priscilla."

"Okay. We make a report, and then head for Caliban, right? We can't do anything for the *Forscher*, so we just give the Wheel what we have and continue the mission."

He nodded. "That's by the book."

She read disapproval in his eyes. Maybe another test of her judgment. "Jake, there's no possibility here of anyone's life being endangered. So we report what we've found and get back to what we're supposed to be doing."

"On the other hand—" he said.

"On the other hand, what?"

"We're close. And our mission isn't under time constraints. We can go have a look and send back additional details."

"Do we really want to do that?" Priscilla was thinking about the shape the *Forscher*'s captain and passengers would be in after nine years.

He straightened and looked down at her. "There's a code, Priscilla. We owe it to them."

"Okay."

"We don't leave people adrift out here if we can help it. It doesn't matter what the book says. We go over to the *Forscher* and take a look at the situation."

WHEN THEY ARRIVED in the vicinity of the radio source, they did not find the ship. What they saw instead was a lander. It was a Voltar II, a later model of which rested inside the *Copperhead*'s own launch bay. "I wonder what happened?" asked Priscilla.

Jake shrugged and looked at the scattered stars on the display. "It explains why they used a radio."

"They had to abandon ship." The lander didn't have a hypercomm.

It looked undamaged. Its registry number, VC112, brightened when the *Copperhead*'s navigation lights fell on it. Its ports were dark although there was still enough power to cause a flicker in the fore and aft warning lamps as they drew near. Priscilla turned her forward lights on the vehicle.

The pilot's seat was occupied.

Jake climbed out of his harness and opened the storage bin. He took out a set of air tanks, the Flickinger gear, and a jet pack. Then he looked at her.

She had an obligation to go with him. It shouldn't have been a problem. She'd done EVAs in training. But she wasn't excited about what they were going to find in the shuttle's cabin. "I'm coming," she said.

FLICKINGER FIELDS HAD long since replaced the cumbersome pressure suits. The generator provided an electronic shield against the vacuum. A passerby, had there been one, would have seen nothing like the astronauts of an earlier era. Rather, there were only two people wearing blue-and-silver uniforms.

They crossed to the shuttle and looked in through the ports. Only one body was visible. It was in the pilot's seat. It appeared in much better condition than Priscilla would have expected after nine years. "The environment," Jake explained. "In a case like this, you don't get all the microbes and whatever else is involved in decomposition. A corpse is more likely to look a bit mummified."

He opened the hatch, climbed into the air lock, and made room for her. She squeezed in beside him. She noticed he'd brought a laser. "Just in case," he said. "You're going aboard a vehicle that has very little power. You wouldn't want to get trapped in the air lock." He touched the control pad, and the outer hatch closed. Next, it should have begun to fill with air. But nothing happened.

"See what I mean?" He used the laser to cut a hole in the inner hatch. There was air pressure inside, and it quickly equalized. Then the hatch opened, and they floated into the cabin.

They turned on their wrist lamps. Jake went up front. Priscilla sniffed the air, told herself it was no problem, and joined him. She recognized the body immediately.

"Simmons," they said simultaneously.

Priscilla stared. Somehow, even now, he was sprawled beneath the restraints in that easy charge-the-hill manner she knew so well. *Good-bye, Dave,* she thought. Growing up, she'd loved the guy. "What do you think happened?"

"We'll have to wait for somebody to find the *Forscher* to be sure," he said. "But whatever the breakdown was, it probably killed Kobayashi and Trelawney." Fudoki Kobayashi had been the pilot. Jake shook his head. "Poor son of a bitch. Die out here, like this."

"I'm surprised he didn't end it," said Priscilla. "He could have walked out of the air lock."

"I suspect he kept hoping somebody would come. He'd sent out a distress call."

"I guess so, Jake. But he must have known nobody would hear it for a long time."

"Maybe. But he was an actor. Maybe he didn't really understand how big it is out here. He got here in a few days. When that happens, you kind of lose the feel for the size of everything. Or maybe he didn't know it wasn't a hypercomm. Whatever it was, it doesn't matter now."

Maybe, she thought, he just wasn't inclined to give up.

SOMETHING HAD BECOME stuck to one of the storage cabinets in the rear of the vehicle. It looked like a notebook. Priscilla removed it, opened it, touched the keypad. Nothing happened. "I think it needs charging."

"We'll take it back with us."

"What do we do about Simmons?"

"We'll put him in the deep freeze." He released the restraints and took a last look around. Pulled the body free, which was of course easy in the zero gravity. "Nothing more for us to do here. Let's go home."

They crossed back to the *Copperhead*, and Priscilla called in the report. Then she connected the notebook to a power source. And began paging through.

"What's it say?" asked Jake.

She frowned at it, scrolled through to the last entries: *Whoever reads this: Get to Talios III by the last week of November.*

And, the last line: *Guess we bombed.*

Jake leaned down, closer to the screen. "I guess they did."

"*Get to Talios by November?* You think they were running an experiment of some kind?"

"Whatever," said Jake. "It's irrelevant now. That would be November nine years ago."

"BENNY, SHOW US anything that deals with what happened to the ship."

He put it on-screen. Simmons described the moment: He had been enjoying a quiet hour, reading the comic novel *Last Man Out*, which was not at all the kind of book she'd have expected. The voices of Trelawney and Kobayashi were just barely audible on the bridge. Then, in Simmons's words, *Everything came apart*. There was a loud bang, screams, and darkness.

"Probably a power surge," Jake said. "It would have knocked everything off-line. Including the AI."

When Simmons got to Trelawney and Kobayashi, they were both dead on the bridge. Electrocuted. The backup lights had come on, and, of course, life support had been maintained. But other than that—

The hypercomm system either didn't come back online, or Simmons didn't know how to operate it manually. Normally, all that's necessary is to give an instruction to the AI, but the AI was down also. Simmons decided his best chance was to use the shuttle radio, send out a distress call in case anybody was nearby, then come back and try to figure out how to work the hypercomm. But he thought the hull would reduce significantly the strength of the radio signal. So he got into the shuttle and launched.

As if things could not have gotten worse, the launch doors closed behind him and wouldn't reopen.

It was hopeless. The last pages were filled with messages left for his two ex-wives, for his kids, and for friends and colleagues. There was no sign of self-pity. Frustration, yes. But if he was frightened, he didn't leave any of it on the record. Incredibly, he remained the action hero so many had come to admire. Except this time, it didn't end happily.

Get to Talios by the last week of November.

Guess we bombed.

Benny broke into her thoughts: "I think," he said, "I've discovered what he's referring to. About November."

"And what's that?" she asked.

"In the Talios system, they encountered an interstellar vehicle."

"Too bad it wasn't around when they broke down," said Jake.

"You misunderstand me, Captain. It doesn't seem to have been one of ours."

JAKE AND PRISCILLA sat frozen while Benny explained. "They were on the surface, doing fieldwork, when their AI alerted them that they weren't alone. She told them there was a spacecraft in the area that did not fit any known configuration. And that it was approaching."

"My God," said Jake.

"Do you want me to put the pertinent sections on-screen?"

The vehicle had been considerably larger than the *Forscher*. It was enormous. Probably three kilometers long, its hull black and smooth. They could see illuminated ports, including an area that had to be the bridge. *We ran for the shuttle,* Simmons wrote. *Ten minutes after we got back inside the ship, they were on the radio. Strange-sounding voices. Not human. Nothing like us. But we responded. We said hello, and I'll admit I used the friendliest tone I could come up with. They answered. One of them did. Don't know what it said. Though it wasn't hard to guess.*

"You know," said Jake, "there should be a complete record of this on the *Forscher*. Pictures, the radio transmissions, everything. We're going to have to find the ship."

"That won't be easy out here," said Priscilla.

She kept her eyes on the screen: During the course of the first day, the AIs learned to communicate with each other. Greetings back and forth. The alien vessel was an explorer from a distant place. Trelawney, apparently beside himself with exhilaration, pointed out that *Forscher* also meant "explorer."

They got a quick reply: "There is little to do out here other than explore."

The aliens had a sense of humor. And another question: "Would you allow us to visit your home world?"

Nobody on board the *Forscher* thought that would be a good idea. There was no way to know the intentions of the visitors. *Above our grade level,* Simmons commented. They didn't dare reveal Earth's location.

The visitors replied: *We understand.*

When Trelawney asked where they were from, they also showed reluctance, and would say only that they'd crossed the galaxy. *We have come a great distance.*

And the biologist gave the same response. *We understand.*

They talked for several days. Simmons and Trelawney both visited the alien vehicle. Apparently, Kobayashi passed on the opportunity. Several of the aliens came aboard the *Forscher,* after the pilot had arranged a trigger that would overload and blow the drive unit—which was to say everything—if a problem developed. "He doesn't say what they looked like," said Priscilla.

Jake shrugged. "The AI probably has all kinds of pictures. I wonder," he continued, "if that's what created the problem going home? Rigging the ship to explode, just in case? When he disconnected, Kobayashi may have overlooked something."

"Could you do that to us?" asked Priscilla. "Rig us to explode?"

"It wouldn't be that hard."

After a week, it ended. The aliens were moving on. *But,* said Trelawney, *we should arrange to meet again. Maybe, given some time, we can get permission to invite you to come to the home system. Though, to be honest, I think that may be unlikely. I suspect there would be political problems. But we have people who would very much want to meet you. It would be a start.*

Simmons quoted one of the aliens: *We would like that.*

But how to do it?

Kobayashi pointed out that two of the planets in the Talios

system, the fifth and sixth, would line up in the "near future." *When they do,* he suggested, *perhaps we could arrange to be here with those who would like to take this farther.*

JAKE WAS GETTING frustrated. "Damn it," he said. "Are they talking about a few weeks or what?"

"Apparently the *Forscher* never reported the incident. Or if they did, it was kept quiet. "

Benny broke in: "Simmons says that they decided to say nothing until they got home. They had time to do that and come back, though he does not say how much time. But he and Trelawney agreed that a hypercomm report would only generate a rejection. That the politicians would want to keep clear of a meeting. Trelawney wanted to be there to fight for the meeting."

"Well," said Priscilla, "it doesn't matter now. It's nine years ago. The aliens are long gone. And everybody's dead on this side."

Jake looked up from the screen. "So what do we do, Captain Hutchins?"

"File a report, hope they can find the *Forscher*, and get on with our own mission."

"You're not interested in going the rest of the way out to Talios?"

"Is that what you're proposing?"

"Why not?"

"Jake." She felt uncomfortable. Priscilla was used to running her life on schedules. "It'll throw us way behind."

"Sure it will. Think anybody will notice?"

TALIOS WAS A class G dwarf, about the same size as Sol, but younger by two billion years. According to the data charts, there were eleven planets in the system. Talios III had life-forms. And that was pretty much the extent of the available information.

Talios V and VI were where?

They needed several more days to track them down. Talios V was small and airless, eight hundred million kilometers from the sun, completing an orbit every twelve years. VI was a gas giant with an entourage of forty-some moons and a magnificent set of rings. It was just over twice as far out. "Orbital period thirty-one years," said Benny. "They were lined up three and a half years ago."

"So we're a little late for the wedding," said Priscilla.

Jake's eyes closed. "Unfortunately, the groom never showed up at all."

"Benny, when will V and VI line up again?" asked Priscilla. "Not that it matters."

"Sixty-five years and a couple of months."

"It's a pity," said Jake.

"You didn't expect them to wait around, did you?"

"I wasn't sure I wanted them to wait around." It was the first time she'd seen him look uncertain. "Still— Well, let's go take a look at Talios III."

THE PLANET FLOATED serenely on the navigation display, but it was hard to believe it harbored life. It did have large blue oceans. White clouds drifted through the skies, and there was snow at the poles. But the continents, the landmasses, looked utterly desolate. No fleck of green appeared anywhere. Nothing moved across its bleak, flat plains.

"According to the database," said Benny, "life got started here less than five hundred million years ago."

"So it's still in the oceans," said Jake.

"That may be correct, Captain. In any case, you would not be able to detect its presence."

"Too small?"

"Unicellular. It will be a long time before there's anything down there that would be visible to the naked eye."

"I wonder if they'll ever figure out," said Priscilla, "why life is so rare."

Jake magnified the images. Large brown patches of land. River valleys. Mountain chains cutting across continents. All empty. "Hard to believe. What've we looked at now, hundreds of worlds with liquid water and stable suns? And just a handful are alive."

"A century ago," said Priscilla, "they thought that almost

any biozone world was likely to produce living things." She was thinking that this was why the meeting at this world had been so important. With life so rare, and advanced civilizations virtually nonexistent—Damn.

So close.

THERE WAS NOTHING to look at. From Priscilla's perspective, they'd wasted time coming here. But she wasn't going to argue the point with the guy who held her license in his hand. "Jake," she said, "do you want to go into orbit?"

"Yes," he said.

"How long do we plan to stay?"

"Not long."

"Okay. What's next?"

"Use your imagination, Priscilla."

She laughed and raised her hands in confusion. "I'm not sure what you're asking me to do, Jake."

"Think about the situation. Look at it from the perspective of the aliens."

She wanted to point out that aliens would probably not think like people. But she let it go. "How do you mean?"

"If you were in their place, and you'd come back here for a rendezvous with representatives from another technological species, something everybody knows is very rare, you'd expect them to show up, right?"

"Yes. Probably."

"What would you do if they didn't?"

She was thinking of the jilted bride. "They'd never see me again."

He laughed. "Assume for a minute you're rational."

"I'm fairly rational."

"All right, then. Let's say unemotional. The failure to show up could not have been personal. Maybe the other side is afraid. Or maybe something happened to delay them. What do you do?"

She exhaled. "I'd leave a note."

"Now answer your own question: What next?"

"Benny," she said. "Commence search for artificial satellite."

"Excellent." Jake looked pleased. "You're going to be good at this yet, Priscilla."

THE SATELLITE FOUND *them.* "Greetings," it said. "We are sorry we missed you."

Jake took over. "We are, too."

"We hope there was no difficulty."

"The people you talked to were lost in an accident. On the way home."

"That saddens us. Please accept our—" It used an unfamiliar word.

"Thank you," said Jake.

"We wish we could do more."

"Are you perhaps still in the area? Is another meeting possible?"

"Unfortunately, not at this time. We are long gone, and will probably not return in the near future."

"I'm sorry to hear it."

"We also have regrets. We waited as long as we could. But there were limitations."

"I understand. Perhaps, one day we will meet again."

"I'm sure we will. Meantime, know that you have new friends. Farewell."

They waited a few moments. Priscilla looked at the planetary images, at the clouds, at the oceans. Listened to the silence. "Do we want to take the satellite on board?"

"No." He shook his head. "Leave it where it is. Take it home, and they'll just put it in the Smithsonian. This is where it belongs." He pointed at the control panel. "Meanwhile, Captain Hutchins, you have a report to file. And some deliveries to make."

"Jake," she said, "Simmons was wrong. He didn't bomb. He went outside in the shuttle. That made all the difference."

"I know."

"I wish he'd known—"

Chapter 2

"PRISCILLA," SAID JAKE, "let's talk about our next assignment. We'll be heading for Groombridge."

Good, she thought. The last stop before they started home. She wondered what the problem, or problems, would be this time. Fuel leak, maybe? Avoiding collision with an asteroid? She was, of course, not informed in advance.

"We can get rolling when you're ready," he said. "Something you might want to think about—"

"Yes?"

"How you would handle a runaway engine? I'm giving you fair warning because—"

It was as far as he got before Benny broke in: "Captain Hutchins, we have an emergency message from Union." He put it on-screen.

> *Copperhead*, we have been warned that there may be an explosive device aboard the *Gremlin*, which is currently en route to Barton's World at Lalande 21185. We do not have confirmation about the bomb. Nevertheless, until we can be certain, we will assume the threat is real. Proceed immediately to

Lalande 21185 and render assistance. Acknowledge.

Priscilla glanced at Jake, who nodded. "Okay, Benny," she
said, "set course. Let's move. Acknowledge and let them
know we're on our way."

"Acknowledging message, Priscilla."

She checked the numbers. Just getting to the system would
require thirty hours. The transmission was already four days
old. "Not good," she said. "How do we help? You know anything about bombs?"

"I think we'll settle for an evacuation. Get everybody away
from the ship and let the experts deal with it. If it hasn't gone
off already."

Priscilla was shaking her head. "What kind of lunatic
would put a bomb on an interstellar?"

Jake sighed. "They've been getting threats for a while
now."

"You mean because of the terraforming?"

"A lot of people are outraged about Selika."

She took a deep breath. "Incredible. Well, whatever the
bosses are thinking, this isn't the best way to respond. They
had to know we wouldn't receive the transmission within a
reasonable time frame. Why didn't they send somebody from
the station?"

"They probably would have," said Jake, "if they'd had
anyone available."

JAKE LISTENED AS they increased power flow to the engines.
"Adjusting course," said Benny. The *Copperhead* swung
slowly toward Lalande and began to accelerate. He put a
graphic of the system on the auxiliary display. He hadn't been
there for several years. Lalande was a red dwarf, about half as
massive as Sol, with six known planets. Barton's was the
second, a living world orbiting at a range of one hundred million kilometers.

Barton's had an ordinary moon, sterile, airless, cold. There
was, however, a second satellite that was not a natural object

at all. It was a *monument*, a four-kilometer-wide ring with a pair of crossbars. The centerpiece, the object that made the monument truly spectacular, was held in place by the crossbars. It was a massive diamond, about a third the size of the ring.

It was the second of the Grand Monuments to be discovered, an event which, twenty years earlier, had stunned the world. The first of the monuments, of course, had been found on Iapetus. Everyone had assumed that the Iapetus sculpture was unique, a solitary piece of art left thousands of years ago on a remote Saturnian moon for reasons no one could imagine. Whatever its purpose might have been, it had changed the human perspective for all time. And it had required almost a century and a half before we'd learned how wrong we'd been. Since then, twelve more of the monuments, each a unique figure, had been found.

"You think that's why the *Gremlin* was going there?" asked Priscilla. "To see the monument?"

"I can't imagine any other reason," he said.

"Have you ever seen it? The Lalande Monument?"

"A long time ago. It's spectacular." He put it on the display. The central diamond glittered in the sunlight. "They think it was made out of an asteroid."

"When I was about twelve," Priscilla said, "my class was given a virtual ride around it."

"That must have gotten everybody pretty excited."

She laughed. "I decided I wanted to go out there one day and touch it."

THEY SLIPPED INTO transdimensional space, bound for Lalande. All sense of movement stopped, and the cold gray fog enveloped them. They moved through the mist like a ship at sea. Occasionally, when he'd been alone under these conditions, Jake had turned off all the lights. The result was absolute darkness. There was no source of illumination whatever outside. Put the navigation lights on, and you were passing slowly through a constant fog whose density never varied. It was, he thought, as close as you could get to hell in the real world, a place where nothing ever changed, where nothing ever happened.

LIBRARY ENTRY

One cannot look at the images of these ancient monuments without wondering, why? They are scattered around star systems with a kind of haphazard glee, left in places where, their creators surely knew, no one was ever likely to see them. They are magnificent pieces of art, the silver pyramid orbiting a terrestrial—though lifeless—world in the Sirius system, the black cluster of crystal spheres and cones rising out of the snows at the south pole of Armis V, the great transparent Cube at Arcturus. The sculpted figure, believed to be a self-portrait, on Iapetus.

Akim Shenoba, in his prizewinning analysis, "Symbiotica," argues that mental development necessarily implies an appreciation for art, a passion for mathematics, a need to know how one came to exist. The Great Monuments, he thinks, demonstrate an angry reaction, an act of defiance, by a single species against an empty universe. He tells us that their existence implies that minds, wherever they are found, will be similar. That, in the end, there will be no true aliens.

I respectfully disagree.

I cannot imagine humans writing symphonies they suspect would never be played. Novels that would never be read. Or wandering around the Orion Arm, leaving titanic sculptures that no one would ever see.

—Soli Chung, *Lost in Time*, 2194

Chapter 3

THE RIDE TO Lalande 21185 took a long thirty hours. Priscilla got no sleep to speak of and developed a seething anger that the authorities at Union hadn't told them more. How did they know there was a bomb? How many people were on board the *Gremlin*? Had they succeeded in warning the pilot?

"Relax," Jake told her. "We can't do anything until we get there. There's a decent chance it's all a false alarm anyhow. Consider it part of the certification process. If you get your license, there'll be other emergencies. Nothing matters more than how you respond when things go wrong."

She got the message.

PRISCILLA HAD SPENT the morning reading while Jake watched a romantic comedy with himself in the starring role. Then they decided to do a virtual tour of the pyramids, which evolved into a round of the game That's My Mummy. They were near the end when Benny froze it and sounded a few notes from "Love in the Dark" to gain their attention. "Captain Hutchins," he said, "we are five minutes from transiting back into normal space."

Priscilla had cornered Jake's Egyptologist and was about to finish him off. "Give up?" she asked.

"His prospects aren't good, are they?" He shrugged, threw up his hands, and switched the system off. They started for the bridge. Tawny, a cat they'd rescued earlier in the flight, appeared from somewhere and began following her. She paused to gather her into her arms. "You guys have really bonded, haven't you?" said Jake.

"She likes to keep an eye on me."

They took their seats, Priscilla still functioning as pilot. "Two minutes," said Benny. Jake hoped they'd surface reasonably close to Barton's World.

"You ever do a rescue before, Jake?" she asked.

"Not like this. Pulled a couple of guys out of a ground station once on the Leopard Moon."

"Sirius," she said.

"Very good."

"One minute," said Benny.

The Leopard Moon had derived its name from a darkened area that, if one had an active imagination, looked like a leopard. Or maybe a tiger. Take your pick. Its picture had reminded Priscilla of the Horsehead Nebula, which she'd often seen at the Drake Institute, where her father had worked. She'd loved going into one of the observation rooms, where Daddy would switch on the stars and ask what she wanted to see. And she'd tell him and sit there in her chair, apparently afloat in the night, surrounded by the vast shining clouds, the Horsehead and the Eagle and the Flame and the Cat's Eye, all almost close enough to touch. It was where she'd fallen in love with the sky.

Tawny was wearing her magnetic booties. Priscilla put her on the deck. She'd have felt more comfortable restraining the animal during maneuvers if she could hold on to her. But it wasn't really a problem. Tawny was good at reacting to the unexpected.

"Activating," said Benny. The lights dimmed, and everything went briefly out of focus. Then the navigation display showed a starry sky. "Transition complete," Benny said.

"Okay. Scan for the *Gremlin*."

"Roger that, Captain."

"Also, see if you can locate Barton's World and put it on the display."

They were moving slightly under twenty thousand kilometers per hour, relative to the sun. That seemed to be a standard rate when a ship emerged from Barber space. It didn't matter how slowly or quickly you were moving when you jumped in; you always came out at approximately the same velocity.

Jake looked at the mike. She nodded. "Benny," he said, "let's try to talk to them. Go to broadcast mode."

"Done."

He signaled for her to take over.

"*Gremlin*," she said, "this is the *Copperhead*. Do you read?" They sat for a moment, hoping to get lucky, hoping for a quick response. But except for static, the radio remained silent.

"I have Barton's position," said Benny. "Range is a bit less than 750,000 kilometers."

"Not bad," said Jake. It was probably as close as they could have hoped for.

The seconds ticked off.

Jake was saying something about how it would help if they could make the jump system more accurate, but Priscilla was watching the time, not paying attention.

And they got a reply: "Copperhead, *this is the* Gremlin. *We are in orbit around Barton's World. Code five. Repeat, code five.*" The response had come in at forty-seven seconds.

"What's the status of the bomb?" she asked.

While they waited for the reply, Jake took a deep breath. "We got one break," he said. "That's Joshua Miller. He's the right guy to have in charge."

"Glad to hear it," said Priscilla. "Let's hope we can get him out of there." The clock counted off the seconds again. The signal crossed to the *Gremlin*, and the reply started back.

Benny broke in: "Switching to directional transmission."

"Good. Set intercept course. Let's move."

"Captain, I have Barton's World on the scopes. The signal is coming from that direction."

"Copperhead," said Miller, "*the bomb exploded thirty-two hours ago. Took out the engines. Fortunately, no casualties. But we are at Barton's World in a failing orbit. Repeat, failing orbit. Estimate twelve to thirteen hours before we go down."*

They angled to starboard, assuming a new course. "Benny," said Priscilla, "how long to get there?"

"If we had sufficient fuel to sustain acceleration and braking, we could make it in approximately six hours."

"I'm not interested in theoreticals. Give me a practical estimate. How long to get there and still have some fuel left?"

"*Twelve* hours, with prudent fuel expenditure."

"*Gremlin*," said Priscilla, "how reliable is your estimate?" She sat with her jaw propped on her fist, waiting for the response. Jake sat quietly, watching.

"*Copperhead, the estimate looks good.*"

"All right, *Gremlin*. We'll be there in ten hours."

"I was suggesting *twelve* hours," said Benny.

"Burn some fuel. Do it in ten." Jake nodded agreement. "Make it happen, Benny."

He leaned in and took the mike. "Josh," he said. "This is Loomis. How many people do you have on board?"

They waited. Then: "*Hello, Jake. Glad you're here. We have twelve total.*"

Twelve? Priscilla glanced up at the overhead air duct. No way their life support could handle that.

Jake took a deep breath. "I thought you were hauling *cargo.*"

"*That was the original plan, Jake. But we got pressed into service to run a tour.*"

"Okay, Josh. We'll see you in a bit." He stared at the display, which showed the relative positions of Barton's and the *Copperhead.* "Benny, we'll start acceleration in four minutes."

"Yes, Jake."

"Priscilla, if you need to do anything, this would be a good time."

PRISCILLA HIT THE washroom, then checked on Tawny. They'd put her in what they now referred to as her acceleration closet, where the blanket and sheets would protect her. She meowed when the door opened. Let me out.

Priscilla wanted to give her a hug but was afraid she'd get loose. "We'll do a couple of breaks along the way, Tawny," she said. "But for now, you're going to be stuck in there."

Meow.

She had a plastic bag with kernels and a slit that allowed her to get at them. Her water was in a flexible plastic bottle. With a soft nozzle. Priscilla secured an imager to the inside wall so she could keep an eye on the animal. "See you later, pal." She sighed and returned to the bridge. Jake was waiting. She slipped into her seat and told Benny to move out.

The acceleration pushed her back.

She put Tawny on the auxiliary screen. The cat was pressed against the back side of the closet. The blanket and sheets seemed to be providing sufficient cushioning. But she did not look happy.

"Incoming," said Benny. "From Union." He put it on-screen.

> *Copperhead*, we have just received a code five from the *Gremlin*. They've suffered loss of power and are currently in a failing orbit around Barton's World. We're not sure how long they can maintain orbit. Best estimate three days from this transmission. Acknowledge.

It was well over two days old.

"Josh," Jake said. "I assume another ship is coming?"

Priscilla closed her eyes and just concentrated on breathing while she waited for the answer. Benny asked if she was okay.

"Yes," she said.

Then, finally, Josh: *"Yes. The* Thompson's *en route. Coming in from Ross 128. Should be insystem in about thirty hours."*

PRISCILLA'S JOURNAL

We can't move very much. We're at 2g acceleration, so all we can do is sit here and watch the instrument panel and try to breathe. It's too much effort even to talk, and my eyes are getting pushed back into my head. Heartbeat is up. I'd sleep if I could, but I'm wide-awake. Every once in a while, Jake tries to relieve things with a joke, but at the moment, nothing seems funny. And it doesn't help that I can't hear him very well because it's hard to do anything more than mumble.

We take a four-minute break from the acceleration every once in a while.

(Written during one of the breaks.).
—November 16, 2195

Chapter 4

"LOCKING IN BARTON'S World on the forward scope," said Benny. "Full mag."

It was a misty disk, mostly dark because it was facing away from the sun.

Priscilla looked over at Jake. "How do you put a bomb on an interstellar?"

"It would be pretty difficult unless you're one of the techs with access. Or the pilot."

"Priscilla," said Benny, "it's time to go to cruise."

"Okay," she said. "Do it."

Benny shut down the thrusters. It was like having a heavy weight lifted off her chest. "Gotta do that again sometime," she said.

Joshua called from the *Gremlin*: *"We see you."*

"Better let me do this," said Jake.

Priscilla nodded.

"Josh," he said. "Who are your passengers?"

"High-school girls, Jake. They're from the Middle East. They've all won science awards. This was supposed to be their prize, a flight to the Lalande Monument. Oh, and there's a teacher."

Jake closed his eyes. "Where'd the bomb come from? Any idea?"

Priscilla listened to the faint whisper of moving air and the occasional bleep of the electronics.

Then Joshua was back: *"If I'd known that, we'd never have left port. It was low yield. Just enough to take out the engines. The* Gremlin *has been hauling supplies for one of Kosmik's terraforming operations."* Jake growled something about the antiterraformers. *"It looks as if somebody just wanted to disable us. And send a message. But the mission was changed at the last minute, and we were pressed into service when the tour ship that was supposed to carry these students didn't pass the maintenance inspection. Whoever put the bomb on board discovered what had happened, apparently didn't want to risk killing a bunch of high-school kids, and called in a warning. That's how they found out."*

"We have a problem," said Jake.

"I can guess," Joshua said. *"You can't support twelve more people, right?"*

"That's correct."

"That was the first thing I looked at when I heard you were on the way. But if the Thompson *gets in reasonably close on its jump, we should be able to make everything work."*

"Most of his passengers are teens," said Priscilla. "They won't use as much oxygen as adults, will they?"

"In fact," Jake said, "they'll use more. Kids breathe deeper, or something."

"So what the hell are we going to do?"

"Don't panic, okay?" Jake's voice was cold. "No matter what happens, stay calm."

"I'm not panicking."

"Good."

"Benny," she said, "how many can we take on board?"

"The maximum we can support, Captain, including you and Captain Loomis, would be ten. No more than that. Assuming everyone breathes normally."

Priscilla turned frightened eyes on Jake. "That means we have to *leave* four of them? To go down when the *Gremlin* falls out of orbit?"

Jake shook his head. "The *Thompson*'s due here in, what, another day or so? We just have to buy some time."

"How do you suggest we do that?"

"The *Gremlin* should have a lander. We can put a couple people in their lander and launch it. Then bring the rest of them over here and put two more in ours. That should work fine, as long as the *Thompson* gets here reasonably quickly."

"Oh. Sure," she said. "I wasn't thinking."

"Why don't you ask him about the lander?"

She took a deep breath and called over. "Josh, this is Priscilla Hutchins. I'm working with Jake. Do you have a lander?"

"Yes. But it was damaged in the explosion, Priscilla."

"Would we be able to use it?"

"Not without causing another explosion."

She looked back at Jake. "That shoots that idea." Her training hadn't incorporated anything like this. "Barton's is a living world, isn't it? Is there any chance we could just get them out and take them down in *our* lander? To the surface?"

"Unfortunately not, Priscilla," said Benny. "The atmospheric mix here isn't breathable."

"There's still a way out," Jake said. "We can support three people in our lander for about nineteen hours. That's a little tight, but we should be okay."

"That still leaves one unaccounted for."

"We'll have to squeeze one more on board. It'll be a strain on life support, but we should be able to manage until the *Thompson* gets here."

JOSHUA SENT PICTURES of the students, a group shot of them at the spaceport just before they boarded the shuttle, another photo of them gathered around a model of the monument. Everybody was smiling. One of the girls was a blonde. Joshua stood in the middle, in his silver-and-blue uniform. She'd seen him several times in the Cockpit and Skyview. He was a big guy with a loud laugh, one of those people who thought he could do anything.

There was also the teacher, identified as Shahlah, the daughter of Jamal Touma, who was the sponsor of the program. She was about Priscilla's age. Attractive. *"This is the first year for the award," said Joshua. "It's to be an annual grant, and Shahlah wanted to be present. She's apparently the person who persuaded her father to make it all happen. The award. The ride to Lalande. The whole game."*

THE *GREMLIN* WAS a Delta-class freighter. It had a reputation for reliability, and it had become a favorite carrier for Kosmik. Its hull, steel gray with an oversized cabin, was imprinted with the Kosmik logo, a hawk carrying a scroll.

The ship gleamed briefly in the light from the distant sun, then disappeared across the terminator into the nightside of Barton's World. "Benny," said Priscilla, "how long do you estimate it can remain in orbit?"

"Two and a half hours. I would say three at most."

Barton's World looked remarkably terrestrial. Big continents with long mountain chains, lush green forests, wide oceans, and snowcapped poles with large, white, fur-bearing animals. Enormous lizardlike creatures prowled jungles and plains. "What's wrong with the atmosphere?" she asked.

Jake passed the question to Benny. "Too much carbon dioxide. And only about half of the requisite amount of oxygen. Biologists believe that something killed off early life-forms that absorbed carbon dioxide. The local equivalent of plankton. Oxygen concentrations dropped to half, carbon dioxide concentrations rose, and forests spread. That pushed the temperatures up, and the oceans warmed. The result was to drive the carbon dioxide out of the ocean and into the sky, where it became a fixture. Unbreathable." He paused. "I can go into a detailed explanation if you wish."

"That's okay," said Jake. "Thank you."

Priscilla had already turned him off.

"All right." Jake pointed at the display. "Let's concentrate on getting lined up with the *Gremlin*."

TAWNY WAS OUT of the closet, and Priscilla was waiting as the *Gremlin* came around the rim of the planet, back into the sunlight. Shahlah appeared on-screen and delivered a tight smile.

"*Welcome to Barton's World, Priscilla,*" she said. She was gorgeous. The photo hadn't done her justice.

The kids cheered when they looked outside and saw the *Copperhead*. Then the captain appeared. The all-right-I've-got-it attitude she remembered from the Cockpit was down a notch. "We're glad to see you guys," he said.

Priscilla nodded. "Glad to be here. We ready to start, Captain?"

"*Sooner the better. One thing, by the way: The kids don't know we're going down. They've been told they're being moved to other ships because of the engine damage. I haven't gone into any additional detail.*"

"Okay. They're going to have to do a spacewalk to get over to us. Will that be a problem?"

"*They already know about that.*"

Had the *Copperhead* been one of the newer vehicles, say, a Mariner-class, they could have docked the two ships and taken the children off directly. But Priscilla didn't even have direct access to the *Gremlin* with the lander.

JAKE CLIPPED AN imager onto his vest so Priscilla could watch everything. Then he put on one of the Flickinger units, picked up the second one, which constituted their entire supply, and went out through the air lock. Priscilla watched him cross to the *Gremlin*. Joshua, Shahlah, and the girls were waiting for him.

The students all appeared to be about seventeen or eighteen, and they looked both relieved and worried. Relieved, she guessed, because Jake was there; worried about doing a spacewalk.

Jake turned off the Flickinger field. "This is Captain Loomis," said Shahlah. "He's come to give us a ride."

He shook hands with her and with Captain Miller, and turned to the passengers. "Hello, ladies," he said, as if they were all cruising on the Nile. His manner suggested this was all routine stuff. No problem. We do this all the time. "It's good to see you. Weren't there any boys who won a prize?"

Several of the students smiled. Others frowned, indicating they hadn't understood.

"Captain Loomis," Shahlah said, "the boys get a separate flight. We've come a long way, but we haven't come that far."

JAKE AND JOSHUA had gone onto the bridge and were talking in low tones.

"I know," Joshua said.

"But we can take everybody. You and I should stay with the *Gremlin* until it's ready to go down. That'll save some air on the *Copperhead.*"

"We've already talked about that," he said. "Shahlah will stay also."

"You sure?"

"She insists."

"All right. We stay as long as we can. Then we'll cross over and move three people into our lander. We'll be pushing life support a little. But it should be okay."

"I hope so." Joshua took a deep breath. "If we get through this, Jake, I'll take you to dinner."

They laughed. "We'd better start moving the kids. How many suits do you have?"

"Two."

"Okay. I brought an extra one with me. Priscilla, you listening?"

"I'm here."

"Some treats would be nice. I'll be over with the first batch in a few minutes."

PRISCILLA'S JOURNAL

This does not feel as if it's going to end well. The *Sydney Thompson* is still more or less twenty hours away.

—November 17, 2195

Chapter 5

JAKE ARRIVED WITH three girls and their luggage. All were breathless after doing a spacewalk wearing no protection other than their air tanks and a harness that seemed to do nothing more than produce a soft glow. They filed into the passenger cabin, rolling their eyes and laughing and exchanging comments in Arabic. At that moment there was no need for a common language. Priscilla and Jake helped them out of their gear.

Priscilla brought out juice and cookies, and they did introductions. The girls were Adara, Lana, and Ishraq. "Make yourselves at home," she said.

Jake was putting the Flickinger units and air tanks into a plastic bag when Priscilla asked him to join her on the bridge.

"Something wrong?" he asked.

"No. I just need to ask you something." When she was sure no one was close enough to hear, she lowered her voice. "Listen, Jake, I can go over and stay on the *Gremlin*. There's no need for you to do it."

Jake took a deep breath. He looked impressed. "Well, that's very generous of you, but no. Let's leave things the way they are. Anything else?"

"Jake, you're the real pilot on this flight. If there's a problem, you need to be here."

"We've got a problem, and I'm here. This is what I get paid for."

"Jake—"

"Forget it. Your job, whatever happens from here on out, is to get these kids home." She opened her mouth to respond, but he held up a hand indicating she was to be quiet. "This is *my* responsibility. We're all going to survive, so don't worry about it. In any case, I don't want to have it on my record that I allowed a student pilot to board a ship with problems." He looked back at her without cracking a grin. "If I did that, I'd never be able to set foot in the Cockpit again."

"Jake, if there's a problem, I'm not certified to solo with this ship."

"Doesn't matter. I'm certifying you now."

"All right. How about we flip for it?" One of the girls, Adara, was watching them through the open hatch.

"Keep your voice down, Priscilla. And no." He looked at the overhead. "We're not flipping for anything."

"Why not?" Somewhere in a deep, dark place, she wanted him to refuse her. To keep saying no, he was the senior officer, it was his responsibility. "Jake—"

"Because it's my call. Because you're a woman."

That was irritating. "Women and children first."

"That's the tradition."

"It's a bit old-school, isn't it?"

"Listen, just take care of things here, all right? Do that, and we'll be okay."

"You have a plan?"

"Yeah." Jake waved at Adara. Smiled. She smiled back and turned away. "It's simple enough. When we've got all the children over here, Shahlah, Josh, and I will stay with the *Gremlin* as long as we can. Then when we have to, we'll come over here and move into *our* lander. We should be able to live off its air supply until the *Thompson* shows up. That way we won't put any additional pressure on the ship's life-support system."

"I don't think that's a good idea," she said.

"Why not?"

"How are you going to know when you have to come over? You wait a few seconds too long, and you'll all go down with the *Gremlin*."

"You have a better plan?"

"Why not put the lander alongside the *Gremlin*? You'd be able to get to it quicker."

"We can't run the engines. There's too much chance it would get blown away when we start running into atmosphere. No. It's okay. We'll be careful, and we'll leave in plenty of time."

"How long—?"

"We've got a couple of hours on the *Gremlin*. Then our lander should be able to sustain three people for about nineteen hours. If the *Thompson*'s still not here, we can fall back on the Flickinger units. We've got five sets of air tanks between the two ships. That'll give the three of us an extra four or five hours each. We should be okay."

"What happens if it *doesn't* get here in time?"

"You know, Priscilla, I never realized you could be so negative. We are doing what we can. If you can't handle your end of this, you should find another line of work." He looked down at her. "Anything else?"

She stared into Jake's brown eyes. Shook her head. "No, sir."

He turned away and went back to gathering the Flickinger equipment. When he'd finished, he pulled the bag into the air lock. Then he said good-bye to everybody. "Be back in a few minutes." He activated the field, and the hatch slid down. Priscilla heard the low, muffled sounds of decompression.

Ishraq appeared beside her. Her smile turned into a frown. "Priscilla," she said in English, "are you okay?"

"I'm fine." She was grateful her offer to go in his place had been rejected. And it embarrassed her. Coward, she thought.

THE THREE GIRLS wore jumpsuits with GREMLIN emblazoned on the back, and the scroll-carrying hawk on the front. They spread out on the seats in the passenger cabin. "We have some games in the library," Priscilla said. Ishraq translated for Adara. Lana apparently had enough English to get by.

They seemed happy to hear about the games although nobody made a move to consult the library. They were pretty, the way teenage girls always are. Adara said something and

Ishraq translated: "How serious is the problem with the *Gremlin*? They don't want to tell us."

Priscilla sat down with them. "It's serious, but they'll be okay."

Lana chewed her lip, and Adara raised both hands to her mouth and switched her gaze to Ishraq while assuming an I-told-you-so expression. Then all three were talking. What's going to happen now?

"We're playing it by ear," said Priscilla. "The important thing, though, is that you're safe here."

"I mean," said Ishraq, "is something going to happen to the *Gremlin*?"

"I'm not sure what'll happen with the *Gremlin*. But you won't go back to it. You'll be going home with *me*. Or on the *Thompson*."

Lana's eyes showed anger. "All this trouble," she said, "because a lunatic put a bomb in the engines. Captain Miller thinks it has something to do with terraforming."

"That's the general suspicion," said Priscilla. "Listen, would you guys like more to eat?"

That promoted another exchange. But they decided they'd had enough. And then they began to laugh and point at something behind her. When she turned, she saw Tawny.

The cat distracted them for a few minutes. But eventually Ishraq began looking around and frowning. "Priscilla, are we going to be able to fit everybody in here? This ship seems kind of small."

"We'll be okay. As soon as the *Thompson* gets here, we'll be able to spread out a bit." She smiled. "One day, you'll be telling your grandchildren about this."

Lana folded her arms.

"Are you cold?" asked Priscilla.

"Oh, no. It's very comfortable in here. I was just thinking—" She hesitated. "Coming over from the *Gremlin* was scary."

"Was that the first time you've been outside a ship?"

"Yes. For all of us."

"Well, you guys did pretty well. The first time I went out, I had heart palpitations."

"Really?" said Ishraq. Tawny had climbed into her lap. "You don't look like somebody who'd scare very easily."

"You don't know me well. But I'll tell you, if somebody walks out of an air lock out here, and her heartbeat doesn't pick up a little bit, she's a pretty tough cookie."

Barton's moon hung in the dark sky. She wished the diamond monument were visible somewhere, but she'd already checked. It was on the other side of the world.

COPPERHEAD LOG

So far so good.

—November 17, 2195

Chapter 6

JAKE CAME THROUGH the air lock into the *Gremlin* passenger cabin to the sound of raised voices. One of the girls was in tears. Another was pointing angrily at Josh. *"Limaza satutru-kuna huna?"*

Shahlah interpreted for the captain: "She wants to know why you and I are staying behind."

"Tell them it's all right, Shahlah. Nobody's staying behind. We just have some reports and things to take care of." Then Joshua smiled at Jake. "Hi, partner."

The girls looked at Jake. "It's okay," he said, trying to keep it light. "We're all going to cross over. Look, I'll be here with them." Then, with a laugh: "Believe me, I wouldn't do it if it weren't safe."

Shahlah translated, but the girls' suspicions did not subside.

"Jake," said Joshua, "did you enjoy the trip over?" He grinned at the girls. "Captain Loomis likes to spacewalk."

"It's exciting," said Jake. He looked toward the young lady who'd asked the question and seemed to be at the center of the growing concern. She was the tallest in the group, almost as big as he was. Her name was Nadia. "It might seem a little scary at first, but you'll enjoy it."

"Alkull sayakunu bikhair," said Shahlah. *"Laisa hunaka*

ma yad'u lilqalaq." Then she looked at the two captains. "I told them everybody will be okay. That there's nothing to worry about."

One of the girls was wearing a crescent necklace. She was watching Jake with no sign of approval. *"Min fadlika fassir lana limatha lan ta'tu ma'ana."*

"Karida wants to know," said Shahlah, "if the *Gremlin* is going to crash."

"Yes," Joshua said. "It is. We won't be able to save the ship."

Karida stayed with it. "How long have you known?"

"We've known for a while."

"Why didn't you tell us?"

"We didn't want to say anything until the *Copperhead* got here."

The students looked at one another. Priscilla, watching via the imager, thought they lost a degree of trust in their captain. And possibly in Shahlah.

Another of the girls was shaking her head. *"'Ana 'ash'oro bil'asaf li'annani 'atait."*

"Layla says she's sorry she came."

Joshua tried to take Layla's hand in his. But she backed away. "I understand," he said. "This isn't the kind of flight we'd planned. And I'm sorry. But everything will be okay."

No translation of his comment was needed; the meaning was clear enough. There were some tentative smiles. Shahlah picked up one of the Flickinger belts and held it out for the nearest girl. "Let me help you, Ashira," she said, alerting Priscilla that Ishraq had not been the only student who spoke English.

PRISCILLA DECIDED THAT, since everyone else now knew the fate of the *Gremlin*, she should share the information with her three passengers. "I don't think they wanted to go into specifics while you were on board because they were concerned that it would be a bit scary."

"We're adults," said Lana. "They could have told us."

"Look at it from their point of view, Lana," said Priscilla. "They were trying to make it as easy on you as they could."

When Jake and three more girls came through the air lock, the reception was subdued. "To be honest," one of the newcomers said, "I'm glad I didn't know. I was afraid something like that was happening."

The new passengers wasted no time removing the Flickinger units and returning them to Jake. "I see you told them," he said. "Everything okay?"

She nodded. "They're fine."

"Good." He collected the belts and air tanks. "I'll be back in a few minutes."

"Okay."

"If there's anything of yours in the lander, Priscilla, you might get it out now." He went back out through the air lock.

THE CLOUD-WRAPPED PLANET below him seemed closer than it had been. He stared down at it as he drifted between the ships. *Next time somebody takes a bunch of kids on a trip, they should pick a world with a breathable atmosphere.*

He found himself thinking about his life back home. His father, who'd been so proud of him when he qualified. And his mother, who'd left them when Jake was only six. Ran off with a banker.

Jake had never married. He'd been swept off his feet a couple of times and proposed once. To Jeri Lockett. The woman he always thought about the moment after the lights went out. They'd been sitting in the Cosmopolitan in Atlanta, and he'd been about to leave on a two-month flight. So he'd taken the plunge. But she had declined. He never saw her again after that night.

He regretted that he'd never had a family. It hadn't been by design. He'd just been too busy. Or maybe because the right woman had never shown up. Or because, when she had, he hadn't been able to hang on to her. Now, somehow, it seemed as if those details didn't really matter very much.

And why, just now, was he entertaining thoughts like these?

"HOW'D IT GO?" Joshua asked when he reentered the *Gremlin*.

"Good. Everything's under control." He glanced at the

four remaining students. "We can only take three on this next run."

One of them would have to wait. The blonde Priscilla had seen in the photo stepped forward. "I'll stay," she said. Her name was Kareema. There was a brief debate while the others also volunteered to wait. But in the end, Kareema got the nod. The others strapped on the belts and pulled the air tanks onto their shoulders.

FIFTEEN MINUTES LATER, Jake returned to pick up the last of the students. He asked Joshua if he wanted to escort his last student.

"It's okay," he said. "You're doing fine, Jake."

Jake shrugged. "I thought you might want to say something to them. Just in case."

"Not a good idea," he said. "It would scare the devil out of them. Don't worry. We're not going down with this thing."

When it was time to go, Kareema hugged Shahlah. "Good luck," the student said. Then she turned to Jake. "Don't let them stay too long."

"Thank you, Kareema," said Josh. "We'll be fine."

"We'll join you in a couple of hours," said Shahlah.

Finally, they activated the force fields, went into the air lock, and crossed to the *Copperhead*.

WHEN HE'D RETURNED to the *Gremlin*, Shahlah informed him that Joshua had gone below to get pictures of the damage. "He's been transmitting everything back to Union."

"Well," he said, "I hope they got the idiot who did this."

"Let's also hope we all get home okay."

"Amen to that."

"I've got a question for you, Jake."

"Fire away, kid."

"What exactly are our chances of surviving this?"

"I think we'll be all right."

"That sounds fairly tentative." She took a deep breath. "Josh's been evasive about it. He says the right things, but his eyes are telling me something else. Be straight with me."

"We should get through it okay," he said. "We can't be sure about anything until we see when and where the *Thompson* shows up."

"All right." She read his eyes. "Thanks. Joshua kept saying there was nothing to worry about. I knew that wasn't true."

"What did the girls think of the monument?" Jake asked. "I don't guess they got a chance to enjoy it."

"Not really. I'll tell you what they *did* get excited about, though. The animals down there." She pointed at the deck, meaning, of course, the surface of Barton's World.

"You really think so?"

"Are you serious? They've got big furry creatures. The size of mastodons. And whole herds of animals that look like pandas. And giant snaky things that make your skin crawl." She led the way onto the bridge, looking for something. "He set a countdown running here somewhere. How long we had before we could expect to go down."

Shahlah touched a pad, and the AI responded: "It would be prudent to stay no longer than forty-five minutes."

GREMLIN LOG

Finally, the girls are safe. Now we have to see whether our own luck holds. Let the record show that a quicker response, however that might have been arranged, would have been seriously helpful.

This will probably be our last entry. The log will be recorded on a chip, and the chip will be delivered to the *Copperhead* and made available to those inquiring into a more effective methodology for responding to emergencies.

—Joshua Miller, November 17, 2195

Chapter 7

THEY TALKED ABOUT their favorite assignments, about the ineptitude of the people who ran Union, about politics, about the silliness that reigned on holovision. About the lunacy of people who planted bombs on interstellars. "They go on about the sanctity of life, then they kill innocent people."

They did *not* mention the occasional bumps and nudges as they descended closer to the atmosphere.

Shahlah described her feelings when she was assigned to deliver the good news to the winners of the Jamal Touma Science Award. Joshua recalled a run-in he'd had with police after taking umbrage with his sister's husband, who had attacked her. "I wound up in jail," he said. "For doing what someone needed to do."

"You hit him?" asked Shahlah.

"Of course. *He's* the one who should have been arrested."

"Why wasn't he?" asked Jake.

"My sister wouldn't press charges."

And they talked about the *Thompson*. Where was it?

They interweaved bouts of silence with comments about what they'd do when they got home. (Nobody said "if.") Shahlah announced that it would be a long time before she tried something like this again. "I thought these things were safe. Otherwise, we'd never have allowed the girls to come on this flight. My father wanted it to be something special. He'll be heartbroken when he hears what happened."

"Nevertheless," said Josh, "I think everyone will appreciate his generosity."

"Oh, yes." She paused. "Jake, speaking of appreciation, I'm glad you were in the area. Don't know what we'd have done—"

"Well." He wasn't sure how to respond. If the *Copperhead* hadn't been available, maybe they'd have sent a ship with appropriate capacity. "I'm glad we've been able to help," he said.

She approached him, looked into his eyes, and pressed her lips against his cheek. "Thank you," she whispered.

"YOU GUYS ARE waiting too long," Priscilla said. *"We're starting to hit some atmosphere."* But Jake told her to be patient.

And, finally, the AI warned them that the situation was deteriorating and it was time to go. They were crossing one of the oceans, which was bright and gleaming in the sunlight. Jake let Priscilla know they were coming. Then they got into their gear. Jake and Joshua both wore jet packs. When they were ready, the *Gremlin* captain took a last look around. "I've been here almost two years," he said. "This has been my home." He sighed, took Shahlah's hand, and led her into the air lock. "Don't worry about anything," he told her. "Just stay with me when we get outside."

"I'll be fine," she said.

The last thing Jake saw before they closed the inner hatch was an image on the navigation monitor. One of the telescopes was pointed down, high mag, at the ocean. Something with a long neck seemed to be looking back at him.

The lock went through the decompression cycle and opened. The *Copperhead* was about a hundred meters away.

"IT'S NOT AS frightening as I'd expected," Shahlah said.

"That's because there's no *down*," said Josh. "No way you can fall."

She and Joshua pushed off together. Jake followed close

behind. "I've never felt anything like this," she said, sounding almost giddy.

They floated across, talking about how they'd hoped to hear from the *Thompson* before they left, and how impressed everybody was that the kids had done this without any problems, and how breathless a world was from this angle. Joshua spotted the monument, then lost it as he closed on the *Copperhead*. The air-lock door was open, and they floated smoothly inside. When they stepped into the passenger cabin, the girls clapped their hands, everybody said hello and how good it was to be together again, and Jake couldn't help enjoying the moment. Now, if the *Thompson* would just show up.

The air had already gotten thick. "Listen, everybody," said Priscilla from the bridge, "please belt down or hold on. We need to do a little acceleration. Just for a few minutes."

Jake was pleased. She continued to show good sense. He grabbed hold of one of the safety grips that lined the bulkheads.

WHEN THEY RESET for cruise, he led Shahlah and Joshua below to the cargo deck. They climbed into the lander, closed the hatches, and settled into the seats. It felt good to get back to decent ventilation. But they looked at one another while everybody came to the same realization. Jake shook his head. Shahlah and Joshua both nodded. Do it.

He touched the commlink. "We need to rethink this, Priscilla."

"What do you mean?"

"Well, the air's better in here than it is in the ship. Bring three of the girls down, and we'll change places."

"Okay, Jake. Be there in a minute."

Shahlah glanced around the interior of the lander. "Why are the windows blocked?" she asked.

"Because," said Josh, "it gets used sometimes in areas of heavy radiation."

She shook her head. "This is depressing."

"I'm sorry," said Jake. He explained about the flare star.

"I'd like to see that," she said. "But *live*. Through a window. Not on a display."

"Sorry," said Jake. "Windows won't work."

"Nice interior, though," she said. The seats were imitation leather, the lighting was soft, and the controls were padded. The vehicle was designed to accommodate five, plus the pilot.

"But we need to conserve the air," said Josh. "No idle chit-chat." So they sat quietly, waiting for Priscilla. Shahlah found a book, *FutureTalk*, in which experts predicted what the next century was likely to bring. Joshua simply closed his eyes. Jake stared at the back of his hand, thinking how nice it would be to be on a mountaintop somewhere, with unlimited fresh air.

Priscilla arrived with Nadia, Layla, and Sakeena. "We're going to rotate the girls through every four hours," she said.

They took over the lander, and Joshua showed them how to access the library. "Same rules here as elsewhere. Breathe normally. Don't talk, okay? And keep the hatch shut except when you're going in or out. Washroom is down at the far end of the bay." Shahlah translated.

They closed the hatch and started back topside. It was 1311 Greenwich time. They had until about noon tomorrow to get some people on board the *Thompson*.

"By the way," said Priscilla, "you timed your exit from the *Gremlin* pretty closely."

"It's going down?" said Joshua.

"A few minutes ago."

JOHARA WAS ASLEEP in the passenger cabin. The others were reading. "I've never seen that happen before," said Joshua. "Usually, they spend their time playing games."

Ishraq looked up from her screen. "Priscilla asked us not to."

"Of course," he said. "Game-playing gets people excited, and you use more air."

"I guess," she said.

Jake and Joshua took seats while Priscilla and Shahlah went onto the bridge. "How about some music?" said Shahlah.

"You think we'd be disturbing anybody?"

"I think they'd love to hear some noise."

"Okay. What do you suggest?" She put the library on-screen.

"Oh," Shahlah said. "You have the Cairo Five." She looked at Priscilla, who nodded.

Shahlah made the selection in English.

THE MUSIC BOUNCED and banged along in a gallop until Priscilla turned the volume down. Don't want anybody getting excited. But the Cairo Five rolled in perfect harmony. The rhythms could have been directly out of Manhattan. A few of the instruments were unfamiliar, more strings than would have been used in a Western rendition, and of a different timbre. But Shahlah smiled and Priscilla was on board from the start. And even Jake, who appeared at the hatch.

> *The Desert Express, oh, the Desert Express,*
> *She rides each night on the Desert Express,*
> *She waves hello then she waves good-bye*
> *Every night on the Desert Express.*

JAKE NEEDED SOMETHING to keep his spirits up, so he fell back on a collection of commentaries by a young journalist named MacAllister. The guy attacked everybody, college professors, women, clerics, Boy Scouts. Nobody was safe. *I can imagine no worse condition than being married to a perfect spouse,* he wrote. What the hell was *that* supposed to mean? MacAllister thought he lived in a world populated by blockheads. He recommended voting to reelect President Norman even though he was an idiot. *Not good,* he admitted, *but a step up from Governor McGruder.*

The reality was Jake could not keep his mind off the clock. And the *Thompson.* Joshua sat across the cabin. His display was off, and his eyes were closed though he was not asleep.

Eventually, the *Gremlin* captain brought up the library, inserted an earpod, and started the *Blake Ocala Show.* Ocala bored Jake. He was enormously popular back in the U.S., but the guy was smarmy at best. His routines consisted mostly of leering at his female guests, poking fun at politicians, and falling down. "You really like that guy?" he asked.

"No," said Josh. "He's pretty dumb. But right now, he's a diversion."

EVENTUALLY, JAKE WENT back onto the bridge. Priscilla was doing a crossword puzzle while Shahlah was reading. "What is it?" he asked.

"A biography of Toraggio," she said.

"The historian?"

"Well, he was more than a historian. He was a futurist."

"I think I saw him once," said Jake. "At Union. Wasn't he the guy who thought we had to set up off-world colonies if we wanted to survive?"

"Yes," she said. "He's largely the reason we're having the battle over terraforming now."

"Wonderful."

"He was also worried about ideologies. He thinks we need to get rid of them."

"Bear with me, but isn't that an ideology?"

She dimmed the screen. "I guess. Did you get a chance to talk to him?"

"Not really. Somebody pointed him out to me. He was checking into the Starlight. He's dead, isn't he?"

"Two years ago," she said.

Jake nodded. And pressed his index finger against his lips. They shouldn't be talking.

Priscilla's clock chimed. Seventeen hundred hours. She got up and went into the passenger cabin. "We're going down to the lander again, ladies. Who wants to come? I can take three."

The kids had already decided. She took Adara, Lana, and Ishraq down and returned a few minutes later with Nadia, Layla, and Sakeena.

"How was it?" asked Josh.

Sakeena wrinkled her nose. "It's great down there. But you can hardly breathe in here."

"Yeah," he said. "I guess it's a bit stuffy." He glanced at Jake but said nothing further.

PRISCILLA'S JOURNAL

The things we take for granted: like being able to breathe. It's almost impossible to sleep when getting enough air becomes a struggle.

—November 18, 2195

Chapter 8

THEY CONTINUED TO rotate the girls through the lander every four hours. The quality of the air was so much better that there was no shortage of volunteers. But when they changed over at 0500 hours, when the air in the lander was also becoming hard to breathe, and there was still no sign of the *Thompson*, the general mood was darkening. "We'll be watching from the bridge," Jake told the girls as they slipped into their seats. "But if you start having a problem, just open up and leave. Okay?"

"What are we going to do after this, Captain Loomis?" Johara asked. She was seriously frightened. They all were.

"We have air tanks," he said. "Don't worry. We'll be all right."

He hated lying to them. Well, maybe he wasn't lying. Not really. *They* would probably be all right. He was less sure about the adults.

He returned to the passenger cabin, where Shahlah took him aside. "You said there's five hours in each of the air-tank units?"

"That's correct."

"Can't they be refilled?"

"They could. But it wouldn't do any good because we'd just be taking the air out of life support."

Kareema and Lana were in the passenger cabin playing with Tawny. Ishraq and Sakeena sat off to one side, tapping messages to each other on their notebooks. The others were scattered around the *Copperhead*.

Jake went up onto the bridge. Joshua was there with Priscilla. "Nothing yet from the *Thompson*?" he asked.

Priscilla shook her head. "Negative, Jake."

He went back and wandered through the ship, trying to look upbeat, everything's okay, we'll be out of here soon. He wished he believed it.

He returned to the passenger cabin. Had a soft drink. Sat down next to Ishraq and Sakeena. They were exchanging information electronically about their science projects. They showed him their notebooks. Sakeena had been doing gravity experiments, and Ishraq had been teleporting particles. Ishraq typed a note: "One day these big ships will be obsolete."

He got his notebook and typed a reply: "You really think that's going to happen?" The idea seemed utterly outlandish. It had shown up occasionally in books and films, but there was no way he could take it seriously.

She responded with one word: "Yes."

He looked at Sakeena: "What kind of gravity research are you doing?"

She had dark intelligent eyes. "You will not laugh?"

"No."

"Artificial gravity."

"Impossible?"

She shook her head.

Jake typed again: "It's supposed to be impossible."

"People used to say that about faster-than-light travel."

He smiled. Raised his hands, conceding the point.

She sent him another message: "You will live to see it."

He was about to reply when he heard Benny's voice. "There it is!"

And Priscilla: "Let's have it, Benny."

Jake got up and strode onto the bridge.

"*Copperhead, Gremlin.*" It was Drake Peifer's voice. *"This is the* Thompson. *We've arrived insystem. Do you read me?"*

"We read you, Drake. We're at Barton's World. Running short on air."

Jake took the right-hand seat, cautioned her to lower her voice, and turned down the volume. A minute ticked by. Longer. Not a good sign. Then: *"Are you able to meet us?"*

"Yes," said Priscilla. "We're mobile."

"Good. Looks like about twenty-one hours to rendezvous."

"That won't get the job done, Drake. Where are you?"

"We're feeding the information now. What's the Gremlin's *status?"*

"It went down."

"How much air do you have left?"

"We need you here within seven hours."

"Hold on." It was a long pause. Then: *"We'll have to try another jump."*

She looked at Jake. He nodded. "Do it," she said.

Transdimensional jumps were notoriously inaccurate. They usually put you within approximately a million kilometers of your target. That was good if you were going to Canopus, and nobody was in a hurry. But it wasn't very helpful if you were already in relatively close. Another jump would take time and might gain nothing. Or even *lose* ground.

THE BETTER PART of an hour passed before they heard from the *Thompson* again. *"We're not much closer,"* Drake said. *"A few hours less. But not enough. We can try another jump."*

"Negative," said Jake. "How's your fuel?"

"About half a tank."

"Hold on. Benny, do we have the *Thompson's* new position?"

"I'm getting it now."

"What's the best rendezvous time?"

"There are fuel limitations. And the sustained acceleration would almost certainly cause injuries. But taking all that into consideration, we can meet in just under five hours."

"Thank God," said Priscilla. "That's tight, but it works."

Jake heard movement behind him and turned to see Josh.

"All right," said Jake. "Priscilla, let's get moving."

"No," said Josh. "The high-acceleration rendezvous is not a good idea."

"We don't have a choice."

"Jake, the pressures generated by all the accelerating and braking will increase everyone's oxygen intake by a substantial margin. I can't be positive, but I'd be surprised if we didn't lose life support during the process."

"We can manage a meeting without excessive acceleration in seven hours," Benny said. "Perhaps a bit less. But we have to get started."

"We don't have a seven-hour air supply," said Jake.

"Do it, damn it," said Josh. "Let's get moving."

PRISCILLA'S JOURNAL

. . . Darkest moment of my life . . .

—November 18, 2195

Chapter 9

"THIS IS NOT going to work," said Jake. "We'll lose the lander at about 0800."

Joshua shook his head. "We have a fifteen-hour supply of oxygen in the air tanks."

"That doesn't add up to seven hours for three people."

"But it's enough for *two*."

"I'm not sure what you're suggesting," said Priscilla, "but I think we should try another jump. Maybe we'd get lucky."

"No." Joshua shook his head. "At this range, the jumps are just wasting time." His eyes narrowed. "It would mean putting everybody at risk. We can't do that."

"So what *do* we do?" she said.

"I have an idea," said Josh.

"What's that?"

"Give me ten minutes. Then come down to the lander."

"What are you going to do?" asked Jake.

"I'm not sure yet. Just let me take a look at our options."

Priscilla thought she saw something pass between the two captains, an understanding. But then the girls were grouped around the hatch asking, *What's happening?*

When are they going to be here?

Is everything okay?

And Joshua was gone.

"We'll be fine," said Shahlah in both languages.

"What's he going to do?" Priscilla asked.

"I don't know," said Jake.

She knew Jake pretty well by then. And he seemed rattled. But she let it go.

JAKE SAT STARING at nothing in particular.

"We have to get going," said Priscilla. "We're wasting time."

"Try a little patience," he said. His voice was flat.

Finally, Priscilla got up. "I've had enough of this. I'm going down to see what's going on."

He put a hand on her wrist. "Wait. He asked for ten minutes. Give it to him."

So they sat. The girls backed away. Shahlah had disappeared, too. Then suddenly she was on the circuit: *"Priscilla, I can't get into the cargo bay."*

"Why not?"

"I can't open the hatch. Can you put air into it from up there? I think Joshua is in there."

Priscilla was already doing it. *"Don't know how I missed it,"* she said. *"It's been decompressed."*

SHAHLAH WAS STILL waiting at the hatch when they arrived. It wouldn't open until the air pressure equalized on both sides. She was in tears.

When finally they got through, the first thing Priscilla saw was Josh, floating a foot or two above the deck, his wrist tied to a frame. They tried to revive him, although Priscilla thought it was probably a cruel thing to do. If they succeeded, he would only feel that he had to go through it again.

But she needn't have worried. He was gone.

Shahlah was sobbing. "No, no, no. He was our captain. There was no way he was going to allow one of his passengers to die. I should have known."

Priscilla looked accusingly at Jake. It was hard to believe he hadn't realized what was happening.

LIBRARY ENTRY

Courage is of no value if the gods do not assist.

—Euripides, *The Suppliant Women*

Chapter 10

EVENTUALLY, THERE WERE lights in the sky, and the *Sydney Thompson* came out of the darkness and eased alongside. Priscilla faced the girls in the passenger cabin. "Who wants to go over to the *Thompson* with Shahlah for the ride home?"

Ten hands went up. Priscilla wasn't surprised. No happy memories here. And, of course, they liked Shahlah. "All right. But we can only send five."

"We do not wish you to misunderstand," said Ishraq. "It's not because we didn't enjoy our time on the *Copperhead*—"

"I know," she said. "I think I'd want off, too. But we need five of you to stay here. Food and water issues on the *Thompson*. Can you guys decide? Do it quickly so we can get everybody some fresh air again."

Ishraq and Ashira volunteered to stay. Layla raised her hand. And Karida and Kareema.

"Okay," Priscilla said. "Good. Get your luggage. The *Thompson* shuttle will be here in a few minutes. No spacewalk this time."

Johara pretended to be disappointed.

There were hugs and a few tears and an agreement that they'd all try to get together back at Union. That was speculative. Depending on where the ships were when they surfaced in the solar system, there could be as much as three days' difference in arrival times.

Jake looked as if he were in a distant place. He returned the embraces with the emotion of a robot and watched the five girls, escorted by Drake Peifer, pass through the cargo-bay air lock into the *Thompson* lander. Shahlah was the last to leave.

"Thanks, guys," she said. "I hate to think where we'd have been without you."

Priscilla helped carry the baggage. Then Shahlah took her aside. "Is he all right?" she asked, meaning Jake.

"He's a bit rattled. But he'll get past it."

"I hope so." She wiped away a tear. "Let me know if I can ever do anything."

"Of course. Thank you. I just wish things had turned out differently."

"So do I, Priscilla. So do I."

They embraced, and Priscilla returned to the cargo bay. The air lock closed, and the lander was gone.

THE *THOMPSON* LEFT first. Priscilla was just taking her place on the bridge when a message came in from Union. *"Jake."* A male voice. *"Hope everything is going okay at your end. We've been worried. Appreciate everything you guys have been doing."*

"That's Frank Irasco," said Jake. Irasco was the assistant director for WSA at Union.

"We were glad you were in the area," Irasco continued. *"Keep us informed."*

That was it. Jake sat down beside her but said nothing. The air being dispersed by the vents had already begun to feel breathable again. Priscilla switched on the mike. "Girls," she said, "the flight to the home system will take three days and about six hours. Then it'll be probably another couple of days to get back to Earth. We'll be moving out in five minutes, so you should take care of any last-minute business and get belted down." She switched off and turned to Jake. "I've never been more happy in my life to get away from a place."

* * *

THE SOMBER REACTION that had taken hold of the girls when they learned of Captain Miller's death subsided. They played games, watched holos, laughed about boys. They especially enjoyed the space-adventure series *Deep Skies*. They had an Arabic version. Priscilla watched an episode with them, and was fascinated by the visuals and the show's distinctive score, suggestive of intergalactic space and cosmic mystery. She tried it in English, got hooked, and became a fan on the way home. She was especially taken with Ryan Fletcher, who played the daredevil skipper of the *Excelsior*, Captain William L. Brandywine.

Ishraq often joined her on the bridge. "I'd love to do this when I grow up," she said.

"Keep going the way you are, Ishraq, and I suspect you'll be able to do anything you please."

"It's very nice of you to say that."

"You've already done pretty well. You've won a science prize. You've been off-world."

"That's not exactly the same as operating an interstellar." She squeezed her hands together. "I'm just not sure—"

"You can do it. All you have to do is make it happen."

"You really think so?"

"Of course."

The hatch opened behind them. Ishraq turned to see who had come in. It was Jake. Escorted by Tawny. "Hello, Captain Loomis," she said.

"Hello, Ishraq. You keeping Priscilla out of trouble?"

She smiled. "Oh, yes." Then back to Priscilla: "You know the ship I'd really like to have?"

"No. What?"

"The *Excelsior*." She got out of the chair to make room for Jake.

"From *Deep Skies*?" Jake said.

"You watch it, too?" Her eyes shone.

"I've always been a big fan." That was hard to buy.

Ishraq turned back to Priscilla. "May I ask a favor?"

"Sure."

"In a few years, when I start training, would you be willing to teach me?"

"Of course. I'd love to. By the way, that's what Captain Loomis has been doing for me."

Ishraq gave Jake a shy smile but continued speaking to Priscilla: "I think you're very lucky."

"I'm the one who got lucky," said Jake.

Ishraq's smile widened. "Yes," she said. "She is very pretty."

PRISCILLA HAD NOT known Jake before the qualification flight. But when you spend three weeks alone with someone, especially when the nearest other human being is light-years away, you get to know him pretty well. Jake had been easygoing, patient, amiable, a guy who did not take himself seriously, and who seemed able to adjust readily to setbacks. But the experience with the *Gremlin* had changed him.

It wasn't that he'd become angry, or that he spent a lot of time staring at bulkheads. He didn't retire to his cabin and remain there. In fact, he spent as much time on the bridge and in the passenger cabin as he ever had. But he didn't laugh easily anymore, and when he did, the laughter was forced. His voice and, indeed, his entire bearing had leveled off into a monotone. The vitality was gone.

It would have been difficult in any case to join in games with the girls because of the language difference. But Priscilla sensed that the Jake who'd been with her originally would have found a way. He didn't even try, however, and because he didn't, she also abstained. Instead, they sat on the bridge, talking about trivia, or rerunning the same dialogues, about the bright futures that surely awaited their passengers, or grumbling one more time about the kind of maniac who'd put a bomb on an interstellar.

The conversations were marked by long pauses, uncomfortable moments when no one could think of anything to say. When the best she could come up with was how much she'd enjoyed the scrambled eggs that morning.

She just wanted it to be over.

TWO OF THE girls, Karida and Layla, had become competitive with each other. It wasn't about anything in particular, Ishraq explained. They'd decided they didn't like one another much.

"If you want the truth," she said, "I think they're just tired. They want to get home."

"I don't guess," said Priscilla, "you can put a bunch of kids into a tin can and keep them there for a couple of weeks and not expect them to get tired of it."

"I think you're right, Priscilla," said Jake. "Even if there'd been no bomb, I'd have suggested a different kind of award next year. No more long-range space journeys. Or maybe—"

"What?"

"We could take them to the one in the solar system. The monument on Iapetus."

She shrugged. "It would take a couple of days to get there, too. Anything like that, for teens, is maybe too much. What we need is a more precise long-range drive. Something that could really take you in close to the target instead of just getting into the general area. Something faster than the Hazeltine would help, too."

"Yes, Priscilla, it would. So what kind of award do you think we should give the prizewinners next year?"

"If I were running it—"

"Yes?"

"I'd take them to Moonbase and throw a party."

LAYLA WAS SITTING on the bridge with her when they arrived in the solar system. By then they'd learned enough of each other's language to be able to communicate reasonably well. She looked at the navigation screen and saw the distant sun. "How much longer," she asked, "before we get back home?"

Priscilla hated to answer the question. "Three days. We're kind of far out."

Layla groaned.

But a flood of messages took some of the sting out of the wait: They began arriving within an hour after they'd surfaced, coming from family, friends, teachers, and even from groups of schoolkids who had no direct connection with the girls. "Welcome home," said the third grade at St. Gabriel's elementary school in Kansas City. And West Park High, in Nottingham, promised that chocolates would be waiting when the *Copperhead* docked. Greetings came in from Jerusalem, Cairo, Belfast, Tokyo, Bangalore, Port Blair, Morocco, and several dozen other places.

"How do they know we're back in the solar system already?" Layla asked.

"I suspect," said Priscilla, "we've been making news, so a lot of people are tracking us. Even if they weren't, ship arrivals get posted online as soon as Ops picks them up."

"Well," she said, "I certainly didn't expect anything like this. It's great to be back."

NEWSDESK

SIX DEAD AFTER ATTACK BY GUNMAN
AT CORNINE UNIVERSITY
Killer Angry at Cornine Support for Terraforming
Statewide Search Under Way

MCDERMOTT BILL PASSES BY WIDE MARGIN
All Federal Elections Will Be Financed by Government

UNEMPLOYMENT RATES DROP
SEVENTH STRAIGHT MONTH
GDP Hits New High; Stocks Soar

NEW CLAIMS FOR INTELLIGENCE DRUG
Can a Daily Pill Really Make Us Smarter?

EVIDENCE MOUNTS THAT INCREASED
IQ LEADS TO SOCIAL DYSFUNCTION
Research Indicates There's a Reason It's Set Where It Is

RUSSIA MAY DEFUND UNION ORBITER
Cites Growing Debt Problems
India May Be Next

TANK NOBE MAY BOYCOTT SEASON
Baseball Fans Outraged; Ticket Prices Rise
Across All Four Leagues

RESEARCH DESCRIBES BASEBALL FANS AS ADDICTS
"They Need to Back Off, but They're Helpless."

STARSHIP CAPTAIN DIES DURING RESCUE
Joshua Miller Sacrifices Life for Passengers
Memorial Ceremony Planned

JENNIFER HOPKINS ARRESTED AGAIN
Drunk and Disorderly after Hollywood Party

Chapter 11

THE *THOMPSON* HAD beaten them into the space station by almost twelve hours. They'd been greeted by a large crowd, and the pictures of the ecstatic homecoming had been relayed to the *Copperhead*. Now *they* were docking, and the crowd had returned. It appeared to be even louder and more enthusiastic. Priscilla opened the air lock, looked out at them, and waved. People cheered and waved back. Cameras locked in on her. Shahlah and Johara and Drake Peifer were in the crowd. She retreated back inside to make room for the girls. "Just follow the tube," she said. "Stop when you get to the concourse but don't leave the area."

Each of them took a moment to say good-bye to Jake, who stood off to one side. They thanked Priscilla and hurried away, delighted to be home. When the last of them had gone, a staff assistant appeared, carrying a small cage. "You wanted this?" she said.

Priscilla took the cage back to her cabin, collected Tawny, and put her inside. The cat didn't exactly approve, but Priscilla had owned two of the animals when she was growing up and knew precisely how to do it. When she came back out, carrying the cat, Jake was still waiting. "Turn her over to General Services," he said. "They'll take care of her."

Priscilla shook her head. "I'm not going to do that."

"What are you going to do? *Keep* her?"

"Yes."

"And how will you manage that? You won't be around here very much."

"I can take her home. Back to New Jersey. I'm pretty sure my mom would be willing to take her in."

"Well," he said, "your call."

She looked across at Jake. His bag was secured to one of the seats. "However it works out, I'll see that she gets a good home."

He let her see that he'd have expected nothing less. "Here, Priscilla, why don't you let me take the cage?"

"That's all right. I can handle it. But thanks." He stood aside, and she led the way out. "So what are you going to do now?" she asked.

"Take some time off. I think I'm just going to relax for a while." He still looked distracted.

She wanted to tell him again it hadn't been his fault. But she thought she'd probably only make things worse. "Well," she said, "have a big time."

They passed through the connecting tube and came out into the concourse, and the place erupted. Whistles, cheers, shouts of *Shukran!* and *Thank you!* She recognized the senator from New Jersey, and the House Speaker, who was from Ontario. Nadia and Adara waved. The reporters moved in close, shouting questions. "How does it feel to be back home?"

"How did you know Captain Miller?"

"Are space missions so dangerous that we shouldn't be sending children?"

Cameras followed them. Lana and Sakeena showed up, embraced them, and said how glad they were to see them again. Everybody was taking pictures.

A few people paused to shake her hand or get their picture taken with her. But Jake was engulfed. They crowded around him, clapped him on the back. Some had tears in their eyes. He tried to explain that the credit for the rescue should go to Joshua Miller, who'd given his life to ensure everyone else survived. But they weren't really listening. There was too much noise, too much excitement.

A woman in Arab garb appeared out of nowhere and thanked Priscilla for saving her daughter. She slipped away before Priscilla could identify her. Another woman wanted to give her money, and a reporter asked how it had felt to rescue the kids off a ship that was about to go down. Dumb question. How the hell did he think it had felt? But Priscilla knew the sacred principle about not irritating the press, so she explained that it felt very good.

Shahlah greeted her with a large smile. "Priscilla," she said, "if there's ever anything I can do, don't hesitate—"

"Thank you, Shahlah. Let's stay in touch."

"By all means." Then: "One other thing—"

"What's that?"

"Jake."

"What about him?"

"He went through a lot out there. Keep an eye on him. He's going to need help." She left as a staff assistant approached.

"Ms. Hutchins?" he said.

"Yes?"

He was about twenty, a good-looking kid, in a work uniform. "We've set up a room for you at the Starlight. The information has been sent to your link. Are you planning on leaving the Wheel?"

"Eventually."

"I mean like tomorrow? The director wants you to stay on for a bit. She'll be in touch."

"Okay. What about the girls? Have we provided for them?"

"We've set aside a couple of rooms. But I don't think you need be concerned. They all had relatives waiting for them."

"Thank you."

"My pleasure, ma'am."

Ma'am? Priscilla stared after him. She felt about ten years older.

JAKE HAD SEEN Matt Carstairs waiting for him the moment he'd come out of the tube. Then the crowd had closed in, and Jake lost track of him. But in the end he was still there, tall and well dressed, wearing his standard pensive expression, with a trace of a smile. Matt was retired Marines, and of course, as they say, once a Marine—

"Boss wants to see you, Jake," he said.

"Okay."

He reached for one of the bags. "Can I give you a hand?" said Matt.

"Sure." They started toward the elevators.

"Tough flight," he said.

"Yeah, Matt. I've seen better."

They got into the elevator, and Matt pressed the button for the third level. Cleared his throat once or twice as an uncomfortable silence took over. He finally asked Jake if he was okay.

"Yeah. I'm good."

"You must be glad to be back."

"I'm just glad it's over, pal."

"Yeah," he said. "I guess I would be, too."

MATT TURNED HIM over to a secretary, who informed the director of operations that Captain Loomis had arrived. She listened to a response that Jake couldn't hear, nodded, and asked him to have a seat. "Director McCoy will be with you shortly."

Jake sat down. The secretary went back to her view screen. He suspected that elsewhere, Priscilla and Shahlah were in similar situations.

He waited a couple of minutes, took out his link, and brought up Worldwide News. A Christian church had been bombed in Senegal. Japan was still trying to recover from a tsunami. Off-season hurricanes continued to ravage the American coast. A nitwit trying to create a biobomb in Scandinavia apparently activated the thing prematurely and killed himself in an otherwise empty corridor at a hotel that was serving as the site of an international law-enforcement convention. And the nominations for the year's film awards had been released.

The secretary pressed her fingers to an earpod, looked across at Jake, then at the director's door. The door opened. "Go right in, Captain," she said.

Jake had known Patricia McCoy for twenty years, from

the days when they were still testing robotic versions of alternate jump systems, none of which had ever worked without killing the test animals or disappearing into Barber space, never to be heard from again. Patricia had been a flight engineer then, and they had orchestrated a couple of missions together. She was, he thought, one of the few managers he'd seen who wasn't in over her head.

She stood just inside her office, wearing a wistful smile. "Jake," she said, "how are you doing?" She was still trim, still looked good. She had thick chestnut hair, dark brown eyes, and a methodical manner that never left him in doubt who was in charge.

"Hi, Patricia. Okay, I guess." He switched off the link and got up.

Patricia signaled her secretary. "No calls, Gina."

"Yes, ma'am."

He followed her into the office. Pictures of early interstellar ships circling alien worlds covered the walls. There were space stations and Moonbase and shots of Patricia welcoming President Norman to the space station. And, on her desk, he saw photos of her husband and two kids. "Good to see you again, Jake." She closed the door. "It's been a while."

"A couple of years," he said.

Three armchairs faced her desk. She settled into one and invited Jake to sit beside her. "You have no idea how scared we were that some of those kids wouldn't come back. Before I say anything else, I want you to understand that we are in your debt."

"Thank you," he said. "It's a good thing Drake and Joshua were there, or it would have been a disaster."

"Well, you and Priscilla what's-her-name, Hutchins, got them off the *Gremlin*. Thank God for that."

"It was touch-and-go for a while. What the hell happened out there? How did a bomb get planted on the *Gremlin*?"

"The official story is that we don't know."

"What's the unofficial one?"

She chewed on her lip. "We're getting a lot of threats lately."

"Because of the terraforming."

"Right. We've got people telling us they are going to blow

up the *Wheel.* Take us all out. Usually, we have no way of knowing where they're coming from. But in this case, yes, we know who bombed the *Gremlin.*"

Jake leaned forward. Waited.

"It goes no further."

"I won't say anything."

"He's an old friend of yours, Jake. Leon Carlson."

He stared at her. "That's not possible. Leon wouldn't hurt anybody."

"Well, apparently that's not so."

Jake had known Leon for the better part of twenty years. "What makes you think it's him?"

"When he found out that the *Gremlin*'s assignment had been changed, that instead of carrying supplies out to Selika, it was taking a bunch of high-school kids on a tour, he called in to warn us."

"Who talked to him?"

"*I* did. He called *me.* He said he wanted to be certain we got the message. He was trying to disguise his voice, but it was him."

"You're certain?"

"Yes, Jake. No question about it."

"My God. Where is he now?"

"We don't know. He's gone." She took a deep breath. "He thinks we're monsters, Jake. That we're aiding and abetting. Anyhow, we were able to warn Joshua. He found it and began trying to dismantle it. That's what set it off. The thing warned him first, told him if he touched it again, it would explode, and that in any case it would go off in two minutes or something like that. It gave him time to get out of the way. And, fortunately, to get the kids clear."

"The *Thompson* was originally scheduled to go to Selika, wasn't it?"

"Yes. We think the bomb was intended to wait until he docked out there and explode at the station. We got a break when Kosmik donated the ship for the awards flight, and Carlson called in."

Jake shook his head. "Better not let Kosmik do any more favors for anyone."

"I guess not. Anyhow, the Feds are looking for him." She

leaned back in her chair. "You don't have any idea where he might be, do you?"

"No. I haven't actually seen much of him this last year or so."

"Pity," she said. "Well, it was a shot."

"Sorry."

"If you think of anything, let us know."

"Sure."

Her expression changed. Became even more somber. "There's something else."

"Okay."

"Tell me what happened out there."

Jake described it, how they'd brought everyone over to the *Copperhead* and the *Gremlin* had ripped into the atmosphere, how they'd rotated the kids in and out of the lander so they got some decent air periodically, how it had seemed as if the *Thompson* would never arrive. And, finally, how Joshua had walked into the cargo bay and drained all the air out of it.

When he finished, she sat unmoving, eyes closed. "That must have been horrifying," she said. "When we first got the report, I couldn't believe it. Joshua seemed like one of those guys who—" She hesitated.

"—Were immortal," said Jake.

"Yeah." She opened her eyes and took a deep breath. Looked out a window into the night sky. "I'm reluctant to broach the next question—"

"You want to know how the decision was made."

"Yes. Sorry, but I need to complete a report. That's one of the questions that will come up."

Jake replayed the scene in his mind. He remembered the moment when he understood that there wasn't enough oxygen to allow everyone to survive. And that it would come down to the two captains. One or the other. And with the impact had come the numbing reality that it had to be done quickly. There'd been no time to waste. "Joshua said he had an idea," he told Patricia. "That maybe we could still keep everyone alive. He said he was going down to the cargo bay, and I should meet him there ten minutes later."

The look in her eyes wasn't even skeptical. She *knew* he'd understood what Joshua intended to do.

"Okay," she said. "And then what happened?"

"A little while later, maybe ten minutes, we got a call from Shahlah. She's the daughter of the guy who sponsored the awards. She had no way of knowing what Joshua was going to do. She was worried, so she went down to the cargo bay. But he'd already drained the air, and she couldn't get the hatch open."

"Okay."

"By the time we were able to get to him, he was dead."

Neither of them moved. At last, Jake asked if she needed anything else.

"No." She managed a weak smile. "We'll want you to complete a written report for us by the end of the day."

"All right." He got to his feet.

"So we're clear, nobody's blaming you for what happened."

He nodded. Said nothing.

"One other thing, Jake. Talios."

"Yes?"

"Forget it, okay? We've recovered Simmons's body. And the official story will be that you found the lander adrift. That's it. Decisions will be made at a higher level. Okay?"

"Sure. Whatever you want."

"Look, Jake, this has been a stressful experience for you. Why don't you take some time off? I'll fix it so it doesn't cost you anything. But you've been through a lot."

"No," he said. "I'm fine, Patricia. But thanks. I appreciate the offer."

"All right. Have it your own way. Let me know if you change your mind." She got up. "How about Hutchins?"

Jake got to his feet. "I've already filed my report on the qualification flight. It was cut short, but Priscilla passed easily. She's good. She knows what she's doing. In case you're asking a different question: During the emergency, she did everything we could have asked of her."

"Okay. I'm glad to hear it. Thanks, Jake."

LIBRARY ENTRY

Why would we shed tears that death is inevitable?
For if life has been good, and filled with joy, and if
all these happy memories have passed through our

mind, leaving an awareness of constant good for-
tune, why then would we not, like a welcomed guest,
rise cheerfully when our time has come, and with a
sense of gratitude go quietly to our rest?

—Lucretius, *De rerum natura, III*

Chapter 12

PRISCILLA CHECKED INTO the Starlight and had some warm milk sent up for Tawny. It was unlikely that the Banter Exchange would have cat food for sale. But she called them anyway. They apologized and explained that people rarely brought pets up to orbit. So she ordered some turkey from the hotel restaurant. Then she called her mother. "Just wanted to let you know we got back okay."

"Priscilla, I'm so glad. We were worried the whole time," she said. "I'm so proud of you."

"I didn't really do much, Mom. It was Jake and Captain Miller and a teacher traveling with the kids who took all the chances."

"You were there, too, darling."

"And that was pretty much my total contribution. I guess you know we lost Captain Miller."

"I know. That must have been an awful experience."

"It was."

"I saw you on HV."

"The reporters were waiting when we got off the ship. Anyhow, my training is over. I'm getting my license."

"Well, good, love. When will you be coming home?"

"I'll stay on the Wheel tonight. But I expect to get some time off. When I find out what's happening, I'll let you know."

"Okay. Do you have enough money, dear?"

"Yes, Mom. But there *is* one more thing: I need a favor."

"Okay."

"A cat got stranded at one of the stations. We had to rescue it."

"A *cat*?"

"Yes."

"You want me to take it off your hands?"

"Ummm, yes, Mom. Maybe not so much take it off my hands, but just take care of her until I can figure out how to handle this myself. You'll like her."

She laughed. "Okay," she said. "We haven't had a pet around here since Loopy died."

TAWNY WAS ENJOYING her turkey when the link sounded. "Ms. Hutchins?" A male voice.

"Yes?"

"Would you come up to the operational offices, please? Room 307. We have a few questions for you."

PRISCILLA'S INTERVIEW WAS conducted by Emil Gadsby, whom she'd met on the day of the *Copperhead*'s departure. Emil asked about the students, whether there'd been any problems with life support, presumably other than its being inadequate to keep everybody alive. He asked whether anyone had complained of breathing difficulties at any time, whether there had been any other health issue, and, in general, how the passengers had reacted to the experience. Finally, he looked at her pointedly. "How about you, Priscilla? Any problems?"

"No, Emil," she said. "I'm fine."

He might have been expecting a different answer. Emil was an ordinary-looking man, a little smaller than most guys, with receding black hair and brown eyes that seemed a bit too close together. He spoke slowly, methodically, in a basso profundo that was a complete mismatch with his quiescent appearance. If she looked away, Priscilla could easily imagine she was talking to the head of the gunrunning mob in the latest Brad Halloway adventure.

"Okay," he said. "Good. You've been approved for certification. You'll receive your license at a ceremony in the Starlight on December 22."

"Thank you."

"You're welcome. Good luck, Priscilla. Enjoy your career."

SHE CALLED JAKE.

"Congratulations," he said. "You performed under a lot of pressure. I think you have a serious future in this business."

"Thanks, Jake. Do they know anything yet about the bomb?"

There was a pause at the other end. Then: "They're working on it. I think there'll be an announcement in a couple of days."

He knew more than he was saying, but she let it go. In the end, it didn't much matter *who* did it. Joshua was lost, and that was all she really cared about. "I hope they catch him," she said. "Times like this, I think we should have stayed with capital punishment."

TRADITIONALLY, ON HIS first night back from a mission, Jake would have enjoyed a quiet dinner at the Skyview, with its eighty-foot-long portal, which provided a magnificent view of the Moon, the Earth, or whatever happened to be in the sky. Then he'd head for the Cockpit and hang out there for the balance of the night. But he would inevitably run into friends at the Skyview, and he knew *everybody* at the Cockpit. He wanted to be alone on this night. He wasn't sure why, or maybe he didn't want to face the reason. Nevertheless, he had no inclination to eat in his apartment. He *never* did that. After spending days or weeks in the belly of a spacecraft, he needed people around him. Just, hopefully, not any of his colleagues.

He went down to the North Star. And, of course, in difficult times, we never get what we want. Erin Shoma was seated just inside the front door. Erin was an attractive young woman with lush brown hair and beautiful eyes. She worked for one of the game dealers on the Wheel, and she showed up periodically with Preacher Brawley at the Cockpit. She was sitting with three other women when he walked in. She looked up, saw him, and delivered a painful smile.

The host led him past her table, headed for a corner booth. One of the women was talking, something about the presidential race. Erin seemed to be listening while simultaneously studying her napkin.

Jake saw three or four other people he knew, but nobody else seemed to notice his presence at all.

HE WAS GOING to have to deal with it eventually. So he decided what the hell. He ordered a drink and a sandwich, finished them, and headed for the Cockpit. This was the hangout of choice for employees of the World Space Authority. There were about fifteen people present when Jake walked in. Mostly, they were technical-support people. A few from the admin section. Only one pilot. Some smiled, others nodded, a few looked away. He sat down at the bar and ordered a gin and tonic.

The bartender gave him a thumbs-up. "Glad to see you got back okay, Jake," she said.

A security officer seated around the curve of the bar formed the words *Hi, Jake* with his lips and quickly went back to the conversation with the comm op beside him.

The pilot was Rob Clayborn. At this point in his career, Rob did only occasional assignments. He ran the *Baumbachner* when it was needed, assisting with maintenance and doing periodic flights to Moonbase. When he saw Jake, he came over. "You had us worried," he said.

Jake nodded. "I think we were all worried, Rob. We lost a good man on that one."

"Yeah, I know. Can I buy you a drink?"

Rob was probably the smallest pilot in the interstellar force. He barely reached Jake's shoulders. But he'd received the Collins Medal for disarming one of the antiterraforming lunatics who, a year before, had gotten a gun aboard a shuttle. He wondered how Rob would have reacted had he been present when Joshua started talking about going down to the cargo hold.

There wasn't room for them to sit together at the bar, so they ordered and retreated to a table. Rob wanted to talk about the *Gremlin* rescue, which they did until Jake was able to change the subject. "How's life on the *Bomb*?" It was shorthand on the Wheel for the *Baumbachner.*

"Okay, I guess. I'm getting ready to retire."

"I'm sorry to hear it, Rob."

"Julie's gotten tired of the routine up here. And I have to admit that I'm bored with the job. Kosmik offered me a slot, but that would mean being away weeks at a time. Well, you know how that is. If I start that, Julie's going to see a lawyer."

He was kidding, of course. Jake knew Julie. She'd never walk out on him. "So when are you planning to step down?"

"As soon as they can find a replacement, Jake. You don't know anybody who wants to stay close to home, do you?"

The drinks arrived. "No," he said, "I don't think so. But if I hear of anybody, I'll let you know."

Rob lifted his glass. Studied it. "Is it all right if I say something personal, Jake?"

"Sure." Jake felt his stomach beginning to churn. "What is it?"

Rob put the glass back down without tasting the contents. "I suspect your experience up there must have put you through hell. I wanted you to know that nobody here thinks you did anything wrong."

THE FOLLOWING DAY, a memorial for Joshua was held at the Union Chapel. Priscilla and Jake attended, of course, both in the blue-and-silver uniforms of the World Space Authority. Priscilla stayed in the rear while Jake took a reserved chair near the front.

Priscilla hated funerals. And memorial ceremonies. They were too painful. She knew they were supposed to be the only way to get past the loss of someone who mattered. (Or maybe didn't, so you had to pretend.) But they never made her feel any better. She just flat-out didn't like them. She wanted people to stop pretending the deceased was in a better place. That he'd gone home to some city in the clouds. She didn't understand why she was so cranky that evening. Maybe too much guilt.

Chaplain Truscott entered through a side door. He exchanged a few words with Frank Irasco, the assistant director, and shook some hands. Then he came to the center of the chapel and waited for all movement to stop. "Ladies and gentlemen," he said, "we're gathered here today to pay tribute to one of the most courageous people it's ever been my privilege to meet."

Jake sat quietly, frozen in place.

The chaplain offered condolences to the family. He added that Joshua had also been a member of a wider family. That his loss had brought sorrow "to all those who wore the uniform of the WSA." He was obviously affected himself. "We don't know why these things are permitted to happen," he said in a voice he was having trouble controlling. "We can only have faith and carry on as Joshua would have wanted us to do. Would have done himself."

Friends and colleagues came forward to speak of how they were affected by Joshua's loss. They talked about his walking in the green pastures, about how they would miss him, how they'd have trusted him to carry them anywhere. "He was," said Easy Barnicle, "as he eventually proved, the ultimate captain. He took his responsibilities very seriously, and in the end, he gave his life for those who rode with him."

Eventually, Jake stood, went to the front of the chapel, and turned to face the mourners. "Joshua Miller," he said, "was the ideal of what I would want to be. Without his selflessness, I would not be here today."

Joshua's wife was in front. She did not speak during the ceremony, but when it was over and she started down the center aisle, everyone cleared space for her. She shook hands, thanked some, hugged others. But she never looked at Jake.

HE CALLED PATRICIA McCoy in the morning. "Yes, Jake?" she said, sounding as if she knew bad news was coming. Though maybe, from her perspective, it would provide a sense of relief. "What can I do for you?"

"I've been thinking, Patricia." He was in the Starlight lounge, staring out through a port at an approaching ship. "I'm going to put in for early retirement."

LIBRARY ENTRY

The details of what happened at Lalande are not yet clear. We know that one of the captains, Joshua Miller, died, but that all of the passengers returned unharmed. And we should consider that taking children on flights to other stars, while it may present extraordinary educational opportunities, nevertheless entails a substantial level of risk. Assistance, should they need it, is simply too far away. If the World Space Authority had been able to launch a rescue vehicle from the space station when it first learned a bomb had been planted aboard the *Gremlin*, Captain Miller might be alive today.

The hard reality is that, had the *Copperhead* not happened to be close to Lalande, where the bomb exploded, there might have been no survivors. The death of Captain Miller constitutes a clear statement of the courage and dedication of those who operate the interstellars. But that courage and dedication may not be enough to prevent a greater disaster eventually. Are we going to wait until we lose, perhaps, an entire vehicle filled with young people, as almost happened here?

Children do not grasp the hard fact that their lives are being put at risk. It is one thing for adults to take their chances on a flight for which aid, if it is needed, may simply not be available. It is something else entirely to put our sons and daughters on such a flight. Either we should call a halt, or we should provide the Authority with the means to ensure reasonable protection for interstellar travelers.

—*The New York Times*, November 25, 2195

ON THE NET

I guess there will always be loons who want to bomb people they don't know.   —Brickoven2

We need the death penalty back.   —Bobmontana

Brickoven's right. We'll never run short of maniacs.
—MariaY

Hard to figure how you get a bomb on board a starship. Last I heard, they had weapon detectors. Haven't heard an explanation, but obviously somebody wasn't paying attention. —Sollyforth

Sollyforth doesn't seem to be aware that this is the first time ever somebody tried to bomb a spaceship. I'd have been surprised if they *had* intercepted the bomber. —billreever

Billreever obviously doesn't know they do routine checks at the shuttles. —Sollyforth

Hey Solly, the shuttles don't provide the only access to the Wheel. Some people, insiders I guess, are able to use landers. The search procedures only apply at the terminals. —billreever

Well, whatever the reality is, when they catch the guy who did this—and it will be a guy, it's never a woman—they should fry him. —Bobmontana

That's sexist, Bob. Women are just as capable of behaving like lunatics as guys are. They just don't do it as often. Remember that mother in the Middle East a few months ago whose kid blew himself up in a temple and killed a dozen people? She said she was proud of him. That's as loony as it gets. —MariaY

Chapter 13

THE CERTIFICATION CEREMONY was a month away. Until then, Priscilla's time was her own. The normal routine for a new pilot was to lock down an assignment with one of the deep-space corporations and take some leave. Priscilla needed to get away. Go home and put Lalande behind her rather than spend a week or two on the Wheel. She was tired of being closed in, of the centripetal halfhearted gravity generated by the spinning space station, and of being so far from the nearest beach. Yes, it was November, but she liked beaches. So she called home. Then she called Jake to say good-bye.

"Enjoy yourself," he said. *"Have a big time."*

"I'll give it my best shot."

"How's Tawny?"

"She's good."

"Your mom going to take her?"

"Absolutely. Tawny and I will be headed for Princeton in the morning."

"Good. She's a lucky cat. Oh, by the way, I have news."

"You're going to be the new WSA director."

He laughed. *"No. Even better: I'm retiring."*

"You're kidding, Jake."

"No. I'm pulling the plug."

"You spend a few weeks with me, and it's all over, huh? Well, that's pretty much the way I've always affected good-looking guys."

That broke him up. *"Priscilla, you're priceless."*

"So where are you going?"

"The Blue Ridge. I'm going to settle in Virginia."

"That's kind of sudden, isn't it?"

"It's time."

"Why Virginia? I thought you were from Pittsburgh."

"I have a cabin up there. It's been my vacation spot for years."

"Well, I'm happy for you, Jake. But I'll miss you."

"I'll miss you, too, Priscilla. If you ever need me, just call—"

HER LIFETIME AMBITION went beyond mere piloting. She wanted more than simply taking an interstellar into deep space. There was nothing intrinsically interesting about that. She expected to go farther, to get onto the exploration side. Head for places no one had ever seen. Most of the pilots did nothing more than haul passengers and cargo between research stations and, in a couple of cases, service people working at extraterrestrial archeological sites, places where civilizations had once flourished but which, for reasons not yet clearly understood, had grown dysfunctional and died, taking the inhabitants with them. There was only one known world with living intelligent beings. That was the awkwardly named Inakademeri, an attempt to render in English one of the inhabitants' own names for their world. Priscilla could never understand why the experts hadn't settled on something a bit less difficult to pronounce. Surely, the natives had other names for their world. In any case, it had been shortened to Nok.

Nok was not a place anyone would want to visit. The aliens were bipeds whose appearance was not wildly different from that of humans, but there was a problem. They were impossibly boring. They were locked in a centuries-old series of conflicts arising out of politics and religion and anything else they could think of to fight over. Fortunately, their technology was nineteenth-century, more or less. But, as one of her teachers had put it, they lacked history majors.

Reproductions of their art hung in museums, and translations of their literature had been made available. But they wrote long-winded novels, painted abstracts that Priscilla could make no sense of, and practiced religions that, in some instances, advocated killing nonbelievers. Their advocates claimed it was simply a matter of giving them time to develop. The bad news was that they'd had roughly a ten-thousand-year head start over humans. Maybe in the end, she thought, we would discover that whatever occupants on other worlds looked like, they would all behave uncomfortably like us. Except possibly worse. There might, in the end, be no aliens worth getting to know. At least none close enough for us to find.

But she was forgetting the Monument-Makers. And whoever had been at Talios.

Priscilla had sat in on a conversation in the Cockpit the night before she'd left on her qualification run. She'd heard Preacher Brawley, one of the most respected pilots in the business, going on about how the age of exploration was over. The various governments, after two decades, saw interstellar flight as nothing but a drain on resources. And private corporations were exclusively involved in making money. Tours, orbiting hotels, and potential colonies. But the corporations did not want to make investments that had only a long-term payoff, let alone do any blue-sky science. She suspected that Kosmik would gladly sell off their interstellar operations if they could find a buyer. And the governments were doing everything they could to withdraw funding.

So now, mostly, we weren't doing much other than transporting cargo and passengers. There were several small, privately funded operations, like the Academy Project, that were actually trying to move farther out. But they needed resources.

She would, for the time being, have to settle. Kosmik, Inc. had an office just off the main concourse. She'd submitted a résumé within hours of getting back from the certification flight. Her shuttle didn't leave until four, so she had plenty of time. Why not take some good news home?

She called them. "My name's Hutchins," she said to the

young man who answered. "I'd like to work for Kosmik. As a pilot."

He passed her along to an older guy with heavy eyebrows and a receding hairline. He looked out at her from the display. "You look a little young, ma'am. How much experience do you have?"

"I'll be receiving my license next month."

"Are you on the Wheel now?"

"Yes, sir."

He looked away momentarily. Seemed to be speaking to someone else. "When can you come in?"

HIS NAME WAS Howard Broderick. He was chewing his lip. "So you want to do missions for us, is that right?"

"That's correct, Mr. Broderick. I'd like very much to be part of Kosmik."

He took a couple more chews, glanced down at a notepad, then looked up at her. "Why?"

"Because Kosmik is leading the way in an age of discovery. They're making history. I'm not sure that we've ever done anything more significant than what is happening right now. I want to be part of it."

"I see." His eyes narrowed. "You were on the mission that came in yesterday, weren't you?"

"Yes, sir."

"You're smiling. Why?"

She was wondering how he'd react if she told him that she'd helped rescue a cat. "I was just thinking how much I've looked forward to this moment."

"Yes. I'm sure. It says here you lost Captain Miller. Not you, but the mission you were part of."

She nodded. "Yes. I'm sorry to say that's correct."

"Do you mind telling me what happened?"

She ran through it again, avoiding some of the more difficult details. And again she faced the question she suspected she'd hear a few more times before this was over. "How did they decide who was going to go down to the cargo bay?"

"Captain Miller simply went down without telling anyone what he intended to do." That was, of course, the truth.

"And nobody understood what was going on?"

"Mr. Broderick, I've told you as much as I know."

"I see." He wasn't impressed with her answer. As if she *should* have been aware. He exhaled. Nodded. "Is there anything else we should know?"

"I think that's about it."

"If we decide to take you on, when would you be able to start?"

"The certification ceremony's December 22."

"That's irrelevant, Priscilla. You're already certified. The ceremony's just a ceremony. So when could you start?"

"It's been a long haul. I'd like to get a few days off."

"Okay. Make sure we have your code. We'll see you back here next Friday. December 4."

"Thank you." She tried to keep her voice level. "I can do that."

"Excellent. Congratulations and welcome aboard."

NEWSDESK

After all these years, it's difficult to see what possible benefit can come out of space exploration, with its enormous costs and assorted risks. We've known for a long time that there are other intelligences in the universe although after more than thirty years of looking around, we've yet to find anyone we can talk to, other than the barbarians on Inakademeri. And we clearly have nothing to learn from them.

Our explorers have gone out more than sixty light-years. We've seen some ruins, and we've discovered the Great Monuments, probably the one serious benefit we've gotten from all this. But the reality is that we've had better sculptors at home though no one wants to admit it.

We live on a crowded planet, beset by widespread famine and plagued by the environmental meltdown caused by ancestors who ignored the problem until it got out of control. And we are still charging around bombing each other.

There is no intent here to belittle the accomplishment of those who gave us the means to reach out and conquer the vast distances that separate us from other worlds. But the hard reality is that the resources being used to send vehicles to the stars are desperately needed at home. Let's take care of our own world before we go looking for others. Let's not repeat old mistakes.

—Gregory MacAllister, *Baltimore Sun*,
November 26, 2195

Chapter 14

IF YOU SPEND twenty-seven years in space, nineteen of them piloting interstellars, you tend to lose contact with the bonds of Earth. Friends wander away, your family dissipates until only a few cousins and nephews remain, and the neighborhood in which you grew up changes so much that it's no longer recognizable. Visit, and you're a stranger. Consequently, Jake had no reason to return to Pittsburgh. Instead, he'd always liked remote places. Growing up, he'd thought that one day he'd like to live on an island. Or a mountaintop. It was probably the same drive that took him to the stars.

The Blue Ridge was a natural place for him to settle. His cabin was located halfway up a mountain, near Radford, Virginia, with a spectacular view of Claytor Lake. He had a few acquaintances but no friends in the area. It was his kind of country—rugged, beautiful, a place where you could expect to be left alone. It had never occurred to him that when the day came on which he actually settled into the cabin, he might not *want* to be left alone.

He'd visualized a different sort of retirement, one in which his colleagues, over the course of his last few months, would tell him how much they'd miss him, in which his bosses would acknowledge his work with a certificate, which he'd frame and hang over the sofa. There'd be a farewell party at the end. He'd expected to come to it with a sense of satisfaction, knowing that he'd done exactly what he'd wished with his life and with the knowledge that it had counted for something. He would arrive on the Blue Ridge bearing the respect of the professionals with whom he'd worked. Of people who'd been around awhile. And of people like Priscilla, who were just starting and would form the next generation. Instead, he couldn't even look into the eyes of those whom he'd known all these years. Least of all, into Priscilla's.

She'd pretended everything was okay. But she knew what he'd done. And God help him, if he were put in the same situation today, he'd probably do the same thing. Stall and pretend he didn't know what Joshua was really saying until he went below and shut off the air.

It was raining when he arrived at the cabin. He'd never been here before for more than a couple of weeks at a time. But it had officially been his home for nine years. He dropped his bags on the front deck, listening to the downpour and the wind while the lock clicked open. No other building was visible although at night a few places across the slopes would light up. And, of course, if he was watching at the right moment, he'd be able to see the maglev going through the valley on its way to Roanoke.

He went inside and closed the door. A sudden rush of rain swept across one of the windows. Jake crossed to the liquor cabinet, opened it, and poured himself a glass of rum. Then he settled into a chair, sipped his drink, put the glass down on a side table, and let his head sink back. It's not always a good thing, he thought, when you run into desperate circumstances and find yourself in the presence of a hero. You may come out alive, but it was possible nothing else that mattered would survive.

He was a different person now than he had been when he was called to go out and take over Priscilla's certification flight. He knew more about himself than he had then. He'd been tested and found wanting. And he'd have to live with it.

Well, okay. How many other guys would have been willing to step up in that kind of situation?

He showered and got into fresh clothes. There was nothing

in the refrigerator, but he didn't want to have dinner alone anyhow. Not today. So he went down to Earl's, where he routinely ate when he was in town.

IT WAS EARLY, and there were only three or four other customers in the place. He knew the waitresses, and David the bartender. David was a heavyset African-American who knew what Jake did for a living and consequently treated him like a VIP. Earl himself was an invisible presence, a guy who lived in Richmond and owned a chain of bistros.

"What'll you have, Jake?" asked David. "Been a while."

"Hi, David." He sat down at the bar. "A light beer would be good. How've you been?"

David gave him a big smile. "Pretty good, actually." He picked up a glass, filled it, and set it down in front of him. "I'm opening my own business."

"Really? You're not leaving here, are you?"

"Yes. This is my last week."

"Well, congratulations," said Jake. "You bought a bar?"

"A restaurant. In Charlottesville. I'll be moving down there next week." He was muscular, a guy who might have been a linebacker in his earlier days. And he looked happy.

"Good luck with it, David." He picked up the beer and took a swallow. "What kind of restaurant is it?"

"It's going to be a Bumpers." He handed Jake a flyer. "It opens the weekend after next."

"Knockout waitresses," said Jake.

David laughed. "Just like here."

"I hope you make a million up there, David."

"I hope so, too." He glanced at the overhead. "How's life on the space station? I see you helped rescue some girls last week."

"More or less."

He had to break off to pour drinks for a couple of customers. Then he was back: "How long you going to be here this time, Jake?"

"I'm home permanently. I've retired."

"Really? You're pretty young to be doing that, aren't you?"

"I wish."

"Are you going to be living here?"

"For a while, anyhow."

"Well, good. I hope you'll come over to Charlottesville to see me occasionally."

"I'll do that, David."

"I'll tell you something, though. If I could fly one of those things that *you* do, I don't think I'd ever quit."

WHEN HE'D FINISHED his dinner, Jake went back up to the cabin and turned on the HV. He needed to get a couple of women in his life. Maybe that would help him break out of this mood. There were a few places in the area he could try. But not tonight.

He settled onto his sofa and looked for something to watch. He skimmed over cooking shows, talking heads going on about the presidential campaign, more talking heads discussing a woman who'd gotten dumped and responded by murdering her boyfriend, the boyfriend's father, and a pizza-delivery guy who'd gotten seriously unlucky. He found an Ed Brisbane comedy, but he'd seen it. And a science-fiction thriller with a man and woman crawling through a pipe pursued by a spidery beast.

Yuk.

He was still looking when his link sounded. He lowered the volume on the HV. "Hello?"

"Mr. Loomis? This is Sheila Pascal. I'm calling for ITI." Interstellar Transport, Inc. *"We understand you've retired."*

"That's correct."

"Mr. Loomis, we need an experienced pilot. We'd like very much to talk with you. Maybe bring you on board."

"No, thank you, Sheila. I have no plans to go back."

"Well, yes, that's what we heard." Her voice warmed. *"We'd make it worth your while, Mr. Loomis. We are moving people and cargo out to several stations. You'd find the work interesting and rewarding—"*

"Thanks, Sheila. But I'll have to pass."

"Okay, Mr. Loomis. I'm sorry to hear it. We expect to keep the job open for another forty-eight hours or so. So you

*have time to get in touch with us if you change your mind. I'll
hope to hear from you."*

JAKE WAS STANDING on the front deck in a heavy jacket watching the sun dip below the mountains. It was cold. November in the Blue Ridge. A steady wind was roiling the tree limbs. He was about to go inside when his link sounded. The ID signaled an unknown caller. *"Jake?"* A male voice. Familiar.

"Yes," he said.

"This is Leon."

"Leon?" His jaw dropped.

"I need to see you."

For a long moment he stared at the link. "Leon, you didn't really *do* that, did you?"

The wind murmured in the trees. *"Yes,"* he said. The word hung in the vast mountain desolation. *"God help me, Jake, yes. I did it. It wasn't supposed to happen the way it did."*

Jake was surprised that he felt no sudden rage. Only a cold lack of emotion. "You know about Joshua?"

"Yes. I know." Something cackled. *"Jake, I'm just a couple of minutes away. Can I come by? I need to talk to you."*

"You know where I am?"

"Yes. Please, Jake."

"All right. Come on over."

DESPITE THE COLD, he waited on the deck. The view was spectacular. Snow-covered mountains, Claytor Lake trailing away to the southwest. The woods were silent, but somewhere he heard kids laughing. Probably the Conway cabin, the only one nearby, though it wasn't visible. Gradually, the laughter subsided and was replaced by the sound of a car coming up the mountain road. The only thing he could think of at that moment was the pleasure it would give him to throttle Leon Carlson.

The car came in through the trees and pulled off into the driveway behind his two-door Ford Lance. Leon got out, looked up at him, closed the car door, and simply stood with slumped shoulders. "Hello, Jake," he said.

"You know the Feds are after you?"

"Yeah. I know."

They stood staring at each other until finally Jake reached back, opened his door, and held it. Leon climbed the three steps onto the deck. He hesitated at the entrance until Jake motioned him inside. "Jake," he said, "I'd give anything if I could go back and change what I did."

"Yeah. I don't guess you get a do-over, do you? Not when you kill somebody."

"No, you don't. I'm going to have to live with that. I thought— Well, Jake, you don't know what we're doing out there. We're destroying an entire world. Everything on it is dying."

"I understand about that, Leon. But how does that justify your putting a bomb on a goddam interstellar?"

"I—I just got it wrong. Nobody was supposed to get hurt."

"You could've taken out those kids, too."

"Damn it, Jake, there weren't supposed to *be* any kids. There was only supposed to be Drake and the shipment. I had it set up so he'd dock at the Selika station, and an alarm would go off and warn him about the bomb. There would have been time for him to get away from it. I was trying to make a statement. It's all I wanted to do. Find a way to alert people about what's happening."

They sat down in the living room. Jake got some scotch and filled two glasses. "Here." He set Leon's on the side table. "What do you want me to do? You want me to help you get out of the country somewhere? Is that what this is all about?"

"No, Jake. My life is over. I just want you to cut me some slack."

"In what way?"

"I want to apologize. I know what you went through."

"No, you don't. You have no idea what I went through. I stood aside out there and let Joshua kill himself. Who do *I* get to apologize to?"

"I'm sorry, Jake. That's why I'm here. I couldn't just let this thing hang. I can't do anything now except this—" He finished the drink in a swallow and stood. "I'm sorry. I'd change it if I could." He started toward the door but stopped.

"If you want to call the police, they can pick me up on the road." His voice broke. He was almost in tears. "Or, if you want, I'll wait here for them to come for me."

"You're right, Leon. You really screwed it up." Jake stayed unmoving in his chair.

Leon opened the door and looked back at him. "Good-bye, Jake," he said. Then he was gone.

NEWSDESK

HOMICIDE RATE IN CITIES RISING AGAIN
Philadelphia Worst in Nation with 63 Dead So Far
Projected to Reach 70 by Year's End

EBERLE HAMPTON DEAD AT 122
Cause of Death Uncertain
Beloved Vocalist Founded Child Rescue

SPACE STATION TO UPGRADE SECURITY
New Systems Already in Place

PRESIDENT NORMAN PARDONS TURKEY
Representatives from Both Parties Attend
New White House Dinner

HIGH IQ LINKED TO COMIC BOOKS
Early Childhood Activities May Count More Than Genes

RED SOX SIGN BOOMER LYSON IN RECORD DEAL

ISRAEL, PALESTINE HOST WORLD CHESS TOURNAMENT

MCGRUDER BLASTS NORMAN ON ECONOMY
AS RACE HEATS UP
Tells Supporters "It's All About Jobs"

DENTIST DROWNS WHILE RESCUING KIDS
Helps Two Girls Survive Overturned Canoe

CHURCH ATTACK RENEWS PLASMA WEAPON DEBATE
NLA Resists Attempts to Impose Ban

ZANZIBAR FERRY OVERTURNS
Six Dead; Captain Sought

Chapter 15

JAKE LISTENED WHILE Leon started his car and pulled out of the driveway. Joshua's killer, and *he* was just sitting there. Wonderful. He removed his link, a silver bracelet, and put it on the side table. Cars were not silent, though the noise was artificially created, consisting of a standardized droning so people could hear them coming. He stared at the link as the car descended the mountain road until, finally, he couldn't hear it anymore. What would he tell Patricia if she found out he'd just sat while Carlson drove off? He didn't work for her anymore, so technically she had no claim on him. Except maybe that he behave in a decent manner.

He could happily have strangled the guy, but he couldn't call the police.

He put on the HV, located a talk show, three people debating whether the general public should have unfettered access to plasma weapons. The HV was valuable in that it filled the cabin with noise. But it did no more than that when he had to watch it alone.

After a few minutes, he shut it down, pulled his jacket on, and went outside. The sun was gone, and the temperature was dropping rapidly.

* * *

HE MET ALICIA Conner the following evening at the Round-house. She was sitting with two other women when she caught Jake looking at her. She dropped her eyes, but she didn't suck in her cheeks or tighten her lips or show any of the other turn-off reactions. It was come get me if you want me—

Alicia was a brunette, energetic, bright, obviously a woman who enjoyed herself. Jake asked her to dance. She pretended to think about it, smiled, and got up. They floated around the floor, exchanged names and compliments, and found a table where they could sit and talk. "I work down at the bank," she said.

"An accountant?"

"No. I'm in security. What do *you* do?"

"I used to be a pilot." He didn't want to use the word *retired*.

"What kind of pilot, Jake? A boat?"

"Interstellars," he said, trying to sound modest. Her eyes went wide. Then skepticism flowed into her smile.

"Come on," she said. "What do you *really* do?"

He returned the grin. "May I buy you a drink?"

ALICIA WAS JUST what he needed after the interaction with Leon. She was energetic, funny, and she grew more attractive as the evening wore on. She was about thirty, was a graduate of the University of Georgia, and had been living in the Radford area for about a year. She was a computer geek, charged with overseeing the protection of customer accounts.

And she *loved* talking about outer space. What stars had Jake been to? Had he really seen some of the Great Monuments? Had he *touched* any of them? When he said *yes*, she squealed and wanted to know which one and how it had felt. "I've always wanted to go out to Iapetus," she said. "I just haven't gotten around to it yet."

She was full of questions. What was the farthest place he'd ever visited? Had he seen any of the ruins on—where was it?—Quraqua? Then she connected his name to the *Gremlin* incident. Wasn't he the captain involved in the rescue of the schoolkids? "Yes," he said. "That was me." It was a tense moment while he waited to see whether she'd dig deeper. But she moved on. What was the most compelling astronomical object he'd seen? (That one was easy: Earth, when you were coming home and got close enough to make out the oceans and continents.)

So they danced and talked their way through the evening.

WHEN IT WAS over, and she commented that it had been a lovely night but she needed to get home, he made no effort to talk her into going back to the cabin. He liked her too much to chance spoiling things. They had by then visited several of the nightspots. He took her back to the Roundhouse, where she'd left her car. "Alicia," he said, "I wonder if we could get together and do something like this again?"

"It *has* been nice, hasn't it?" she said.

"Absolutely." He looked down into those brilliant eyes. "Would it be okay if I called you later? Maybe we could set something up?"

"I can live with that." She smiled and gave him her code.

They kissed, gently, with carefully contained passion on his side. He escorted her back to her apartment complex. He watched her park and waited until she was at the front door. She waved and went inside. Then Jake returned happily up his mountain road. Sex would have been good, he thought, would have been *outstanding*. He suspected he could not have made it happen, though. But it wasn't what he needed at the moment anyway.

What he needed was a friend.

The guys in the Cockpit would have thought he'd lost his mind.

ALICIA'S DIARY

Tonight, I might have struck gold. We'll see.

—November 26, 2195

Chapter 16

PRISCILLA AND TAWNY rode the shuttle down to the Philadelphia spaceport. She got off and gloried in the familiar tug of gravity, in being able to walk without paying attention to every step, in not having to be careful about the way she handled her coffee. One of the other passengers, a large middle-aged woman, read her eyes and smiled agreement. A young couple, probably finishing a honeymoon, were actually jumping up and down, deliriously happy to have their weight back.

She took a taxi to the Thirtieth Street Station, where she boarded a glide train. Twenty-five minutes later, she got off in Princeton. Her mother was waiting in the station and greeted her with a big hug. "It's so good to have you home," she said. "We were following the news reports, but nobody seemed to be sure what was going on."

"It's great to be back, Mom."

Mom had news. Reporters had been calling, asking how she felt about the way Captain Miller had died. "I didn't get into that. Told them I didn't know anything about it. They were also hoping to find you, but I didn't tell them you were coming home." She smiled.

"Thanks, Mom."

Her eyes clouded. "I have to say that I wasn't impressed by Loomis's behavior."

"It was an impossible situation, Mom. We didn't know. You might as well blame me."

"That's hardly the case, love. But let it go. Did I tell you that Uncle Phil is finally going to get married? To a doctor, no less. Her name's Miriam. You'll like her. And Cousin Ed finally quit his old job with the city. He's working over at Margo's bakery. A chef. I think he's finally satisfied. It's really what he's always wanted to do."

Ed was, in fact, the best cook in the family. He'd been a history major in school, but it hadn't worked out. He'd tried teaching, had been a naval officer, and had talked about writing a history of the post-Islamic wars. He'd admitted to Priscilla that the era was too complicated and too chaotic for anybody to make sense of. "It might need twelve volumes," he'd told her. When she'd left, he'd been a clerk at the county unemployment office. "For a while," said Mom, "we thought he'd just gone around to the other side of the counter." They both laughed.

They left Tawny in the car and stopped for a snack at the Delmore Pizza. It was almost 3:00 A.M. for Priscilla, who'd been living on Greenwich time for almost three months. But the aroma of pizza had always been enough to keep her awake. They sat down at a table, and Mom said something about going off her diet, but it was worth it to have her daughter home again.

Her mother, fortunately, had stopped calling her "Prissy." Priscilla had never liked the name. Mom was the only one who used it, but, although Priscilla never said anything directly, she'd made no effort to hide her feelings. Obviously, the message had finally gotten through.

She was living alone now. Had been since Daddy's sudden death two years earlier. Sitting at the Delmore, trading stories with her mother, talking about Barton's World and the frightened students, she realized that her mom was proud of her.

HER BEDROOM HADN'T changed much. The framed photo in which she stood between her parents in front of one of the monitors at the Drake Center still commanded attention from the top of her bureau. A photo of the *Galileo*, an early super-luminal, hung over the bed, and a picture of her with her old boyfriend Charlie Cartwell at a Wildwood beach stood under a lamp. A calendar featuring a wide-eyed parrot hung near the window. It was still set at September, when she'd left for her final weeks in training.

Like anyone's childhood bedroom, it encapsulated a lot of memories. Jerry the Hamster waving at her from the lamp shade, the upper shelf of her closet where she'd hidden Christmas gifts for her parents, the child's desk in one corner where she'd started her first diary.

On that night, because she was still running on Greenwich time, she awakened long before dawn. She started thinking about breakfast and decided to get up. It seemed like a good day for a bagel topped with strawberry jelly.

She put on the HV and got a shock: The FBI had held a press conference and named the suspected bomber in the *Gremlin* incident. It was *Leon*.

That was simply not possible. He was a friend. She'd shared meals with him and knew he would never deliberately injure anyone. But she remembered the evening on which there'd been the altercation in Skydeck. Still, it could not have been him. The interstellar pilots and techs had a sacred bond of sorts, a commitment to one another that everything was secondary to the safety of their passengers and each other. The notion that one of them would deliberately put a bomb on a ship was counter to everything she'd come to believe.

She shook her head. *Can't trust anybody.* But she just couldn't buy it.

SHE CHECKED HER link, hoping to see a message from, maybe, Interstellar Transport attempting to buy her away from Kosmik. But there was nothing. She got up and looked out the window at the McClellands' house across the street, clothed in darkness. A three-quarter Moon was framed just over its roof.

Even now it was hard to believe she'd walked on its surface.

* * *

SHE GOT A call from Wally Brinkman that afternoon. She and Wally had run an on-again, off-again romance over the past year. Wally had been shocked that past summer when she'd announced her intention to leave Princeton. *"Princeton?"* he'd said. "Priscilla, you're going to be leaving *Earth*. You really sure you want to do that?"

Wally had gone into investment banking. He was a good guy, but he thought life was exclusively about money. That was what his education had been for. He'd told her that she could do much better at home. "There's no money in piloting," he said. "For one thing, even if you had some resources to start with, you're too far away from everything to be able to keep up with what's going on. So you have to trust somebody else to manage your investments." He'd shaken his head. "It's just a shortsighted way to do things."

"So, Wally," she said, when his face blinked onto the screen, "how is it going?"

"Just fine," he said. *Just fine* was a kind of mantra with Wally, who didn't believe in putting his emotions on display. *"I see you're a hero now. Well done."* Big smile.

"Well," she said, "it was really Jake Loomis and Captain Miller who were the heroes. All I did was mind the ship."

Wally had black curly hair that was never quite trimmed properly. He liked to portray himself as a guy who didn't worry about details, who played for the big score. She was saddened that he always seemed fearful of being himself. *"Modesty,"* he said, *"is one of the signs of true greatness."* His smile suggested he was kidding, but not really.

"No," she said. "I was never in danger. It was the two captains who took their chances. And a teacher."

"Yeah, I heard about all that. Heard about Loomis." His tone hardened.

"What did you hear?"

"That he stood by and let the other guy go down to the chamber where they didn't have any oxygen."

"Wally, that's not exactly what happened."

"Okay. I'm just repeating what I'm hearing."

"Who's saying *that*?"

"I saw it on the talk shows." A chill touched her heart. *"Are you saying that's not the way it happened?"*

"It's not. It isn't that simple, Wally."

"Okay. I've never trusted the media anyhow. Listen, the reason I called, I wanted you to know I was really glad to hear that you'd got through all that and were coming home for a while. How long are you going to be here?"

"I'm not sure. Probably just a few days."

"When you go back, will you be stationed somewhere?"

She smiled. "I assume I'll be *somewhere*, yes."

"But not anywhere near Princeton?"

"Probably not."

"Well, I'm sorry to hear it." He appeared uncertain. *"I was wondering if I could take you to dinner tomorrow evening? Maybe we could go to Talbott's?"*

She heard cars pulling up outside. "Sure, Wally. I'd enjoy that. What time?"

"Pick you up at seven?"

"See you then."

THE HOUSE AI was George. George was her grandfather on her mother's side, but no one had ever claimed he'd been the reason for the name. She'd met an old boyfriend of Mom's once with the name. "Reporters, Priscilla," George said.

"Okay." Two cars had parked in the driveway. They carried emblems from Worldwide News and CBC. Central Jersey News was pulling alongside the curb as she opened the door. "I've got it," she said. Several reporters were hurrying up the walkway. "Hello," she said.

They all began speaking at once. The first to get through to her was a tall, African-American woman. "Hi, Priscilla," she said. "I'd like your take on what happened to Captain Miller. Did they cut the cards to see who'd go into the cargo bay? Or what? How did they make the decision?"

"Look," she said. "It wasn't anything like that. Nobody knew Captain Miller was going to take his life. We were still trying to figure out what to do."

"So he just *did* it?" said a guy who looked too young to be out of high school. "He didn't warn anybody what he was going to do? He just killed himself?"

"I can tell you that we had just gotten the news that we wouldn't have enough air, and we were trying to figure out what we would do. Why don't you ask me why *I* stood by and let it happen?" Priscilla knew it was a mistake before the words were out of her mouth.

"Why *did* you?" asked another of the reporters. A large male this time.

"Let me try again," she said. "I didn't know what he intended to do. Nobody did."

"Can you tell us where Jake Loomis is now?"

"I have no idea."

"You must have known someone was going to have to fall on his sword. Was it a choice between either Loomis or Miller?"

"Hey," said a female reporter off to one side. "Give her a break. What the hell are you people doing?"

Priscilla handled the other questions about as well as could be expected. She gave credit to Jake and Shahlah, and said that the girls had been exemplary. "They were in a scary situation when we got there, but they kept cool. Couldn't have been better." She stood out there in front of the house, not dressed for November weather, not feeling the cold though, not even aware it was cold because all she could think of was how she was coming across and what a terrible politician she'd have made. "As for Captain Miller," she said finally, "we owe him everything."

More cars arrived and finally her mother realized what was going on and came out and called a halt. It was the perfect finish: Here's the intrepid interstellar captain, or captain-to-be, facing suspicion of cowardice, and she needs her mother to bail her out.

THEY RAN THE clip a few minutes later. Priscilla's mother was furious. "What's wrong with these people?" she demanded. "Didn't they ever hear of chivalry? Anyhow, it's the captain's responsibility."

"Mom, I *was* technically the captain."

"Loomis was your senior officer."

Priscilla had to swallow her frustration. "Let it go, Mom, all right?"

Her mother sighed, sat back in her chair, and crossed her arms. "I'm sorry. I certainly didn't want to offend you."

"It's okay. I'm just a little bit rattled right now."

"There's no need for you to be, love. You're a hero. Despite what those nitwits say."

HER FAMILY THREW a welcome-home party for her that evening. It was supposed to be a surprise, but Mom warned her in advance when Priscilla started talking about going to see a couple of her girlfriends. "Uncle Phil set it up," she said. "Everybody's so anxious to see you."

They all showed up, uncles and aunts and cousins, some of whom she hadn't seen in years. Mark Hutchins had been six years old at their last meeting, a curly-haired kid chasing a puppy around. Now he was taller than she was, and he'd become a heartbreaker. Uncle Phil looked very much like her father. And his prospective bride, Miriam, was everything Mom had said. Her aunt Chris Parroff, who had filled Priscilla's early years with the world's finest chocolate cakes, provided another one.

Her relatives had come from all over New Jersey and Pennsylvania. They had seen what Aunt Chris called Priscilla's news conference. Everybody took offense. Cousin Gregory said he would write a letter. "I was glad that one woman spoke up," said Miriam with a note of satisfaction in her voice. "Somebody needed to put those ding-dongs in their place."

"I wish *I'd* been there," said Uncle Phil. "Those guys will do anything to come up with a story. They don't give a damn about what really happened."

Mark delivered a snort. "Well, whatever. I was glad somebody there defended Priscilla."

"Priscilla didn't need defending," Mom said, visibly annoyed. "She did fine."

Priscilla was relieved when the subject, finally, got dropped.

* * *

THERE WERE A few surprises during the course of the evening. Old friends stopped by. Girls with whom she'd hung out during her high-school and college years. Guys she'd dated. Even Harmon Baxter, who'd walked away from her for a blond cheerleader. Harmon was careful about approaching her. But she had no hard feelings. Wouldn't have given him the satisfaction of being annoyed. He didn't bring up the cheerleader, and, of course, neither did she.

It was during the conversation with Harmon that her link activated. She excused herself, grateful to get clear. The call was from Kosmik. "Hello," she said.

"Priscilla, this is Howard. I wanted to let you know that we need you back on the Wheel. We have a problem."

"I'll try to get a shuttle out tomorrow."

"We've already taken care of it. You'll be on the morning flight out of Philadelphia. And by the way, I know this isn't the way we planned things, but we'll reimburse you for your trouble."

When she heard, Mom was upset. "Is this the way it's going to be?"

"I don't think so. They just need somebody on short notice."

"Where will you be going?"

"I didn't think to ask."

SO THE WELCOME-HOME party became a farewell party. They sang and danced and told jokes and reminisced about the old days. About how Grandpop used to say he didn't mind flying as long as he could drag one foot on the ground. And Cousin Aggie, whose behavior suggested she'd come from Mars. They asked Priscilla what it felt like to slip into that other kind of world, Barber space. And where did they get that name from anyhow? Was it because somebody had had a close shave in there once?

Jackie Tensler, a friend since the seventh grade, asked whether there were "any available guys on the Wheel?" And another cousin wanted to know if Priscilla could arrange to take her along on one of the missions.

Uncle Phil wondered how long it would take to get to Alpha Centauri in his car. And Priscilla's seven-year-old niece Teri told her she was going to pilot starships when she grew up. "Just like you, Aunt Priscilla." Everybody told Priscilla how it was a pity her father hadn't lived to see this day.

She was dancing with Arlen Hoxley when the link activated again. She liked Arlen. Always had. He claimed to have fallen in love with her when they were both in kindergarten. They'd done occasional dates through the years, but he'd never really made a play for her. And she had never really invited his attention. Born to be friends, she thought. Nothing more. But it was enough.

Ordinarily, she'd have shut the link down during a social occasion, but she'd given it instructions on that night to block everything except calls from Kosmik and Jake. And Wally, just in case.

It was Wally. *"Priscilla,"* he said. *"About tomorrow evening—"*

She thought he'd watched the press take her on and was going to back off. "Yes, Wally?"

"We talked about dinner. But I can get tickets for Family Affair *at the Corel tomorrow night. How about we eat early and go to the show? Would that be okay?"*

The Corel was live theater. "Wish I could," she said. "But they've called me back to work."

"Tomorrow?"

"Yes, Wally. I just got the word. Sorry."

"Okay. I'm sorry, too."

"I wish we could have gotten the evening together."

"Priscilla, you are the loveliest woman in Princeton. But I suspect you know that."

Wally *did* know how to get through to her.

AT AROUND MIDNIGHT, the party got suddenly quiet. People were whispering and turning to look at her. "What?" she said. "What's going on?"

Uncle Phil was staring at his link. "He's dead!" he said.

"Who's dead?"

"Carlson."

Mom looked at him and shook her head. *Please don't bring that up in here.*

"No," said Priscilla. "Let's hear what it's about."

"George," said Mom, "turn on the HV. *Newsworld*."

Marilyn Jakovik, the anchor, materialized in the middle of the room. "—Early this evening," she was saying. "He was living in an apartment under a false name. He is, of course, the man authorities were looking for in connection with the interstellar-bombing incident last week that nearly killed a ship full of high-school girls from the Middle East. The cause of death has not yet been released. But Carlson posted a statement earlier today on the Internet. The statement revealed where he was, his remorse over the incident, and his intention to take his own life.

"We are going to run the statement as soon as we come back from commercial. In the meantime, we want to warn you that it may be painful to watch and that parents may wish to exercise discretion with children." Despite the nature of the tragedy, Marilyn managed a smile.

"I have no sympathy for him," said Priscilla. She wasn't sure she meant it. "I'm glad he's gone."

Mom nodded.

"Maybe," said Uncle Phil, "you should wait to see what he has to say."

"I can't imagine anything that could possibly justify what he did."

Her mother paused the commercial, which was pushing a law firm. "Did you not want to watch it?"

"No. I'm just glad it's over."

IN THE END, she changed her mind, or more likely realized she had not meant what she'd said, and they watched.

"There is no rationale for what I've done," said Carlson. He had a deer-in-the-headlights look. "I'm responsible for the death of my friend Joshua Miller. And, because I couldn't keep track of schedule changes, I endangered the lives of ten innocent students and their teacher. And two more people in the *Copperhead*. Both also friends." He was wearing a black pullover shirt. "I've no excuse, and I'm not able to live with what I've done. So I'm going to end it tonight. But before I do that, there's something everyone needs to know.

"I'm sure everybody listening to this is aware of the process called terraforming. It's a process that tries to convert the environment of a world to make it more friendly for human colonization. That sounds good. They're experimenting with it on Selika. Unfortunately, in changing the atmosphere, we are killing off most, and probably *all*, of the life-forms."

His image was replaced by pictures of birds and lizards and whalelike creatures. And animals that might almost have been Scottish terriers and cats and monkeys and other creatures that resembled nothing Priscilla had seen before except that they all had eyes, and they all somehow looked wistful. There were even some plants, shrubbery that *moved* as she watched. She was reminded of the occasional pleas that asked viewers to assist animals currently maintained in shelters or discarded by their owners.

"These are all being killed off, in *your* name, by large international corporations, led by Kosmik, Inc., and aided and abetted by the World Space Authority. If we allow this process to continue, our grandchildren will look back at us and hold us in contempt for standing around and permitting it to happen. Even the people who want to move out to Selika, to colonize it, will find it sterile and repulsive. It won't be the *Eden* they're being promised.

"There's no justification for what I've done. I'm aware of that, and I've had to live with it. But I saw no other way to draw attention to this problem than by doing *something* that would get public notice. Petitions go nowhere. Postings on the Internet accomplish nothing. Appeals to the people who run Kosmik have been turned aside. So I took a chance. It went terribly wrong, and Joshua Miller paid with his life. I will now pay with mine. But I beg you, those of you with any sense of decency, make your voices heard. Stop the terraforming. Whatever it takes, get it stopped."

He was replaced by Marilyn Jakovik, who switched to news of a murder trial. Mom turned it off. "What do you think?" she asked.

Priscilla shook her head. "Incredible," she said.

Her mother's eyes had fastened on her. "Who did you say you're working for now?"

NEWSDESK

VICE PRESIDENT: WE NEED INTERSTELLAR FLIGHT
"Confining Ourselves to This Planet Endangers the Species."

KORMANOV ARGUES FOR EXTENDED INTERSTELLAR EXPLORATION
"To Do Any Less Is to Forget Who We Are."

MAGLEVS KILLING DEER
Wildlife Protection Agency Appeals to Congress
Magnetics May Be Reducing Reproduction

MANITOBA ENGLISH TEACHER FIGHTS OFF BEAR
Distracts Animal from Children; Wounds Not Life-Threatening

TORNADOES HIT DAKOTAS
No Fatalities, Several Towns Wrecked

MALKAVIA INSERTING IMPLANTS INTO DISSIDENTS

AVERAGE LIFE SPAN IN NAU TOPS 150
Finland Leads the Way at 161

CANCER RESURGENCE IN EAST ASIA
Doctors Baffled

GOLD PARTY DEBATE TONIGHT

LIFE GUARD SOCIETY: TERRAFORMING KILLS EVERYTHING
Martin Pleads for Total Ban
Decries Use of Violence
Bomb on Gremlin *"Inexcusable"*

SOCIAL SKILLS HIT NEW BOTTOM
Virtual Reality Comes with a Price
Parents Urged to Take Control

STAR PILOT BOMBER COMMITS SUICIDE
Posts Attack on Terraforming

Chapter 17

WHEN SHE CHECKED into the Starlight, a message from Broderick was waiting. *"Priscilla,"* it said, *"you are assigned to the* Venture. *Depart tomorrow 0900 for Amity Station. You'll be carrying supplies. No passengers. Pick up Dr. Monika Wolf at the station and bring her home with you. You have time to complete the flight and get back for your graduation ceremony. But do a quick turnaround. Congratulations again. Call me if you need anything."*

Amity was the Selika station, located in the 107 Piscium system, just over twenty-four light-years out. Selika, of course, was the world that was igniting so much controversy. The hope was that it would be ready for human colonists in another six to eight years.

Priscilla called Ops. "What will I be hauling?" she asked.

One of the comm officers was on the other end. *"Basic supplies, Priscilla,"* he said. *"Food and water. Some hardware. And"*—he paused—*"hold on a second. It says here superalgae. It's contained in specially modified kelp. Whatever all that means."*

"Okay," she said. "Thanks."

She went online and did a search. The problem on Selika was that the atmospheric oxygen level was only about 16 percent. Earth-based life likes it at 21 percent. So it had become necessary to increase the content. They were doing it by placing the kelp in the oceans. The superalgae grew fast and began producing oxygen immediately. The kelp has large broad leaves that serve as bladders, which protect the superalgae. It also has leaves that do photosynthesis and thereby support the metabolism.

Well, okay. She'd take their word that it actually worked.

She called Broderick. "How's the security on the *Venture*? Are we sure there won't be a bomb on board?"

"Yes, Priscilla." He let her see that he was being patient with her. *"No need to worry. We've put very good security in place. We are certainly not going to permit a second incident. And we'll go over the ship again before you leave."* He smiled. Nothing to worry about.

SHE WASN'T ESPECIALLY sleepy, so she went down to look at the *Venture*. A security station had been set up. They wouldn't even let *her* on board without a second call to the Kosmik watch officer.

The ship had been connected to feeder lines, and the kelp-algae mix was being pumped into storage tanks belowdecks.

She stood at the dock for several minutes, admiring the vehicle, its smooth silver hull, the pair of slotted wings that would allow her to maneuver in an atmosphere if necessary, the sleek bridge wraparound, the arrow-shaped prow. And, most of all, the twin engines, mounted on either side of the hull. Dream come true.

She went inside and checked out the passenger cabin. It was about the same size as the one on the *Copperhead*, but it was more luxurious, with leather chairs and walnut bulkheads. Not bad. It had four individual cabins, a washroom, and a workout area.

And, finally, she went onto the bridge. She'd been saving it for last. Or pretending it wasn't all that big a deal. She wasn't sure which. Lights were moving out in the dome. A work crew. The bridge was dark save for a single lamp on the control panel. She sat down in the pilot's seat.

"Lily," she said, addressing the AI, "hello." The ship remained silent. "You're not activated yet, are you?"

She listened to the low hum of the life-support system.

Top of the world.

WHEN SHE ARRIVED next morning, they were loading food and equipment. She went inside, picked a sleeping cabin, and stored her bags. She came back out and found Broderick entering through the air lock as the last of the techs left. Two security guards were with him, carrying what she presumed were bomb detectors. "All right, gentlemen," he said, "it's all yours."

One of the guards descended into the cargo area, the other went aft. "All set, Priscilla?" Broderick asked, lowering himself into a seat.

"I will be in a few minutes," she said.

"Good. We're going to be working together, so you might as well call me Howard."

"All right, Howard."

"And you can relax. I don't bite."

"I'm aware of that." His manner was relentlessly formal. Not an easy guy to take on a first-name basis. She was glad he wasn't coming along.

"You know how to get to Selika?"

"Yes, Howard." She made no effort to keep the annoyance out of her voice.

"I'm just kidding."

"I know."

"Okay. You should get back here several days before the ceremony. But don't push it, okay? I suggest you don't stay out there to visit the way some of our people do."

"Okay."

"And don't forget you'll be bringing Dr. Wolf back with you."

"Sure. Is she okay?"

"She's fine. Just wants to come home."

"Anything else?"

"That's about it. And, Priscilla, I appreciate your willingness to take this on at short notice. I know we interrupted your plans. But I won't forget." He got to his feet. "Enjoy your trip. And I'll see you when you get back."

They shook hands. His grip was firm and somehow encouraging. A smile flickered across those thick lips. Then he turned and left.

Fifteen minutes later, the two security guys told her the ship was clean. Then they, too, departed. She closed the air lock, did a quick inventory, and went onto the bridge.

Time to get started. She put on her cap, squared her shoulders, grinned at her own exaggerated sense of accomplishment, and sat down in the captain's chair. "Ready to go, Lily?"

"Yes, indeed, Captain. At your pleasure."

"Very well." Priscilla leaned over the mike. "Ops," she said, "this is the *Venture*." She smiled. "Ready to move."

A male voice responded: *"Very good,* Venture. *There's nothing in the neighborhood. We're opening the launch doors now. Depart at leisure."*

"Roger that."

She sat quietly for a few moments. Unlike the *Copperhead,* Venture did not have shielded ports. She could actually see outside. The docking area, illuminated by sunlight, was big, large enough to accommodate eight vehicles.

My first solo. "Ready to go, Lily?"

"Whenever you are, Priscilla."

They were facing into the docking area, so she'd have to back out.

A couple of guys in chocolate-brown work suits, protected from the void by Flickinger fields, were outside moving boxes from one storage unit to another. They turned toward her to watch. She paused, enjoying the moment before giving her first order as a ship's captain: "Lily, start engines."

She heard the low rumble as they came to life.

"Release the lines."

Lights blinked on the control panel, and she felt a slight tremor as the magnetics shut down and the *Venture* began to drift away from the dock. "Lines released, Priscilla."

She pulled her harness down over her shoulders. "Activate forward thrusters, Lily. Back us out."

The dome's vast curved interior began to move past.

God, this felt so good. She was tempted to take the ship out herself, but standard protocol leaving the station was to turn everything over to the AI. So she did.

Somebody behind one of the observation ports waved. Priscilla would have liked to blink her lights, but that would have been unprofessional. Not that anyone would have taken offense, but *she* would have known. It was time to play the role.

Only one other ship was present: the *Baumbachner*, lying dark and inert on the far side of the port. She watched it pass out of view as they approached the launch doors. The *Venture* moved through into the void. Lily waited the requisite six minutes. Priscilla adjusted course toward the target star, 107 Piscium. Then she fired the engines and began to accelerate.

Forty-eight minutes later, with the Earth and Moon both dominating the sky behind her, the *Venture* jumped into transdimensional space.

IT WOULD BE a long ride out to Selika. Eight days submerged, and another two or three days after arrival to get to the world itself. At least, this time, she had ports and a wraparound that weren't blocked by shielding. That was the good news. Unfortunately, there was nothing outside save the dark mist, which moved slowly past. The *Venture* could easily have been traveling at about two knots.

Located in the direction of the constellation Pisces, 107 Piscium was an orange-red main-sequence star. It was about six billion years old. The planetary system consisted of two gas giants and two rocky worlds, one of which was two billion kilometers from the sun, frozen beyond any possibility of life.

The other rocky world was Selika. It was in a Goldilocks situation, orbiting at a range that provided a temperate climate. The name derived from Roger Selika, the billionaire explorer, who'd designed and built his own ship and had been first to arrive in the system. He was rewarded by the discovery of what was then, other than Earth, only the fourth known living world.

The ship's library was loaded with material about the

planet, pictures of vast forests and broad prairies, of rolling hills and jungles with vegetative growths that looked like nothing she'd ever seen. There were beautiful images of inordinately high mountains, broad oceans, and a snow-covered landscape, often illuminated by two or three of Selika's moons. And of a swirling chaotic surf, its confusion probably caused by the multiple satellites.

Priscilla was intrigued by the animated vegetation. It was somewhat disorienting when she first looked at it, vines and branches and sometimes even stems that stretched and weaved and literally reached out for her. And the animals: Some looked lethal—creatures that might have been crocodiles walking on two legs, others with large claws and feline grace bearing a resemblance to tigers except that they, too, were bipedal. And there was something that seemed to look out of a web of six tentacles with eyes that were eerily human. That was the sexapod. Somebody had shown a sense of humor. The sexapod was by far the most chilling creature Priscilla had ever seen. She couldn't help noticing that none of these monsters had shown up in Leon Carlson's appeal. After she'd turned off the sexapods, which had watched her as holograms from the other side of the passenger cabin, she found herself listening for strange sounds elsewhere in the ship.

Enough of that. She took to concentrating on friendlier animals. And there were plenty. Some looked as if they would indeed have made exquisite household pets. Furry, cuddly creatures that would nuzzle you, that would want to share a bed with you.

WHEN SHE'D BEEN on the qualification flight with, first, Harry Everett, and then Jake, they'd watched a lot of HV. They'd enjoyed concerts, watched episodes from the new Sherlock Holmes series, and laughed at the antics of *Venable High*, which recorded the adventures of the students at a private girls' school who, definitely, were not to be taken lightly. "Here at Venable High," the headmistress said at a graduation ceremony, "we expect that anyone who underestimates our young ladies will pay an appropriate price."

Jake had set the shows up to portray Priscilla in the role of

Maggie, one of the more aggressive students, and himself as Charles, the inept local police chief, who was terrified of the girls. In her favorite episode, a few gangsters make the mistake of kidnapping two boyfriends and holding them for ransom. The police are effectively helpless, but the thugs have no chance against the girls, led by an outraged Maggie.

When she'd finished her research, she decided to go back to *Venable High*. But she became quickly bored. It should have come as no surprise. Priscilla had never been much interested in watching HV or going to the theater alone. She needed company to make entertainment work. Though maybe she had an option. "Lily?"

"Yes, Priscilla?"

"Would you be interested in watching a show this afternoon?"

"Absolutely. What did you have in mind?"

She thought her best bet was to find something that would be intellectually challenging for Lily. "How about *The Broken Seal*?" she said. "It's a murder mystery."

"That sounds good."

She put it on. Grant Seagal was a homicide detective who always seemed overmatched by the killer. But the killer's tendency to underestimate the inspector inevitably proved his undoing. The audience always knew from the start who had committed the murder, and it never took Seagal long to figure it out. The suspense always lay in discovering how the detective would establish the truth.

The Broken Seal was a good show. But watching it with an AI who was effectively invisible turned out to be not much different from watching it alone. Priscilla stayed with it, but she was glad when it ended.

IN THE MORNING, she had breakfast in her pajamas and sat down on the bridge and gazed out at the mists. She played a couple of games of chess with Lily, and, when the eggs and toast had settled, got into her workout gear and did her daily physical routine. Then she went looking for a book and came up with a collection of plays by Jason Woodwell, the celebrated dramatist whose career had spanned the early years of the century. She decided to try *Square Pegs*, in which a pair of government workers decide to opt for honesty and efficiency and discover there's an innate danger in an effective bureaucracy. She could read it, or watch it, as she preferred. She didn't feel much like watching another show, so she stayed with the book version.

"Lily," she said, "I need some music."

"What would you prefer, Priscilla?"

"Rachmaninoff," she said.

"Are you serious?" Lily sounded shocked.

"Yes. Why, is that a problem?"

"You seem rather young to have a taste for classical music."

"Put him on the piano," she said. "Nobody's better."

"How loud do you want it?"

"Keep it soft. It's for background." And she started on the first act.

THEN SHE READ *Paper Tiger*, another Woodwell play, a political drama that had won the Americus Award. It had been one of her assignments in college, but Priscilla had not been able to get past the first act. This time she enjoyed it thoroughly. Background music came from Joel Martin, the string guitarist who had brought in a new era a few years back with his light-speed rhythms. She read Woodwell's other plays as well, *Firelight*, *Taking the Plunge*, *Gift Horse*, *The Last Virgin*, *Harmony Island*, and kept going, usually at a rate of two per day. She also read several of his essays, which weren't as much fun as the plays, but they were interesting and helped pass the time.

She talked about her reactions with Lily, who showed, of course, a complete familiarity with Woodwell's work. And that was the problem. She knew all the facts but didn't really grasp what the plays were about. She did not understand why, for example, characters would want to cling to belief systems not supported by evidence. Unlike people, Lily had no fear of being turned off. Or proven wrong.

Each morning, Priscilla arrived on the bridge, asked Lily if anything had changed since the previous night, heard the negative response, and went back to the passenger cabin, where she had breakfast. Two hours later she was in the workout area. She hadn't expected to miss Jake as much as she did. Or miss having *somebody* on board. Thank God, she thought, for Monika Wolf.

PRISCILLA'S JOURNAL

This is the first time I've been out here by myself. I thought I understood about the solitude, when I was alone with a few other cadets, or with Jake. But when there's actually nobody else in the ship, nobody within light-years, it takes on a whole new aspect. I can't help wondering whether, eventually, being alone under these conditions might not have a deleterious effect on emotional stability.

—December 5, 2195

Chapter 18

JAKE WAS SITTING with Alicia at Burstein's German Restaurant in Roanoke, enjoying sauerbraten and red cabbage, when she surprised him. "Are you doing anything tomorrow evening?" she asked.

"Well," he said, "I can't say I have any plans that can't be broken. Why? What's going on?"

"I was wondering if you'd be interested in watching a basketball game?"

That sounded as if she had a nephew or someone playing for one of the local high schools. The prospect of spending two hours watching teenagers run up and down the court wasn't exactly appealing. "Who's playing?" he asked, making no real effort to hide his feelings.

She delivered a mischievous smile. "*I* am."

"*You* are?"

"I play for the Christiansburg Hawks. We're playing Pulaski tomorrow evening."

"I didn't know you were a basketball player."

She produced a ticket and held it out for him. "It's at the Pulaski Recreation Center. If you're interested."

"Sure," he said. "I love watching beautiful women play basketball."

* * *

THEY DROVE OVER in Jake's car. "I don't usually start," she said.

"They put you in when the game's on the line."

"Right. You should also know that the Jets—that's the Pulaski team—are in first place."

"And you guys are right behind them?"

"I wish. No, we're down in the middle of the pack."

"Well, knock this crew over, and I'll treat for drinks afterward."

"How about if we don't knock them over?"

"That's not exactly a championship attitude, Alicia."

She laughed. "Call it reality."

Maybe it would be just what he needed, now that he had a second death to feel guilty about. He was trying to persuade himself Leon's suicide wasn't his fault, either. It wasn't. Not really. But had he met his responsibility and turned him over to the Feds, he'd still be alive.

"You okay?" asked Alicia.

"I'm fine." He hadn't told her about Leon's visit, hadn't told anyone. He'd hated Leon after he found out *he* was the culprit. He'd never forget those terrible hours on the *Copperhead* while they waited for news of the *Thompson*. And the moment when he'd stood silent while Joshua went down to the cargo bay. Nobody had actually confronted him about that. Even Patricia had ducked. Or tried to. But she'd been the one who had framed the words that had cut him so deeply: "To be clear, nobody's blaming you for what happened."

Leon's body remained in the hands of the FBI. His church refused to provide a memorial ceremony because he'd died by his own hand. (Apparently it had been an overdose of some kind.) But his family announced there would be a farewell event at a veterans' club in Vineland, New Jersey.

He was thinking about attending. It was ridiculous. But he *wanted* to go. Maybe, he thought, it would give him some release from the dark shadows that haunted his nights. Leon, the Leon who'd been a friend for more than fifteen years, would not have deliberately harmed anyone. And Jake could not forget the desperation of that visit the day before he'd ended it. There was, in the end, no way he could not attend. "No, Alicia," he said, "I'm fine. Couldn't be better."

SNOW HAD BEGUN falling during the ride to Pulaski, and there was an inch or more on the streets when they arrived at the recreation center. It was the first storm of the season. He left her off at the front door, parked, and joined a decent-sized crowd inside.

The Pulaski team was already on the court. They looked pretty good. In any way you wanted to interpret that. And a couple of minutes after he sat down, they were joined by the Hawks. Jake recognized one of the other women who'd been at Alicia's table the night they'd met. He began to realize he was going to have a seriously enjoyable time. Finally.

During the warm-up, Alicia stood outside the foul circle and sank some jump shots. She was better than he'd expected. So were her teammates. He noted also that the basketball court looked considerably longer than he remembered from his high-school days. *Good thing I'm not out there*.

Approximately two hundred people were present to watch the game. Whistles blew, and the crowd listened, with some clapping, as the starting five for the Hawks were introduced. The loudest reaction came for their center, who must have been six and a half feet tall and exceedingly mobile. How could they possibly be only a mediocre team with that woman on their side? Then it was the Jets' turn, and the crowd applauded and whistled.

The answer to that was that the Jets, at least, had a balanced offense and two players who were blindingly fast.

The Hawks fell behind early but stayed close. Alicia got into the game midway through the first quarter. She was a guard. Jake was impressed with her running and ball handling. She scored twice on inside jump shots, and passed off for a couple more scores. Not bad for a backup.

The Jets increased their lead to seven as the game approached halftime. The Hawks got most of it back with a pair of three-pointers. They'd stolen the ball and were headed back down court for a third try when Jake's link vibrated. Usually, when he was out on the town, he shut it off. But he'd forgotten. He glanced at it. Unknown caller. "Yes?" he said, trying to get over the noise.

He heard a woman's voice: *"Captain Loomis?"*

"Speaking."

But the place was getting loud, and it was impossible to hear. "Hold on," he said. He sighed, got up, and left the gym. Out near the front doors, he apologized and asked if the caller was still there.

"Yes," she said. The noise level from the gym rose to a roar. Then faded. *"Can you hear me, Captain Loomis?"*

"I hear you." He walked out into the street.

"I'm Sandra Coates. I'm calling you for the Astro Society. We'd very much like you to be the guest speaker at our monthly luncheon next week. Would that be possible?"

"Who's the Astro Society?"

"Oh, yes," she said. *"I should have explained. It's a group of academics and scientists. We have a branch in Roanoke. We'd love to have you come and have lunch with us."*

"Why me, Sandra? What would you want me to talk about?"

"Some of your experiences with the interstellars. What you've seen. Where you think we should be going."

"Where in Roanoke?"

"At Carmody's Restaurant. It would be next Wednesday. We start at noon."

THE HAWKS MANAGED to grab the lead just before halftime. Alicia started the third quarter and the game seesawed through the balance of the evening into the final six minutes. But then the Jets, fueled by perfect ball handling and a withering shooting game, took control of the flow. They applied full-court pressure, shut down the Hawks' offense, and even neutralized their center. When the final buzzer sounded, they led by nine. But Jake was impressed by the level of play on both sides. Especially by the fact that no one on the Christiansburg team showed any inclination to give up. The crowd cheered and yelled and, at the end, stood and applauded both teams.

And Jake left the building realizing he was in love with Alicia. How could you not be with someone who could break down court the way she did?

THE CARLSON MEMORIAL was scheduled the following day. He flew to Philadelphia, rented a car, and crossed the Delaware into South Jersey. He was early, so he stopped for a snack. An hour later, he pulled up in front of the Veterans Association Hall just off Valentine Avenue in Vineland. It was a squat, gray structure, originally intended as a manufacturing site. But it had been reconfigured for social events. There were about a dozen cars in the parking lot.

A middle-aged couple were loitering at the entrance. The woman appeared to be wiping her eyes. They went inside as Jake climbed out of the automobile.

Just inside the door, a register had been placed on a table. A young woman sat behind it. Jake signed in, and the woman thanked him for coming. A lectern had been set up on the far wall, which was dominated by a flag, with its sixty-three stars. Two sections of folding chairs faced the lectern. Approximately twenty people were present, most already seated. He was surprised to see Clyde Truscott, the Union chaplain, standing off to one side talking with a few people.

Then it was time to start. Quiet, soulful string music seeped into the room. Those who were still standing took their seats. And a man who resembled Carlson got up and advanced to the lectern.

"Ladies and gentlemen," he said. "For those who don't know me, I'm Shockley Carlson, Leon's father. I'd like to thank you for coming. This is a difficult time for all of us, made especially painful because of the nature of what happened. Anyone who knew Leon knew he would never have deliberately injured anyone. He constantly went out of his way to help other people. During his college years, he was a volunteer at the Vineland animal shelter. He used to joke that if you took care of animals in trouble, you got extra credit at salvation." He paused and looked up at the flag. "Ironically, it was his sense of humanity and decency that got him into so much trouble.

"I'm not saying that what he did wasn't wrong. There's no way I can defend his action. What I *am* saying is that the Leon I knew, that I suspect we all knew, wasn't malevolent. What he did was commit a serious error in judgment, a result of desperation brought on by what's been happening on Selika. He was heartbroken that his actions resulted in the death of Captain Miller, who'd been both a colleague and a friend. He admitted that he'd made a terrible mistake, and he's paid for it.

"Another friend of his, the Rev. Clyde Truscott, who is the chaplain at the space station, has asked for an opportunity to speak with us. Reverend?"

Truscott was a small man with a big voice. "Ladies and gentlemen," he said, "we've lost a good friend, a member of our family, under the worst of circumstances. The one fortunate thing we can be sure of is that, whatever we might believe about an afterlife, we know that Leon is in a better place now than he was a few days ago."

WHEN IT WAS over, they filled a table with sandwiches and strawberries and snacks. Jake looked for a chance to express condolences to Leon's parents. They seemed surprised when he gave them his name, but they thanked him for coming and apologized for what he'd been through. "He was devastated," his mother said, "by the damage he'd done."

Jake wandered over to the table, not actually planning to eat so much as doing something other than leaving the building, which was what he wanted to do. He picked up a pretzel, gnawed on it, and began to edge his way toward the door. Then the young lady who'd been overseeing the register was at his side. "Captain Loomis?" she said.

"Yes. What can I do for you?"

She smiled. "My name's Olivia Patterson. You probably don't remember me. I'm Leon's sister."

He did vaguely remember a sister. "Of course," he said. "I knew I'd seen you before."

She had dark brown hair, blue eyes, and good features

made doubly attractive by their vulnerability. "I was happy when you came in, that you were able to find time for us. I wish Leon could have known that, if something like this happened, you would still come."

Jake looked into her eyes. She seemed nervous. "What do you mean, Olivia? I'm an old friend. Why—?"

"He thought, because of all this, that you—" She stopped, managed to look even more uncomfortable, and continued: "He thought you would hold it against him. The other captain's death. He didn't think you'd forgive him. Didn't think *anybody* from the Wheel would ever forgive him. Wouldn't hate him for what happened."

"It wouldn't really have been up to me to forgive him, Olivia."

"I probably used the wrong word, Captain Loomis."

"*Jake* will work fine."

"Jake. I guess I should have said that he didn't believe you could overlook it. That you could recognize he'd screwed up but let it go."

"I'm sorry he felt that way."

"I'm glad you came. He would have been relieved to know you would be here. He knew his reputation was ruined with the pilots, but he said *you* were the one who was always actually *there*. And he wanted you to tell him it was okay. If that makes any sense."

"Sure it does. And I'm here. He was a good man. I know that. We all do."

"I'm so glad to hear you say it, Jake. I tried to talk him into going to see you. To tell you how he felt. But he thought it would be useless. I wish with all my heart that he'd done it, that he'd talked with you. If he'd done that, he might be alive today."

ON THE NET

You read all these idiot science-fiction novels about invading aliens, and it turns out *we're* the ones showing up and killing everything. I can't believe we're doing this.
—Mickey R.

I'm not particularly religious, but I don't think God would approve of what's happening out there. And I know there are a lot of people who would say there is no God. But even if that were true, the decent thing to do is to live as if there *were* one. I can't see how we'd go wrong if we did that.   —Louie-in-back

Maybe Carlson had it right. Maybe using a bomb was the only way to get their attention.
                                    —JennOnTheLine

So, Jenn, what you're saying is that it's okay to blow up a bunch of schoolkids who have nothing whatever to do with what you're unhappy about.
                                    —OregonAnnie

I'm not saying that, and you can't be that dumb as not to know it. What I was trying to say was that it's a pity we're so blind and deaf that we don't pay any attention to what's going on until a bomb goes off.
                                    —JennOnTheLine

If you're really worried about this stuff, stop talking about it and go to pdy776 and sign the petition. It's the only way to get the attention of the pols.
                                    —Joaquin12

So they get a few million names on a petition. It doesn't do any good. The only thing the pols are scared of is that one of the corporations that keeps them in the Congress will pull its support. It's all about money. Bombs may be the only alternative. I'm not saying we should go that route, but I think we either do something that focuses attention on this issue or forget it.   —HannahMoonlight

Mickey's right: *We're* the aliens.   —Mostafa22

Petitions work, damn it. It just means we have to get enough people behind them. If you idiots would stop complaining and sign the damned things maybe we'd get some action.   —YokaiTao

This is the silliest argument I've seen in a long time. Why do we care what happens 25 light-years away? Let's concentrate on some of our more immediate problems. Like maybe the population problem? Or global warming? Or religious extremism?

—Big George

Chapter 19

ON THE EIGHTH day, the *Venture* surfaced, and thirty hours later Priscilla was approaching Selika. It was a gorgeous green-and-blue world, floating serenely in bright sunlight, accompanied by its three moons. Priscilla looked down at broad oceans, a continent stretching nearly from pole to pole, and a host of island chains. Ice caps were considerably larger than they were on Earth. The average temperatures, she knew, were three degrees lower than those at home. That, of course, would not be a problem for settlers.

Several groups were already vying to colonize the world when it became available. An organization calling itself the Nativists wanted to come out and live in the wild. To get back to nature and escape the dreary routines of modern, civilized life. Two religious congregations wanted also to free themselves from the temptations of the modern world. And there was a band of people who claimed the title Freedom Fighters who thought the NAU had been taken over by socialists, and a group of Chinese who wanted out of a country that they said had become a dictatorship.

All five claimed to have enough money to cover their transportation and get their colony launched. Priscilla suspected some of that might have been contributions from people who wanted to see them leave.

"Priscilla," said Lily, "we have contact with Amity."

"GOOD TO SEE you," said a female voice from the space station. *"Welcome to the cultural center of the universe."*

"We're glad to be here, Amity."

"You should be in time for the party tonight. Just ride the wave in." She was referring to the directional signal Lily had already locked onto.

"Is there really a party?" Priscilla asked.

"It's in your honor. We always party when somebody new shows up. Or when we have any other kind of excuse."

"I'm for that," Priscilla said. When she got closer, she turned control over to Amity Operations, and they brought the *Venture* in alongside the lone vehicle docked at the station. That was the *Kandari*, a ship with several external tanks. An access tube reached out from Amity and connected with Priscilla's air lock. She opened up, and a pair of technicians— a tall, broad-shouldered man and a young Asian woman— waved hello and asked permission to come aboard.

"Absolutely," Priscilla said. "Come on in."

Both were probably in their midtwenties. "Captain," said the male, "this is Tonya. And I'm Rick. We're here to relieve you of your cargo."

"My name's Priscilla," she said. "You guys can have it. You need any help?"

"No, we're good. You should probably go inside. They're waiting for you."

She took her bag, went into the access tube, and was met at the other end by a young woman and a short, stocky man with thick gray hair. "Hello," he said, offering a hand. "I'm Joe Chappell. And this is Wilma Barrister. We're happy to see you, umm—"

"Priscilla Hutchins," she said.

Wilma's eyes sparkled. "Welcome aboard, Priscilla." She was the comm operator.

They were in a lounge with a door in every bulkhead. A dozen chairs were scattered about, and a couple of small tables. A pennant reading PROJECT RAINBOW was fixed over the entrance. "How was the flight, Priscilla?" Chappell asked.

"Long," she said.

"Yeah, we know about that. If there's anything we can do to make you comfortable while you're here, don't hesitate to ask. Wilma will show you to your quarters and provide anything you need."

"Thank you," said Priscilla.

"It's no trouble. We're always glad to have a visitor. Especially one so charming." The comment sounded automatic. Chappell started for one of the doors, but stopped. "Oh, you're aware that you'll be taking Monika Wolf back with you?"

"Yes, Joe. I know about that."

"Very good. She'll be ready to go in the morning. I expect about nine. Now, if you'll excuse me, I'm in the middle of something." He tried another smile, gave up, turned, and left.

"Problem?" asked Priscilla.

"No. Joe always has something important to do. He's a good guy at heart." She led the way out. "He's our director, but I guess you know that." It had been hard to miss.

"I thought that," she said. "Wilma, what's Project Rainbow?"

"That's the terraforming operation."

"How's it coming?"

"All right, I guess." She led the way through a door and down a corridor. "Be careful," she said. "We have some spin but not much." It was effectively zero gee. But they couldn't have produced anything stronger without getting everyone dizzy. Wilma took a side corridor, stopped at a door, and opened it. "This one's yours."

The cabin was a bit compact, smaller even than the quarters on the *Venture*. But it wasn't going to matter. She expected to be out of there within ten hours.

"Thanks, Wilma."

"You're welcome. And I wasn't kidding about the party. Take whatever time you need. When you're ready, come back to the lounge and meet everybody."

IT WASN'T EXACTLY a party. The two cargo handlers, Rick and Tonya, were there. They were obviously lovers. A guy who seemed to be Wilma's boyfriend showed up, and three or four others. "What are you drinking?" asked the boyfriend, whose name was Ben. "Here's the wine list." It was all nonalcoholic.

"Joe," said Wilma, "doesn't believe in alcohol on space stations."

"I can understand that," said Priscilla. "Drunks in orbit. Probably not a good idea."

"You were alone in the ship?" asked Rick.

"Yes," she said.

He made a face. "I don't know why they do that." Rick wore a shirt with a rainbow and the project name. "I don't know how you guys manage it. I'd go nuts if they sealed me alone in one of those things for a week."

"You get used to it," she said, speaking like a veteran pilot and immediately regretting it. Somebody here might know this was her first mission. So she grinned. "At least, that's what they tell me."

"You new?" asked Wilma.

"Just a couple of weeks."

Wilma introduced her to two physicists, Hal and Agnes. Hal was middle-aged, balding, and looked generally bored. He made it immediately clear that he'd been out there a long time. "We don't get many visitors like you."

Priscilla's alarms went off. "I guess not, Hal. So you guys change the weather patterns, right?"

"We do more than that. Basically, what we do is climate adjustment."

"In what way?"

He passed it over to Agnes, whose age and reactions signaled she could easily have been Hal's mother. "We've had to modify the mix of gases in the atmosphere," she said. "This place has good potential for human habitation. It's one of maybe three worlds we've seen where people could actually live comfortably. But it needs some modification. Usually, if we get a decent climate, the gravity level's too much. Or too little. Cilia II, for example, would be a great place to live. Standard gravity and an ideal atmosphere. But it's unstable."

"How do you mean?"

"There's a ton of junk floating around in the system." She laughed. "It gets whacked regularly by asteroids. In a billion years or so, the problem will go away on its own."

Priscilla poured herself an apple juice. "What kind of adjustment do you need here?"

"A higher level of oxygen."

"And you do it with superalgae?"

"Very good," said Hal, trying to look impressed. "You've done your homework."

She nodded. Looked back at Agnes. "How long have you been at it?"

"I don't think anybody, except Hal, has been here longer than a year," she said. "Project Rainbow, though, is about six years old."

"How's it been going?"

"Okay," said Hal. "Oxygen content has gone from fifteen to almost sixteen percent. For better or worse. Or were you talking about the social life?"

Wilma's eyes moved from Hal to Priscilla. She pursed her lips, as if Hal had told an inappropriate story. He shrugged. Smiled. Drank whatever was in his cup.

"Something wrong?" asked Priscilla.

"Well," said Wilma. "Nothing critical. The nitrogen-oxygen balance seems to be having an adverse effect on some of the lower-level life-forms. No big deal."

WILMA CONTINUED INTRODUCING her around, and one of the women made a play for her. As did one of the young males. Social reality in a place like Amity, she realized, was going to be a completely different ball game from anything she'd experienced before. Maybe that was why Monika Wolf was heading home. Priscilla actually felt guilty declining the offers. She almost felt as if she had an obligation to provide a break from the vapid existence. *Amity.* It brought a sad smile to her lips.

Toward the end of the evening, she heard raised voices somewhere in the station. One belonged to Chappell, the other to a woman. Priscilla couldn't make out what it was about. The disruption lasted only a minute or so. But the

lounge grew quiet. And when it was over, everyone behaved
as if it had not happened.

SHORTLY AFTER SHE'D retired, Hal showed up at her cabin
and asked whether she needed anything. She thanked him
and assured him she was fine. He let her see his disappoint-
ment.

Priscilla was up early, packed her bag, and stowed it on the
Venture. Then she joined a couple of the techs for breakfast in
a conference room that also served as the dining area. She
was finishing a plate of pork roll and eggs when she heard the
same two raised voices that had interrupted the party the previous evening. "—No choice," Chappell was saying. "I really
wish you'd rethink things, Monika." The director walked in,
accompanied by a tall, intense woman with black hair and
angry eyes. She wore a white blouse and green slacks, in contrast to the gray work uniforms everyone else had.

"Maybe," said the woman, "you should think about the
potential consequences of all this."

"Try to be rational," he said. "The chances of its happening are remote."

"You don't know that."

"Look, I wish you could just give it some time. If you
leave—"

"Good-bye, Joe. I hope you're right. But I doubt it." She
looked around, spotted Priscilla, and approached the table.
"Hutchins?" she asked.

"Yes. You're Dr. Wolf?"

"I am. I'm ready to leave whenever it's convenient." She
turned on her heel and walked out the door in the direction of
the launch platform. Chappell watched with mounting frustration as she left.

Then he turned to Priscilla, who had just said good-bye to
her companions and was getting up. "Have a good flight," he
said in an accusing tone as though *she* were somehow responsible for Wolf's decision.

Priscilla was thinking that being alone on the *Venture* suddenly didn't seem like such a bad idea.

* * *

TWO BAGS HAD been left by the access tube. Wolf picked up one of them and left the second for Priscilla. She collected it and followed her passenger into the ship. When they cleared the air lock, Wolf stopped and gazed down the passageway at the closed doors. "Which one is mine?"

"Pick one," said Priscilla. "Any but the first one on the left."

Wolf took the middle cabin on the right. "Thank you," she said.

"Anything else you need before we get started?"

"No. We can leave whenever you're ready." She went into the room and closed the door.

Priscilla took her seat on the bridge, said hello to Lily, and started going through her preflight. She was about two minutes into the process when she became aware of movement behind her. Wolf was standing back there watching her. She was several inches taller than the captain and probably twenty years older. "You seem awfully young," she said, "to be a pilot."

"You know," Priscilla said quietly, "this is beginning to feel as if it will be a long flight."

"There's no need to get obnoxious, Captain. I've—" Her voice shook. "I've had enough of that for one day." She turned away, started to retreat, but returned within seconds. "I'm sorry if I've offended you. I didn't intend to. None of this is your fault. I just—" There were tears.

"Can I get you anything, Dr. Wolf?"

"No, I'm okay." She was still having trouble with her voice. "Sorry. I'm behaving like an idiot."

"It's all right."

She nodded. Nodded again. And, finally: "By the way, my name is Monika."

"We'll be leaving in a few minutes, Monika. You can sit here if you like." She indicated the right-hand seat.

"No. That's okay. I'd better just get out of your way." She smiled weakly and left.

Priscilla connected with Wilma, who gave her clearance for departure. *"Enjoy the flight home,"* she added, with an unmistakable note of sympathy in her voice.

Priscilla was tempted to ask for details about what had gone wrong, but she wasn't sure whether Monika was close enough to overhear. Anyway, it was probably better not to have someone else's interpretation. She'd undoubtedly hear about it on her own.

They released the *Venture* from the dock. She told Monika to belt down, eased away from the station, turned onto her course, and began to accelerate.

MONIKA REMAINED SUBDUED. She was polite enough, but she simply didn't want to do much other than read and juggle mathematical displays. Still, Priscilla was pleased to see that she spent most of her time in the passenger cabin rather than in her own unit. That suggested she didn't really want to be alone.

They ate together, and gradually the tension subsided. They talked about how they'd both chosen careers that took them to remote places. "When I was a kid," Monika said, "I got intrigued by aliens. Read too much science fiction."

"So you were a natural choice for the Selika project," said Priscilla.

"I suppose. Though I'm not a biologist."

"What *is* your specialty, Monika?"

"Artificial intelligence. I got hung up on information software pretty early, too." She smiled and, for the first time since she'd come aboard, looked relaxed. "When I discovered we hadn't found anyone we could talk to, nor were likely to, I took the next best bet: create our own aliens."

"But apparently you never lost your interest in exploration."

"No. I guess not. My parents didn't care very much for what I was doing. My father wanted me to become a doctor."

"Your experience sounded a lot like mine. My mom wants me to be a lawyer."

"It was probably the Gene Black novels as much as anything," Monika said. Gene Black had been probably the preeminent writer of deep-space adventure thirty years earlier.

On their fourth morning together, while the ship swam

through the transdimensional fog, Priscilla came into the passenger cabin on her way to the bridge and found Monika in tears.

"It's nothing," she said. "I'm just a little upset, I guess."

"It's all right. We have some medications. I can get something for you. Help to calm your nerves."

"My nerves are fine. I'm just tired."

"Okay. Whatever you say."

"You know, Priscilla, you give up too easily."

Priscilla tried laughing, and it worked. Monika calmed down. But she got the medications for her. When she'd finished taking them, Monika sat with her eyes closed.

"Feel better?"

"Yes."

"Good. We're going to be out here for several more days. Why don't you tell me what's going on? You need someone to talk to."

"I didn't realize you also had a psychiatric license."

"It's required for bartenders and pilots."

"I've heard that. Well, the truth is that I probably need a lot more than talking, love."

"So I assume all this is connected with the terraforming?"

"Ah, yes. Right to the heart of the matter." She was quiet for a long minute. Then: "You know, the way we're going, we'll probably kill off everything on the planet."

"I've heard about that. How, exactly, is it happening?"

"The superalgae. They're increasing the percentage of oxygen in the atmosphere."

"I know. That's the point of the project, isn't it?"

"The extra oxygen is devastating some of the more basic life-forms."

"You mean like, what? Ants?"

"Yes, like ants. Nothing more complicated than that as far as we can determine. And maybe not even at that level."

"That's not the way I understood it. I thought the higher life-forms were being decimated."

"That's all projection. There've been some reductions among some of the higher species, but we're not certain of the connections yet. The problem is that if it's happening, and I'd bet my life it is, we can't wait until the final numbers are in before we back off. And I don't think we'll back off even then. There's too much money involved." She took a deep breath. "So some of us are getting desperate."

"Leon," Priscilla said.

"Yeah. He had it right. Poor bastard. Did you know him?"

"Yes. I never thought he'd have been capable of something like that."

"I guess we never really know anybody."

"You're saying nothing on Selika can adjust to the change in the atmosphere?"

"No, I'm not saying that at all. Many of the life-forms, maybe most of them, can adjust. But some don't. We think only a few, actually. But they're part of the food chain. Knock off some species, and everything that feeds on that species goes, too. And everything that feeds off *that* level. All the way up the chain. We don't know what we're starting here. We don't know where it's going to end."

"Weren't studies done on this stuff before they started these programs?"

"Of course, Priscilla. But there are too many variables. You can't predict everything. You can't catch everything. What's worse, the guys who did the studies knew ahead of time what kind of results management wanted. And I'd be amazed if there weren't payoffs. Anyway, the problem now is that Kosmik has too much invested in Selika to back away."

"Has Chappell reported this?"

"He claims he has. But who does he report to? People who have an interest in keeping the program moving."

"So you're not going to be part of it anymore?"

"That's correct."

"Are you going to blow the whistle?"

"I am. I'm going to blow the lid off."

"Good."

She shrugged. "Right."

Priscilla smiled. "You're supposed to feel a little better now."

"I know. I probably would if I thought—"

"What?"

"It would matter. By the time we get back, Kosmik will have destroyed my reputation. They'll accuse me of being a lunatic, Priscilla."

"They can say what they want. But the facts are on your side."

"No, love. Only the suppositions are on my side. I could turn out to be the woman who went down gallantly defending alien ants. And unfortunately Leon Carlson didn't help matters. Or some of the nutcases who make us all look like lunatics."

"Oh."

"The problem is that we don't have enough information to make a calculation. From what I can see, there's a better than fair chance we'll take out every living thing on the planet. But it will take a while. Maybe centuries. Once it starts, though, once the process gains a foothold, we'd have a very difficult time shutting it down."

THAT NIGHT, SOMEWHERE after midnight, Priscilla thought she heard Monika moving around. She got up, left her quarters, and made her way barefooted to the passenger cabin. There was a light on the bridge.

"Monika?" She called the name softly, as if not wanting to wake anyone else.

She heard a barely audible click. Like a panel closing. And her passenger's voice: "I'm up here."

Priscilla went onto the bridge. Monika was seated in the pilot's chair, but everything seemed in order. "What are you doing?"

"Playing mind games. Pretending I'm the pilot. I'd love to be able to run one of these things. I envy you."

Priscilla sat down beside her. Tied herself in so she wouldn't float away. "Can't sleep, Monika?"

"I've been tossing around all night." She grinned. "I've looked forward for a long time to going home. To the *ride* home. I wish, though, that I could be the pilot."

They sat quietly for a minute. Finally, Priscilla asked about her career plans.

She shrugged. "Get a job on the ground, I guess."

NEWSDESK

Worldwide News has learned that a member of the scientific team living in orbit at the distant world Selika has been sent home for psychiatric assistance. The person's identity is not known, nor is the exact nature of the malady. Kosmik, which oversees the operation, had no comment this morning, but has since released a statement that at no time was any member of the staff in danger.

Kosmik is attempting to terraform Selika, which has been at the center of the terraforming controversy for more than a year. Selika is approximately 24 light-years away.

—December 15, 2195

LIBRARY ENTRY

We have collected, in two days, more than seven million signatures demanding that Congress move to stop further exploitation of living worlds. The activities of Kosmik and its collaborators is unconscionable.

—The Public Action Website,
December 16, 2195

If they will not stop, then we must consider alternative action. We may have no option other than to follow the lead of Leon Carlson.

—Calltoarms.ca, December 17, 2195

Chapter 20

JAKE ARRIVED EARLY at Carmody's. The back room had been reserved for the Astro Society. Approximately twenty people had gathered so far, and they were still drifting in. Sandra Coates recognized him immediately. She was in her thirties, with amiable features, auburn hair, and energetic brown eyes. "Captain Loomis?" she said. "So nice to meet you. We appreciate your coming. Just give us a few minutes, and we'll be getting started."

She introduced him around, identifying the participants as archeologists or botanists or nuclear physicists. It was clear she thought the specialty mattered to him. Nevertheless, they got quickly past the formalities, and Captain Loomis became *Jake*.

The place filled up, the servers arrived, and Jake was escorted to his place at the head table beside Sandra and Mike Hasson, the psychology chair at Brockton University. Sandra seemed genuinely delighted to have Jake in attendance, and she pointed out that the invitation had been Hasson's idea. "I don't think people really understand how the world changed," Mike told him, "after we got into space. Well, maybe not so much got into space, but developed FTL. Some of us remember when we had our hands full getting out to Mars and Europa. But faster-than-light really changed the game."

The meal was pretty much standard luncheon fare, potato salad and sandwiches and grilled carrots and an unidentifiable dessert that had cheese in it. When everyone had finished, Sandra ascended to the lectern and introduced Jake, "who has been to places most of us only dream about." She held out a hand for him, the audience applauded with enthusiasm, and Jake took the mike.

"Thank you, Sandra." He looked out over the diners. "I'm not sure what I can say that you're not already aware of. I can tell you that I feel honored to be here, and how fortunate I've been to have been allowed to navigate our interstellars. It's permitted me to visit places that we once thought were completely beyond our reach. I don't know what I can tell you that you don't already know, but I'll say this: Once you've traveled to another world, once you've walked on different ground, looked out across a new ocean, you can never be the same. The reality, though, is that *you* provided the opportunity. You provided the technology. And I want to take this opportunity to say thanks.

"What we have, we've received through the efforts of the world's scientists. Starting back with the Greeks, I guess. You guys got us out of the caves and gave us the sky. In the end, we owe everything to men and women like yourselves, who explore the reality in which we live." He described how it felt to watch a ringed world rising out of an ocean, to ride with a comet, to watch a star hurling giant flares into the night. "And maybe especially," he said, "to go to a place like Iapetus and look at the figure left there thousands of years ago by someone I suspect you folks would like very much to have met."

After about twenty minutes, he thanked his audience for listening and asked if anyone had a question.

Hands went up around the room. "Captain Loomis, do you think we'll ever find a seriously advanced civilization? By that I mean one that's maybe a million years old?"

"Where do you think we'll be in another hundred years?"

"What's the most spectacular thing you've seen out there?"

"Captain, Marian mentioned the possibility of a million-year-old civilization. What do you think that would look like?"

"Why do you think we're so fascinated by the possibility

of finding someone else we could talk to? I mean, high-tech aliens could be dangerous."

The Talios story had not been released, so Jake did not mention it. "It's in our genes," he said. "What wouldn't any of us give to sit down and have a beer and pizza with someone from the other side of the galaxy?"

The remark brought applause. Then a young woman seated near the front raised her hand. Jake looked in her direction, and she got up. "Captain Loomis, how do you feel about Project Rainbow?"

"I'm sorry. What's Project Rainbow?"

"Selika," she said. "Where they're killing off the planet."

"I think they should wait until they have better research. Until they can accomplish what they want without harming anything."

More applause. And more hands went up. He was about to signal someone else, but the woman stayed on her feet. "Would it be fair," she said, "to describe your feeling as outrage?"

"Well, I'm not sure I'd go that far. But I'm not happy with what they're doing."

"You're not happy? They are probably killing off everything on that world, everything on Selika, and you're *not happy*?" Her voice was rising. "I wouldn't want you to take this the wrong way, but I won't sleep much better tonight knowing that people like you are in charge."

NEWSDESK

SHOOTER MISSES SENATOR BELMAR AT AWARD DINNER
Two Dead; Senator Shielded by Killer's Aunt

HOPKINS DROPS OUT OF GOLD RACE
Belmar, McGruder Lead in Nomination Fight
Collins Stays in Despite Sex Scandal
Wife Expected to Provide Support Tonight

BOOKS LOSING GROUND IN WESTERN WORLD
Does Anybody Read Novels Anymore?
Nonfiction Down Slightly

GROUP MARRIAGE LAW PASSES IN CALIFORNIA
Governor's Veto Overridden

ASTEROID PASSES BETWEEN EARTH AND MOON

NAU MURDER RATE DOWN 17TH STRAIGHT YEAR
Chicago Safest City

LAST MAN STANDING LEADS OSCAR HOPEFULS

NORMAN: NAU WILL STAY OUT OF
SOUTH AMERICAN TURMOIL

NFL MAY EXTEND SEASON TO 24 GAMES IN 2198
Players' and Fans' Unions May Oppose

Chapter 21

PRISCILLA SURFACED NEAR midnight on the seventeenth, five days before the licensing ceremony. Within an hour she received a relay of *Jack Kelly's Late Night* reporting that unnamed sources had confirmed that Monika Wolf suffered a breakdown at Amity and was being returned for treatment. "Well," said Monika, "I suspect that might leave you wondering where the truth is in this matter."

Kelly added that Kosmik was denying the report. They had a clip from an interview with Howard Broderick. "Ridiculous," Broderick said. "Monika's coming back, yes, but it has nothing to do with mental issues. I don't know where this story came from."

Monika sneered. "Right, Howard, you wouldn't have any idea, would you?"

"Our guest tonight," said Kelly, "is Senator Hollins of Ontario, a sponsor of the Life Guard Amendment, which would prohibit terraforming on any world where it can't be done without harming the local life-forms. Senator, welcome to *Late Night*."

"Thanks for having me, Jack."

"I wanted to ask you about this Monika Wolf story. She's coming home from Selika, which is the scene of the terraforming operation that's causing so much uproar. Are they *really* killing the local wildlife? Edward Kepinjer, a biologist who's been working on Quraqua, the other world where they're doing terraforming, says they are not having any problem there. Can you explain what's going on?"

"Jack, this is unknown territory. We don't really have solid evidence yet that we're doing serious damage on Selika. Quraqua *seems* to be okay. But different worlds—?" He shrugged. "What we're learning about Selika *does* suggest there might be a problem."

"If that's the case, Senator, why don't they just relocate to somewhere else?"

"Because, at the moment, there *is* nowhere else. Not if you're talking about establishing a colony. There are, in fact, about twenty living worlds. But in some cases the atmosphere is beyond reclamation. In other places, the gravity index is too high. Or too low. And I know that sounds strange, but most of us don't adjust well if we have to spend a lot of time in low-gravity situations. Where it's too high—" He smiled. "I don't think many of your listeners would be much interested in putting on an extra two hundred pounds overnight. A couple of worlds might have been okay except that they have unstable ground conditions."

"So we have to look some more."

"That's correct. Finding the right world is going to cost money. And it takes time. So far, we only have Quraqua. We thought we had a second place in Selika. Unfortunately, Jack, it looks as if that may not be working out."

Monika raised a fist.

THEY HAD JUMPED in unusually close to the Wheel. Ten hours later, the *Venture* pulled into dock. And it was, finally, time to say good-bye. Monika got her gear and paused at the air lock. The return voyage had been considerably easier than the outbound flight. "You want to ride with me next time," Priscilla said, "just let me know."

"No charge?"

"None at all."

"Good. Where are you going next?"

"I have no idea."

Monika smiled. "Me, too. Look, let me know when you're headed for Andromeda." Priscilla offered her hand, but Monika embraced her. Then she stepped back. "One thing before I go: Don't trust these people. Kosmik. Where they're concerned, it's strictly about the money."

PRISCILLA WENT TO the Skyview for lunch. She was being shown to her table when her link chimed. It was Howard. "I'm glad to hear you're back. How'd the flight go?"

"It went okay," she said.

"No problems?"

"No."

"All right. Good. What are you doing now?"

"Just sitting down to lunch."

"When you're finished, how about coming over to the office for a few minutes? No hurry."

HE LOOKED UP from his desk, apparently happy to see her, and pointed to a chair. "You have another mission coming up. In six days. You have any problem with the schedule?"

"No," she said. "That sounds okay."

"Good. I just wanted to give you some advance warning." He leaned forward and frowned. "There's something else. You'd already left Amity before I found out why they were sending Monika back. I apologize for that. I wasn't aware there'd been a stress-related problem, or we'd have handled things differently. She didn't give you any trouble, did she?"

"No. Not at all. She was fine."

"Okay. Good. I'm glad to hear it. We're usually more careful." He showed her a big, happy smile. "Anyhow, you'll be leaving Wednesday, the twenty-third. You'll be on the *Venture* again."

"I like the ship."

"I was sure you would. Obviously, you'll be gone over Christmas. That's okay?"

"What's the mission?"

"Amity again."

Priscilla stared at him. "Amity?"

"Something wrong?" he asked.

"May I ask why?"

"More supplies."

"More chemicals, you mean?"

His good cheer faded. "Oh, come on, Priscilla. You're not buying into all that nonsense, I hope? I guess that was the real risk of leaving you alone with Wolf for a week. It's hard enough dealing with bomb throwers and crazy politicians. We're trying to do what we can. But there's no hard evidence for the charges. We're doing the research, and there's nothing solid."

"So you're saying it's not true?"

"I'm saying nobody's been able to show that it *is* true. Listen, we wouldn't be doing this if we thought anything like that could happen. We've had a lot of experts look at the project. They say there's no danger of anything like what people are talking about. We're not killing off anything. Well, maybe some cellular stuff, but it's not a planetwide extermination like they're saying on the news shows."

"I did some research on the return flight, Howard. There are a good many experts who don't agree with what you're saying."

"Oh, listen, Priscilla, people always line up on both sides of any controversial issue. It gets them attention by the media. That's all a lot of these people want."

She was trying to stay calm. "I couldn't help noticing," she said, "that most of the people who say there's no problem had connections of one kind or another with Kosmik, or one of the other companies that are involved."

"I think that's an exaggeration."

"You're free to think what you like."

"Look, Priscilla, you have to understand that the Life Guard people have gone way over the top on this. We get threats all the time from lunatics who claim to be pro-life, but they don't mind trying to kill anybody who doesn't agree with them. My God, they're *shooting* people. Did you hear about Senator Belmar?"

"No." Belmar was the pro-spaceflight candidate, running for the Gold nomination. "What happened?"

"A kid with a plasma gun walked into a dinner where he was speaking. Killed a couple of people, and wounded, I think, seven or eight others. Fortunately, the senator wasn't hit. The shooter's aunt jumped in front of him. But he was the target. And, of course, Carlson put a bomb on the *Gremlin* and could have killed all those schoolkids. Is that really the side you want to be on?"

"Lunatics are everywhere," she said.

"So you see my point."

"For the record, Howard, I'm not interested in being on anybody's side. The kid with the plasma gun was a nutcase. That has nothing to do with what's happening on Selika."

"Of course it does. It's people like Monika, the true believers, who stir them up. Who are giving them a cause."

"I thought she made a lot of sense."

"Bear with me, Priscilla, but you're not a climatologist." There were voices in the corridor. And footsteps. The gravity level at the station was so light that one seldom heard people walking around. Somehow the sound seemed to add resonance to voices. His eyes cut into her. "Now, can I rely on you to be here next week?"

Had he not asked the question, she might have gone ahead, said no more, and taken another load of superalgae out to Amity. But the question, somehow, turned everything into a confrontation. He was challenging her. He didn't realize it, but he was making it impossible for her to duck the decision and simply do her job.

"No, Howard," she said. "I can't do that."

"You're being foolish, Priscilla."

She got up from her chair. "I guess I am. But what they're doing out there—it's something I don't want to live with."

"You understand what this means? We can't keep you on if we can't depend on you."

"I'm sorry to hear it. But I can't accept any Selika assignments."

"All right. Have it your way. We'll issue a closeout payment to you later today." He got up. "Good luck, Priscilla. I'm sorry it has to end like this."

She looked at him for a long moment. "Me, too."

SHE NEEDED A job again. Blackwell was one of two long-range-touring companies. They specialized in taking their clients, as they referred to their passengers, to see the Great Monuments. And, of course, a few of the other spectacles within three days' travel time. She called them.

"And what is your name, please?" asked a middle-aged woman with blond hair and a bored expression.

"Priscilla Hutchins. I'd like to apply for a pilot's position."

"I see." The woman's gaze locked on her. *"Do you have any experience?"*

"I returned this morning," she said, "from my first flight. Out to Amity. For Kosmik."

"You've separated from Kosmik?"

"Yes, I have."

"Voluntarily?"

"Yes."

"Why?"

"I have a problem with the terraforming issue."

"I see."

The woman pressed a few tabs, looked away at something Priscilla couldn't see. Came back. *"I'm sorry, Ms. Hutchins, but we aren't accepting applications at the moment."*

"It doesn't say that at your Web site."

"Yes. Well, that situation fluctuates a good bit. We'll keep your name on file."

Interstellar Transport told her that, unfortunately, they just had no need of pilots at this time.

Wagner DeepSpace regretted they had no openings.

United Transport would call her if anything developed.

STARGATE TOURS, BLACKWELL'S competitor, invited her in for an interview. But by the time she arrived, they'd changed their minds. They were polite but pointed to her inexperience as the reason she would not be a good fit and apologized for wasting her time. She called Jake and asked what he thought was happening.

"I think they're not happy with a pilot who quits her first employer after one mission."

"Even if I had a good reason?"

"Priscilla, there probably is no good reason."

* * *

A FEW DAYS before the certification ceremony, she saw Carlos Ashwan in the Cockpit. Carlos was tall and lanky, the guy who always played the piano at parties. He would be one of the new pilots receiving his license. "You catch on with anybody yet?" she asked him.

"More or less," he said.

"How do you mean?"

"I've signed with the Academy Project."

"The deep-space explorers?"

"Yep. It's sponsored by Wilson University. In DC. I really like what they're doing. All they're interested in is what might be out there. Blue-sky science. But of course there's always a downside."

"What's the downside?"

"Funding. They don't pay real well. And the missions are long. You spend a lot of time in the fog. At least that's what they tell me. I'll be leaving on my first flight next week."

"Where are you going?"

"To 23 Librae."

"What's 23 Librae? Where's that? I never heard of it."

"It's eighty-five light-years out."

"Carlos, you're going to need a month to get there."

"Actually twenty-four days."

"What do they expect to find?"

"As far as I'm aware, the only thing they know about the place is that it's got a planetary system. They think one of the worlds will have water."

Priscilla ordered a tuna sandwich and coffee. "Enjoy the trip."

"I hope. How've *you* been doing?"

"I just walked away from one job."

"Really? What happened?" She explained, and he shook his head. "Well, you shouldn't have any trouble finding somebody else."

"Carlos," she said, "you think the Academy Project might have an opening?"

He passed their address to her and smiled. "Tell them I recommended you."

* * *

SHE RODE THE shuttle down and arrived the following morning at the Academy grounds in DC. Christmas shoppers were everywhere, birds were singing, and a warm off-season breeze was coming in from the Potomac. She strolled across the campus of George Wilson University, which of course was named for the president who'd forged the North American Union. A few people were at the Memorial Wall, taking pictures or just enjoying the weather. The Wall, of course, was dedicated to those who'd lost their lives during Academy operations. Names and dates were engraved, along with a brief account of the final mission on which they'd been embarked. Here was Chan Ho Ling, who'd died when his lander was caught in a horrific storm on a world orbiting Beta Comae Berenices. And Lyn Benedetti, stranded at Delta Pavonis and dead for lack of air before anyone could get to her. John Yaniwicz and Andrea Khoury, who'd constructed a boat and launched it into a river on Epsilon Reticuli III. Neither they nor the boat had ever been seen again.

Five passengers and the captain of the *Vigilant*, which disappeared without a trace during a mission to Aldebaran.

William Kostner, lost near VanMaanen's Star. And Leonard McCutcheon, only twenty-five when he'd died during a lightning strike while trying to get his crew to safety.

There was space for more names, for heroes yet to come. She imagined *Priscilla Hutchins* listed there. *When the Buckner Asteroid hit the Wheel, she stayed behind so others could live.*

She stopped by the Galileo Fountain. Benches circled the area, and she sat for a while, listening to the sound of the water, and of the wind in the trees.

THE ACADEMY OFFICES were located inside the Volcker Building. She walked into a lobby. An AI greeted her and asked her business. "My name's Hutchins," she said. "I'd like to speak with someone about obtaining a position with the Academy Project."

"May I ask specifically which type of position you're seeking, Ms. Hutchins?"

"I'm an interstellar pilot."

"One moment, please. You may sit if you wish."

She settled onto a divan. Framed photos of unworldly landscapes and gleaming interstellars filled the walls. Two windows looked out over the campus. Music was playing in the background, a tune Priscilla remembered from her childhood.

Then a small, middle-aged man with a smile appeared. The smile didn't reach his eyes, which told her immediately how this would end. "Ms. Hutchins," he said, "I'm glad to meet you. My name's Barkley. Why don't you come on back for a minute?"

He led the way down the corridor and ushered her into a modest office. More interstellar pictures on the walls, and a photo on a desk of Barkley, a woman, and three kids.

They sat down on a couple of plastic chairs, and he asked if she would like some coffee. She passed, and he nodded. "I understand you'd like to sign on with us as a pilot."

"That's right," she said. "I'd like very much to work for the Academy."

"Yes. Of course." The smile faded. "I wish I could offer you some encouragement, Ms. Hutchins. Unfortunately, we only have three full-time pilots. Occasionally, we pick up someone else for a special mission, but we just don't have a regular position open at the moment. I'll be happy to add you to our list of applicants. If—when there's an opening, we'll get in touch with you."

ANOTHER OF THOSE who'd received accreditation with her, Mukarram Fakhouri, had been picked up by Celestial Transit. Two of the cadets had signed on with United Transport, one had replaced her with Kosmik, and one was still looking. Priscilla was already on United Transport's list of hopefuls. She sent copies of her résumé to Celestial and to the Stellar Express. And that was it. There was no other corporate entity operating off the Wheel. Stellar Express called her in for an interview, and they actually seemed optimistic at first, but they, like Stargate, apparently just needed time to check the record. They declined without explaining why.

She was sitting in the Skyview on that final evening before the licensing ceremony, finishing off a dish of strawberries and listening to recorded piano music, when Frank Irasco came in, spotted her, and walked over. Irasco was the assistant director of Union Operations. "Mind if I join you, Priscilla?"

"Sure, Mr. Irasco. How are you doing?"

"I'm fine, thanks. How about you?"

"I'm okay." She didn't like Irasco. He always looked as if he understood quite clearly that he was superior to everybody else in the room. Mostly, it was the smug smile and the eyes. Despite his short stature, he always seemed to be looking down at you. Jake hadn't liked him, either. But at the moment, she could use a friend.

"I heard what happened over at Kosmik," he said. "Have you signed on with anyone else yet?"

"No, I haven't."

Irasco ordered coffee and a grilled salmon dinner. Then he turned back to Priscilla. "I assume you know that we're being sued."

"The Space Authority? No, I wasn't aware of that. Why?"

"Joshua's wife. She wants twenty million. It's a waste of her time, of course."

"I would think so. Her husband worked for Kosmik."

"She's suing them, too."

"Why is she after the WSA?"

"She thinks our response time was too slow."

"We got there as quickly as we could."

"She has a point, though. We responded with the closest ship. That was you. We should have sent out something with more capacity. Something that could have taken everyone off. The *Kruger* could have done that."

"But would it have gotten there in time to evacuate them before the *Gremlin* went down?"

"Well, that's the problem. It probably would have. If it hadn't, we'd be getting sued for not sending the closer vehicle. In fact, we should have sent both. The truth is that we screwed up. But in any case, the legal action's a waste of time."

"Why?"

"There's a no-liability clause. It's in everybody's contract.

So she won't get anything. But when it's all over, we're not going to look very competent. That's why she's doing it."

Priscilla sighed. "I'm sorry to hear it."

His coffee arrived. It was, of course, in a cup designed to accommodate the centripetal swing of the station. He tasted it. "I have an offer for you, Priscilla. I need a staff assistant. You know your way around here pretty well. It doesn't pay much, and you probably won't get off the station, but you'll be close by if something develops."

She hesitated. "Mr. Irasco, did you see the Leon Carlson statement?"

He nodded. "I saw it. Terrible thing, that. I still can't believe it."

"Is he right? Is the WSA complicit?"

"You mean about helping Kosmik? Of course it's true. That's why we're here. Our job is to assist anybody who's traveling off-world. That's the whole point of our existence. As long as they're not breaking the law, we are bound to do what we can to help."

"Regardless of what they're doing?"

His eyes closed, and he shook his head. "Priscilla, we aren't empowered to make ethical judgments." He looked suddenly tired, and she realized he'd been having this conversation on a regular basis since Carlson went viral. "Look, we have no choice in these things. What they're doing does not break any laws. Until they do, we can't refuse to assist them."

"Okay," she said.

"Now, let me ask you again: Would you like to work for us?"

"Mr. Irasco, I appreciate the offer, but I'm not sure I'd be a good fit for a staff job."

"Priscilla, I want a backup pilot. Somebody who can jump into a ship and get things done if there's a problem. We've been taking a beating because we don't have that capability. It doesn't look very good when the Authority has an emergency, and we don't have a pilot available."

"Mr. Irasco, you don't have a *ship* available."

"Call me *Frank*. And sure we have a ship available. We have the *Bomb*." Priscilla couldn't resist a tolerant smile. The *Baumbachner* was a maintenance vehicle. It had a

Hazeltine drive, but it was ancient. And it was the ugliest ship in service. "Jake tells us you're pretty good. Understand, you probably won't really be going anywhere. Maybe to Moonbase once in a while. Or out to L2. The reality is we almost never have any emergencies. Despite this recent series of events. But I want to be able to say that at least we *have* a pilot ready if we need one. Mostly, what you'll be doing is sitting in front of a computer. And we're going to set you up to do some tours, too. We don't have those yet, but we want to start them."

"Tours of what, Frank? The solar system?"

"The space station. If you can live with that, and the possibility of being on hand to respond to an emergency, we'd be happy to offer you a position."

PRISCILLA'S JOURNAL

It's an office job. But I guess I'm going to have to take what I can get. I just never would have believed that I'd wind up sitting behind a desk on the Wheel. Tomorrow, I'll take a picture of the *Baumbachner* and send it to Jake. With my love.

—December 21, 2195

Chapter 22

PRISCILLA CALLED HOME that evening—it was midafternoon in Princeton—to let her mother know she had picked up a staff job. Mom tried to sound enthusiastic, but what came through was relief that her daughter wouldn't be hanging out near black holes. *"At least,"* she said, *"you've got something. I'm happy for you."* She passed the news to someone else. Then: *"You know, I've never been excited about any of this, Priscilla. But in the end, I can't believe you won't get everything you want."*

The following morning she reported to the Yuri Gagarin Ballroom at the Starlight to receive her certification. She wore the blue-and-silver uniform of an Authority pilot but without the symbolic rocket clip. She joined the other five cadets, who were seated on a small stage. They constituted the year's entire class of newly minted interstellar pilots. There was an audience of about sixty-five people, mostly parents and family members.

Jake showed up for the ceremony, not wearing a uniform even though he was entitled to do so. He sat down in the rear. When their eyes met, he gave her a thumbs-up. Moments later, she was shocked when her mother came in, accompanied by

Uncle Phil, Cousin Ed, and his bride, Miriam. Incredible! How on earth had they gotten Mom onto the shuttle? It was probably a good thing Miriam was there in case she passed out. But her mother looked as happy as Priscilla could remember ever having seen her. They raised their hands in guarded waves. Priscilla returned a smile.

Then, finally, Patricia McCoy entered, swept down the aisle, mounted the stage, and took her place behind the lectern.

Patricia provided a tall, smooth, commanding presence. "Ladies and gentlemen," she said, "welcome to the twenty-first certification ceremony of the World Space Authority. Today, we will recognize those who have qualified during the past six months as interstellar pilots. These are the people who will literally take us to the stars." She glanced at the cadets, seated to her right. "Our future lies on other worlds, places where no one has walked, places that, at this time, no one has yet seen. These young women and men will show us the way." She described qualities needed to pilot interstellars and stated that the six cadets on the stage had demonstrated those qualities. She went on in that vein for several minutes.

Jake remained expressionless throughout, his eyes seemingly gazing at another place.

"When we talk about the cosmos," Patricia said, "we don't know how far, in the end, we'll be able to go. But we can be certain that as long as we continue to produce young men and women like these, the road lies open." She looked across the stage at the candidates. "Please stand and raise your right hands."

They got up and raised their hands.

"Repeat after me." The audience leaned forward as one. Mom's eyes touched hers. "I solemnly swear to abide by the code of conduct prescribed in the official statutes."

Priscilla, with the others, delivered the line and waited.

"To use all due care to maintain the ship entrusted to me and to complete the mission."

Again, they followed the lead.

"And especially to make every effort to ensure the safety of the passengers and crew who are given over to my care."

When they'd finished, the room was silent for a few

moments. Then Patricia said, "The pilots may be seated. We will now present the certificates." That brought a stirring in the audience. "Visitors will please hold their applause until we are done." She reached down and produced a scroll. "Carlos Ashwan." He was from Vera Cruz. "Carlos, please come forward."

She handed him the scroll and the rocket pin that designated his grade, and shook his hand. "Congratulations, Captain Ashwan. Make us proud."

He accepted the document and returned to his seat.

"Mukarram Fakhouri." Patricia waited with a smile while he approached. "Perform to your capabilities, Captain Fakhouri, and all will be well."

Priscilla knew she was next. She tensed.

"Priscilla Hutchins."

She stood, went to the lectern, and accepted her scroll.

"Thank you," Priscilla said.

Patricia nodded. "Captain Hutchins," she said, "continue as you've begun."

When the ceremony had ended, her mom, Uncle Phil, and Ed engulfed her. Miriam smiled her approval. They presented her with a diamond necklace in honor of the occasion. Eventually, Jake also got to her. "Congratulations, kid," he said. "Enjoy yourself. And call me if you need anything."

THE CELEBRATION HAD barely begun when the whispering started. Priscilla was sitting with her family when Carlos came over. "You hear about it yet?" he asked.

"Hear about what?"

"The news reports. They've got more stuff about the animals."

There was an HV in the ballroom. Mack Keever, one of the network anchors, was running images of alien creatures, some fur-bearing, some reptilian, many with feathers, all with eyes that somehow connected them with the animals one might see in a shelter. Except that these were dying.

"It's all over the Internet," Keever said. "And it's not only animals." They switched over to desiccated forests. "This is what we're doing on other worlds."

PRISCILLA'S JOURNAL

This was the day I've been looking forward to as long as I can remember. I'd expected it would be the happiest day of my life. It has been happy. But there's a shadow over it.

—December 22, 2195

Chapter 23

THEY PARTIED INTO the night. Mom had a glorious time, Uncle Phil drank a little too much, and Ed turned an ankle trying to dance in the near-nonexistent gravity. Miriam formed what would turn out to be a lifetime friendship with Denise Peifer, Drake's sister.

Meantime, Preacher Brawley took Priscilla aside and told her he understood she didn't have quite the position she'd hoped for. "But Jake has told me about you. Just be patient, Priscilla. Your day is coming."

Jake had gone missing.

They spent the next several days on the Wheel, sightseeing, hitting the restaurants and gift shops, and touring the launch bay. When the *Exeter* arrived on Christmas Eve, carrying tourists who'd been looking at one of the monuments—Priscilla was so caught up in the celebration that she didn't pay any attention to which one it had been—they had front-row seats. Mom especially liked Skyview, and said it was the wildest place for hamburgers she'd ever seen. And, finally, it was time to go back to Princeton. Priscilla went with them.

She was still on the shuttle when Wally Brinkman called. *"Congratulations,"* he said. Wally had sent chocolates to her at the Starlight. *"I was hoping we could get together when you get home. I'd love to see you again."*

"Sure," she said. "I'd enjoy that."

"How about we do dinner, then go to the Corel? They're doing Midnight Special." Live theater. *Midnight Special* had been a major hit a half century earlier. The Corel featured an amateur troupe, but they were good. "Absolutely," she said.

TWO NIGHTS LATER they were headed for the theater, with a stopover at Maroni's Italian Restaurant, where she treated herself to a fettuccini alfredo. Then it was off to watch the show. She'd seen *Midnight Special* performed when she was in college. It hadn't exactly been the laugh riot her teacher had promised, but it was okay. Maybe, she thought as she and Wally took their seats near the front, it would work a bit better tonight.

One of the lead characters, Mark Klaybold, is a public relations guy who takes special pride in his ability to create markets for worthless products. He generally has his way with women until he meets Amanda, with whom he falls in love. Amanda, however, finds it impossible to take him seriously as anything other than a scam artist. "The world is all about perception," Mark tells her when they first meet. "If you can get people to believe something, *anything*, that makes it true."

They were only a few minutes into the first act, though, when her mind began wandering. How long would it take her to get a serious position? Could she talk her way into the Academy Project within the next year or so? Occasionally, she tuned the show back in, laughed at Mark's fumbling efforts to persuade Amanda he sincerely loved her. That she could trust him not to lie.

Despite everything, Mark was a likable character, a charmer, good-looking, but constantly overreaching. Constantly in trouble. He meant well but even when he tried to be honest, communication breakdowns left him looking not only deceitful but clumsy.

THE TRADITION AT the Corel was that, after the performance, the cast lined up outside to shake hands and talk with the patrons. It was, for Priscilla, a major part of the show, meeting the people who'd been onstage. She'd envied her classmates in high school and college who'd participated in the theater programs. She would have loved to play Erica in *All for Love* or Maureen in *Moonbase*. Any of the romantic roles in the school shows. But the prospect of memorizing a part and getting out in front of the curtains without forgetting her lines and making a fool of herself overwhelmed her. No. It was never going to happen. And it never had.

So she smiled pleasantly at the director, and at each of the six actors, congratulating them and telling them how well they'd performed. From her perspective, if you got through without blowing the material, you'd done all that could be expected.

Mark had been played by a young man whose name was Calvin Hartlett. Somehow, the good looks that carried Mark to his various conquests had disappeared. He was tall, with brown hair and gray eyes. But offstage and out of the lighting, he looked rather ordinary. Maybe it was that the energy had drained out of him. He was at the end of the line, with his leading lady. Priscilla smiled at them. "Nice performance, guys."

Hartlett looked at her oddly. "Aren't you Priscilla Hutchins?"

"Yes," she said.

His eyes brightened. "Princeton's own star pilot."

She nodded. "More or less."

"It's a pleasure to meet you." Remarkably, Mark Klaybold seemed to have returned. "I'm glad you enjoyed the show."

"It was a solid performance."

"Thanks," he said. "I hope you come back to see us." He glanced at Wally, and she knew she'd hear from him again.

IN THE MORNING, she'd finished breakfast and was out on her daily walk when her link chimed. It was Jake.

"The man of leisure," she said. "Where are you now?"

"In the Blue Ridge. Not far from Roanoke."

"Nice country."

"You looked good at the ceremony."

"Thanks. I wish you'd stayed around."

"That was your party, babe."

"You should have been part of it."

"Thanks. I was."

She was going to ask when he'd gotten home, but she didn't want to go plunging off into small talk. "Jake, is there anything I can do for you?"

"No," he said. *"I don't need anything. As far as the WSA is concerned, I've gone away, never again to be heard from. And good riddance."*

"I wanted to thank you for going out of your way for me with Frank."

"Irasco? What do you mean?"

"You apparently said some pretty nice things about me."

"I didn't tell him anything that wasn't true."

"Whatever. Anyway, I appreciate it. I'm working for him now."

"So I heard. I think, Priscilla, you just need to be patient. I know you're probably not very excited about sitting behind a desk, but just stay with it. You're a damned good pilot, and I'd trust you to take me anywhere."

CALVIN HARTLETT DIDN'T disappoint her. *"Is this Priscilla?"* he asked when she picked up. *"We didn't really have much of a chance to talk last night. I'd love to get to know you better. We're off this evening. I know it's short notice, but it's the only night I'm free all week. And I suspect you won't be in town long. I was hoping you'd let me take you to dinner."*

PRISCILLA'S JOURNAL

No sign yet of Monika going after Kosmik. All that talk about taking a stand.

Headed for the high country. I get the leading man. And an unbridled vote of confidence from Jake. When I started my qualification flight a couple of months ago, Harry Everett had been my instructor. But he got ill during the first week and had to be replaced by Jake. Jake showed up, and his first comment was whether my piloting skills had brought Harry down. It was supposed to be a joke, but I was in a sensitive place and took him seriously. I thought he'd seen something in my record he hadn't liked, or someone had said something to him. It was one of the most unsettling moments in my life. Tonight, though, I feel like that Amazon on the HV show.

—December 29, 2195

Chapter 24

PRISCILLA HAD HOPED, naturally, that she'd be going to dinner with the handsome, devil-may-care Mark Klaybold, the character Calvin had played in the show. He'd pretend to be an ordinary guy, though with extraordinarily good looks. He'd take her to a pricey restaurant, probably the Tablet, show how impressed he was being out with someone who'd been to other worlds, point out that her eyes sparkled in the candlelight, and, at the end of the evening, try to coax her into bed.

Instead, she got Cal, who, except for his car, seemed quite ordinary. He picked her up in a sleek white Benson, obviously impressing Mom, whose jaw dropped when she saw him. Or maybe the car. Priscilla wasn't sure which. But her hopes visibly soared. Calvin might be the very guy Mom had been looking for, someone who'd completely entrance her daughter and help put this interstellar craziness on a back burner.

Cal had expressive eyes and broad shoulders and a square jaw. But they needed stage lighting. Or animation. Something. "Priscilla," he told her while holding the car door for her, "I'm really glad you came to the show last night. It was so nice to meet you." Mark would have said, *"Priscilla, you must be the most gorgeous pilot on the planet."*

En route to the restaurant, they talked about what had led

her to her career and how enthralling it must have felt to help rescue those kids. She asked him about his acting ambitions. "I'd like to go to Hollywood eventually," he said. And, as if the notion were ridiculous, "What I'd really like is to take over when Brace Hopkins retires." The prime action star of the era. His smile suggested he was kidding. But not really.

"What do you do for a living, Cal?" she asked.

"I'm a financial advisor."

"Really?"

"Sure. I'm the guy you go to when you want to pick up some securities." They pulled into the parking lot at Gilmore's. It wasn't the Tablet, but it was nice. "I've fallen in love with the theater, though." He turned off the engine and sat staring out at the gathering dusk. "I don't think I'd ever realized before how pedestrian managing stock portfolios can be."

"You don't want to do that for a lifetime?"

"Lord, no. But it's hard to find anything that pays as well."

It was an unusually cold night. They got out of the car and hurried inside. The doors closed behind them and cut off the chill. He took her jacket and checked it for her. The host came over, a small man with a neat mustache. "Hartlett," Cal said, "we have a reservation." A fire crackled in a grate, and a pianist across the room was playing something soft and romantic.

Gilmore's was filled with people dressed for an evening on the town. In the center of the table, a small candle burned inside a red globe. They were seated by a window looking out across Nassau Street. The University Chapel was lovely in the moonlight.

"How long will you be here?" asked Cal.

"Just a few more days."

"Must be great." His eyes locked on her, full of hope. "I imagine riding around all day in one of those starships makes everything else seem pretty pedestrian."

"Yeah," she said. "It can have that effect."

He smiled, and she caught a glimpse of Mark Klaybold in there somewhere.

WHILE THEY ATE, Cal confessed that he suspected he'd spend the rest of his life with Martin Gable Finance. "Unless my movie career takes off." Again, she saw that self-effacing smile that somehow nevertheless suggested he still hoped good things would happen.

"You know, you'd make a good Rick Cabot." Cabot was, of course, the superspy who'd leaped from the pages of Carol Goldwin's novels.

"Ah, yes," he said, mimicking Cabot's British accent, "just keep smiling, Ms. Hutchins, and don't make any sudden moves." He was perfect.

"Very good," she said.

"Thanks. So what do you expect to happen with you? Where will you be going next?"

"I'll be working at the station for a while. Nothing very exciting."

"If you had a choice, where would you *like* to go?"

"Someplace where there's another civilization. Where there's somebody we could talk to."

"Really? Wouldn't that be kind of scary?"

"I suppose so. But it would be nice to sit down with someone who'd never heard of Earth. And maybe find out whether he enjoys music. Whether *it* enjoys music."

"That's very poetic. But aliens on HV aren't usually very friendly." He took a moment to sip his coffee. "Well, it sure sounds more exciting than tracking security equities." He tried the coffee again. Hesitated. "Will you be coming back once in a while? To Princeton?"

"I expect so," she said. "My family lives here. Are you from this area originally?"

"I was born in Cherry Hill. Grew up there."

"Where'd you go to school, Cal?"

"Princeton. How about you?"

"Same," she said. "Did you major in finance?"

"Of course. But I did some theater, too."

Priscilla smiled. "You were beautiful last night."

THEY HIT A couple of the nightspots. And, finally, the evening tiptoed to an end. He made no overt move, took her home in the Benson, and told her how much he'd enjoyed being out with her. Priscilla pulled her coat around her. Cal climbed out and opened her door. The wind seemed capable of taking a couple of the trees down. Had she been traveling with Mark, he would have said something to her in the restaurant about how he'd miss her, how he wanted to make something happen. The piano and the fireplace would have provided the background. But Mark had never really shown up. She was disappointed.

He hovered beside her, apparently trying to decide whether to attempt a kiss. "Priscilla," he said as they walked slowly up to the front of the house, "I'd like to do this again. If that would be all right."

"Sure," she said, withholding any sign of enthusiasm. "I won't be back for a while, though, Cal."

"That's okay. I just—"

"What?"

"Well, I don't know. I just don't want you to walk out of my life after one evening." He leaned forward, pressed his lips against her cheek, and backed off.

Oh, Mark, where did you go?

LIBRARY ENTRY

Yung Sun Yeun, speaking last week in his State of the World address, outlined the endless problems the World Group faces in confronting widespread famine, peacekeeping issues, and climate change. The global population is completely out of control. Numerous species are dying off. And these were, of course, only the tip of the iceberg. Dr. Yeun, fortunately, is a realist. He understands the planet's resources are limited and should not be wasted on initiatives that contribute nothing toward global survival. We do not need more maglev train routes, he said. We have no use for enhanced space-born energy systems when the ones in place are performing more than adequately. We can get along without bigger navies. It's hard to see how we profit from interstellar exploration. We don't even need, he says, to ensure the survival of the human race by establishing off-world bases. Our first obligation, he maintains, is to take care of our home world. Any action that diverts resources from that single objective should cease. Our prime concern is the people we have, not the ones who may one day be running around the Orion Arm. It's clearly time for the members of the World Group to follow Dr. Yeun's leadership. We're discovering that intelligent life seems to have gone missing among the stars. Unfortunately, we don't see many signs of it here, either.

—Gregory MacAllister, *Baltimore Sun*,
December 30, 2195

Chapter 25

FOR JAKE, THE good life had arrived. He loved spending time with Alicia, whether it was in the Ferrante Club in Roanoke, or wandering through the woods, or watching movies at his place. He went to the Hawks' games, at home and on the road. She claimed she played better when he was in the stands. "You provide a little extra energy, Jake," she'd told him one night after they'd won on her last-second jump shot. The reality was that no woman in his life had ever affected him the way she did.

Everything else was falling into place also. There was a Thursday poker game in town, which he attended except on those evenings when the Hawks were playing. Several of the local schools asked him to talk to their students about space-flight. He put together a show that included a virtual trip to some of the local stars, and to Iapetus. He made a change in reality, though, by coordinating it so that Iapetus was no longer in tidal lock. That allowed the students to gather on a ridge and watch Saturn rise in the east, with those magnificent rings jutting vertically into the sky.

He became a volunteer at the local animal shelter (where, coincidentally, Alicia also served). He went for long, solitary walks, and felt the difference immediately in his muscles, which had absorbed too many years in low or zero gravity.

The food was considerably better than the fare to which he'd become accustomed. He never ate in the cabin, though, unless Alicia made the meal. He visited every restaurant within sixty-five kilometers. And for the first time since he was about twelve, he played occasional bingo, with Alicia, at one of the local churches.

He had blundered into a golden age. He'd always expected that, when he retired, he'd sleep late and spend most of his time just lying around. Maybe do some bowling. But Alicia wasn't a bowler, and he just didn't have time.

She took him to an indoor swimming pool in Roanoke. The woman looked glorious in the water, smooth and synchronized, moving swiftly, leaving Jake to manage as best he could. Jake could swim reasonably well, but he'd fallen out of practice. "I'm going to suggest to the people on the Wheel that they need one of these," he said.

Both *The Roanoke Times* and *The Christiansburg News* interviewed him and did stories. He became a local celebrity.

NEVERTHELESS, HE'D BEEN there barely three weeks before a disquieting restlessness set in. He didn't want to admit it to himself, but he missed the interstellars. Missed looking down on other worlds. Missed the admiration that the silver-and-blue uniform commanded from passengers and anyone else who happened to be in the neighborhood.

He missed the occasional voyage during which he started with no idea what waited at the other end. He missed the simple things, the exhilaration that came during the first minutes after launch, when the acceleration pressed him back into his seat. The shocked reactions of passengers who were, for the first time, looking out the portal at an alien moon or a star cluster or a passing asteroid.

And as the weeks went by, he became more aware of what had gone missing from his life. But there was something else: He had not been able to let go of Joshua Miller.

It was not that he was still overwhelmed by a sense of guilt. He'd been able to convince himself that he had probably not been aware of what Joshua had intended. But even if that were so, he knew that somehow, a set of scales was out of balance.

Whatever the exact nature of what he was experiencing, he was unable to keep it hidden from Alicia. She knew something was wrong. Life was not going off the track completely, but rather it was out of sync. "Are you okay?" she would ask occasionally, even when he was not conscious of contemplating whether he needed to feel the push of the star drive, or perhaps owed something to Joshua. "Is everything all right, Jake?"

It wasn't.

But he assured her it was only her imagination. *I'm fine.*

When he was alone in the cabin, however, he felt the weight of solitude as he never had when he was riding the interstellars.

LIBRARY ENTRY

What we do is who we are.

—Marissa Earl, *Narrow Roads*, 2025

Chapter 26

PRISCILLA HAD NOT been able to get Monika Wolf out of her mind. On her way back to the Wheel, she decided to call her. Monika sounded pleased to hear her voice. *"I've been wondering how my favorite pilot's been doing,"* she said. *"Wish we were close enough to manage an occasional lunch."*

"Me, too," said Priscilla, as they rose above some storm clouds. "Have you gotten a job yet?"

"Oh, yes. I'm with Baxter Intelligence. Not as interesting as what I used to do for Kosmik, but at least I'm not causing any harm anymore."

"I quit them myself," she said.

"Good for you. I wish we could get everybody to walk out." It was strictly an audible conversation, but Priscilla sensed that she was smiling. *"Political pressure is building. A lot of people are unhappy about what's going on. I think eventually we'll be able to shut them down."*

"I hope you're right," Priscilla said.

IN THE MORNING, she checked in with Frank Irasco. *"I'm glad you're back. I hope you enjoyed your vacation."*

"Very much," she said.

"Good. We're ready to put you to work. Can you come in today?"

Twenty minutes later, she took the elevator up to the third floor. He was standing in the passageway talking to a couple of staff people when the doors opened. He looked toward her, finished the conversation, and came over. "Welcome back, Priscilla. You ready to start?"

"Absolutely."

"Excellent. Let's go this way." He showed her a small office just around the curve of the corridor. "It's yours," he said.

"It looks nice."

"Your formal title will be *support assistant*. You'll have a variety of responsibilities." He invited her to sit down behind the desk. She did, and he leaned over and pressed the comm pad. "Janna," he said, "would you bring us some coffee, please?" Then he settled into one of the two chairs. "Your most critical job is to be our backup pilot. Which means, if there's an emergency, and there's nobody available to send out, you'll get the assignment. Are you okay with that?"

"I can live with it," she said.

"What's wrong?"

"Why backup? Why borrow somebody else's pilot and ship if we're having a problem?"

"Priscilla, I understand how you feel. But we have an established method for dealing with emergencies. The method is that we use whatever vehicle might be available. The deep-space corporations have an obligation to assist. And they do. When something happens, we want to get someone to the site as quickly as possible. Usually, that means somebody who's already within a reasonable range. We could keep an emergency vehicle here at the Wheel, and years might go by before it would get used. So we can either use the corporate vehicles that are scattered around, or we can construct a fleet and spend a hell of a lot of money maintaining them in strategic locations."

"Okay," said Priscilla.

"Good. I'm glad we have that settled."

"What will I be doing when I'm not functioning as a backup pilot?"

"You'll be doing administrative work."

That sounded exciting. "All right."

"You'll be keeping track of every underway mission to ensure that our support facilities know well in advance what's going on. There'll be some interesting stuff crossing your desk, so don't think of it as just an office job. For example, you'll have access to the reports from the Quraqua dig sites, and there'll be information coming in from Pinnacle. You know what that is?"

"Yes," she said. Pinnacle had been home to a high-tech civilization three-quarters of a million years ago. "Have we figured out yet what happened to them?"

"No. It's going to take a while. Anyway, we'll also be getting reports on the Noks. On Orfano. On Barton's World. Wherever we have a presence. Your job will be to scan them to make sure they get correct distribution. It's all in the manual. Anything that looks interesting, especially if there's an indication something has gone wrong, make sure you get it to me."

"Okay, Frank." Orfano, she knew, was a world adrift. Torn from its sun millions of years ago.

"You'll be responsible for tracking the maintenance work on the *Baumbachner*. Rob Clayborn will handle the actual maintenance, making sure it gets done and whatnot. Rob's our pilot. He's the guy you're backing up. But he doesn't go out on any long-range missions. He's strictly local."

"Why?"

"Because, technically, the job doesn't exist. Don't push it, okay. We don't want to get involved in operations run by the corporates if we can help it."

"Okay, Frank."

"You'll also be responsible for managing schedules and accommodations for VIP guests, for maintaining personnel records, for setting up tour groups through the station and making them happen, and for assorted other stuff." He paused. Looked at her. "Think you can handle it?"

"I can't see where there'd be a problem," she said.

"Okay. And I know what you're thinking: that it sounds like make-work. Basically, you're on hand to help in an emergency. The office job has been created so you actually have stuff to do. But that doesn't mean we aren't serious about the work. Okay?"

"What does Rob do?" she asked.

"Well, the truth is he's getting ready to retire. His health has been a problem, and I'll be surprised if he doesn't bail out within the next month or two. By the way, he hasn't said anything like that, so I'd appreciate it if it doesn't leave this room."

"One other thing. There'll be a staff meeting"—he glanced at the time—"at one. In the Altair room."

NIKKI WAS HER office AI. Every day, as Priscilla came into work, Nikki greeted her with a sparkling "Good morning, Priscilla." The AI was relentlessly cheerful. Priscilla thought of herself as being reasonably upbeat, but there were limits to what she could endure. When she got buried in routine administrative matters that stultified her brain, the last thing she needed was that happy gurgle from Nikki. She asked her finally to tune it back. But that seemed to be beyond Nikki's capability, so Priscilla made the adjustment as best she could.

Despite whatever desperation she might have known at becoming an office worker, she was still able to feel some satisfaction when, at night in her apartment, she could look up at the framed certificate, hanging on the wall over her working table, which stipulated that she was competent to direct the movement of an interstellar.

Her mother was happy with the situation. "Well," she said, "I think it's a distinct improvement from running all over the place in those rockets. At least I don't have to worry about your getting lost out there somewhere." And then: "We can still get you into law school in the spring if you like."

She'd been six days on the job when she got a call from Calvin. *"I miss you,"* he said.

"How's the show going, Cal?"

"It's okay. The audiences like it."

"You have any more coming up?"

"Well," he said, *"the Players do, but I won't be auditioning for the next one."*

"Why not?"

"It takes a lot of time. Anyhow, they've decided to do Hamlet.*"*

"*Hamlet*? And you're going to pass on a chance to perform in *that*?"

"You want the truth, Priscilla?"

"Sure."

"I don't think we're anywhere near good enough to pull it off. You need professionals for something like that."

"You guys are pretty good."

"Priscilla—"

"Yes, Cal?"

"Any chance you'll be coming home again soon?"

"Probably not right away. I'm trying to adjust to a new job."

"What kind of ship are they giving you?"

"Actually, I'm not really going anywhere. I'm in an office. And in a couple of weeks, I start taking tour groups around."

"Oh. Sure. Well, listen, when you do come home, I'd love to take you out again. Okay?"

THE FOLLOWING DAY she was adjusting paychecks to fit the new standards being applied by the financial services division when she got a call from Irasco. *"Priscilla,"* he said, *"can you come over for a minute?"*

The boss was relaxed behind his desk, bathed in sunlight. "Good morning," he said. "Come on in." She took a seat. Irasco was reading one of the news sheets. He asked if she had seen the latest statement by Andy McGruder. McGruder was revving up his presidential campaign. He was a former Minnesota governor running for the Gold Party nomination. His platform seemed to consist mostly of trying to scare the voters about the size of government. And especially the cost of maintaining what he saw as a nonproductive space program. "As if the country doesn't have real problems—" He shook his head.

"The reason I called you, Priscilla: There's a load of parts in the *Bomb* that they'll be using to refit the scanners." He pointed at the overhead. "The big ones. On the roof. Rob was

supposed to take care of it, but he woke up with his head spinning this morning, and the medics want us to get someone
else to make the delivery."

SHE WOULD HAVE enjoyed wearing one of her two uniforms
for the assignment. But they'd have laughed at her.

The *Baumbachner* had a pathetic appearance. Even considering the age that had spawned it, the thing looked clumsy.
It could have been an oversized barrel with thrusters. A laser
was attached to the hull, which made it, as far as she knew,
the only armed vehicle in the fleet. Its name was inscribed
across the hull in pretentious Celtic script.

Myra Baumbachner had been a billionaire who'd donated
enormous sums and her life to getting the space program up
and running after the national efforts had all, to one degree or
another, failed. She was the prime force that came to the
rescue when the Iapetus monument was discovered. It was a
pity they couldn't have named a better-looking ship for her.

You and me, Myra, thought Priscilla as she went into the
air lock, crossed the passenger cabin, and settled onto the
bridge. Actually, the interior looked much better than the outside. Of course that simply meant the cabins weren't awful.

"We have an AI here?" she asked as she took her seat.

"Right here," a female voice replied. "Who are you,
please?"

"Priscilla Hutchins. Rob had a dizzy spell, so I'll be taking his place."

"No one has informed me, Priscilla. You won't object if I
seek confirmation?"

"No. Of course not."

"Good. My name is Myra."

No surprise there. "Hello, Myra. Can you connect me with
Ops?"

Two clicks. Then: "Done, Priscilla."

"Ops," she said, "this is the *Baumbachner.* We're ready to go."

"Very good, Baumbachner. *There's nothing in the neighborhood. You're free to depart when you're ready."*

"Roger that." She flipped a couple of switches, activating a
scope and a monitor. "Myra, start engines."

"Just a moment, if you please, Priscilla. I'm— Ah, yes, here it comes now. Very good. You are approved." The engines came online with a rumble.

So here she was ready for her second solo. All the way to the roof of the space station. "Release the lines."

Control-panel lights blinked. "Release confirmed." The magnetics binding the *Baumbachner* to the dock shut down.

"Move us out. Gently." She activated her harness and pulled it over her shoulders.

Scopes mounted across the hull provided views in all directions. The port thrusters switched off. The bow began to swing toward the launch doors, and the navigation thrusters came on. The ship moved toward open sky.

When they'd cleared the launch doors she looked out across the top of the station. "Myra," she said, "do you know where the equipment is to be delivered?"

"No, ma'am. I have no idea."

"All right." Dumb. She'd assumed the AI would have the information. "I have control, Myra."

"Okay."

She took the vehicle slowly higher until she could get a good look at the rooftop. It supported two facilities used for storage and maintenance, and multiple clusters of scanners and scopes. At one of them, a group of technicians was at work.

She switched back to Ops. "Have you any idea where I'm supposed to make delivery?"

"Negative, Baumbachner. *Let me give you to Tao."*

"Tao is the person in charge?"

"He is. Hang on a second."

Then a baritone: *"Priscilla?"*

"Yes, Tao."

"All right. We can see you." One of the technicians waved. *"Bring them here, okay?"*

"On my way."

"You stay at the con. Don't turn it over to the AI. Come in as close as you can. Then just open up. We'll take care of the rest."

"Will do, Tao. Keep everybody back."

"We'll stay out of your way."

They needed her to go in under the scanners. *I hope I can do this without hitting one of the damned things.* She swung slowly to starboard and moved forward with as much deliberation as she could manage.

THE SCOPES DIDN'T provide sufficient perspective. But Tao apparently realized that. *"Back off a little more, Priscilla. That's good. A little more."* Her screens were filled with support beams and dishes and cables. *"Okay. Keep coming."*

It didn't seem as if there could be any room left.

"You're doing fine. Stay with it. Just a little closer." Something bumped under the deck. *"All right. That's good. Lock in."*

She used the magnetics to attach the *Baumbachner* to the roof. *"Perfect, Priscilla. You relax. We've got it now."*

"Anything I can do to help?"

"Negative. Take it easy. We'll need about an hour."

SHE WAS HUNGRY. "All we have," said Myra, "is tuna casserole. And there's some cherry pie."

She went back into the passenger cabin, collected the casserole and a tomato juice, and sat down. Unfortunately, since she was sitting on top of the spinning space station, the centripetal force, which acted as a slightly-off-center gravity if you were walking around Union, tended now to drag her toward the starboard bulkhead. But she belted in. The Moon was visible through one of the ports.

The only sounds in the *Baumbachner* were the blips and bloops of the electronics. It wasn't exactly paradise, but it felt good to be back on the bridge.

LIBRARY ENTRY

. . . When Governor McGruder poses his trademark question to the voters—What is the point of running around out there?—someone should show him the Great Monuments. He doesn't really have to go out personally to look. Just pick up the Haversak collection and run the images. Let him examine the golden pyramid orbiting Sirius, or the Procyon Monument, a circular pavilion with columns and steps that would have accommodated something a bit larger perhaps than a human. Show him the crystal cones and spheres apparently arranged arbitrarily in a field of snow at the south pole of Armis V, but which reward the careful observer with an elegant pattern. Let him see the magnificent obelisk rising out of battered ridges on the Moldavian moon, otherwise a completely pedestrian satellite circling a featureless world. There's no need even to mention the compelling self-portrait on Iapetus.

If the governor can look at these stunning images and still ask why we have gone to the stars, then it should be clear to all there is no hope for him. And if the voters send him to the New White House, there may be no hope for us.

—*The Washington Post*, January 12, 2196

Chapter 27

PRISCILLA WAS IN her office, going through financial documents, when Frank called. *"Just so you're aware,"* he said, *"Governor McGruder will be stopping by tomorrow. I doubt he'll show up* here, *but you never know. Anyhow, in case he does, we want to look sharp."*

Sure. I'll look sharp checking over last month's expenditures. "Okay, Frank," she said. "Thanks for the warning."

"Something else, Priscilla. We're throwing a party this evening for some visiting VIPs. You're invited."

She wasn't excited by the prospect. But if she hoped ever to get away from her desk, she'd have to play the game. "Sure, Frank. Where and what time?"

"The Gagarin Room," he said. *"Can you be there at eight?"*

PATRICIA MCCOY COULD look good when she wanted to. On that evening, she wore sparkling cobalt slacks and a silver blouse. Her hair, usually tied back, hung to her shoulders. She was talking with a handful of visitors in a room filled mostly with strangers.

Frank saw Priscilla come in and signaled the director, who

turned and motioned her over. The conversation in the room diminished. All eyes were suddenly on her. "Ladies and gentlemen," said Patricia, "I'd like to introduce Priscilla Hutchins. She's the young lady who brought the students home safely from the Lalande Monument a few weeks ago."

The guests applauded, nodded in approval, and smiled warmly. Several came forward, shook her hand, congratulated her on her performance, and said things like how they hoped she'd be around if they ever got into serious trouble. It was a glorious moment, and she was able to conclude that maybe she'd been a contributor to the outcome after all.

Patricia indicated she should join her group. "Priscilla," she said, "this is Alexander Oshenko." She knew the name. Oshenko was a Russian physicist who'd won the Americus a few years earlier.

"I'm honored," said Oshenko.

"And Maria Capitana. From Pamplona. Maria is a human rights activist. And Niklas Leitner. Niklas is from the University of Heidelberg. If you have any serious hopes of living for three centuries, he's the guy you want to get to know."

She also met a prizewinning novelist, the president of Oxford, and, most significantly, Samantha Campbell, the director of the Academy Project.

Campbell was in her sixties, with black hair and an amiable smile that contrasted sharply with intense blue eyes. "Beautiful effort, Priscilla," she said. "I envy you. You've certainly gotten your career off to a rousing start."

"Thank you, Dr. Campbell—"

"I hope," said Patricia, "you won't be trying to steal her from us."

"Oh, no." She flashed that smile, implying she'd do no such thing. "Unfortunately, we couldn't come close to matching what you must be paying her."

"Actually," said Priscilla, "I *did* apply."

"Really? And we missed the opportunity? Well—" She shrugged. "Our loss."

Patricia passed her to Frank, but not before suggesting that she needed a name that sounded a bit more heroic. "*Priscilla* doesn't really work, does it, Frank?"

"No," he said, "not really. If you're going to move seriously ahead, we need a guns-up version of your name. *Priscilla's* a touch too fashionable."

"My mom used to call me *Prissy*."

Patricia laughed. "Oh, that would be good."

"Something like *Sundown* would fit the bill," said Frank.

"That's taken."

"I know. But *Backwater* might work."

"Magnificent," said Priscilla with a straight face. "When I was a kid, I tried to get everybody to call me *Hutch*."

"Pity it didn't take," said Patricia.

"These are all people," Frank said, "who support the Academy Project. If they get their way, it could result in some serious exploration being done. We brought them here to reinforce their attitude and give them a chance to meet one another. Some of them made their reputations as organizers. So who knows what might come out of this?"

"Did you invite Governor McGruder?" she asked. "He could use a little influencing."

"No way we could do that. If he found out about this, he'd use it against us. The party would become another example of wasteful spending. In fact, when we heard he was coming, we wondered whether he *had* found out. But I think it's a coincidence. I hope so." He glanced around the room. "I have to mingle," he said. "Enjoy yourself. And, Priscilla?"

"Yes?"

"Don't leave early, okay?"

SHE HADN'T EXPECTED the VIP treatment. That Frank entertained even for a moment the notion that she'd take off prematurely when people were under the impression she was a hero demonstrated how little he knew about her. She had felt somewhat intimidated when Patricia started the introductions, but as they'd worked their way around the room, and the assorted guests had all seemed to assume she was a celebrity, the disquiet had faded. Now she felt like a queen.

In the lopsided gravity, dancing can be something of a challenge for those not accustomed to it. Consequently, Priscilla found the guests somewhat reluctant about stepping out on the floor with her. But ultimately, they were willing to try their luck. The Amazon biologist Leandro Santana told her, "Once you've seen a crocodile smile, nothing else will ever scare you." Nonetheless he followed her tepidly into a *lucinda*. And then caught fire.

She danced with almost every male in the place, traded jokes with the women, and even got some laughs from Patricia. The music, of course, was provided by a sound system. "If we'd brought in a band for something like this," Frank told her, "it would have been all over the media."

She thought about making her case with Dr. Campbell, but it was possible she might be perceived as rushing things if she did. Campbell now knew who she was, and that was maybe enough for the moment. In any case, she wouldn't have felt comfortable about walking away from her job after Patricia and Frank had gone out of their way for her.

She was usually a cautious drinker. But everybody wanted to toast her, and then they toasted each other. By the end of the evening, she was pretty thoroughly toasted herself. The reason some of the guests stayed extraordinarily late was that the station operated on Greenwich Mean Time. And 2:00 A.M. in Greenwich was only 9:00 P.M. on the east coast of the NAU.

SHE OVERSLEPT, WOKE with a headache, and finally staggered into the office. Frank stopped by and suggested she might want to take the rest of the morning off. "You look a little wiped out," he said.

He had left the party only shortly before she did, and Priscilla had no interest in letting him think he was tougher than she was. The guy was, after all, only a bureaucrat. "I'm fine, Frank," she said. "No sweat."

He looked at her for a long moment. "Okay. You know best. But let me know if you decide to head out, all right?"

"I'll be here," she said.

She got some coffee, put the operating-area-maintenance files on her display, and propped her chin in her right palm. "Nikki," she said, her eyes closed.

"Yes, Priscilla."

"Let me know if you see Frank heading back this way."

"Of course, Priscilla."

* * *

SHE DOZED OFF for a few minutes. But it was no way to sleep. She got up, went to the washroom, and wiped her face with cold water.

More coffee helped. She got through the morning okay, skipped lunch, and sat for an hour in the lounge. The afternoon went on forever. No more parties, she decided. Not like that. Not on a weekday.

She was about to quit for the day when Nikki called. *"Priscilla, Mr. Irasco asked if you were still here. I told him you were. I hope that was all right. Anyhow, he wants to see you in his office."*

"HOW'RE YOU FEELING?" he asked.

"Oh, I'm fine," she said. "What do you need, Frank?"

He looked doubtful. "Governor McGruder wants to meet you."

"The governor wants to meet *me*, Frank?" Her throat tightened. "The *Gremlin* again?"

"Enjoy your time in the spotlight, Priscilla. I've seen this before. It can go on for weeks. But once it fades out, it's gone."

Lord. "When?"

"Usually a couple of weeks. This is going on a bit longer."

"No, I mean when does he want to see me?"

"Oh." He glanced at the time. "As soon as we can get there."

"You're kidding."

"I never kid, Priscilla."

Her eyes slid shut. She wanted to scream. "How do I look?" she asked.

"You look fine." He hesitated. "I *could* tell him you're sick."

It was obvious he didn't want to do that. "No. Let's go." He led her through the door but didn't turn, as she expected, toward Patricia's office. "Where are we headed?"

"He's on his way to the dock." The elevator was open when they got there. "Look," he said, "you know how this guy feels about us, right?"

"Sure. He wants to close us down."

"Don't give him anything he can use."

"I won't."

"Just tell him the truth, whatever he asks, but don't embellish. Okay?"

ANDREW Y. MCGRUDER—Big Andy to his constituents—was appropriately named. He was about six-five, and, on Union, had probably shed 260 pounds. His black hair was turning gray around the temples and thinning on top. He wore khaki slacks and a white pullover sweater. Priscilla had seen him often enough on HV to know he was not the usual sort of politician, who would tell voters anything to keep them happy. He was capable of learning and had shown it by reversing himself on some issues, like the general-purpose tax. And he seemed perfectly willing to admit he'd made mistakes. Not qualities she expected to see in a politician. He'd paid a price for it. His opponents routinely accused him of being a flip-flopper. Nevertheless, she didn't like the guy. And it wasn't just his stand on space exploration. There was something in his eyes that told her he couldn't be trusted.

He was standing by one of the portals, surrounded by about forty people, half of them techs. The *Sydney Thompson* was docked outside, its prow visible to the reporters, who were taking his picture and asking questions. "It's good to be here," he said. "Don't misunderstand me. These people have performed some incredible feats. I mean, you look out there and think about what we've accomplished and—" He shook his head. "It makes me proud."

"Then why," asked one of the reporters, "are you trying to close them down?"

"I'm not." He shook his head adamantly. "I'm trying to save the program. But you know as well as I do that the country can't sustain the current costs. Nor can the other members of the WSA. As it's now constituted, the space effort is a drag on everybody.

"I know the argument: Kosmik and Celestial and the Stellar Express and the other private corporations are doing pretty well. But it's happening on the backs of the taxpayers.

If the corporations want space travel, that's fine. But *they* should be paying for it.

"Look, we haven't really learned how to do this yet. We lose people, and we lose resources. We had that pilot killed a few weeks ago. We don't like to admit it, but we have to face reality. We can stagger ahead a few more steps. But if we do, it's all coming down. And I assure you, if the WSA collapses, if we have to close down the Wheel, it will be the end. We will not be coming back. At least not in the lifetime of anybody here. So I say let's use some sense. Let's draw down now. We can wait, give it some time, and eventually"— he raised both arms to encompass the docks, the *Thompson*, the operations area, the Wheel itself—"eventually, maybe we can restore and reinvigorate all of this."

Patricia McCoy stood off to one side, watching. Frank headed directly for her. "How's it been going?" he asked, in a whisper.

"Could be worse." She looked at Priscilla. "You okay?"

"I'm good, Patricia."

"All right. Be careful what you say." She led her over to a guy who was obviously part of the governor's team. "Here she is, Claude."

Claude was an elderly African-American. He glanced at Priscilla, apparently appraising her, and signaled approval. Their eyes never met. He held up his left arm in McGruder's line of sight and signaled this was the one.

McGruder didn't react. He finished what he was saying, something about how the resources we save now will grow and ultimately rescue the space effort down the line. Then he broke off. "There's a young lady who just came in that I'd like you all to meet. Priscilla Hutchins, would you come up and say hello, please?" He delivered a smile that had become, because of its charm, a significant factor in the campaign. The guy, she thought, would get a considerable slice of the women's vote. The reporters backed away and made room for her. Claude gave her a gentle push.

"I'm sure everybody here," said the governor, "knows Priscilla Hutchins. She's the young lady who brought the students home safely last month after the loss of the *Gremlin*."

He held out a hand for her. "Hello, Priscilla. It's good of you to come by, and it's a pleasure to meet you."

"Thank you, Governor. The pleasure's mine."

"It's always nice to share some time with a bona fide hero."

"I'm not a hero. I just happened to be there when the heroes showed up."

"And you also *happened* to ride home with those kids. We're all grateful for that." He grinned and looked out at the reporters, then at the *Thompson*. "I'm glad they didn't need *me* up there to bring one of those things home."

Priscilla didn't know what to say, so she simply stood looking at the crowd and feeling foolish.

McGruder's eyes narrowed. "You look tired, Priscilla."

"I'm fine," she said.

He turned again to the audience: "Look at her. She has all she can do to keep her eyes open." He sighed. "It's the effect I always have on beautiful women."

Everybody laughed. Priscilla smiled defensively. "I doubt," she said, "you'd put anybody to sleep, Governor."

"That's very kind of you." He looked absolutely in charge. A guy who loved having an audience. "I'd hoped to meet you today, Priscilla, because it's through people like you that we've been able to reach out, literally, to the stars. And I understand fully why you might be inclined to resist my proposals that we cut back on our investment in space. If I were in your place, I would probably feel the same way." He was looking directly into her eyes now. "The reality, though, is that the government is deeply in debt, the economies of India, China, Russia, Germany, Britain, all the nations who have contributed so much to make this effort a success, all their economies are stressed. We have serious problems with overpopulation, climate disruption, fresh water, species going extinct, and all kinds of other things. If we are eventually to become a starfaring world, which I know is what we all want, we are going to have to pause now and catch our breath. We need to back off, not only from our space program, but in other areas as well. If we fail to do that, if we keep pushing mindlessly ahead, running up the national debt, it's my conviction that we will lose everything." He looked genuinely in pain. "Wouldn't you concede, Priscilla, at least that I might have a point?"

"I understand what you're saying, Governor," she said. "But we have a tendency, once we shut something down, to leave it that way."

"You're right. That's why we need to act now. I'm not proposing we abandon the WSA. What we need is to trim it back. Keep it active, keep it in place, but don't put it in a position where it's draining our resources so much that we have to, as you say, Priscilla, shut it down." He glanced again at the *Thompson*. "Let's hope we can arrange things so that, one day, I'll be able to ride that ship out to Alpha Centauri as part of an ongoing interstellar program. And when that day comes, I hope you'll be my pilot." He shook her hand and thanked her.

Priscilla stepped away from him as another voice was raised. "Governor, if you will—" A female reporter. "When you talk about a payoff for the investment in spaceflight, you always talk about money. What about the level of cooperation we've seen among member countries since we started the World Space Authority? It's been eighty years now. We've had no wars among the founding nations. And sure, they're still competitive, but you could argue that they don't try to undermine one another anymore."

"Ms.—?"

"Michelle Worth."

"Is there a question in there somewhere?"

"Aren't you missing the most important benefits we get from all this?" She looked around at the portals, the *Thompson* and the launch area, framed pictures along the bulkheads of nebulae and planets and space vehicles. "Isn't the human race, largely because of the space effort, finally showing signs of drawing together?"

The governor sighed. He'd been through all this before. "I wish it were so. Ladies and gentlemen, I don't want anyone here to misunderstand what I'm trying to say. I'm aware that we've gained a lot from what the people here have done. They have my deepest respect and admiration. What I *am* saying is that if we want to keep the program from dying, we have to make some hard decisions. Cut back now, and we can still look forward to a bright future. And that's it. That's my message. It's all I'm saying."

More hands went up. "Yes, Harvey?"

Priscilla turned and headed for the elevator. Frank joined her there. He looked pleased. "Nice job, *Hutch*," he said.

She couldn't head off a grin. Still, she was not happy. "How can you say that, Frank? He's explaining why they should slash our funding, and I helped him."

"No, you did fine. You put a face on the organization, Priscilla. It was all we could hope for."

NORMALLY, THE PEOPLE who hung out at the Cockpit were staff from Union, the operations guys, the administrative types, the maintenance workers. Priscilla suspected they all enjoyed being in a place the general public assumed was limited to the men and women who took the interstellars into the night. After all, in this era of expansion out of the solar system, the pilots were the ultimate heroic figures. They'd replaced military people and detectives and emergency medical workers. More HV shows featured their adventures than those of any other character type. They showed up in commercials explaining how Poltex provided more energy when energy was seriously needed. They told you which lawyers you could trust. They retired, ran for Congress, and usually won. And it was inevitably a huge story when one of them was caught cheating on a spouse.

Rob Clayborn showed up the day after the governor's visit. He looked okay. The dizzy spells had apparently gone away. That afternoon, Frank told her he'd been pronounced ready to resume his duties aboard the *Baumbachner*. "The doctors think it had something to do with his diet," he said. "He's been trying to lose weight and may not have been getting enough nutrition. Anyhow, we've got him back."

"That's good news," she said. "Thanks."

"I'm sorry, Priscilla."

"Hey, don't be. I'm glad he's all right."

CAL CALLED AGAIN. *"I miss you. It's never happened to me before. Never really missed anybody. Not like this. I was thinking maybe I'd come up to the Wheel for a couple of days. If that would be okay with you."*

Priscilla wasn't quite ready to move to that stage of a relationship she wasn't sure she wanted at all. So she explained how busy she was, that she almost never had any time off, and why didn't they wait until she got home?

Her mother also called, still pushing law school.

THEN CAPTAIN BRANDYWINE arrived at the station. Mike Brandywine, played by Ryan Fletcher, was, of course, the heroic starship captain in the series *Deep Skies*. The studios were shooting a sequence in the launch area. In this episode, a time traveler had landed on the *Valiant*, warning its crew that, in seven hours, terrorists would seize the space station and be waiting to take control of the ship when it docked. "Unless we can change things," she told them in a halting voice, "they'll be successful. They'll use the *Valiant* to destroy London. Eventually, the attack will destabilize the UK, and, within two years, bring down the entire Western World." They wouldn't allow anyone to watch the actual filming, but the *Catherine Perth* was in port, and Fletcher and some of his colleagues asked to tour the ship. Priscilla was a fan of the series and she took advantage of the opportunity to go see him. Also present were the actors who portrayed Jason Petrie, the half-French, half-alien engineering officer, and Barbara Cole, the knockout security chief. Every staff worker not on duty must have been in the launch area when Fletcher and the others arrived, escorted by Patricia. The crowd applauded, collected autographs, and applauded again when Fletcher told them what an honor it was to be there with the people "who were actually making it all happen, rather than just pretending."

When they came out of the *Perth*, accompanied by its captain, Arnold "Easy" Barnicle, Patricia brought them in Priscilla's direction. "And this young lady," she said, "is Priscilla Hutchins. *Hutch* to her friends. She's one of our pilots."

Fletcher looked at her. "Hutch," he said, "I didn't realize our pilots looked so good." Then he flashed that killer smile and turned away for more introductions.

It was a heartbreaker.

NEWSDESK

FOUR CLIMBERS DEAD IN COLORADO AVALANCHE
Ignored Warnings to Stay off Mountain

SENATE VOTES TO DISMISS CASTOR
Corruption Charges Filed; Indictment Believed Imminent
Other Senators May Be Involved
Historic Term Limits Bill Introduced in House

BANCROFT COMPLETES CROSS-COUNTRY BIKE RIDE
Pledges for Homeless Pass 5 Million

GENETIC GOOD-LOOKS BOOST NOT WORKING
No Real Change in Glamour Generation
It May Be All in the Smile

INCREASES IN TEST SCORES
ATTRIBUTED TO ROBOT TEACHERS
In Classroom, Robots Consistently Outperform Humans
Hold Inherent Advantage in One-on-One Instruction

INCOMING SOLAR FLARE MAY DISRUPT TECHNOLOGY

POLICE KILL VIOLENT CHIMP
Three People Injured in Southsea Park

FERAL CATS STILL A MAJOR PROBLEM ACROSS COUNTRY

MCGRUDER CHALLENGES BELMAR TO RELEASE IQ SCORE

SPACEPORT SECURITY FLUNKS CHECK
Reporters Board Flights with Fake Bombs
Coordinated Test Gets by Flaws in London, Berlin,
Tokyo, New York
Peking & Paris Block Entry

DROUGHT CONTINUES IN MIDWEST
Water Rationing in Effect in Eight States

Chapter 28

"HI, *HUTCH*."

She heard it several times next morning before she even got to her desk. One of the medical guys used it to say hello while she was at breakfast; Joan Kung sang it out as they passed in the Starlight lobby; a staff member whose name she didn't even know used it coming out of the elevator. Frank, who was going the other way in the corridor outside her office, raised a hand but said nothing. Though maybe the smile said it all.

She picked up her coffee and went into her office. Nikki greeted her: "Good morning, Hutch."

"You, too?"

"I'm sorry. Couldn't resist."

"You need some new material."

"I sense that you are annoyed."

"Hey, they introduced me to one of the biggest stars of this generation, and they made it a point to screw up my name."

"I'm sure Patricia meant no harm."

Priscilla sank into her chair and set her coffee on the desk. "I know. And I'm acting like an idiot."

"May I ask why, Priscilla?"

"Love your tact."

"Thank you."

"Was that sarcasm?"

"Sarcasm is a purely human response."

"Okay. Look, if you have to know, I spent a large chunk of my childhood trying to get rid of *Prissy*, which was the name my mom used for me most of the time. I never much cared for Priscilla either."

"May I ask why not?"

"I just didn't like the sound of it. So I tried to get my folks to change my name. To give me a nickname."

"And what nickname would you have preferred?"

"That's what annoys me. I wanted *Hutch*. It never really caught on. Until, apparently, yesterday."

"I do not have a laughter capability."

"I'm sorry about that."

"So why don't you cash in on it now? Take *Hutch* as your own. There will never be a better time."

"Nikki, I've gotten used to *Priscilla*."

"It's your call. By the way, *Priscilla*, we have an organization chart that needs updating."

SHE WAS TRYING to get some accounting records together when Parik Simpkins came in. Parik was a construction worker. She'd met him only once before and had to scramble to come up with his name. He had dark skin, dark eyes, and an easy smile. He held out a pair of earrings. "Are these yours, by any chance?"

They looked like pearls. "No," she said. "What makes you think they might be mine?"

"They were found on the *Bomb*. You were the last person to use the ship."

"Not mine," she said. "Rob might know something." There were rumors that Rob Clayborn entertained occasional lady friends aboard the *Baumbachner*. Which maybe explained the dizziness.

"Okay, I'll check with him." He started to leave. Hesitated. "Did you hear about the problem at Teegarden?"

"At where?"

"Teegarden's Star."

"Oh. No, I didn't. What's going on?"

"You know the Academy Project has a research station on the ground, right? Well, anyhow, they can't get the lander started. They're running out of food and water. The *Proxmire*'s in orbit, with plenty of supplies, but they don't have any way to deliver them."

"That's not good. Is the lander on the ground?"

"Yes."

"When did we find out?"

"Yesterday," he said.

"So what are we doing?"

He shrugged. "I thought *you'd* know."

THREE MINUTES LATER, she was in Frank's outer office. The staff assistant looked up. "He's busy," she said. "I can call you when he's available. It shouldn't be long."

"How about if I wait?"

"Suit yourself."

She sat down, looked out the window just in time to see the rim of the Moon disappear. The Moon was back in the window when Frank's door finally opened. Patricia came out. She smiled at Priscilla, said hello, and left without waiting for a response. Frank saw her, rolled his eyes, and waved her inside. "Something wrong?" he asked, as the door closed behind her.

"I just heard about the Teegarden problem."

"Sit," he said as he lowered himself onto his desk. "Yeah. Well, we're working on it."

"May I ask what we're doing?"

His jaws tightened. "Priscilla, I'm kind of busy right now. We're taking care of it, okay?" There was an edge in his voice.

"Is someone on the way there?" she asked.

"Not yet. We sent a message to the *Grosvenor*. Actually, to the *Grosvenor*'s destination. It's headed for the station at Ross 248. As soon as it surfaces, they'll let it know what happened."

"As soon as it surfaces? When will that be?"

"Two days. More or less."

"Frank, they're not much closer to Teegarden than *we* are. So the *Grosvenor* gets the message two days from now, and *then* it starts for Teegarden?"

"That's correct. Yes."

"Our flight time to Teegarden is about the same as theirs. If we start now, we'd save two days."

"Priscilla." He was getting annoyed. "Look, why don't you leave this to us? You must have something better to do."

"Why don't we send somebody from here?"

"Because we don't have anybody to send. Now please just leave it alone."

"What about the *Baumbachner*?"

He laughed. "The *Baumbachner*? That's our *maintenance* vehicle." He took a deep breath. "This is not a life-and-death situation. They won't run out of food for another day or two. So relax and let me handle it, okay?" He looked toward the open door.

SHE WONDERED HOW he could be so sure no lives were at risk. Interstellar communication was reliable, but there was no guarantee. It wasn't hard to think of ways the *Grosvenor* rescue could go wrong. In any case, a couple of extra days without food and water could be a fairly negative experience. Why put people through that if it wasn't necessary?

Priscilla went back to her office and sat staring at her display. Accounting records. *Eventually, unless we change the system, there are going to be more casualties. And nobody really seems to care. The only thing that matters is who gets blamed.*

She put Teegarden's Star on-screen. It was a brown dwarf, with a miniscule fraction of the sun's luminosity. It possessed a single planet, in close, barely one and a half million kilometers out. Remarkably, the world had life. Which was why a base was being established on the surface. The animals consisted mostly of spidery stuff, creatures with multiple legs and wings, bulging eyes, beetle husks. She looked at pictures of the ground. There were no trees, just bushes and thickets and brambles, almost white rather than green, twisted and strung together. The skies were always dark, black at night, dusky gray when the sun was in the sky. The data said there was a moon, but it took a serious effort to locate it in the visuals.

And there were pictures of the ground staff. Five people, led by an Alexander Quinn. Quinn reminded her of a history teacher she'd had back in high school. Tall, thin, with a long nose and a take-no-prisoners attitude. His opinion was always on display.

Quinn and his people would not be happy trying to get by for a few days without meals. His team all looked pretty young. Two guys and two women. There was no question what the WSA *should* be doing. And if something went wrong because they hadn't given maximum effort, she'd be as guilty as Irasco. She checked the schedule to see who was on duty in operations. It was Yoshie Blakeslee. Priscilla knew her but not well. "Nikki," she said, "connect me with Ops."

The green light blinked, and Yoshie responded: *"This is Operations. What can I do for you, Priscilla?"*

"Yoshie, I need a favor."

"Sure."

"I want you to prep the *Baumbachner* for departure. Do a complete refueling. I'll need two weeks' supply of food and water for one."

"Priscilla, why do you need to refuel? It has plenty of fuel."

"I'd just as soon you not ask too many questions. But I'll be making a jump."

"On the Baumbachner?*"* She sounded reluctant.

"Yes."

"Destination, please?"

"I'm still working on it. Just get it ready. Posthaste. I'll be there in a half hour."

"Who's the ordering official, please?"

"Mr. Irasco."

SHE LEFT THE office, strolled casually down the corridor, said hello to Patricia, who was just coming out of the conference room, and descended to the main deck. Then she hurried to her hotel room, packed, and ten minutes later showed up on

bravo dock, where the *Baumbachner* was secured. A second
ship had arrived and was being unloaded on the far side. She
thought of Frank's comment: *"We don't have anybody to
send."* Well, it was possible Frank had asked, but the carrier
had other uses for the vehicle and declined. It wasn't hard to
imagine its happening that way. *After all, it's not life and
death.* Frank asks for help and has to show somebody's in imminent danger. Out here, where you're dealing with interstellar distances, by the time the danger becomes imminent,
it tends to be fairly late.

She stopped at the departure desk. Nobody was there, but
an AI asked her name.

"Priscilla Hutchins."

"Priscilla, have you determined a destination yet?"

"Teegarden's Star," she said.

"Purpose of visit?"

"Rescue operation."

"Will you be carrying any passengers?"

"Negative. I'll be alone."

"Very good, Priscilla. You're clear to go."

"Thank you." She went into the access tube, hurried down
to the dock, and boarded the ship. She closed the air lock,
stowed her bag, and went onto the bridge. "Hello, Myra," she
said.

"Hello, Priscilla." The AI sounded cheerful. "Where are
we going?"

"Teegarden's Star."

"Teegarden's? Why are we going there?"

"To bail out an Academy team."

"Really?"

"Yes."

"Excellent. I've never done a bailout."

THE ENGINES CAME on. "Ops, this is *Baumbachner*. We are
ready to go."

The launch doors began to open, and Yoshie was back on
the circuit. "Baumbachner, *proceed at your leisure. Priscilla,
there are no other vehicles in the area."*

"Roger that, Yoshie. See you when I get back." She switched off the mike. "Okay, Myra, let's move. Just like last time."

"Lines released, Priscilla. Thrusters activated." They began to back out of the dock.

"Bring us around until we face the launch doors, Myra."

Gradually, she lined up with the exit, and the ship moved forward.

"Hutchins!" Irasco's voice exploded over the commlink. *"What the hell do you think you're doing?"*

She stared at the mike. Made a noise deep in her throat. And responded: "Frank, I'm headed for Teegarden."

"No you're not. Priscilla, bring it back."

Myra's voice: "What do we do, Priscilla?"

"Keep moving."

The doors began to close. "We do not have time to pass through, Priscilla."

"Okay," she said. "Hold it."

Someone exhaled on the commlink. Yoshie. Then Irasco said, quietly, *"After it's docked, stop by my office."*

"HAVE YOU LOST your mind?" Frank sat behind his desk, glaring. "What the hell were you trying to do? Show me up?"

She was standing in front of his desk. "It wasn't about *you*, Frank. It was about the people at the other end. They're waiting for somebody who may or may not get the word that they're in trouble."

"All right." He shook his head. "Priscilla, I just don't understand you. But you haven't left me much choice. You're terminated. Please go away."

"Frank. We lost Joshua because we didn't get to him in time. Eventually, we'll be forced to establish a response unit of some kind. Do you want to wait until somebody else is killed?"

"Damn it, Priscilla, back off. You think I *like* this arrangement? It's the system we have. You go out there in that wreck, and something goes wrong, *you're* dead." He took a deep breath. "You're lucky, by the way."

"How's that?"

"I'm not going to take your license. But I doubt if, after this, anybody will hire you."

PRISCILLA'S JOURNAL

Five people stranded out there, and all I can do is think of myself. Why is it always about *me*? But the reality is that, eventually, I may turn out to be the only casualty of this thing.

—January 19, 2196

Chapter 29

PRISCILLA RETURNED TO her office, dropped into a chair, and stared at the link. Maybe she should call and apologize. Assure Irasco she'd stay in line from now on. Cause no more problems. She did not want to walk away from this job. Did not want to go back to Princeton, where she'd probably spend her time waiting on tables at the Chicken Stop. But there was no way she could bring herself to do that. Anyhow, he probably wouldn't back off even if she did.

Good-bye, Alpha Centauri.

She called the shuttle terminal and asked for a reservation. The afternoon flight was full. They could accommodate her in the morning. She locked it in and started gathering her personal belongings. It was easy enough; she hadn't really moved much stuff into the office. There was a *Liberator* desk calendar, with a fresh cartoon every day. The *Liberator* had the funniest cartoons on the planet. The current one showed an idiotic-looking clerk assuring his boss that he shouldn't worry about a thing. "I'll take care of it personally."

She kept a change of clothes in the closet. She gathered her notebook and her pens and took down the wall calendar. It was all pictures of animals. January featured two kittens. (She liked paper calendars.) She picked up her toothbrush and, finally, the framed photo of the six graduating cadets, taken at the ceremony.

She put everything into her bag and decided to avoid saying good-bye to her coworkers. There was no way that could turn out well. As angry and frustrated as she was, she didn't want to leave in a trail of tears.

Maybe she could take advantage of her meeting with Dr. Campbell and get a position with the Academy Project. Though, probably, they wouldn't hire her once they learned what had happened. But she had nothing to lose.

Jolie Peters, a data-scan specialist, was outside in the corridor. "Hi, Hutch," she said.

That meant she probably hadn't heard yet. You don't do jokes with somebody who's just been terminated. She said hello, took the elevator down, walked past more offices on the main deck, and went out into the concourse. A couple of hundred tourists were wandering around, looking out through the portals, filling the gift shops and the restaurants and the game centers. Maybe Frank had been right, maybe she should have stayed out of it. Done what she was told.

But she was still too close to the people caught in the lander to assume that it was okay to take chances, not worry too much about the details, just have faith that everything would be all right.

She went into one of the game centers and spent half an hour shooting down space invaders. They were evil-looking creatures with enormous eyes and crocodile snouts, and they kept landing in gravity-defying saucers and emerging in walking tripods, like the ones in H. G. Wells. She had never played the game before, had in fact not bothered much with shoot-out games after she got past twelve years old. But on that occasion she took considerable pleasure in mowing stuff down.

SHE STAYED AWAY from the Cockpit that evening. And the Skyview. Best, if she wanted to eat alone, was probably the North Star, which mostly served tourists. It was pricey, but she owed herself a good meal. She ordered turkey and mashed potatoes and cranberry sauce and carrots, added a glass of burgundy, and ate by candlelight. There was music, of course, and a handsome young man tried to pick her up. He could not have chosen a worse night.

She had a second glass of burgundy, drank it slowly, and wondered when she'd be back. *If* she'd be back.

She was not ready to return to her hotel room, so she walked the concourse, lost in regret, and hardly noticed when she passed the North Star again. The concourse was circular, somewhat more than five kilometers around. She wondered what Jake was doing. Imagined what her mother's reaction would be when she heard the news. Speculated about whether anything would have been different had she been able to get the *Baumbachner* out through the launch doors. Her father would have been disappointed in her getting fired. Or no, maybe he wouldn't. He'd have been proud of her. Do the right thing regardless of consequences. It had been his mantra. Don't get caught up in the bureaucracy. Sometimes, you just have to take your chances.

She stopped in one of the viewport lobbies and looked down at Earth. They were over the Atlantic. Nothing but ocean down there, illuminated by starlight. The station was on the dark side of the planet, and there was no moon. She thought how nice it would be to buy a cabin cruiser and go to sea for a year or two. Pity she wasn't wealthy.

IT WAS GOING to be a long night. She arrived back at her apartment, thinking about the time she'd spent on the *Copperhead*, waiting while they tried to ride out the fragmented rescue attempt. Then, she'd been distracted by the presence of the girls. And the truth was that she'd never been able to accept the idea that somebody would not survive even after she knew the numbers wouldn't work. Somehow, there'd been a sense that someone would show up, charge in while there was still time. She hadn't believed any other outcome was possible until she saw Joshua in the cargo bay.

Maybe not even then.

She got out of her clothes, showered, set the alarm, and climbed into bed. There was nothing on the HV, just political talk shows, reruns of comedies and police procedurals, cooking directions, and how to upgrade your real estate. But she didn't want to deal with a silent room. So she left one of the talk shows on while she lay quietly staring at the overhead.

Some dark part of her *wanted* the rescue to go wrong, the *Grosvenor* to decline the assignment, to blow an engine, something that would prove her right. She realized what that would probably mean for Quinn and his colleagues, and that brought a rush of guilt, but on that night the guilt seemed secondary to everything else. She wanted to get even with Frank and Patricia. The director had to be involved, too. There was no way Frank would have terminated her without clearing it first with the boss. And Priscilla *did* have an option: She could go to the press. The downside to that was that she'd mark herself as a whistle-blower. That would destroy whatever remaining chance she might have to hire on with *anybody*.

In the morning, she dragged herself out of bed, dressed, and packed. Then she called her mother. "Coming home, Mom," she said.

"When? What happened?" She sounded, and looked, alarmed. *"Is something wrong?"*

"I'll tell you about it when I get there."

"When will that be?"

"Today," she said.

"Today? Priscilla, what's going on?"

"It's just not working out, Mom. Listen, I'll talk to you later, okay?"

She went down to the lobby and checked out. "We're sorry to see you leaving, Ms. Hutchins," said Laura, the lady at the desk. "We thought you were going to be staying with us indefinitely."

"My plans have changed," she said, "I'm sorry to say."

She went outside and hailed a cab. They were small electric vehicles, automated, with open sides. Her bags went on top. She climbed in, touched her link to the connector, and told it to take her to the launch terminal. Mukarram came out of the Cockpit, which was located directly across the way. He waved, and she waved back. He looked happy.

She arrived at the terminal, got out of the cab, and went inside. It was early yet, and the place was almost empty. She checked in, dropped off her bags, and went back across the concourse to get some breakfast. Best for a quick meal was Belly Up.

She was just starting on some pancakes when Irasco walked in. He smiled weakly. "Mind if I sit down, Priscilla?"

She looked at him. Looked at the empty chair opposite her. "Good morning."

"You're not always easy to get hold of. I've been trying to call you for an hour."

"I was turned off."

"Oh."

Her waiter came over. A young man, ginger-colored hair, green eyes, nice smile. Much more likable than Frank. "Is there anything else I can get for you?" he asked. Then he turned to her former boss: "Did you want a menu, sir?"

"Just coffee," he said. "Thank you." He glanced down at Priscilla's pancakes. "And make it one check."

"Separate checks, please," said Priscilla.

The waiter smiled uncertainly and backed away.

Frank toyed with a fork. "I'm sorry about what happened."

"What is it you want?" she asked.

"Well," he said, "we talked it over last night. I probably acted a little abruptly. Priscilla, we'd like to keep you on board. Start over." He gazed across the table at her. "If it's all right with you, we'll forget the whole thing happened."

"Why?" she asked.

"I don't think you understand what we're dealing with here, what's at stake. You know there's a movement out there to shut the space authority down. Everybody's economy is in a shambles. Even the Germans are suggesting the space program's a waste of resources desperately needed elsewhere."

"I'm aware of that, Frank. I don't live in a box."

"Okay. Bottom line: I don't want to do anything to support their argument."

Priscilla was tired of the debate. "Something goes wrong at Teegarden, and those people die; you think that won't be one more nail in the coffin?"

"I overreacted. Sorry." He tried to rearrange himself in his chair. "We want you to stay with us. The only thing I'm going to ask of you is that you promise not to go off half-cocked like that again. Do we have a deal?"

"I don't think I can make that promise, Frank. Not if somebody's life is at stake."

"Look, I don't want to restart this thing, but it wasn't a life-and-death situation. The question was whether they might miss a few meals. To be honest, I think we *both* over-reacted. But I'll tell you what: If something comes up, and you feel that strongly again, just warn me first, okay? And so we're on the same page here, the drive unit on board the *Baumbachner* hasn't been used for years. There's no way to know how reliable it is. The only life that was at risk yesterday was *yours*."

She looked at him. Into those frustrated eyes. "Okay, Frank."

"Then you'll come back?"

"Yes."

"Excellent. Take the morning off and get yourself together." His coffee arrived. He tasted it, paid both bills, and got up. "I'll see you this afternoon."

"All right. And Frank?"

"Yes?"

"Just for the record."

"I'm listening."

"You remember who you assigned responsibility to for maintaining the *Baumbachner*?"

"Sure. *You.*"

"Right. And you can take my word for it that, if we need it, the *Baumbachner* will be ready to go."

"I hope it doesn't run up the bill."

NEWSDESK

INVISIBILITY BAN GOES TO COURT
Do Potential Benefits Outweigh Risks?
Brockmoor Labs: Ban Unconstitutional

AFRICAN FAMINE INTENSIFIES
World Group Aid Insufficient

GLOBAL POPULATION PASSES ELEVEN BILLION
Churches, Religious Groups Break Tradition,
Urge Use of Contraceptives

PRIEST TALKS WOULD-BE SUICIDE OFF
CHICAGO EXCHANGE LEDGE
They Sit Together Forty Stories Over North Ave for Three Hours

ECONOMY: PRESIDENT NORMAN REASSURES NATION
"It's Just a Burp."

CUBS PUT BOOM-BOOM ON WAIVERS
Age, History of Injuries Factors
Fifth Straight Title Now a Long Shot

MTB OUTBREAK IN WESTERN INDIA
Crippling Disease Strikes Millions

SAUDI ARABIA ELIMINATES CAPITAL PUNISHMENT

FOUR DEAD AS GUNMAN ATTACKS
EX-WIFE AT CHURCH SERVICE
She Survives; Pastor Among Victims

WATKINS OUT OF GOLD PARTY RACE
McGruder Continues as Likely Nominee

TERRAFORMING RESEARCH CENTER
ATTACKED BY SPRAY PAINTERS
Six Nuns Among 17 Arrested

FINANCIAL DIRECTOR OF NEVADA
SCHOOLS CHARGED WITH FRAUD
Wrote School-System Checks to Cover Gambling
Debts in Las Vegas
Nobody Noticed for Three Years

THUNDERBOLT OPENS TONIGHT
Captain Brandywine and the Valiant *Back in Action*

JAMAICAN TRAWLER SINKS
Search for Five Fishermen Called Off Until Dawn

HIPPOPOTAMUS GIVES BIRTH IN SEATTLE ZOO
Provides New Hope That Species Might Survive

TORNADOES HIT MIDWEST
Seven Dead, Thirty Hurt as Storms Rake Plains

SERIES OF SHARK ATTACKS ON SOUTH FLORIDA COAST
Beaches Closed; Warm-Water Currents Blamed

GUNMAN KILLS WESTRUM
Kosmik CEO Led Terraforming Effort
Life Guard Society Denies Link

Chapter 30

"MOM, EVERYTHING'S OKAY. I won't be going back to Princeton after all."

"All right, dear. I guess I'm glad to hear it. What happened?"

"Well, it was just a misunderstanding. The problem's gone away."

"Listen, love, it was the boss, wasn't it?"

"What makes you think that?"

"It's always the boss, Priscilla. I met him that night at the party. I don't think you want to work for somebody like that. I'll tell you, you'd be a lot better off if you were a lawyer. Then you're your own boss."

"It's not that big a deal, Mom. I did something he didn't want me to. It was my own fault."

"What did you do?"

"Well, we had an incident. Some people needed help, and I tried to go after them without proper authority."

"Priscilla," she said, *"always play by the rules. Isn't that what we taught you?"*

"Yes, Mom, it is."

"All right. If you're going to stay there, please be more careful."

"Okay."

"And you know you always have a place to land if you need it."

"I know, Mom. Thanks."

"By the way, I think Tawny misses you."

HER FIRST ACT when she arrived back in her office was to order an inspection of the star drive on the *Baumbachner*. "And affiliated systems," she added. "If anything's broken or questionable, fix it."

Then she went in to ask Frank how the rescue was going. "Ross 248 should have received our message by now," he said. "*Grosvenor* will be getting there by midafternoon tomorrow. At Ross 248, that is. They'll be informed of the problem when they do, and they'll make their turn and get started for Teegarden."

"Tomorrow," she said. "They'll need four days to reach the system, and probably two more to get to those people after they surface."

"Are we going to start again, Priscilla?"

"Damn it, Frank, we need a better way to do this stuff."

"The system that's in place works pretty well."

"It doesn't work at all."

"All right. Look, that's enough. I understand how you feel. To be honest, I feel the same way. But there's nothing I can do. So let's just back off, okay?"

FRANK HAD BEEN right about the star drive. The *Baumbachner* needed a new one. And, unfortunately, they didn't come cheap. Priscilla forwarded the request to his office for approval and was surprised when he signed on.

At the end of the day, she wandered over to the operations center. Yoshie Blakeslee was on duty again. She was an attractive young woman, Asian, with black hair, dark eyes, and a captivating smile. She looked up when Priscilla walked in. "Hi, Hutch," she said. "I'm surprised they let you in here."

"What do you mean, Yoshie?"

"Usually, when they let somebody go, they revoke her clearance."

"Oh. Well, it's all right. They were just kidding. I'm back."

"You're serious?"

"More or less."

"Well, I'm glad to hear it. I was rooting for you yesterday. Too bad you didn't get out the door."

"I think if that had happened, they *would* have let me go."

A supervisor came into the space. He was an African-American, tall, bent, wrinkled, with a ridge of gray hair around a bald skull. "You're Hutchins?" he asked.

"Yes, sir."

He nodded. "I thought you were older." His features softened, and he reached out to shake her hand. "I'm Morgan White."

At that moment, she felt pretty good. "Pleasure to meet you, Morgan."

"I owe you a drink."

"Why's that?"

He looked as if she'd asked a ridiculous question. "Talk to you later." He passed a chip to Yoshie and left.

"That because of yesterday?" she asked.

"I think you made a few friends, Hutch. Is it okay if I call you that?"

She thought about it. Why not? "*Hutch* is good. I wanted to say thanks for the assist yesterday."

"It was my pleasure."

"You didn't get into any trouble, did you?"

"No, I'm okay."

"Yoshie, do we have any news on the Teegarden thing?"

"Nothing new. They have probably been trying to stretch their food supply, but we think they'll have used the last of it by tomorrow." She put the Teegarden ground module on the display. "This is about three days old. Taken from the *Proxmire*." The shelter consisted of a double dome. Lights were on, but they were smeared in the murky twilight.

"Not the most cheerful place. Is that as bright as the sky gets?"

"That's it, Hutch. The planet's almost in tidal lock. A day there is about three weeks long."

"Yoshie," she said, "if anything changes, let me know, okay?"

* * *

THE STORY ABOUT the marooned biologists at Teegarden made the news that evening. Rose Beetem, on the Black Cat network, talked with a retired pilot, Aaron Abdullah, about the dangers of spaceflight. "This stuff still seems to happen," she said, "despite all the technology."

"That's true," said Abdullah. "We're in an exploration era a little bit like the fifteenth century was for ocean travel." He was speaking from home, seated in an armchair in front of a wall decorated with a portrait of a forest at night with two moons overhead. "We don't really have the technology or the resources to make these flights safe. People go out there, they're a long way from anybody else, and just getting a message where it'll do some good can take days. The people at Teegarden need fifty-two hours, roughly, to get a subspace transmission to the Wheel."

"How long," asked Beetem, "would a standard radio transmission need to get here?"

"Thirteen years," he said. "It's a long way. And we tend to forget that because we can take shortcuts through space. When you go out there, you take your life in your hands. Eventually, I think that'll change, but I don't expect to see it in our lifetime, Rose."

Priscilla stared at the images. Abdullah was tall and sounded authoritative. There was something vaguely intimidating about him. But we *could* make it safer, she thought. *If we tried harder. Made a serious effort. Tell them, damn it. Aaron, you have a platform. Say something.*

MORE PICTURES ARRIVED from Teegarden Thursday morning. They were images from Tuesday, interiors from the ground station, clips of Alexander Quinn and his team, looking worried, weary, fragile. One of the two women commented, with a wry smile, that she'd been wanting to lose weight for years but not like this. "We'll be able to eat until about Thursday," she said. "Then we'll be switching to the gelatin desserts."

Quinn looked at the woman, then out at Priscilla. "Martha

made another effort today to get the lander started. She's our pilot, as you may know." Martha smiled helplessly. "But the thing's flat-out dead. In case anyone's wondering, we can't eat anything that grows here. So all we can do is wait." His anger and frustration were palpable.

The transmission had been sent two days ago.

SHE BROUGHT UP the Teegarden mission file and read a little about the objective, which had something to do with cellular-energy restoration. She'd hoped the mission purpose would sound consequential. And probably it was. But it wasn't anything that would excite the general public.

Quinn was one of the pioneers in his field, author of several books, and apparently one of the people who'd set the Academy Project in motion seven years before. Martha Manning, the pilot, was, coincidentally, also from Princeton. Well, almost. She had grown up in Bagwell, a small town a few kilometers east.

The other woman was Esther Comides, a biology professor at the University of Athens. She looked good, or probably would have with a decent meal under her belt. She had red hair and dark eyes. It was hard to imagine her male students concentrating on cellular reproduction while she was standing in the classroom.

And the two guys. They were postdocs, Gustav Lisak, from Oxford, and Bojing Chou, from Shanghai University. Both on their first assignments since getting their degrees. Bojing was another potential candidate for a leading-man assignment. Lantern jaw, intelligent eyes, good smile. It wasn't hard to imagine how much enthusiasm they must have carried with them on that first visit to another world. She wondered how much they'd take home.

SHE WENT INTO her office Friday morning hoping to hear that the *Grosvenor* had surfaced at Ross 248, gotten the message, and was now on its way to Teegarden. But her inbox was empty, so she called Ops. *"Nothing yet, Ms. Hutchins,"* they told her. *"We'll get back to you as soon as something comes in."*

She was staring out at the stars when Jake called. *"Able to talk?"* he asked.

"Sure. How's life in the Blue Ridge? You still on track with Alicia?"

"Pretty much," he said. *"I was happy to see you got your job back."*

"How'd you hear?"

"The Authority isn't very good at keeping secrets, Priscilla. But I wanted to congratulate you on what you did. It was a gutsy move. And what Frank should have ordered in the first place."

"Thanks."

"Be careful, though. The only reason you're still there is because they don't want to be back on the news shows again. They screwed up, and it cost Joshua his life. If something were to happen at Teegarden, they wouldn't want it to come out that they'd fired the young lady who tried to go to the rescue. They had *to put you back on. But they'll be looking for an excuse to get rid of you. Don't give them one."*

"I'll try not to, Jake. But I can't make any promises."

"How's it going? You have word on the Grosvenor *yet?"*

"We're waiting for it now. It should have arrived in the Ross area Tuesday. Let's hope."

"Other than that, how are you doing?"

"Okay."

"You don't sound enthusiastic."

"Well, I'm still behind a desk."

"Those people are idiots. But your time will come, Priscilla. Just hang in."

AN HOUR LATER, Yoshie called: *"Ross is reporting that the* Grosvenor *came in on schedule, Priscilla. They got the message. So they should be well on their way by now."*

PRISCILLA'S JOURNAL

I was glad to hear about Alicia. I didn't think Jake would ever be happy down on the Blue Ridge. But he's fallen in love, and that's great. I was seriously worried about him when he left, but he seems to be adapting pretty well. He tells me he still misses life up here, but he sounds perfectly content. I can hear it in his voice. I hope he's smart enough to hold on to her. She looks good, but she's a lot younger than he is. So who knows? Well, I guess I should have realized all along that he would find somebody. I'm happy for him. And I don't want to admit this, but I'm almost jealous.

Still no explosion from Monika. I guess she was all just talk.

—January 22, 2196

Chapter 31

SHE COULDN'T GET them out of her mind, Quinn with his electric features, his annoyance and frustration written all over them; Martha, the pilot; Esther, the leading lady; Bojing, who'd admitted to the media that he was scared about going so far from home; and Gustav, who'd said that he wanted to devote his life to fighting disease and that he believed researchers could profit by what was being found at Teegarden.

Quinn and Martha both were married, and both had kids.

Bojing had lost a sister a year before during a robbery attempt. Esther was an only child. And Gustav—well, he'd come out of a poor neighborhood, first in his family to go to college, and now he was sitting on another world.

At the end of the day, she stopped by Frank's office. He didn't look happy to see her, but there was nothing unusual about that. "Frank," she said, "is there any provision to keep the families informed?"

"What do you mean?" he asked.

"The families of Quinn and his people. When we hear something, do we contact the families, let them know what's going on?"

"It's not our responsibility, Priscilla," he said.

"Whose is it?"

"We pass everything to the Academy people. It's up to them."

SHE DIDN'T PUSH it. Maybe he was right, and they were better advised to stay out of it.

Her appetite had gone away, so she passed on the Cockpit for dinner, passed on dinner altogether, and went into a game room. She sat down in front of one of the displays, and chose Destiny, which allows participants to explore the stars, where they discover glittering civilizations, hungry aliens, and hi-tech structures designed to trap interstellars like flies in spiderwebs. But she couldn't keep her mind on it and shut it down after ten minutes and a close call with a white dwarf, which very nearly sucked her ship out of the sky.

There were other games: takeover efforts by runaway robots, interstellar wars, experiments gone awry producing dragons that threatened to gobble down New York or Geneva or wherever if you don't step in with your laser cannon and stop them. But they were all boring futuristic shoot-outs. It was as if the manufacturers, or the players, didn't recognize the sheer drama in looking down at a stretch of ground that had never been touched by a human foot. How about, she thought, a game in which you play God? Design a new set of rings for Saturn? Or put together a new nebula? Maybe the Butterfly Nebula?

Well, no, none of that would be very popular. But maybe a game involving rescue missions?

She was still sitting in front of the screen when Cal called. *"Priscilla,"* he said, *"I was hoping you'd be home this weekend."*

"No, I'm still at Union, Cal. I won't be getting back to Princeton for a bit."

"Okay," he said. *"You know, I'm discovering how much I miss you."* She sensed a transformation into his alter ego, Mark Klaybold. *"This place feels so empty without you."*

"Cal, I'm sorry." She almost called him *Mark.* "There's just not much we can do about it."

"Well, that's not necessarily true. I'd love to take you to dinner Saturday."

"That would be nice. I wish we could manage it."

"So we can do it?"

She wondered if he hadn't heard her. "Cal," she said, "I won't be in town."

"No, no." Across the room, someone cheered. Apparently they'd blown up an alien star cruiser. *"Where are you, Priscilla?"*

"In a game room."

"Oh. Okay. Anyway, I was thinking of going up there. To the Wheel. I've never been in orbit before. And this seems like the perfect time. I'm not involved in the show right now, so—"

Not a good idea, she thought. She liked Cal, but inviting him up for the weekend had some obvious drawbacks. "Have you looked at the price of shuttle tickets?" she asked.

"Yes. They aren't cheap, are they? But you've *had to spring for them."*

"I'm part of the organization, Cal. I get a pretty good rate."

"Oh."

"Look, I'm not going to have much time this weekend. My schedule's loaded. But I'll be going down for a few days next month. If you want, maybe we can get together then."

"Promise?"

"Sure," she said. "Absolutely."

SHE'D HAD ENOUGH of the games. She wandered over to the Cockpit and ordered a barbarossa. The news channels were showing pictures of Quinn and his people. They looked okay. Almost content, actually. Which meant the pictures weren't recent.

On one of the talk shows, Miles Conover and his gal pal Ivy sat around discussing current topics with assorted guests, and she got a surprise. One of the guests was Michelle Worth, the reporter who'd challenged Governor McGruder.

"—Are you saying that the death of Captain Miller could have been avoided?" Ivy was asking. The question was directed at Michelle.

The reporter shook her head. "I'm not saying that. I *am* saying that there's *no* provision for taking action when things go wrong. Ivy, look at what's going on now at Teegarden. People are stuck out there with no supplies, and they had to wait three days for the *Grosvenor* even to get the news that they were in trouble. Three days to *start* the rescue effort. It's shameful. Suppose those people were running out of air. Like Miller. Look at the attitude you get from the bosses: *Well, you guys just hang on. We'll be there in a week or two.* Why isn't there somebody at the Wheel ready to go?"

"That's simple enough," said the other guest, whom Priscilla did not recognize. "It costs money. You try to buy an interstellar recently?" He was blond, overweight, and liked to roll his eyes.

"All right," said Michelle. "But there's more to the story. You know who Priscilla Hutchins is, right?"

Priscilla's hair rose.

"She's the pilot," said Conover, "who brought back some of those kids."

"Right. I have it from a reliable source that Hutchins tried to leave for Teegarden a couple of days ago. When news of the problem first came in. You know what happened?"

"I have no idea," said Conover.

"She was stopped by the bureaucrats. From what I understand, they have an established procedure, and she wasn't following the procedure. So the people at Teegarden will have to wait a few extra days with no food."

Great, she thought. *That's going to enhance my situation around here.*

HER DRINK ARRIVED. She tried it, and her link chimed. *"Priscilla? This is Morgan White."*

The supervisor at Operations. "Hello, Morgan. Anything wrong?"

"No. I just got word about something, though. Thought you should know, if you haven't heard already. When they went through the Baumbachner, *the results weren't so good. The techs are saying that there's a good chance if you'd activated the drive, it would either have exploded, or made the jump and exploded the next time you tried to use it."*

"YEAH, PRISCILLA," FRANK said, with a smile playing on his lips. "I heard about the *Baumbachner* an hour ago."

"I wanted to say thanks."

"It's okay. You've been right all along. We should have an emergency vehicle. They're trying to fix the *Bomb* now, but I still don't trust it. We need an emergency vehicle, but we just don't have the funds for it. And this is why we need to stay within the system. Okay?"

PRISCILLA WAS TASKED with composing a reaction to the news reports. She put together a statement that, when Frank and Patricia had finished tinkering with it, pointed out that the *Grosvenor* was proceeding to the rescue and was expected to arrive in the Teegarden system in about three and a half days. It added that the *Baumbachner* had not been permitted to proceed earlier because it was no longer capable of interstellar flight. "An attempt to take it to the Teegarden system," someone added, "would have done nothing more than kill the pilot." It also noted that the ship was being refitted and would be maintained as an emergency vehicle. Priscilla had been instructed not to mention the fact that the actual rescue was still probably five days away. The pundits brought that issue up on the talk shows, however, and the WSA was beginning to take another beating when they caught a break: Mickey Alvin, then at the peak of his comic career, got involved in a bar fight and was arrested early that evening. That became the next day's main story.

Priscilla got back to her apartment just in time to watch Alvin being hauled off in cuffs. They followed with a picture of the captain of the *Grosvenor*, Easy Barnicle, who was wearing his no-nonsense face and assuring everyone they'd get to Teegarden in record time.

She wanted to throw something at the screen. Priscilla thought of herself as cool and even-tempered. But that night she was angry with the world. With herself, most of all, for neglecting the maintenance of the *Baumbachner*. With Frank, who didn't even understand how she'd felt; with Easy Barnicle, who was doing what *she* could have done if the system worked decently, and with the people on the talk shows, who were beginning to picture her as a comic figure. "Lucky she didn't blow herself up," Ivy said.

Quinn and Martha, and Esther Comides—that name rolled off her tongue for some reason—and Gustav Lisak and Bojing Chou. She'd never met any of them, but she felt as if she knew them.

What was it Frank had told her? *We almost never have any emergencies.*

"PRISCILLA," SAID FRANK, "we're all set to go with the platform tours. I've sent you the details. We want to get the program up and running as soon as possible. Think you can manage that?"

"How soon did you have in mind?"

"If you could start the tours a week from Monday, that would be good. What we'd like you to do is to conduct them three times a week, Monday, Wednesday, and Friday. Mornings would be best. Probably about ten. Take everybody around the platform, let them see the dome, get a look at Operations. If possible, it would be a good idea to show them the inside of a ship. We could use the *Bomb* for that. And do whatever else you think might be good. We'll run them for a couple of months, see how they go, then make an evaluation."

"Okay," she said. "I'll take care of it."

"Good. Let me know if you have any questions."

LIBRARY ENTRY

The prime objective of any bureaucracy is to ensure its own survival and proliferation. Whatever its stated function may be, whether ensuring the democratic operations of a nation or arranging the periodic pickup of the trash, nothing matters so much as its own continuity. It is the first consideration in time of crisis and the ultimate goal of whatever strategy is devised. Protect the organization. Those who are engaged in this immoderate pursuit are seldom conscious of any other reality. They believe they are performing their assigned tasks for the welfare of those who are theoretically being served. And when they win through, and the bureaucracy lives to engage another day, they feel they have done all that can reasonably be expected. They walk away with their consciences clear.

—Roger Casik, *Organizational Orgasm*, 2177

Chapter 32

TRANSMISSIONS FROM QUINN and his people continued to come in, sometimes as cool analyses, sometimes in frustrated bursts. Priscilla studied their faces, weary, scared, angry, lost, knowing that when these images originated, relief was still several days away.

It was easy enough to see that they felt a need to talk with the outside world, to reassure themselves that they weren't alone. They ran out of water the day after they exhausted the food supply. But there was plenty of ice on the ground. They debated whether it was safe. The consensus was that it was unlikely any local microbe would be capable of doing damage to them. "We should be all right since we're not part of the biosystem," Quinn said. They boiled the water nonetheless, and of course still couldn't be sure. But they knew what the likely outcome would be if they didn't do *something*.

"Hang on," Frank told them while they watched the images. "The *Grosvenor* is coming."

Yes indeed. On their way.

Priscilla would eventually look back on the experience as a time when she might easily have taken to drinking. The media beat the drums and posted countdowns. Two days until the *Grosvenor* could be expected to surface insystem. *One* day. And then, finally, they were *there*.

But it became necessary to explain again that the ship was still almost three days away from the Teegarden world.

Patricia showed up on Jack Kelly's show. "We try to be there when we're needed," she told the host.

Kelly looked skeptical. "But they've been out there with no food for, what, five or six days? And your guy is just now getting into the system. Why'd it take so long?"

She smiled pleasantly, as if Kelly just didn't understand reality. "It's a long way to Teegarden's Star. Twelve light-years, and I know twelve anythings doesn't sound like much. But it's an enormous distance. Jack, you have a son who's, what, about eleven?"

"Jerry? He's ten, Patricia."

"Okay. If, after you went home tonight, you were looking at that star through a telescope and it exploded, you wouldn't see anything different. In fact, he'd be out of college before you'd see the blast." Her voice softened. "The men and women who do the exploring, Jack, who carry out the missions, have a lot of courage. And they know how risky it is. How far they are from help. As I've said, we do everything possible. But there are limits to what we *can* do."

THE *GROSVENOR* WAS due to arrive at the shelter Wednesday, January 27, six days after the shelter ran out of food. Unfortunately, there was no way for anyone to know for certain it had arrived because of the delay in transmissions.

On that day, however, while the media tracked a virtual rescue they hoped was taking place, Priscilla got a call from Michelle Worth. Her defenses immediately went up.

Michelle smiled at her out of the display. *"You look happy,"* she said. *"It must feel good to know the rescue mission's almost done."*

"I hope so," said Priscilla. "Where are you?"

"Durham, North Carolina."

"That your home?"

"It is now. The studio's located here. And you've an open invitation to visit next time you're in the area."

"Thanks, Michelle. What can I do for you?"

"I'd like to do an interview."

"Now?"

"If you don't mind. The equipment's all set."

Priscilla hesitated. "I'm not sure what I can tell you that you don't already know."

"Why don't you let me worry about that? Is it okay with you if we get started?"

"I'm kind of busy, Michelle."

"This won't take long. Or, if you like, I can get back to you when you're free."

No easy way out. "Well," she said. "Let's do it now. But I'd like to keep it short, okay?"

"Absolutely."

"Is this going to be live?" She didn't know why she asked the question. It wouldn't make any difference whether it was live or not.

"No," she said. *"We were hoping to run it in about an hour."*

"Okay."

"Thanks, Priscilla. Just look directly into the screen. Yes, that's it. That's fine. If you're ready, we'll start."

"All right."

"Priscilla, welcome to the show. I wanted to ask you about the people stranded at Teegarden. Everybody knows it takes days to pass messages from one star system to another. You tried to save time by going to the rescue as soon as you got word of the problem out there. But the bureaucrats stopped you. I wonder if you wanted to comment on that?"

"The bureaucrats stopped me?"

She laughed. *"You must be a bit frustrated, aren't you? I mean, the assumption is that the* Grosvenor *got there today, or* will *get there before the day's over. Or maybe tomorrow or Friday. But you could have been there two days ago."*

"Maybe," she said.

"What do you mean?"

Priscilla hesitated. She didn't want to admit that the *Baumbachner* would have blown up if she'd tried to make the jump with it. Of course, maybe Michelle already knew that.

"They didn't want me taking the ship because it wasn't equipped for interstellar travel. I didn't know that. My boss saved me a lot of wasted time."

"You're a pilot, aren't you? How could you not know it couldn't go interstellar?"

"If your viewers have twenty minutes or so, I can probably explain it."

"Let it go, Priscilla. Was there another vehicle on the platform anywhere that could *have been used to make the flight?"*

"No, Michelle. Not at that time."

"Why not? I mean, how does it happen that the World Space Authority doesn't have a single ship that can respond to an emergency?"

"Because we're underfunded," she said. "If we're going to do interstellar travel, we should get serious."

THAT EVENING, A message came in from Easy Barnicle, confirming the ship's arrival in the Teegarden system. *"The good news,"* Barnicle said, *"is that we're only six hundred thousand kilometers out. We've made contact with Quinn. I think they're pretty happy to know we're here. Should be there by Wednesday."*

Minutes later, they had a transmission from Quinn: *"At last,"* he said. *"Thank God."*

It had by then become the biggest story in the media. Barnicle and the rescue mission were all over the newscasts and the talk shows. Relatives of the stranded scientists cried openly during interviews, the Gold Party's hopeful nominees and the president all made it a point to congratulate Captain Barnicle. Senator Belmar and Governor McGruder both assured the voters that, if they were elected, they would, in McGruder's words, "take steps" to reduce the possibility that anyone would ever have to go through this again. McGruder did not elaborate, but Belmar promised to provide "faster vehicles" to the rescue service. He did not seem to be aware there *was* no rescue service or that, if the physicists had it right, interstellar travel through Barber space imposed a speed limit.

The president assured everyone he was "looking into it."

It was a big moment for the Authority, and for the civilized world. And it got even bigger when, on Friday, everyone was watching pictures of the *Grosvenor* making rendezvous with the *Proxmire*, taking off supplies, then, two hours later, its lander coming to rest beside the double-dome module that had protected the ground team for the better part of two weeks. Priscilla watched with tears in her eyes as Quinn and his people, in Flickinger gear, stumbled out to the vehicle and helped carry food and water back to their quarters. Inside the shelter, Barnicle was greeted with a level of energy one would never have expected from the half-starved occupants.

Priscilla was sitting in the Cockpit with eight or nine people from Operations and the admin offices. Somebody started applauding, and they all picked it up. Then they refilled their glasses and drank a toast to everyone involved.

IN THE MORNING, Frank wandered through the Authority admin area, which would normally have been empty since it was a Saturday. But everyone was there, shaking hands, accepting and giving congratulations for a job well done. Willard Falkin, the new CEO of Kosmik, Inc., which owned the *Grosvenor*, was among the many passing and accepting compliments.

Later in the day, they received another transmission. Quinn and the other members of the scientific team were still inside the module. But they looked *good*. Music was playing, they were talking and laughing. Crisis averted. A tech from the *Grosvenor* had restored power to their lander. Easy Barnicle, with Gustav on one side and Martha on the other, waved at the imager. *"We'll be leaving,"* Quinn said, *"in a few minutes."*

Martha leaned over and kissed Captain Barnicle.

LIBRARY ENTRY

In other breaking news, Cameron Richards separated from his longtime girlfriend, Taia Blanchard.

—Western Broadcasting, January 30, 2196

Chapter 33

PRISCILLA CONDUCTED HER first tour the following Monday. But she could not stop thinking that it could have been *her* riding to the rescue instead of Barnicle. *If* she'd taken care of her job and seen to the maintenance of the *Baumbachner*, and if Frank had gotten out of the way and let her go.

Spilled milk. But lesson learned: Be prepared.

Approximately fifteen people showed up in the visitors' lounge for the tour. They were pumped about the rescue and would have loved to board the *Grosvenor*. Unfortunately, it wasn't available, but she was able to do the next best thing. She co-opted Skyview, led her charges into the restaurant at midmorning when it was not busy, and seated them at the long window. Then, using the imagers, she provided a virtual flyby: The *Grosvenor* appeared in the distance, at first nothing more than a dim star that gradually brightened, morphed into several lights, and finally into the vessel itself. It raced toward them, coming so close that they ducked as it passed overhead. When it was gone, they applauded.

Priscilla had been somewhat nervous about that first tour, afraid she'd freeze when she got in front of the group. But the tourists were enthusiastic about seeing the operations center and she took them on a virtual tour of the *Baumbachner*.

They took pictures of one another on the bridge and in the passenger cabin. Some even asked her to pose with their kids. Next they went to the Cernan Room, where she'd prepared a virtual display that featured appearances by original astronauts and cosmonauts. Susan Helms and Pete Conrad took questions; Anatoly Solovyev and Roger Chaffee oversaw a display of spectacular pictures of places around the solar system; Alan Shepard and Neil Armstrong described the early days. The old Saturn rockets once again lifted off from the Cape, and the command modules splashed down in the ocean. There was some laughter, and one teenager, looking at one of the twentieth-century shuttles, commented on how much guts it must have taken to go into orbit "in one of those things."

She took them to the science center, which was devoted primarily to managing the telescopes stationed at L4 and L5. One was bringing in images of a galactic eruption that had been in progress for several thousand years. The other was tracking a supermassive black hole that seemed to be swallowing its galaxy. "Where's the hole?" said one of the kids.

An astronomer standing nearby smiled and offered to explain. Priscilla gave way and saw again how much experts enjoy talking about the idiosyncrasies of their profession.

The reaction to the tour was so enthusiastic that they ran thirty minutes overtime. Priscilla enjoyed it probably as much as anyone. The virtual images were dazzling. She made a note to make the imager an integral part of the program. And she'd add a comet, maybe, as well as one of the deep-space stations. And what the hell, why not do a close encounter with an asteroid? She wouldn't be able to use Skyview on a regular basis, though. Management had made a special effort to accommodate her on this occasion, and she couldn't ask them to do that three times a week. But she might be able to set a program up at the Lookout Lounge. That would work just as well. They even had a snack bar.

TWO DAYS LATER, on the Wednesday tour, as Anatoly Solovyev prepared to take a group of about twenty through the Neptunian rings, she got a surprise. Cal was with them.

He smiled. His lips formed *hi*.

She stared back. Realized her jaw had dropped. Then raised a hand. *Hello*.

He faded back into the crowd when Solovyev's hologram blinked off. They made stops at the science center, the docks, Lookout Lounge, and the *Baumbachner*. The tour ended, of course, at the gift shop. She thanked everyone for coming. One of the children, a boy about eight years old, wanted to know if she'd ever been out in a ship.

"Yes," she said. "I've been out a few times."

"How did it feel?"

The child was an African-American. He wore a huge smile, and his eyes were locked on a picture of the *Thompson*, which adorned the bulkhead. "You'd like it," she said.

CAL WAITED UNTIL the group had dispersed. Then he approached. "You put on a pretty good show."

"Thank you, Calvin. I didn't expect to see you up here."

"I didn't really want to wait until God knows when. I had a few days off, and I thought I'd come see if I could talk the loveliest woman in orbit into having lunch with me." His alter ego, Mark Klaybold, was back. How did he manage that?

"Sure," she said. "That would be nice."

"Good. Do you have a favorite place?"

"How about the North Star?"

"Isn't that a little far to go for lunch?" His eyes sparkled, and they started walking.

"Have you been up here before, Cal?"

"No. I was struck by your line about keeping both feet on the deck. I see what you mean. It doesn't take much to get dizzy in this place, does it?"

"Just try to keep your mind off it."

"That's easy for you to say. I don't like heights."

"My mother's the same way. But you came here anyhow? I'm impressed."

"Well, can I tell you the truth?"

"Sure."

"When you talked about coming to Princeton during the month, you didn't sound very enthusiastic."

"Oh, I was probably tired, Cal. They keep me fairly busy here."

"I see." He hesitated. "I just wanted to make a point."

"Which is—?"

"I didn't want you to forget about me, to consign me to being a happy memory." The grin came back, but he looked uncomfortable. "I know it's pretty early to be talking like this. I mean we actually haven't had much time together. But it would be really easy for us just to walk away from each other, for *you* to walk away from *me*, and I don't want that to happen. At least not until you've given me a chance—" He stopped. Looked at her. "I'm talking too much, aren't I?"

"You're doing fine, Cal."

"I'm glad to hear it." The concourse was experiencing one of its busier days. Usually, you could circle the entire station and see a total of maybe two hundred visitors. But on that morning, sightseers were everywhere. "When do you expect Easy Barnicle will be back?"

"Probably tomorrow," she said, as they walked into the North Star.

The host led them to a table in back. They ordered sandwiches and two glasses of chianti.

While they waited, he said all the right things and brought her in from the distant place she'd been inhabiting. "I wish we lived close enough that we could get out periodically. Maybe just go to lunch. But spend some time together. So we could get to know each other."

"That would be nice, Cal. But I can't see it happening."

"No. Me neither. You ever do any acting?"

"No," she said. "I'm too self-conscious."

"You'd make a great leading lady." He looked out at the concourse. Or maybe at the bulkheads. "What do you do with your spare time? I don't guess there's any live theater here?"

"No, Cal. There's no way they could find a large enough audience to make it work."

"Too bad," he said. "Maybe eventually they'll have one."

"They could call it the Theater of the Stars."

"Good. I like that."

The chianti showed up. He raised his glass to her. "I can't tell you how glad I am you came to the show that night."

She smiled and touched her glass to his. "I enjoyed it."

"Priscilla," he said, "you look kind of sad."

"I'm fine, Cal."

"You sure? I'm hoping it's not because of me."

"No, of course not." She shook her head. "I'm sorry. This has just been a difficult couple of weeks."

"What's wrong? Can I help?"

"You already have, Calvin."

"You know," he said, "you turn that smile on, and the whole place lights up."

PRISCILLA'S JOURNAL

I'm not sure what's changed, but Cal seems different now. I've never before felt about anyone the way I'm beginning to about him. And I know I'll look at this one day, and it will probably seem silly. There've been guys before, Mack, Eddie Ruben, Leo Carstairs, Maury. But they were always pleasures of the moment. I never considered any of them as potentially a permanent fixture in my life. I was going off-world. That was where my life would be, and everything else was secondary.

But I've let Cal connect with me somehow. I think of him when I'm sitting at my desk poring over expenditure reports, when I'm watching the HV, when I'm looking out the window at the Atlantic Ocean. I think of him when I'm in the shower and when I'm standing out on the dock wishing I could go somewhere in the *Baumbachner*. He is getting to be the first thing I think of in the morning and the last thing at night. It wasn't supposed to be this way, and I'm not sure how it happened.

Worst of all: He's mine if I want him. I can see that. But I can't, in fairness to him, accept any offer. Not unless I walk away from the one thing I've always wanted.

—February 3, 2196

Chapter 34

JAKE AND ALICIA had rented a cabin on the shore of Claytor Lake. She'd brought sandwiches, cheesecake, and lemonade and was in the process of pulling the goodies out of the refrigerator. "I love this place," she said. "When I was a Girl Scout, we used to come here. We stayed in the cabins, played games in the woods, went swimming and canoeing, and rode the horses." She gazed across the lake at the line of trees. "I loved camping then."

"You don't do it anymore?" Jake asked.

"Not really. We got away from it. I haven't been camping in years. Haven't been near a canoe or a horse in years."

It had been a long time for Jake, too, but he didn't mention it. He saw no advantage in reminding Alicia about the difference in their ages.

It was a cold, gray afternoon, threatening rain or maybe snow. Perfect for providing a warm, cozy environment in the cabin. Alicia was wearing a Madison University pullover. Her hair was cut short under a Patriots baseball cap. They'd brought sweaters, but both were folded on top of a side table. "Jake," she said, "when you were going to other places, other worlds, did you ever do a boat ride?"

"No," he said. "I can't recall that we ever *had* a boat with us."

"I'm trying to imagine what it would be like to be on a lake in a place where there are no people. No anything, really. Is it true that a lot of those places out there are sterile?"

"Most of them," he said.

"I mean the worlds that are like Earth."

"That's what I meant. Life is rare, Alicia. People used to think they'd find it wherever there was water. That was because it got started so early here. We had living things almost as soon as it became possible for them to exist. So it sounded as if, when you got the right conditions, you automatically got life."

"So what happened?" she asked. "Why isn't there life everywhere?"

"Nobody really knows. There are theories, but—" He shrugged.

"Jake, what did it feel like, being in a place that's absolutely empty, except for you and the people you have with you?"

He laughed. "In the beginning, when I was just starting, it was pretty creepy. But you get used to it. I think Priscilla found it a bit unsettling during a couple of our landings."

"Who's Priscilla?"

"Oh, she's the pilot I told you about. I was the instructor during her qualification flight."

"I don't think I realized that was a woman." She bit into her sandwich, and a light dawned. "Oh. She was the one in the news with you."

"Yes."

"Of course." She paused and fingered her link. It was a necklace. "Priscilla Hutchins," she said. Her image blinked on. She enlarged it, moved it into the center of the room. "She looks pretty good."

He shrugged. "I suppose," he said. "She's still a kid."

"So where did you guys go?"

"Fomalhaut. And we were out near Serenity. And Palomus."

"Palomus?"

"It was a station. It's near a flare star. That's a star that puts out a lot of radiation." He bit into his sandwich. It was tuna. "It's good," he said.

She was wearing an odd smile. "Who else was with you on that trip?"

He tried to let her see there was nothing to worry about. "Nobody," he said.

"That sounds pretty convenient."

"There's a strict code of conduct."

"Well, of course." She was trying to make a joke out of it, but he suspected it could eventually become an issue.

"When I said we were alone, I wasn't counting the AI. It's programmed to report any questionable behavior. If anything happened, we'd both lose our jobs."

"Really?"

"Yes," he said. "Really."

She broke into a wide smile. "It's okay, Jake. I was just teasing."

THE AFTERNOON WARMED somewhat, and they went out and sat on the deck, munching cheesecake while a sailboat cruised past. He was here with the loveliest woman he'd ever known. She pretended to be moderately aloof. But that was how he knew she was his if he wanted her. And he *did* want her.

But he wasn't sure he could spend the rest of his life in the Blue Ridge. On the ground. That was the reality. He was beginning to realize retirement was not really all that he'd thought it would be. Driving up and down the mountain road, living a routine existence in which surprises were almost inevitably bad news. He wondered how Alicia would have responded to his old life.

Most of the pilots were single. You couldn't really keep a family together when you were spending most of your time cruising back and forth to Epsilon Eridani. Some people, from time to time, had made arrangements to bring a spouse along. But that didn't work very well either. The spouse, male or female, needed a special kind of personality to be able to live inside the confines of an interstellar that spent most of its time in Barber space, which is to say barely moving through mist in a dark place with absolutely nothing outside to look at. Not to mention the fact that one could expect to spend long periods of time with no company other than the spouse.

His link chimed. It was Frank Irasco.

"Hi, Frank," he said. "How you doing?" He thought about using the earpod but decided he didn't want to cut Alicia off.

"Okay. How's life in paradise?"

"Not bad," he said. "I'm near a lake with a beautiful young woman." Alicia's grin widened while she simultaneously rolled her eyes.

"The lady obviously has good taste," he said. *"Jake, we need your help."*

"What's wrong?"

"The Vincenti's *missed a position report."*

"Where is it?"

"Last we heard, it was orbiting a nomad."

"Where's the nomad?"

"Four light-years."

All right. That wasn't bad. The jump would take a little more than a day. Figure a couple more days to zero in. Maybe a week altogether, round-trip. "When was the report due?"

"Seven hours ago. I'm hoping something just broke down somewhere, and it'll still come in. But meantime, I need to be sure we're ready to do something if we have to."

"You're not going to just reroute somebody?"

"Nobody's close enough to get there before we could, Jake. And we're under a little pressure these days. As I'm sure you realize."

"Okay, I can understand that."

"We'll make it worth your while."

"Why don't you send Priscilla?"

"Jake, she doesn't have the experience. If those people are in some kind of trouble out there, I need somebody I can trust. Not that I can't trust her, but— Well, you know what I mean."

"Have you talked to her about it?"

"No. She doesn't know anything about it."

"Why me?" he asked. "Isn't there anybody else up there?"

"Not right now. I have to bring somebody in. You're the guy we want, Jake."

Damn. The whole thing with Priscilla was a farce. They claimed she was there in case of emergency. But when they get one, they don't trust her enough to send her out. Alicia was watching him, but her face remained noncommittal. If he declined this kind of request, what would she think of him?

"All right," he said, "I'll make a deal with you. I'll do it, provided you make Priscilla available. Invite her to go along." That got a raised eyebrow from Alicia. "If there's a problem out there," he added for her benefit, "I might need help."

"Okay," he said. *"I'll take care of it."*

"And make it sound like your idea."

"Fine. When can you get here?"

"I'll leave tonight." He caught a sudden bleak look in Alicia's eyes. Jake covered the mike. "I'll only be gone about a week," he said.

She did not look happy.

Frank was saying something and he'd missed it. "Say again, Frank. You broke up."

"If you hustle, you can make the evening shuttle out of Reagan."

"Okay," he said. "One other thing: What ship do we have available?"

"The Baumbachner."

"That thing's a wreck, Frank."

"Actually, it's in pretty good shape. And at the moment, it's all we have."

He signed off and gave Alicia a shrug.

"What's a nomad?" she asked.

"It's a planet with no sun."

"No sun? How does that happen? Does it burn out, or what?"

He was suddenly aware he was gulping down the cheesecake. "Something happens that pulls the world out of orbit. Most likely it would be a passing star."

"Is the mission dangerous?"

"No. There shouldn't be a problem."

"How can you say that when that other ship is missing?"

"It's not *missing.* It just didn't file its position report on time."

"How does *that* happen? Aside from maybe that it crashed? Or got attacked by aliens?"

"Come on, Alicia, relax. There are no aliens. At least none that would be dangerous to us."

"So what's the routine? Does the captain file the report?"

"The captain's responsible, but the report is normally transmitted by the AI. Automatically, every twenty-four hours."

"You ever hear of this happening before, Jake?"

"Yes."

"And what caused it?"

He would have preferred not to respond. "We never found the ship."

"Oh."

And there'd been three other cases. One ship had exploded when the star drive apparently let go. The other two also had never been heard from again. But he said nothing. Oh for four didn't sound good. "Everything okay, Alicia?"

"Yeah."

"What's wrong?"

"Nothing." She shook her head.

"Alicia, I trust Priscilla. I know her. If there *is* a problem, she's the one to have on board."

She looked at him for a long minute. "Okay," she said.

NEWSDESK

NORMAN LOSING GROUND WITH VOTERS
Campaigns Continue Smear Tactics
Belmar: President Looks Other Way as Corruption Mounts

EASTPOINT POWER COLLECTOR DRIFTING
Central Europe Bears Brunt of Outage
Stabilization Mission to Leave Tomorrow

LAST ELEPHANT DIES
Bobo Passes in West African Care Center

BAILEY CHARGED WITH SEXUAL HARASSMENT
Ontario Governor Claims Accuser "Deranged"

SHUTTLE HIT BY GEESE OVER REAGAN
Third Incident This Month at Washington Port
Migrations Taking Place Early

ECHO HARPER DEAD AFTER HEART ATTACK
Olympic Swim Champion "Just Working Out"
No Previous Indication of Problem

DOG RESCUES THREE CHILDREN FROM BURNING BUILDING
"Turbo Led the Way"

MAN KILLS EX-WIFE, BOYFRIEND, TWO
BYSTANDERS, IN NEW YORK BAR
Statewide Hunt on for Burke Caldwell
Had Long Record of Spousal Abuse

PHYSICISTS CLAIM NEW EVIDENCE UNIVERSE IS ILLUSION
Kay Clemens on Tonight Show: *"It's All in Your Head"*

Chapter 35

WHEN THE *GROSVENOR* surfaced a quarter million kilometers beyond the Moon, the media came out in force. The intensity of the coverage didn't quite match what the schoolgirls received when they came back on the *Copperhead*, but it was close. Quinn and his people and their family members had been on HV daily during the rescue effort, and consequently a wide audience had gotten to know them. The ship docked at Union, where Easy Barnicle and the five people he'd rescued transferred to a special shuttle, which they rode into DC. A large crowd was waiting for them, and a band played "The Green Hills of Earth" as they filed into the waiting area. Later that day, parades marched in Shanghai, Boston, and in Barnicle's hometown, Baltimore. They were greeted at the New White House by President Norman and the First Lady. They made the rounds of the talk shows, where Quinn announced that he'd sold a book to Bartram Publishing, and a rumor began to spread that a movie was already in the works.

During an appearance on *Live With Lennie*, Barnicle described his feelings when he'd handed out the food and water and watched everybody dive in. "We'd warned them not to wolf down the chow. Not to eat too much. But I don't think anybody was worrying much about that. I'll tell you,

Lennie, I watched those folks go after those meatballs, and I don't think I've ever felt that good in my life."

THE FOLLOWING MORNING, a summons came in from Frank. Patricia was also in his office when Priscilla arrived. They were talking, but the conversation stopped when she came through the door. Frank pointed to a chair, and the director delivered a wary smile. "Good morning, Priscilla," she said. She smiled again, checked the time, and got up. "I have to go, guys. Frank, it's all yours." And she strode out of the office.

He closed the door. "Priscilla," he said, "you've made it pretty clear you want to get back on the bridge."

"Absolutely," she said.

"Are you familiar with Orfano?"

"Sure. That's the world they found adrift a few years ago."

"That's correct. The Academy wanted to trace as much of its history as they could. So they sent a team out there to take a look around."

"The *Vincenti*."

"Yes." He nodded. "They reached the place five days ago and went into orbit. But they missed their position report this morning."

"It could just be a communication breakdown," she said. "The AI might have malfunctioned. Or maybe a temporary loss of power."

"Of course. Or it could be something serious. We don't know. And the Academy is not happy. After this Teegarden business, everybody's a bit jumpy."

"I assume the Academy's sending somebody out to see what happened?"

"They don't have anybody in position to react."

"They want us to help."

"Correct."

Priscilla couldn't resist. "Is the *Grosvenor* available?"

"There's nothing funny about this, young lady."

"Sorry, Frank. You have more experience with this kind of thing than I do."

"I'm glad you recognize that, Priscilla." He was trying to

be patient and to let her see that it wasn't easy. "We're taking a lot of heat right now."

"So what—?"

"Fortunately, Orfano is pretty close. It's only a little more than four light-years. There's nobody even remotely closer to it than *we* are."

"Frank, I'm ready to go. I assume we'll be using the *Baumbachner*."

"It's all we have."

"Okay. It's going to need a quick maintenance check. And refueling."

"We've started the process, Priscilla."

"What about the tours?"

"This is more important. We're replacing them with the virtual tour that we used to use. It won't be quite as lively as you've been, but—"

"Good enough. I'll be ready to go in a half hour."

The creases in Irasco's face deepened. "I knew we could count on you. But we don't know what you might run into out there. So we don't want you going alone."

"That's not a problem. I can take somebody to help out. One of the technicians. Maybe Ursula—"

"Actually, *you're* the person going along to help out, Priscilla."

She frowned. "How do you mean, Frank?"

"You're going to find out about this anyhow, so I might as well tell you now. You weren't our first choice. We needed someone with more experience. Don't think we don't have the utmost confidence in you, but if we sent someone out there who'd just gotten her license, and anything went wrong—"

"Who is it?"

"We called Jake. And asked him to go."

"Oh." She shrugged. "Okay. So we're both going?"

"Yes."

"And he said that he'd go if I was included?"

He raised a hand in defense. "Don't get me wrong. We were going to offer you a spot as well. And do me a favor: Don't tell him I told you."

"Where is he now?"

"On his way. He'll be here on the evening shuttle out of DC. So, all we need is for you to be ready when he gets in."

SHE MOVED HER gear down to the ship and called Ops. Yoshie answered. "Have we heard yet from the *Vincenti*?"

"Negative, Priscilla. They're still quiet."

"Let me know if anything comes in. Okay?"

"Absolutely. I understand they're sending you on the mission."

"Looks like."

"Well, good luck."

Then she called her mother. "Heading out on a flight, Mom."

"Good for you," she said, pretending to be enthusiastic. *"Where to?"*

"A runaway planet. It's not far. We'll only be gone a few days."

Mom's breathing changed. *"What's a runaway planet, dear?"*

Priscilla explained. *"Sounds cold,"* Mom said.

"I'll take a sweater."

"Okay. Just be careful, all right?"

"Sure, Mom."

"Well, enjoy yourself. When are you leaving?"

"In a few hours."

"Call me when you get back. Okay?"

THERE WAS A better than fair chance that the people on the *Vincenti* would fix the problem and announce that everything was okay. And the mission would be scrubbed. She desperately didn't want that to happen. *But what kind of human being am I that I'm hoping they don't call in? That a potentially lethal situation doesn't turn out to be minor because I don't want to spend the next few days in my office?*

She stowed her gear and tied her link into the ship's comm system. Then she ran a systems check. When she'd finished, she reviewed everything that was known about Orfano.

There wasn't much. The wandering world had been discovered several years earlier when it got between the Marcellus Cloud and the L2 Space Telescope. Nobody paid any attention to the shadow until a researcher going over the records noticed it. They went back to the L2 and, although the operational staff thought the effort a waste of time, instituted a search and relocated the object. It *was*, they realized, a planet that had become detached from its parent sun and was now headed gradually outward toward the galactic rim.

A mission had been dispatched last summer to take a look. They'd spent several days in orbit. The surface temperature was somewhat warmer than they'd expected, reaching, in some places, -170 degrees Celsius. The atmosphere was about 10 percent oxygen, but otherwise they found nothing out of the ordinary. After they'd returned, however, analysts at the Academy detected surface features they found hard to account for. Ridges curved across the landscape with near-geometric precision, almost as if they'd been carved from the rock. Mountains in many places were smoothed, rounded, generally shaped like domes. In other areas, they resembled turrets. The mission reports indicated that the crew had taken a close look but had dismissed the configuration as natural surface features. "No sign of life," they'd concluded. "Life not possible under these conditions."

Nevertheless, there were doubts. So, eventually, a second mission had been dispatched. That was the one that had missed its most recent position report. The *Vincenti*.

PRISCILLA'S JOURNAL

Ready to go.

—February 4, 2196

Chapter 36

FRANK WAS WAITING at the terminal with a tentative smile. He offered Jake his hand. "Good to see you. We hated to disrupt your retirement, but we really needed someone we could rely on."

"You still haven't heard from them?"

"Nothing."

"Okay."

"Does the terminal know to deliver your bags directly to the *Baumbachner*?"

"Yes."

"All right. We want you to get going as soon as you're able. We'll have a room waiting at the Starlight when you get back."

"Thanks." They walked out onto the concourse.

"Jake," said Frank, "I know you blame us for what happened with the *Gremlin*. But—"

"I don't blame anybody, Frank. The system is what it is. It's what we signed up for. Is Priscilla waiting in the ship?"

"Yes."

"Okay." They stopped in front of the elevators. "I assume you guys did a thorough check of the *Baumbachner*?"

"Yes. It's in good shape."

"I hope so."

They reached the elevators. Frank pushed the button. But he never took his eyes from Jake. "Have you been in touch with Priscilla since you left here?"

"A couple of times, Frank. Why?"

"I don't think she's been very happy working for us. I just wanted to let you know so you go easy on her. She tends to get a little emotional sometimes."

The elevator opened. Jake got in. A woman in a station uniform joined him. "I never noticed a problem," Jake said.

"When she was with you"—Frank held the door open—"when she was with you, she was doing what she cared about. But she's had to make some adjustments here. Anyhow, just in case, you may want to cut her some slack."

"All right, Frank. And we'll let you know as soon as we have something."

PRISCILLA WAS WAITING on the bridge. She broke into a big smile as he came through the hatch, got up, and threw her arms around him. "Jake," she said, "you have no idea how glad I am to see you again."

"Just like old times, huh?"

"Umm—I wanted to thank you."

"For what?"

"Well, Frank asked me not to say anything. But I know you put pressure on him to let me go along."

"My pleasure, Priscilla. I figured you were probably tired putting together payrolls."

"I don't have much to do with payrolls."

"Well, making sure they have a decent supply of lubricants, then. Whatever. How's it been going?"

"Okay," she said.

"How's Tawny?"

"Tawny's fine. She likes Princeton." She sat back down, and he climbed in beside her.

"It won't go like this forever, babe. Just stay with it. Eventually, they'll figure it out."

"I don't really have any complaints, Jake. I don't guess I've made it easy for them."

"They mean well, Priscilla. Just try not to alienate them, okay?"

"Sure."

He studied the panel. "You run the check-off yet?"

"We're primed and ready to go."

The bridge was retro. It looked like something out of an old movie. "Is this thing really safe?" he asked.

"I hope so."

"So do I." He looked at the time. "We can get started as soon as my bags show up. I probably should have brought them down myself." Priscilla glanced at the control panel. Then at Jake. "Stay where you are," he said. "You're in command. I'm just here as an observer."

She smiled. "You're one of the great men of our time, Jake."

He actually blushed. "Whatever, but I don't guess I'll be much use if my stuff doesn't show up soon."

She called the terminal, asked about the bags, nodded, and disconnected. "They're on the way."

"You seem to be in a hurry, Priscilla."

She laughed. Cleared her throat. "You want the truth, Jake?"

"Sure."

"I want to get submerged before Wauken calls in, and they cancel the mission."

"Isha Wauken? Is she on the *Vincenti*?"

"Yes. You know her?"

He smiled. "An old girlfriend."

THEY EASED OUT between the launch doors, turned to their assigned course, and began to accelerate. "By the way," she said, "I should introduce you to our AI. Her name's Myra."

"Good evening, Captain Loomis," said the AI.

"Hello, Myra," Jake said. "Nice to meet you."

"The feeling is reciprocal." Her seductive tone surprised Priscilla.

"Does she have a sense of humor?" Jake asked. "Or is that the way she normally talks?"

"It's the first time I've heard her do that. I think you have a fresh conquest." She checked the gauges. Then: "How's it feel to be back?"

"Better than I'd expected. In fact, sometimes I'm sorry I left."

"Jake, may I ask a personal question?"

"Sure."

"Did they force you out? I never had the impression you really wanted to leave. You said you did, but—"

"Well, no, actually I didn't want to leave. But I wasn't forced out. At least not by Frank or Patricia."

"Then by whom?"

He looked at her. Felt a surge of regret. "By *you*, Priscilla." Her eyes went wide, and she stared at him. "It's okay. I just— What? I couldn't face people around here after we lost Joshua."

"Jake—"

"Let's just let it go, okay?"

"So why'd you come back?"

"Because somebody else out there might need help. And they didn't have anybody else." And he realized immediately he shouldn't have said that.

Priscilla turned a laser gaze on him, but she didn't say anything.

"I didn't mean it that way, Priscilla. When Frank called, I thought about backing off, but I wasn't sure they'd have been willing to send you on your own. You're still new at this, and they don't want to take any chances of anything more going wrong. They don't know you the way I do. I mean, you could have gone out there and performed like Captain Brandywine, and they'd still have taken some flak for sending out a relatively inexperienced pilot."

She softened. The anger faded. "Well," she said, "thanks. Especially for getting me included in the deal."

"It seemed like the least I could do. Though I wasn't sure you'd want to go."

"Of course I want to go. You think I wanted to sit in that office back there while you went out and did the mission?"

"I needed to be doing something useful," he said. "I was tired just sitting on the front porch watching the world go by."

* * *

THE EARTH, OF course, dominated the sky. Fleecy clouds floated over Asia, which was ablaze with city lights.

"We'll be making our jump in a few minutes," said Priscilla.

Jake checked to be sure his harness was secure. Sometimes the transition could be a bit rough. "Okay," he said. "Whenever you're ready."

She leaned over the mike. "Ops, this is *Starhawk*. We're ready to make our jump."

"Who?" The guy at the other end sounded startled.

"Kidding," she said. "Make that *Baumbachner*."

"Oh. Okay, Baumbachner. Roger that."

"Has the *Vincenti* reported in yet?"

"Negative. We've heard nothing at all."

SHE MADE HER jump into transdimensional space. "Time to target," she told Jake, "thirty-three hours."

"Who's on the *Vincenti*?" he asked. "Other than Isha?"

Priscilla checked her notes. "Larry Martin and Gunther Hahn, both physicists, and Otto Schreiber, a doctoral candidate from Leipzig University. Martin's described as a planetologist, whatever that is."

"All right."

"Making sure we don't have more people than we can carry back, Jake? Just in case?"

"No. I don't think Frank would make that mistake again. I was just wondering if there'd be any more familiar names."

"Are there?"

"No. Just Isha."

"How close were you?"

"It wasn't much more than a few dinners."

WHEN PRISCILLA RECEIVED responsibility for the *Baumbachner*, she took time to update its library. It had originally been not much more than a sparse collection of thrillers and technobooks. Those were still there, of course. But she'd added thousands of titles: novels, biographies, history, science, even some theological tracts. There were movies dating back two and a half centuries. "It doesn't sound," Jake said, "as if working for Frank takes much of your time."

"The job is pretty much whatever I make it," she said. "Mostly they want me there in case they need a pilot. And to do tours."

"Does Myra play poker?"

It was a facetious question, of course. Myra was capable of playing all kinds of games, including multiple hands of poker, if need be, and doing it as separate entities. She was also capable of faking enthusiasm.

Ultimately, they mostly just talked. They watched a couple of movies, and went on a guided tour of the American Museum of Natural History. Priscilla used one of the ship's imagers and spent hours combing through visuals from its interstellar library, looking for special effects she could plug into her tours back at Union. She recorded spectacular pictures of gas giants poised over mountaintops and dinosaur-like creatures drinking from rivers and explosive bursts erupting from solar surfaces. She played them for Jake, projecting them into the center of the passenger lounge, soliciting his opinion.

She did a few crossword puzzles while he watched football and baseball games that Myra had located for him, featuring the Pittsburgh teams, of which he was a longtime fan.

Jake missed the mountain cabin, the wind coming out of the trees, hanging out with the poker players, and having dinner with Alicia. It just seemed that, no matter how he did things, dissatisfaction crept in. There was always something missing.

AFTER ALL THESE years, he was still fascinated by conditions outside the ship when it was submerged. Though they were covering immense distances in an impossibly short time, one could never have guessed that by looking through any of the portals. The *Baumbachner* seemed to be almost adrift in a dark fog. Nothing else was visible. They might have been moving at possibly two knots. Certainly no more than that.

It was a completely different universe out there. He'd read about Barber space, as it was called. But none of the explanations made any sense to him. The physicists talked of multiple dimensions and quantum relativity. And he was pretty sure that, mathematics aside, they didn't have a grasp of it any more than he did.

But it didn't matter. It was there, it worked, and it opened large sections of the Milky Way to exploration. And that, in the end, was all he cared about.

An hour or so away from Orfano, he sat alone on the bridge, with a book on the auxiliary display. It was a collection of cartoons from *Punch*. Inevitably, though, his gaze would find the quiet mist outside.

PRISCILLA'S JOURNAL

If we're going to do this kind of thing rationally, we're going to need better communications. I don't know if they'll ever be able to reduce the amount of time a signal needs to get from one place to another. I suppose you really can't complain when a transmission covers almost six light-years in a day. And it would be helpful if we could talk to each other while we're submerged. Having to wait until we complete the jump before we can find out what's happening is not convenient. We'll probably eventually get better technology. And this equipment will wind up in museums.

—February 5, 2196

Chapter 37

JAKE HAD LONG since lost count of the number of flights he'd logged. But this was the first time he'd surfaced in an area with no sun. Well, maybe that was something of an exaggeration. He'd been out to Neptune once. Sol, from there, wasn't much more than a bright star. But at least you knew it was there. In this case, light-years from everything, he felt— What? The emptiness? The distances?

"Myra," said Priscilla. "Any sign of Orfano?"

"Nothing yet. It may take some time."

"All right. Let's see if maybe we can get lucky and locate the *Vincenti*. Go to broadcast."

"Okay. Ready when you are."

"*Vincenti*, this is *Baumbachner*. We have just arrived in the area. Do you read?"

She switched over and listened to the silence.

"*Vincenti*, answer up, please."

Nothing.

"I've got Orfano," said Myra. "Range is seven hundred thousand kilometers."

"That's not bad," said Priscilla.

Jake agreed. "Considering how far we've come, that's about as close as you could hope for."

"Unfortunately," said Myra, "It's behind us. We're pulling away from it."

"Wonderful," Priscilla said. "Prepare to do a one-eighty."

"It will require two hours to reverse movement."

"Okay. Hold on a second, Myra." She looked over at Jake.

"No," he said, "I'm fine. Start braking whenever you're ready."

ORFANO WAS SLIGHTLY bigger than Earth, with an equatorial diameter of thirteen thousand kilometers, and a gravity index at 1.1. Reports from the first expedition indicated warmer temperatures than would normally be expected with no sunlight. The experts attributed the condition, probably, to the presence of an iron core warmed by radioactives.

They were braking again, preparing to enter orbit.

Jake was at the controls while Priscilla sat quietly in the right-hand seat, looking out at gray clouds and an icy landscape. It was more exotic than any planetary surface she'd seen before. On terrestrial worlds, mountains usually came in clusters, divided by plains and hills. But the clusters were random, and the mountains scattered arbitrarily. Orfano's mountains and ridges resembled a frozen eruption. They possessed an unsettling symmetry. Long, curving lines of snowcapped peaks and valleys ran parallel to each other, cast in shades and tones of rock that formed circles and triangles. Or maybe not. She found that if she closed her eyes and looked again, the impression went away.

"I see it, too," said Jake.

"What do you mean?"

"It looks as if it was landscaped."

"Oh."

"I'm not especially religious, but that place could have been put together by an engineer."

When the angle was right, the ice glittered in the starlight, and the ground acquired a kind of pristine beauty. Nature in all its fractious, weathered clarity. "Maybe that's where you should have your cabin," she said.

"It does have a certain charm, Priscilla. But it's a bit too exotic for my tastes. Myra, any sign of the *Vincenti*?"

"Negative, Jake." The seductive tone was gone. Games were over. "We're not picking up anything."

"Okay. Keep us informed."

"Of course."

He turned back to Priscilla. "It's early yet."

"What do you think could have happened to them?"

"Well, we know they're not simply on the other side of the planet." They'd been sending out transmissions for hours. "To be honest, I'm not optimistic. But maybe they developed a problem with their comm system. If they couldn't communicate with anybody, there wouldn't be much they could do. They weren't going to go all the way back to fix a transmitter. So they stay on, complete the mission, then go home. They might have done that and already left."

"And we have to wait here until they get home, and Frank lets us know everything's okay?"

"Priscilla, you're a licensed pilot. What do you do if your comm system gives out and you have to return to base?"

She thought about it. "Oh," she said.

"So what do you do?"

"Leave a satellite with a message."

"Very good."

"I'm embarrassed."

You should be. "It's okay," he said.

After her performance with the *Gremlin*, he was almost relieved to find out she could be just as dumb as anybody else.

"THEY'RE NOT HERE," Myra said.

Priscilla looked out at the empty sky. "They must have gone back. And it looks as if I'm not the only one who forgets about satellites."

"Or they went down," said Jake.

She frowned. "I hope not."

Starlight reflected from icy ridges and mountaintops. He could make out a long, jagged canyon near the horizon.

"So what do we do?" asked Priscilla.

"We expand the search. We'll keep looking until we find something or get recalled."

"You think Isha would leave without putting out a satellite?"

"Anybody can screw up. But no, it's hard to imagine. Myra, set up the scanners for a ground survey."

"Okay, Jake."

"The *Vincenti*'s big enough," he said, "that if it went down, we should be able to find it."

THEY MOVED OVER a gray mist. The gorges, ridges, and mountains were hazy under the stars. The ground could not properly be described as rugged. It was rather the sort of terrain one might see in a portrait designed to emphasize the beauty of the natural order. Priscilla could not resist expressing her admiration. Meantime, Myra adjusted the angle of each orbit to expand the coverage, but the hours drifted by without result.

Eventually, they both slept in their chairs while the AI continued to monitor the scanners and scopes. Jake woke periodically only to drift back off, lulled by the murmur of the air vents. Then it was morning on the ship, if not in the world below, and the interior lighting adjusted accordingly. In several areas, the surface appeared to be obscured by storms. Priscilla woke. "Nothing yet?"

"Negative," said Jake. "Let's get some breakfast."

He released his harness, and Myra's voice broke the silence. "Object ahead," she said. "It appears to be in orbit."

"What is it?" he asked.

"I am not sure." She put it on-screen. Jake could make out nothing other than that it was tumbling. "It is much too small to be a vehicle."

Priscilla was in the pilot's seat. "Ready when you are, Jake," she said.

He belted back down, and she changed course and fired the thrusters. The ship began to accelerate.

The object grew larger. It had right angles. "It is about the size of a human being," Myra said.

Jake stared at it. "Probably just a chunk of ice."

"It appears to have four legs," said Myra.

It was acquiring definition. "Holy cats," Priscilla said. Jake gaped. It looked like a *chair*.

BAUMBACHNER LOG

We have found the *Vincenti*.

— Jake Loomis, February 7, 2196

Chapter 38

IT WAS THE same type of chair he was sitting in. Maybe slightly different armrests. It was tumbling slowly, and the restraint that would have secured its occupant drifted behind it. The back of the chair looked broken. No. Not broken. *Twisted.* They stared at it. "How could that have happened?" Priscilla asked.

The chair was slightly ahead of them, a few kilometers off to port, and at a slightly higher elevation. Priscilla adjusted for altitude, matched velocity, and, a few minutes later, they drew alongside. "I assume we want to recover it?" she said.

"Yes. Do it."

She opened the launch doors. "Myra," she said, "I'll need you for this. Take over and get the chair."

"Okay, Priscilla. I have it." They felt a slight change as Myra angled the ship. Then they moved to port again. One of the scopes locked on the chair, and they watched it float into the cargo bay. "Chair is secure," she said. "Closing up."

THEY REMAINED ON the bridge for several minutes, scanning the area while the cargo bay repressurized. But there seemed to be nothing else out there. Then they went down below. The chair was afloat near the storage cabinets at the rear of the chamber.

"You don't think this is another one of those antiterraforming attacks, do you, Jake?" she asked.

"Don't know." The base of the chair was torn apart, as if it had been wrenched out of the deck. "Explosion?" Priscilla asked.

"I don't think so. It's not scorched. And most of it looks okay."

"So what happened?"

"I have no idea. Myra, any theories?"

"No, Jake. I do not understand it."

Whatever it was, Jake had no expectation of finding survivors.

Isha, farewell.

THEY TOOK THE chair topside to the passenger cabin. Jake wedged it between cabinets and secured it with cable. Then he recorded an account of what they'd found, included some pictures, and sent it to Union. "They're not going to be happy," Priscilla said.

Jake grunted his response. There was no way this was going to end well. He hadn't actually ever been close to Isha. He'd taken her out a few times, and even slept with her once, but there'd been no real chemistry on either side. At least not as far as he could determine. But he'd liked her. She'd been a good woman. She'd loved telling stories about how her family had reacted to her career choice. Absolutely crazy. It was a common narrative for pilots. Her dad had been a policeman, and he didn't think riding around on a rocket was a good idea. For one thing, it wasn't safe. For another, he'd argued, there was no future in spaceflight. "It's all going to go away; and then where will you be?"

"How," asked Priscilla, "can you explain any of this? How does this thing get torn out of the deck, but there's no explosion?"

"I don't know," Jake said.

There was fear in her eyes. "At the moment," she said,

"I'm feeling a little bit spooked." She stared at the chair. "What happened to you, anyhow?"

It's definitely not a good sign, he thought, when you start talking to the furniture.

"DO WE WANT to continue the search on the ground?" asked Myra. "Or should we concentrate on looking for other objects up here?"

"Keep the sensors pointed down," Jake said.

They continued shifting from orbit to orbit, looking out at a relentlessly unchanging sky. They ate a listless dinner in the passenger cabin and went back onto the bridge. Priscilla eventually put a book on her display and tried to lose herself in it. Jake played poker with three AI partners. And then, when he was expecting Myra II to lay down a flush against his three queens, she surprised him: "We have lights."

"Lights?" Priscilla looked up from her book. Jake forgot about the game.

"Where?" he said.

They blinked on the display, glimmers in the cloud cover. Six glowing spots in the night. No, seven. In a line. "Off to starboard."

"It's a storm," Jake said. "Lightning. That's all it can be."

"Jake," said Priscilla, "it does not look like lightning." For one thing, it was a steady glow.

"Okay. Lock in the position. We'll take a look next time around."

CIRCLING A COMPLETELY dark world was, for Jake, a new experience. There was a different sense of movement than one would get while orbiting Earth, or any planet in a star system. You did not, as normally happened, pursue the sun across the sky, pass beneath it, and eventually leave it behind. There was rarely any horizon. Instead, you traveled across an apparently flat landscape, which revealed only shadows and mist. It was a flat landscape that went on forever, a place made for ghosts. He wouldn't have admitted it even to himself, but he was glad he wasn't alone.

"The lights must have been reflections," Priscilla said.

"Okay. But reflections of what?"

"I don't know."

"It's a pity," he said, "we didn't find their AI instead of just a chair."

"It would have helped. We should take McGruder on a flight like this. Maybe he'd change his mind about defunding the program."

Jake grunted. "I don't think I'd want to spend a week or two locked in here with a politician."

"That's a point."

"What were you reading?"

"How Laura Kingman saved the space program. Back in the NASA days."

"The woman who took out the asteroid."

"And killed herself in the process."

"I thought," said Jake, "the consensus was that it would have missed anyhow. That it was close, but it wasn't going to hit anything."

"What's the difference?" asked Priscilla. "At the time, she couldn't be sure. So she took no chances."

"Try to imagine your buddy McGruder doing what she did."

"He's not my buddy, Jake. But actually, we have no way of knowing what he would do."

Jake tried to laugh, but it didn't happen. He wondered whether he would have done it himself. He knew how he'd have answered that question a couple of months ago. Not so sure anymore. "Myra," he said, "have you seen any more lights?"

"Be assured, Jake," Myra said, "I'd have told you if I did."

"I know."

"Then why'd you ask?"

Because it had been time to change the subject. He saw that Priscilla understood it as well. "So how's Roanoke treating you?" she asked.

WHEN THEY RETURNED to the site, the lights were still there, seven of them emitting a soft, golden glow. "Are they moving?" asked Priscilla.

"I don't think so," said Jake.

There was a pause. Then Myra: "Negative movement."

Jake split the screen. Compared the lights in the two sightings. "They're brighter now."

Priscilla took a long look. "I think you're right,"

"We are at the same range," said Myra.

It could have been a line of stalled cars in a heavy rainstorm. But the lights in the rear were growing brighter. Then they dimmed, and the enhanced illumination passed like a wave along the group toward the front. And faded.

"Holy cats," said Priscilla. "Did you see that?"

The process started again. The rear of the line of lights brightened, and the effect once more moved forward.

"It's a signal," said Jake.

"You mean for us?"

"I have no idea, Priscilla. Myra, is there any way that could be a signal from the *Vincenti*?"

"Jake, I cannot conceive how anyone on board could have created those images."

"It's probably just a variation of ball lightning or something," said Priscilla.

"I can't imagine ball lightning in this kind of climate."

"Well, I'm open to a better explanation."

"Check with me later." They were drawing abreast of the lights now. "We're going to have to go down and look," he said.

"Okay. We should be able to catch it on the next round."

"Myra, transmission for Union."

"Ready when you are, Jake."

"Ops from *Baumbachner*. We are seeing lights below, in one area only. They're included in the transmission. We have no explanation for them. On next orbit, I'll take the lander down, and will let you know what they are."

Priscilla took a deep breath. "They're just going to be some sort of electricity generated by the atmosphere."

"You're probably right." He was still looking at the images on the display. "I'll send everything back, and you can relay it to Union."

Priscilla frowned and shook her head. No. "Jake," she said, "I'm not going to let you go down there alone."

"Correct me if I'm wrong, but I think there may be some confusion here, Priscilla, about who's in charge."

"Come on, Jake. You going to pull rank?"

"Yes, since I apparently have to. Look, Priscilla, it's just not smart for both of us to go. You know that as well as I do."

"Jake—"

"I'll stay in contact with you the whole time. If anything happens, if we lose touch, give me an hour or so. If you still don't hear from me, clear out. Understand?"

"This feels like what happened last time."

Jake sucked in air. "I hope not, Priscilla."

BAUMBACHNER LOG

This is a futile effort. Whatever dragged the captain's chair off the bridge and out of the ship could not have done it without wrecking the vehicle. It's been almost a week since they were last heard from. Even if someone had made it to the lander and managed to launch, there would not have been enough air to keep him alive all this time. But nobody's going to say we didn't try.

Priscilla thinks it's not a good idea for me to go down alone. Let the record show that she demanded to go along. I have had to order her to stay with the *Baumbachner.*

—Jake Loomis, February 8, 2196

Chapter 39

THE *BAUMBACHNER* LANDER entered the atmosphere and rode down through clear dark skies. The lights were still there, floating lazily in the dark. They were still rippling in that same melodic way. A visual symphony. There was an elegance to it, a glowing softness, as if he were watching an HV show in which they were getting ready to roll the credits.

"*Jake.*" Priscilla's voice. "*Can you make out what they are?*"

"Still just lights, Priscilla. If it weren't for the wave, I'd say they were Chinese lanterns."

"*That would be a shock. Can you tell how high they are?*"

"Looks like ground level. Andrea, what do you think?" Andrea was the lander AI.

"They are close to the surface, Jake. But they are not *on* the surface."

"*Can you see anything else?*" Priscilla asked. "*Anything on the ground?*"

"Priscilla, I can't *see* the ground. It's pretty dark down there."

"*Are they moving at all?*"

"No. As far as I can tell, there's no movement whatever." The sensors gradually acquired the landscape. It was hilly,

with a couple of ravines, and everything rimmed by a circle
of mountains. He was descending into a bowl. "Priscilla,
whatever the lights are, I don't see how they can be natural.
Something's down there."

"They seem," said Andrea, "to be clustered over a fairly
small area, Jake."

"How small?"

"I cannot tell with precision."

"Give me a guess."

"I would say perhaps three kilometers in length. And they
do not appear to be on the ground. But I would say they are
only a few meters above it."

THE BRIGHTENING AND dimming still ran from one end of the
series to the other, which he could not avoid thinking of as
rear to front. Accept that logic, and the line was pointing directly at one of the hills. In fact the lead light was almost rest-
ing on the crést.

He circled the area and trained a spotlight on the hill. The
top consisted of a slice of flat ground. "Something's there," he
told Priscilla.

"What, Jake?"

"Hold on." He got one of the scopes on it. "It's the *lander.*"

"You're kidding."

"Do I sound as if I'm kidding?"

"Okay. Good. It's the one from the Vincenti?"

"I can't really tell yet. But it's hard to imagine where else
it might have come from."

"What kind of shape's it in, Jake?"

"Actually, it looks okay. Except that the wings are off."
How in hell had it gotten there? There was no way a lander
could have come down intact on that hilltop. Even had its
wings been in place. One was lying in the snow halfway down
the slope. "I don't understand this," he said. "It looks as if it
landed without incident. Except for the wrecked wings."

He descended past the lights and looked for an area to
land. He got lucky: There was an unbroken stretch of ground
about a kilometer away. It was, however, covered by snow or
ice, and it was surrounded by mounds and rocks. Getting into

it would be a squeeze, but he could see no easy alternative. "What do you think, Andrea? Can we manage that?"

"I am not comfortable with the selection. The surface will be icy, Jake. We might easily end as part of the real estate. I recommend we abort."

"We can do it," he said.

"I have logged my view on this matter," said Andrea, in a disapproving voice.

"Okay."

"Keep in mind, Captain Loomis, that if this goes wrong, *I* will be left to shoulder the blame." The AI, of course, was not really annoyed. It wasn't a conscious entity although it was easy sometimes to forget that. This was simply the Authority's way of warning against bad behavior.

He swung wide over the battered surface. "Priscilla," he said, "do you see that?"

"Yes. I see it. Jake, it scares me."

"Have a little faith, kid."

"Are you going down?"

"No way I can't."

"Just be careful, okay?"

He lined up for his landing and began his final descent. Gorges, rocks, crevices, and hilltops rose to meet him. He got a better look at the lights, which were only a few meters above the ground. The night was still. That was definitely good. He wouldn't have wanted to attempt this with a crosswind.

"You're approaching too fast," said Andrea.

He eased in until the wheels touched down, but she was right and he pulled back, lifted off, and circled around for another try. *Okay. Just take it easy.* He cut forward speed as much as he could, dropped down toward the rocks, and came in so close his wheels must almost have touched them. Then he was on the ground again. He went into a skid, came off the brakes, and regained control. The rocks and clumps of ice on either side raced past and gradually slowed. The other end of the field was blocked off by more rocks. They came rapidly closer, slowed, and finally stopped as the lander swung to the side and almost tipped over. He took a deep breath. *"Nice landing, boss,"* said Priscilla. Her voice had been getting weaker as the distance between them increased.

He couldn't tell whether it was her cynical side, so he played it straight. "Thanks, Priscilla." He turned the spacecraft around and aimed it back the way he'd come. "Always a good idea to be able to leave in a hurry," he told her. But the only reply was static. He climbed out of his seat, pinned an imager to his vest pocket, and activated his Flickinger gear. A light breeze pushed against the lander. He pulled a radio transmitter out of one of the storage cabinets, to leave at the site so a future mission, should there be one, would be able to locate the downed vehicle.

When he looked outside again, the lights that had guided him in were growing dimmer. Going dark. As he watched, they went out.

What the hell was going on?

He checked his wrist light, attached the oxygen tanks, went into the air lock, and opened the outer hatch. Carefully. He looked around to assure himself he was alone. The only movement came from the wind. After a moment's hesitation, he stepped down onto the ice.

The snowscape glittered. He left the outer hatch open and started toward the hill. He wouldn't have admitted it to Priscilla, but he was scared. Something had led him here, and he wondered if it was the same *something* that had ripped the *Vincenti* apart and brought the lander down into this godforsaken place.

Come into my parlor.

But the night seemed empty.

He was about to turn his wrist light on, but changed his mind. He didn't need it, and there was no point drawing unnecessary attention to himself.

Gravity was high. His weight had gone up by about twenty pounds. He lost his balance once and almost fell on his rear end. He recalled Tracy Blesko, an engineer whom he'd known years before. Tracy had been walking on Europa, in a Flickinger suit, of course, when he slipped and fell. He'd damaged the control unit, the power had shut down, and that had been the end of Tracy. They'd redesigned the unit since then, and claimed a recurrence wasn't possible. But Jake never trusted manufacturers' claims. So, on that icy ground, he moved cautiously.

The climb up the hill was longer than it had appeared from the ship. But eventually, and without incident, he got to the top. The downed lander lay dark and still, half-covered with snow. Nothing moved inside. One of the rear thruster tubes was missing. Cables and support rods hung loose. Jake stared at it. Add the missing wings, and there was no way this thing could have reached the ground without getting splattered.

He looked around again, but in all that wide expanse there was no movement. He walked to the air lock and pressed the pad.

THE INTERIOR WAS warm, and still had power. He saw a body in the after section, lying behind the rear seats. There were no others. He was relieved to see that it wasn't Isha. Death in the lander would have been slow. He looked at the pictures of the passengers and recognized Otto Schreiber, the young man from Leipzig who'd been working on his doctorate. He was about twenty years old. Looked as if he'd been dead for two or three days.

"Hello," said an unfamiliar voice on his commlink.

His heart almost stopped before he realized who it was. "You're the AI," he said.

"Yes. My name is Simon. I am very happy to see you. I was afraid we would never be found."

"You did manage to put yourself in a remote place, Simon. How did it happen?"

"I do not know, sir."

"My name's Jake."

"Greetings, Jake. I wish you could have gotten here in time to save Otto."

"I do, too. Did he suffocate?"

"Yes. It was painful to watch."

"I'm sorry." He looked out at the landscape, still, somehow, half expecting to see something coming toward him. "You say you don't know what happened?"

"No, Jake. We were on the *Vincenti*. Otto was loading the lander. Preparing it for a descent. They were going to go down and take some soil samples, gather rocks for mineral-ogical purposes. Then, suddenly, I heard strange sounds, like metal tearing, coming apart. And people began screaming. The ship lurched, first left, then right. Otto was thrown against a bulkhead. Isha got on the commlink and ordered Otto to get inside the lander. He said he *was* inside the lander. So she closed the air lock and opened the launch doors. She must have overridden the protocol that prevents opening them until the bay is depressurized. The ship sounded as if it was coming apart."

"But you don't know what was happening?"

"I have no idea, Jake. I thought we had probably struck a piece of debris. But it felt like much more than that. I don't know how to describe it. I could see the bulkhead beginning to pull away as if something were *stretching* it. As soon as the launch doors had opened, we were propelled outside. Isha did everything from the bridge. We were spinning end over end, the lander, and maybe the *Vincenti*, too. I don't know. It was impossible to ascertain what was happening. Otto was hurled against first one bulkhead, then the other. One of our wings was torn off."

Jake had never known an AI could be capable of near hysteria. But he heard it in Simon's voice. "You couldn't see what was happening to the ship?"

"No. I couldn't line anything up. We were tumbling the whole time. Once or twice, I caught glimpses of the *Vincenti*. But I couldn't see anything unusual except that it was out of control. The only possibility seemed to be that it had struck something. Or been attacked."

"Okay. Simon, you have things a little confused. You said one of your wings was torn off as you came out of the *Vincenti*."

"Actually, both were. One stayed with us, dangling by a few cables, until we came down. Then it broke loose."

"I can't figure out how you could have landed on this hilltop even if there'd been *no* damage, let alone losing your wings. How the hell did you manage it?"

"I do not know, Jake. We did fall for one minute seventeen seconds. Then the descent stopped. The fall stopped. We continued going down. But it was as if we were under control. As if a cushion of air or something had taken hold of us and was guiding us toward the ground. I know that is hard to believe, but the evidence is here. Otto died days later, when the air ran out."

Jake was struggling with the extra weight. He eased himself down into one of the seats. "Could another ship have taken you in tow somehow without your being aware of it? Would that have been possible?"

"I don't see how. No."

"Okay. Am I also to assume you weren't responsible for the lights?"

"What lights?"

JAKE DEPRESSURIZED THE cabin and opened both air-lock hatches. Then he lifted Otto's body and tried to prop it over his shoulder. But it was too heavy to carry in that manner. Otto wasn't particularly a lightweight to start with. He got the body into his arms and stumbled toward the air lock.

"Jake," said the AI, "you won't leave me here, will you?"

"I wouldn't leave you here, Simon. I'll be back in a while." He got out into the snow, staggered a few more steps, and lost his balance as he started downhill. He had to give it up. No way he could carry the corpse a kilometer across a slippery surface in this gravity. He hauled Otto back up the ladder into the lander and set him in one of the seats. "I'm sorry, pal," he said. "They'll have to come back for you."

"I don't think," said Simon, "he will care one way or the other."

Jake looked out at the icy hills, stretching away in all directions. He knew precisely where the *Baumbachner* lander was, down in that rift off to the right. But at the moment it was lost in the dark. "Simon," he said, "during the time you've been stranded here, have you seen anything out of the ordinary? Anything at all?"

"No, Jake."

"Your landing: From the condition of the vehicle, it was obviously a soft landing."

"Yes, it was."

"You must have seen whatever it was that supported you."

"I am sorry. I did not see anything."

"Were you still spinning during the descent?"

"No. We gained equilibrium. But I cannot explain how that happened."

"Were your own engines on?"

"Negative, Jake."

He sat, staring at the barren landscape. Eventually, he sighed, took the transmitter from the bag, and installed it on the control panel. He was just finishing when Priscilla came back: *"Jake,"* she said. *"What have you got?"*

"Priscilla, only one of the crew made it to the lander. Otto. He's been dead for a couple of days."

"I'm sorry, Jake. I was hoping maybe they had some extra air tanks. Any idea what happened?"

"No. They got hit by something. But I don't know what—Weirdest part of this—"

"What's that, Jake?"

"They came down without wings and landed otherwise intact on top of a hill."

She took a long time to answer: *"Okay,"* she said at last. *"We can try to figure it out later. By the way, we picked up another piece of the* Vincenti *in orbit. Part of an exhaust tube. Jake, it was broken off at both ends. But the really spooky thing—it looked as if it had been* stretched. *Pulled apart."*

"You're serious?"

"You ever know me to kid?" She was silent for a few seconds. Then: *"What were the lights?"*

"I have no idea. They went out after I got here." He got up out of the seat. "I'll talk to you later. Be up as soon as I can. Meantime, keep an eye open."

He removed the AI—which once out of its cradle could no longer speak to him—and carried it back to his own lander. It should have been an easier hike this time since it was downhill most of the way, but the downhill part made it more treacherous. He fell once and almost went down a second time. Whatever the manufacturers had installed in the Flickinger control gear, though, must have been working because the force field didn't shut off.

THE LANDER ROSE into the night. Priscilla sent pictures of the damaged exhaust tube. He looked at it, brought up images of the *Vincenti*, and compared the two. It looked as if a giant hand had seized the rear of the tube, crunched it, and pulled it apart. *Stretched* it, as Priscilla had said.

"What do you think?" she asked.

"The hand of God."

"Seriously."

"I'm being serious. Listen, you don't see anything else up there with you, right?"

"Negative."

"Tell Myra to keep watching. If you see anything, I don't care what it is, stay clear of it."

"You want to tell me what you think is going on?"

"Priscilla, let's just say that if you suddenly got two feet taller, it would do nothing for your good looks."

BAUMBACHNER LOG

It's hard to imagine what could have happened to bring the *Vincenti* lander down more or less intact. The only possibility I can think of is a vehicle with advanced magnetic capabilities. Lock onto the lander and carry it to the ground. But if anything like that *was* in the sky around here, we'd know about it. I've never seen a place in my life that looked less likely to be home to anybody, let alone a high-tech civilization.

—Jake Loomis, February 8, 2196

SHE WAS WAITING for him in the launch bay when he climbed out. "I've sent in a report," she said. "I'm sorry about Otto. He was pretty young."

Jake nodded. "So was Isha. Everybody's too young for something like this to happen to them. But we can talk about it later. Let's get belted down and clear the area."

"So what do you think happened?"

"I can only think of one possibility. If I'm right, it would be a good idea to talk about it somewhere else."

"Let's go," she said.

* * *

JAKE WAS RELIEVED to watch the dark world drop behind them. "So what's your theory?" she asked.

"They were getting ready to send a landing party down. Otto was packing supplies and whatnot into the lander, when—"

"What—?"

"I think they ran into some sort of superdense object."

"You mean a *black hole*?"

"More likely a piece of matter like the kind you'd find in a neutron star. The details don't matter. The bottom line is that there's a good chance a superdense object is orbiting Orfano."

"You think they literally *collided* with it?"

"I don't think you *collide* with something like that. You sort of get sucked in."

"How much mass are we talking?"

"Myra, how much would a baseball weigh if it were made of this stuff?"

"I don't think a baseball composed of that type material could hold together, Jake."

"Forget the theories. Assume that it *does*, what's its mass?"

"I would estimate approximately one and a half trillion tons."

Priscilla shook her head.

"Imagine," said Jake, "what the gravity would be like if you got anywhere close to something like that."

Myra applied the math: "Priscilla," she said, "if you came into contact with the baseball, your weight, relative to it, would be approximately 125 million pounds."

She shook her head. "That wouldn't be good."

"Apparently, assuming that's what happened, when they came within its influence, Isha reacted immediately. She saw no possibility of escape. Probably didn't know what was happening. Except that the *Vincenti* was coming apart. So she told Otto to get into the lander. And she sealed it and launched."

"Heroic woman."

"Yeah. For all the good it did anybody."

"What about the lights? What were those?"

"They really *were* odd, weren't they?"

"The only thing I could think of was that whoever had been in the lander set something up to get our attention."

"Well, Otto was dead. And Simon says he didn't know anything about it."

"Simon's the AI?"

"Yes."

"So what *was* going on?"

"You tell me, Priscilla."

"I have no idea."

"Okay. Here's something else: Simon says the lander was damaged during the launch. It lost its wings."

"How do you mean 'lost'?"

"Torn off."

"Impossible. I mean, the lander was more or less intact on the ground, right?"

"Yes. Except for the wings. One was down on the slope; the other was missing."

"So how'd they get down?"

"That's the question, isn't it?"

"There's somebody down there."

Jake nodded. "I don't see any other explanation."

"And they're friendly."

"Maybe."

"So do we go back to find out who it is?"

"What do *you* suggest?"

She thought about it. "The smart thing to do would be to quit while we're ahead."

Jake adjusted his harness. "Makes sense to me."

"But we'll spend the rest of our lives wondering—"

"I know," said Jake. "That sounds like one of those comments that get engraved on tombstones." He pushed back in his seat. "So, I take it you vote for going back?"

PRISCILLA'S JOURNAL

Orfano is the saddest, most dismal place I've ever seen. We talk about people needing sunlight and we use *sunny* as a synonym for optimism and so on.

Nevertheless, I don't think I ever realized how critical sunlight can be to setting a mood. Remove it, and darkness becomes a palpable force. In Orfano's skies, there are, of course, stars, but they are only glimmers in an overwhelming night. There isn't even a moon. Not that it would matter if there were because a moon needs sunlight, too.

—February 8, 2196

Chapter 40

THE ODDS OF encountering the object seemed remote, but to play it safe, Jake placed them well outside the orbit in which they'd found the exhaust tube and the chair. "I hope you're right," Priscilla said, "about all this. If the *Vincenti* was brought down by some sort of hi-tech weapon, we wouldn't have much chance." She looked genuinely concerned.

"It shouldn't be a problem," said Jake. "If there was a system to take out any strangers who went into orbit, we'd know about it by now." He looked down at the ice-covered world. "It's just hard to believe there'd be anything there. Myra, I know we have no idea how long ago Orfano was expelled from its planetary system. But what's the minimum? What's the least amount of time it's been without a sun?"

"Indications," said Myra, "are it could not have orbited any known star during the last three hundred million years. The consensus, however, is that it has probably been adrift more than one and a half billion years."

"Well," said Priscilla, "if you're right about all this, the *Baumbachner* will go down in history."

"Let's hope it doesn't just go down."

"We should inform Union of our intentions."

"Do it. They'll respond by directing us to use caution."
Priscilla looked uncomfortable. "What's wrong?" said Jake.

"Aside from wondering what we're getting into? If it turns out
we're going to make history, I'd like my name associated with
something that sounds a little flashier than the *Baumbachner*."

"You on that again?"

"It doesn't seem like too much to ask."

"Nothing wrong with going back to *Starhawk*, I guess. But
I don't think it's going to fool anybody."

"*Valkyrie* would be nice. Or maybe *Defiant*. Even *Reliable*. In fact, *Reliable*'s good."

Jake couldn't help smiling. "How about *Reluctant*?"

"You'll be sorry when we become historic figures, and
everybody's laughing at us."

THERE WERE NO lights anywhere. But the sculpted landscape
had taken on a new significance. Jake had been inclined to dismiss it when they'd first arrived as simply natural formations
mixed with an overactive imagination. He thought that the various
symmetries would be explainable without resorting to aliens.
Now it was hard to believe there *wasn't* an alien force at work.

But after thirty hours in various orbits, they had nothing.
No lights. No responses to radio transmissions. No sign of
any activity whatever.

Although, in fact, they *did* come up with something. "I believe we've found our superdense object," said Myra.

"Where?" they both asked.

"It is at a substantial distance." The display lit up, and they
were looking at a swirl of dust. "Actually, I noted it before,
but since it had nothing to do with our objective, I paid no
attention. Error on my part."

"Is it in orbit?"

"Yes."

"Okay. Get it on the record so we can make sure we stay
away from it."

"IF SOMEONE'S ACTUALLY down there," said Priscilla, "they
don't seem to be interested in setting up a conversation."

"Maybe they can't," said Jake.

"How do you mean?"

"They might not have the right technology."

"So how do you think they got the *Vincenti*'s lander down safely?"

"I don't know, Priscilla. Why don't we give them a chance to do another rescue?"

They went down to the cargo bay, where Jake equipped the lander with extra sensors. Priscilla rigged some pillows in the pilot's seat, wrapped them in blankets, and put her cap on the resultant figure, creating the impression of a pilot. "Good," said Jake. "That should work. Now let's go set up the launch."

Priscilla nodded. "We should get near the downed lander."

They returned to the bridge and depressurized the cargo area. "I just can't imagine," Priscilla said, "anything being alive on that world. Maybe there's some sort of automated mechanism at work."

"What would be the point?" asked Jake.

She shook her head. "It could be something left over from another time."

"We're talking hundreds of millions of years, Priscilla. That would be a pretty substantial mechanism."

"Four minutes," said Myra.

Priscilla was back in the pilot's seat. "Open the doors," she said.

Jake opened a channel to the lander AI. "Andrea, after we launch, I want the lander to look as if it's lost partial power. As if you're struggling to keep it from going down. Do that for three minutes. Then shut off the engines, and do a free fall as long as you can without damaging the vehicle. If anything unusual happens, record all circumstances. If nothing intervenes to prevent the fall, restore power and return to the ship. We'll pick you up on the next orbit. Is that clear?"

"Yes, Jake. It sounds simple enough. I wish you luck in this experiment."

"LAUNCH IN ONE minute," said Myra.

Jake turned toward Priscilla. "Wish us luck, kid."

She gave him a thumbs-up. "What do we do if someone walks out of a cloud, grabs it, and takes it down?"

"I think," he said, "we say thank you very much and ske-daddle."

Priscilla sat quietly. Jake watched the timer click off the seconds.

Priscilla leaned over her mike as the time ran out. "Launch the lander," she said.

"Vehicle launched," said Myra.

"Okay, Andrea," Jake said, "you've got it."

"Roger that," said Andrea. She turned on the lander's navigation lights. And one of the interior lamps, whose glow *did* give the impression someone was in the pilot's seat.

"No way they could miss that," said Priscilla.

"Whenever you're ready, Andrea." The lander's engines coughed, died, came back. The vehicle began to struggle.

"Code five," said Andrea. *"Engine failure. Going down."*

Jake watched it slipping through the darkness. "She's putting on a good show."

"Anybody who can see it," said Priscilla, "would have to know the thing's in trouble."

The engines sputtered a few more times and died as the lander went into free fall. Jake held his breath. If there was going to be an intervention, it would have to come quickly.

"Code five," said Andrea. *"Please assist."*

"I don't think anything's going to happen," said Priscilla.

Jake had never really accepted the rescue explanation, had not expected to see something snatch the vehicle and carry it safely to ground. Yet what possibility remained?

The lander was in a death spiral. Moments later Andrea's voice broke the silence: *"Negative results. Restarting engines."* Jake heard the thrusters fire. *"We are pulling out. Returning to orbit."* The rate of descent slowed, but the ground was coming up fast. Jake found himself holding his breath. But the vehicle leveled off quickly, skimmed along hilltops and clusters of rocks, and began to gain altitude.

"Good, Andrea," said Jake. "Come on home."

He sat back and closed his eyes. "Jake," said Myra, "we have a light."

* * *

IT BURNED STEADILY, a soft sapphire incandescence. Nothing like the original lights. "Can't tell what it is," said Jake. "Too much mist in the area."

"Myra," said Priscilla, "will you be able to find it again?" It was already growing dim in their rear.

"If it's still there," she said. "It's in a different area from the original globes."

They'd need an orbit to recover the lander, and another to set up a second launch. "No hurry," said Jake.

"We'll have to go down," said Priscilla.

Jake shook his head. "*I'll* go down."

"Come on, Jake. I'd like to be part of this, too. How about if *I* go down this time?"

"Not a good idea."

"All right. Why don't we both go?"

Oh, hell. Nothing was likely to happen, so it really wasn't worth another argument. "Okay," he said.

The blue light was still there on the next orbit. They brought the lander on board, refueled it, and ran a quick check. Then they waited while the *Baumbachner* circled the planet again. Priscilla tried to get some sleep, but it was useless.

And finally, they were climbing into the lander.

"The light is still there," said Myra.

JAKE CONCEDED THE lander to her. Priscilla took the pilot's seat. The light had gotten lost in clouds when they launched, but Andrea guided them down, taking most of her data from the ship. And eventually it reappeared, a softly glowing patch of mist.

She swung gently to the right and began a circular descent. The mist was rising from the center of a group of low hills interspersed with broad ice sheets. Jake looked her way. The message was obvious enough: Did she want him to make the landing?

She had no problem taking the lander down. Furthermore, she had nothing to prove. "You want to take over?" she asked.

"No," he said. "Just put us on the ground."

My kind of guy, she thought. "What's making the light?" Priscilla asked the AI.

"I can't tell," said Andrea.

She brought them down on the ice sheet, went into a skid, but hung on until they stopped. The blue mist was only about fifty meters ahead. "Priscilla," said Jake, "I think the smart way to do this would be for you to stay here. I'll take a look and see what we have."

"Why is that the smart way?"

"Because it ensures we keep control of the lander. We'll stay in touch, and if something bad happens—I doubt it will, but just in case—you can get out of here, and the people back home won't be wondering where we went." He smiled. "You're glaring at me again, Priscilla. What happened to this Hutch person I was hearing about?"

Jake was pulling on a blue-and-silver WSA jacket with a rocket emblem. The manufacturers of the Flickinger system claimed that the force field provided complete protection against extreme temperatures, but he didn't believe it. People using the equipment inevitably felt more comfortable wearing a coat or jacket.

"I'm just wondering why the safe thing to do always seems to be to leave me behind," she said.

"I'm sorry," Jake said, "but somebody has to stay. You're the pilot."

"All right."

"Thirty years from now, when you're in charge of everything, you'll have to tell people the same thing, that they can't always go where they want." He activated his Flickinger unit and went into the air lock.

SHE GOT UP and retreated into one of the passenger seats to get a better view. The outer hatch opened, and Jake climbed cautiously down onto the hard-packed ice, his weight gain already impeding him. He trudged off across the frozen ground. "How you doing?" she asked.

"It's a trifle windy out here," he said.

He was headed between two low hills. She listened as the ground cracked under his feet.

"Be careful."

"I will, Priscilla."

He'd left the outer hatch open, as he'd done when he had gone over to the downed lander. She knew why, of course: It would facilitate things if he had to leave in a hurry. She watched through his imager. The sapphire glow got brighter as he rounded the hill. The ground was a combination of ice and rock, then suddenly it changed to water!

She caught her breath.

"It's a lake," Jake said. *"How the hell is that possible?"*

But it was there. Solid ice near the shore leading to open water farther out. And it was the water that was exuding the mist. A beautiful cobalt blue.

Priscilla checked the outside temperature: 185 below zero, centigrade. "Stay away from it," she said. "Get out of there."

"Relax, Priscilla," said Jake.

"No." Andrea's voice. "She's right. It's radioactive. Come back."

That was enough. Jake turned and started to retreat. But he wasn't happy. *"What?"* he demanded. *"Why do you say that, Andrea?"*

"It's Cherenkov radiation. It's what happens if you take a star drive and drop it twenty kilometers. The fuel spills out, melts the ice, and turns blue in the water. You get a blue glow."

"Come on, Jake," said Priscilla. "Move."

He was coming. But the Flickinger field protected against radiation. Up to a point.

PRISCILLA'S JOURNAL

I'd never heard of an interstellar coming apart and depositing its drive unit on a planetary surface. When I asked Andrea to take a look at the history, she discovered it did happen once when the *Blackford* collided with an orbiting rock and simply broke open. That, I decided, was what had happened here. Except that the rock had been heavy, really heavy, and had pulled the spacecraft apart. The drive hit the ground. And the chair stayed in orbit.

—February 9, 2196

Chapter 41

JAKE CAME BACK through the air lock while Priscilla held her breath, listening for the radiation alarm. But it remained silent.

"I guess," Jake said, "it's time to fold the tent."

"I have an idea," said Priscilla.

"If," Andrea said, "you are planning to continue this mission, I suggest we return to the *Baumbachner* and refuel."

"What's your idea?" asked Jake.

THEY WENT BACK to the ship, where Priscilla retrieved one of the imagers from the library. Then she sat down in the pilot's seat and connected the unit to the feed. "Myra, I'd like to take a look at the record from Jake's descent to the *Vincenti* lander."

The AI put it on-screen, the line of lights, at first no more than distant sparks seen through wispy clouds. Then a gradual brightening as Jake moved closer, the wave effect taking hold, the sparks growing into stars, then into luminous spheres. A perfect line of lights from front to rear. No way that could be anything but a signal.

Jake watched while she recorded it for the imager. When

she'd finished, she ran a test, reproducing the lights on the bridge. Then she sat back and smiled. "Ready to go," she said.

THE *VINCENTI* LANDER was shrouded on its hilltop.

"You know," Jake said, after he'd turned them around and shut off the engines, "I don't see any point in going back to the wreckage. We're in the general area. That should be enough."

"Okay," she said.

They climbed out of their seats, and activated the Flickinger fields. Priscilla collected her imager. They went through the air lock, and a soft wind pushed at her. "Midnight World," she said. "Where the sun never rises." She looked up at the hill on which the *Vincenti* lander had come to rest.

"When you're ready," said Jake.

She aimed the imager directly ahead, raised it a bit above ground level, and turned it on. Two soft lights appeared, and the landscape brightened.

THEY WATCHED WITHOUT moving. "Jake, I have a question."

"I'm listening."

"If there really *is* someone here, and they did, somehow, bring the lander down, why didn't they make an effort to save Otto?"

"Maybe," said Jake, "they realized they had no way to get to him without killing him."

She was looking around, hoping the lights would draw a response. The wind was moving the snow around.

"Try the entire series," said Jake. "We might need all seven of the lights."

She'd reproduced only two because she'd wanted to maintain the actual dimensions of the display, the size and degree of luminosity and the distance between the lights. In showing all of them, she'd lose that. But—she made the adjustment, and the original seven appeared. She raised the angle, putting them higher overhead.

"Good," said Jake. "If that doesn't do it, I think we're out of options." He turned toward her. "Why don't you let me hold it for a while?"

The imager wasn't heavy, but her arm tired quickly in the excess gravity. She handed it over.

The breeze kept pushing at her. But the landscape remained dark and motionless. "I guess," she said, "it's a fool's errand."

"Maybe."

She walked clear of the lander, so she could see in all directions. "Anybody out here?" she asked. But it was a radio transmission; only Jake could have heard her. After a minute or two, she raised her hands. "Nope," she said. *"Nada."*

"Maybe it's just as well, Priscilla. Wouldn't want a bunch of bloodthirsty aliens sneaking up on us."

"Hey!" she said. "That's odd."

"What is?"

"Wait a minute." She had her right hand out, palm open. "I think it's *raining*."

Jake held out his own hand. Nothing. "Andrea," he said, "what's the temperature?"

"Eleven degrees centigrade," said the AI.

"That's up a little bit," he said.

Priscilla wanted to screech. "Up about 170 degrees."

Now Jake was looking in all directions, including *up*. "Priscilla, I'm not sure what's going on— Hang on a second." He had both hands out.

Something splatted into his palm.

PRISCILLA'S JOURNAL

There have been all kinds of scenarios for first-contact events: aliens show up orbiting Neptune; aliens who are so tiny that when they arrive without preliminary, somebody mistakes their lander for a football; aliens coming in from another dimension, but they're unable to see us, or we them. Some first contacts actually happened. The ancient monument on Iapetus. Ruins on Quraqua. Whoever it had been that Dave Simmons ran into at Talios. The only local functional aliens were on Nok, and they had turned out to be *boring*. Who could have believed that? Now we have this one: Aliens say hello by making it rain.

But Jake thinks the correct pronoun should be *it* rather than *they*.

—February 9, 2196

Chapter 42

THEIR REPORT ARRIVED in the solar system eleven hours before they did. When the *Baumbachner* surfaced, 950,000 kilometers out, they checked in with Ops and, within moments, Frank was on the circuit. *"Jake,"* he said, *"are you sure there were no survivors?"*

"We only found the one body," he said. "But the *Vincenti* was torn apart. There's no way any of them could have gotten through it."

"Were you able to recover the body?"

"No, Frank. It's in their lander. The gravity's too much."

"Okay. There'll probably be a follow-up mission. We can get it then." He sighed. *"We're thinking about what part of this to release. We were hoping— Well, none of that matters. We'll see you when you get here."*

THEY ARRIVED IN port two days later. One of Frank's staff people was waiting at the dock to escort them to his office. Patricia was with him when they arrived. "I've read the report half a dozen times," Patricia said. "Tell us again: How did you guys find the lander?"

"It's hard to explain," said Jake. "There were some atmospheric lights. They were directly over the spot where it had gone down."

"Atmospheric lights? What actually do you mean?"

"I don't know any other way to describe them. They were literally *pointing* at the lander."

Patricia broke in: "Jake, you're not exaggerating?"

"No. It's just the way I described it."

The director glanced at Priscilla, who nodded. "That's correct. We have it all on the record."

Patricia frowned. "Were they the only lights in the area?"

"Yes," said Jake. "As far as we could tell, they were the only lights on the *planet*."

"That's going to be hard to explain."

"I guess," said Jake. "But I'll tell you, without those lights, we'd still be out there looking."

"Okay." Frank's tone suggested the story made no sense. "We'll figure it out later. Tell me how the lander got onto the hilltop."

Jake took a chip out of one pocket and held it out for him. "This is Simon, the lander AI. Giving his description of what happened."

Frank inserted the chip into the projector. They listened while Simon went through it again. When it had finished, Frank and Patricia sat staring at each other. Finally, the director shook her head. "This gets crazier all the time, Frank."

"I know."

"Well, it's not really our business at this point." The director looked frustrated. "You guys complete a report for us. Don't skimp on the details."

"We already have it," said Jake.

"Good." She turned back to Frank. "Let's bring the Academy people up to date. I assume they'll want to figure out a way to retrieve the body. They'll be annoyed at us for not doing it." Her eyes went back to Jake, but she didn't pursue the issue. "Let them know we'll give them whatever help we can." She shook her head. "A superdense rock. And an invisible parachute. What's next?" With that closing comment, she got up and started to leave.

"Wait," said Jake.

She stopped. "There's more?"

"I want to tell you about the rain."

WHEN THEY'D FINISHED explaining, Frank made no effort to hide his smile. "And you think that was, what, a way for an alien force of some kind to say hello?"

"It felt that way," said Priscilla. "Rain in a place that was brutally cold. Or should have been."

"Did you experience a change in the temperature?"

"Yes. It got warmer. A *lot* warmer."

"What's the temperature usually like out there? A hundred and something below zero?"

"Usually," said Jake. "But we're obviously getting some wild fluctuations."

Patricia took a deep breath. "So *it*, whatever it is, was saying *hello*. Don't we usually associate getting rained on as a negative experience?"

"We're not suggesting anything," Jake said. "We agreed before we got home that we wouldn't try to put an interpretation on this. And I guess we got carried away. We're just telling you what happened."

"Still," she said, "that's what you think?"

"Maybe you had to be there," Priscilla said. "But yes, that's what I think."

Patricia nodded. "If someone tossed water at me, I'd read it a little differently." Her eyes seemed focused in a distant place.

"It might be a good idea," Frank told them, "if you didn't repeat this part of the story outside."

"Yes, *please*," said Patricia. "We don't want people thinking we've completely lost our minds. But I think Samantha should be informed." She meant Samantha Campbell, the director of the Academy Project. "Any other surprises?" she asked.

"That's it," said Jake.

"Good." She headed for the door. "I think I'll get out of here while I can."

When she was gone, Frank leaned forward. "One more thing. The families will be setting up a memorial service in a few days. Just so you know. But I don't see any need for you to attend. Jake, you're clear. Thanks for helping. We appreciate it. You, too, Priscilla."

"PRISCILLA," SAID JAKE when they were alone, "you know we're going to hear from the Academy about this."

"I'd be shocked if we didn't. I'm surprised Frank and Patricia brushed it off."

"They weren't there. For them, it's just one more problem." He looked toward the Cockpit. "I could use a drink. You with me?"

LIBRARY ENTRY

MCGRUDER PRESS CONFERENCE

UBS: Governor, as recently as last week, you were saying that spaceflight was an unnecessary expense, that it had no long-term payback. Yesterday, during your remarks at the National Space Center, you said that—let me make sure I have the quote correct—you said that our expansion beyond this planet demonstrates who we are. Could you elucidate on that?

MCGRUDER: Look, Bob, when I discussed long-term payback, I was talking about money. With the present technology, resources invested in space travel are effectively gone. I'm sorry it's that way, but that is the reality. That's not the same as saying there's no reason to do it. It's obvious to us all that we have an obligation to move off-world, to find other places where the human family can live. To go out and explore, to look around and learn everything we can about the universe. It's what we're about, Bob. To find out. All I'm saying is that we should do it without breaking the bank.

—February 12, 2196

Chapter 43

JAKE CALLED ALICIA from the hotel. "We're done here," he told her. "I'll be heading down in the shuttle in a couple of hours."

"I'll be happy to see you again, Jake. How did the mission go?"

"I'll tell you about it when I get there."

"Okay. What time are you getting in?"

"About seven."

"Good enough. Call me when you get home."

HE AND PRISCILLA had lunch at Skydeck. Then they said good-bye. He'd already sent his bags ahead, so there was nothing to do now except stroll down to the terminal. But he was only about halfway there when his link chimed. *"Jake Loomis?"* A female voice.

"Yes, it is."

"Captain Loomis, I'm Margaret Brentwood. I'm with the Academy Project. I wanted to thank you for what you've done."

Jake smiled. "I was glad to be in a position to help, Margaret. I'm sorry we didn't bring home better news."

"Well, we all are. Still, we're indebted to you."

"Thank you."

"Captain, we don't know yet what's going on at Orfano. You found the lander because of some lights, right?"

"That's correct."

"And they were the only lights you saw out there? On the entire planet?"

"Yes, Margaret."

"Were they somehow under the control of one of the crew members? Maybe something they could have set up in advance?"

"I don't see how that would have been possible."

"Then who was manipulating them?"

"I have no idea."

"So we're faced with something of a mystery, aren't we?"

"I'd say so, yes."

He could hear her breathing. *"Captain, we're putting together another mission. We're going to send some people out there to investigate. The plan is to establish a temporary shelter, move in, and try to find out what's going on. In your opinion, would there be any danger to the team members?"*

"You mean other than whatever brought down the *Vincenti*?"

"Yes. Of course."

He was slow to answer. "None that I'm aware of. Certainly nothing presented itself to us. But you'll want to warn them to use caution. Just in case. When will they be leaving?"

"As soon as we can get it organized."

"Well, good. I'll look forward to hearing the results. Margaret, I have to get moving."

"I understand. I've just one more question, Captain. Would you be willing to join the expedition?"

Well, he couldn't say *that* was a surprise. But a second mission wouldn't simply be in and out. He could expect to be there for a while. Still, it could become historic. It was the kind of operation he'd hoped for throughout a long career of routine flights hauling passengers and cargo around to the usual places. And now, when it would be so difficult to take advantage of, it arrives. Damn it.

"We need you," Margaret said. *"You've been there. You know what's going on, as much as anyone does. We'd be extremely grateful for your assistance."*

It would take him away from Alicia for several weeks. Or, more likely, months. "Thanks," he said, "but I'm just not able to do it."

"Sir, you could be the difference between success and failure."

"Take Priscilla Hutchins," he said. "She was with me. And she knows as much as I do."

"You're the experienced pilot, Captain. The one we want. And please don't be too quick to close the door on this. To start with, you know where the Vincenti *lander is. If we're reading the report correctly, Priscilla does not."*

"Actually she does. Anyhow, we left a radio with it. You probably already have the code to activate it."

"Yes, we do. But it still would be advisable to have you there. You may have encountered a completely new life-form. Something unlike anything we've seen before. We have the data, but you *have been on the scene. There's no way we could get it set up within the next ten days or so, so you'd have some time off. And we'd be more than happy to compensate you generously."*

"Margaret, I was under the impression that the Academy Project operated under a tight budget."

"We do, normally. But we've let some of our backers know the potential in this matter. The situation has changed dramatically. Now, let me ask that you think it over for a day or so? Just think about it. I'll get back to you later."

"I'm sorry, Margaret. But I'm not going to change my mind."

"Please, Jake, just keep the door open. It's all we ask."

HE RODE THE shuttle down to Reagan, where he half expected to find Alicia waiting for him. But there was no sign of her. Well, she was too smart for that. It was a long ride from Radford, and, anyhow, the last thing she'd want would be to look needy.

He hauled his bags through the station, boarded the maglev to Richmond, and lowered himself into a seat. The tug of normal gravity felt good after the weightlessness of the *Bomb* and the overloaded gee force of Orfano. Funny how you tend to take things like weight for granted until they go away. Or you get heavier. Until he got involved with space travel, he'd never thought about it.

He changed trains at Richmond, rode into Lynchburg in the late afternoon, and caught the local to Roanoke, where Alicia *was* waiting. She smiled, but she didn't exactly throw herself into his arms. "Missed you, Jake," she said.

"I missed you, too, beautiful." It was great to be home. To be with her again.

"So what happened out there?"

He told her as they came out of the terminal. Her eyes grew wide when he mentioned the superdense object, and even wider as he talked about rippling lights and oddball rain.

She seemed uncertain as they settled into her car. "Do you think it was really a black hole?" she asked at last.

"No. It wasn't actually a black hole. It was *like* one, though."

"So it could have destroyed *your* ship, too, right?"

"If we'd run into it, yes. But we were watching for it. The *Vincenti* probably never saw it coming."

"The rest of that story gives me chills."

"I'm not surprised."

"Well, anyhow, I'm glad you got back okay. I hope you don't get any more calls like that one."

They stopped for dinner at Harvey's, just off the expressway. She loosened up a bit while they waited for the food to arrive. And, afterward, they went up to the cabin.

ALICIA LAY WITH the blanket pulled over her shoulders, eyes closed, her features outlined in the early light. She was the most gorgeous creature Jake had ever seen. In a few short weeks, she had literally overwhelmed him. He wasn't sure, though, that it was real, that it wasn't a reaction to being stuck on this mountaintop. To facing the reality that he was retired, that he could now devote himself to taking care of the magnolias.

The glamour of being in this remote place had gone away. He missed the interstellars, missed the charge that came with sliding out through the launch doors and accelerating toward

Capella or Sirius, missed the sense of doing something. Even if it was just sitting in the captain's chair and feeling the power at his disposal. The reality was that Alicia was now all he had. So maybe he was in love with her. Or maybe he was just clinging to her. The last thing in his life that really mattered. He didn't know. He just didn't trust himself anymore.

The alarm was about to sound. He reached over, shut it off, and pressed his lips against her cheek. "Time to get up, love."

A smile appeared, but her eyes didn't open. "Is it seven o'clock already?"

"Afraid so."

She moaned softly and pulled him down on top of her. He was trying to get the blanket out of the way when his comm-link chimed. He ignored it.

THE DAY AFTER she'd said good-bye to Jake, Priscilla had picked up a tour group. It had been one of the largest she'd seen, probably thirty people in all. And she was surprised to discover they knew who she was. "What was it like out there on Orfano?" a teenager asked. And a young woman: "How many planets are there like that? You know, where they're just drifting around?"

"Well, nobody really knows, of course. But the experts say there are literally billions of them."

"Billions?" The questioner was a nervous-looking older man with white hair. (There was a retirement group among the tourists that day.)

"And that's just in this galaxy," she said.

A middle-aged African-American woman looked shocked. "Where do they put them all?"

Priscilla smiled. "There's a lot of room out there."

Accounts of the strange lights had leaked out, and she was asked about them, and whether she thought there might be something alive on Orfano. As far as Priscilla knew, the rainfall part of the story was still under wraps. When she'd finished with the tour, she took the rest of the day off, wandered over to the Cockpit, enjoyed a dinner with Drake Peifer, and was on her way home when her link sounded.

It was Jake. "Hi," she said. "You called to tell me you're coming back?"

"Not really. Priscilla, have you heard from the Academy yet?"

"No," she said. "I assume they've been in touch with you?"

"They're prepping a new mission out to Orfano. They want to recover Otto's body, but the real reason, of course, is to pin down what's going on out there. They're going to establish a ground base."

"Well, I wish them luck." And she realized why he'd called. "They want us to go with them."

"Well, they need one of us. Do you have any interest in going?"

She stopped and sat down on one of the concourse benches. "Sure," she said. "But they've already talked to you, haven't they?"

He hesitated. *"Yes."*

She was the fallback choice again. "And what did you do? Tell them no?"

"Look, Priscilla, I can go or stay. It could be a wild flight. Or maybe not. Who knows? Alicia wouldn't be very happy if I went. But one of us is going to have to help out."

"You really want to go, Jake?"

"No. But I will if you want to pass."

"You're doing it again, aren't you?"

"Doing what again?"

"Setting things up for me. Listen, Jake, this is your party. It has been from the start. Go ahead and do it."

"You're sure?"

"Yes."

SHE SETTLED IN front of the HV that evening to watch the news. McGruder had all but clinched the Gold Party's nomination. And Gregory MacAllister, appearing as one of Rose Beetem's guests, was asked what he thought about terraforming. He commented that we should do something about the air in Baltimore. So the idiot was making a joke out of it.

And, still, where was Monika Wolf? All that talk about blowing off the roof?

NEWSDESK

GOLDS COMING STRONG FOR MCGRUDER
Hawkins Says Norman "Out of Touch with Reality"
"Lacks Practical Skills to Get Economy Moving"

AI CHESS TOURNAMENT ALL DRAWS AFTER FIRST ROUND
Organizers Suspect Prank by AIs

MEXICAN INVITATION REAL? OR ELECTION PLOY?
New White House Denies Floating
Rumors of Mexican/NAU Merger
Callisto: "No Offense, but We're Not Interested"

NAU PROPOSES CURB OF PULSE WEAPONS
Attacks in LA, Chicago, South Jersey Shock Nation
Baxter: "No Access for Morons"

MAGLEV GOES INTO MISSISSIPPI RIVER
Seventeen Injured; One Missing

INMATES LOVE DANTE
Oregon Literary Program Meeting with Success
Writing Workshops Also Gain Popularity in Prisons

EGYPTIAN CIVILIZATION OLDER THAN WE KNEW
Artifacts Shock Historians

REST IN PEACE COMPLETES FIFTH YEAR ON BROADWAY
Jane Pinkerton Comedy Sold Out Through August

DEAD MAN SHOWS UP AT MEMORIAL SERVICE
Mistaken Identities After Hotel Fire in Atlanta
Fire Department Sued

BASEBALL OWNERS WANT MORE TEAMS IN PLAY-OFFS

ALL-OUT EFFORT TO SAVE PANDAS
Numbers Continue Downward Spiral
Estimates Sink Below Four Hundred
Natural Habitat, Bamboo Forests, Gone

EDUCATION STATS LOOK GOOD
Achievement Gains in Latin America, Europe, NAU, Eastern Asia
Science, Math, Language Skills Soaring

Chapter 44

THE BLACKSBURG WILDCATS had regularly rolled over the Hawks for two years, and in fact seldom even had to run hard while doing so. At least that was Alicia's description of the situation. But on that one night, the Hawks showed up with a withering attack, got fourteen points from Alicia, and withstood a determined fourth-quarter rally to come away with a 67–63 victory. Jake sat behind their bench cheering his head off. Afterward, most of the players—everyone who didn't already have a prior commitment—trooped over to the Roundhouse and partied until midnight.

When the celebration was over, and almost everyone had left, Alicia put down her drink, looked at him, and asked what was wrong.

"You're pretty good at reading me," he said.

"You're not exactly Voltaire, Jake. What's going on?"

"They're sending another mission to Orfano. The Academy wants some questions answered. And there's a body to recover."

Her eyes darkened. "You're going with them, aren't you?"

"I'm sorry, Alicia. They need me."

"Why?"

"Because I was there before. I know where the wreckage is."

"Why don't they send what's-her-name? Hutchins?"

"They need somebody more experienced."

"You going to be gone a week again?"

"I don't know how long, love. It'll probably be more than that. Probably a *few* weeks."

All the light had gone out of the room. She just sat, watching him, making up her mind how to react. "You told me last time it was a one-time thing. That when the mission ended you wouldn't be going out anymore."

"I don't think I ever said that."

"It's what I heard. But let's get it settled. After this one, will you be doing it again?"

God help him, he didn't know. He didn't want to live the rest of his life on that mountaintop. On the ground. "Alicia, I love you."

"That's not what I want to hear at the moment, Jake."

"I know."

"So what is it going to be?"

"We could make it work. I mean, I wouldn't be going out very often. Now and then, maybe. When they need me."

"Great."

"Alicia, it's what I do."

"Okay. And I'll sit it out here while you go riding around. Have I got that right?" There was steel in her voice.

"You're making it sound worse than it is."

"Am I? When we first met, the story was that you *used to be* a pilot. But that was in the past. You'd come to settle in Radford. The outer-space thing was over. If I'd known you were going to keep going back out, I'd have been a little more careful about letting myself get involved with you."

"I'm sorry, Alicia. That *was* the plan. I'm not sure what happened."

She closed her eyes. Nodded. Bit her lip. "Good night, Jake."

"You need a ride home."

"It's okay." She looked toward the bar. "Janet's over there."

LIBRARY ENTRY

The only difference between a caprice and a life-long passion is that the caprice lasts a little longer.

—Oscar Wilde, *The Picture of Dorian Gray*

Chapter 45

CAL MEANT WELL, but he seemed to have trouble with time zones. When the link sounded at midnight, she was willing to bet it would be him. Inevitably she was right. *"How are you doing, love?"* he asked.

"Actually, Cal," she said, "I was doing fine. Sleeping, though."

"Oh. I did it again, didn't I? I'm sorry, Priscilla. I keep forgetting."

In fact, usually she didn't mention it. "It's okay," she said.

He took a deep breath. *"I'll skip the small talk."*

"Don't worry about it."

"No, no. Look, Priscilla, I'd really like to see you this weekend. Maybe Saturday? Would it be a problem if I came up? To the station?"

"Sure, Cal," she said. "That would be good."

HE ARRIVED CARRYING chocolates. He waved at her from the exit ramp, and she somehow automatically fell into his arms. "I hate not seeing you for long periods of time," he said. "I've been thinking about getting a job up here. I understand Kosmik's looking for an accountant."

"You're not an accountant."

"I could fake it. They'd never know." He managed an absolutely charming smile. *I'm kidding, but just say the word.* He really did look happy. Something more than what you normally saw with a guy on the make. "Did you get some pictures from Orfano?" he asked.

"Yes, we got some."

"A world in the dark. It sounds like a seriously creepy place."

"It was pretty cold."

"I guess. How far away is it?"

"We only needed a couple of days to get there."

He looked good. She'd forgotten how charming he could be. Her leading man. "It's really nice to see you again, Priscilla."

"And you, too, Cal."

"Have you eaten yet? How about we go have some breakfast? The food in the shuttle is kind of sparse. What time is it here?"

"We're still on Greenwich time, Cal." It was midmorning for him, midafternoon for her. "But sure. Let's get something to eat."

THEY WENT TO the Cockpit. When all the trivial questions about how they were doing and when Cal's next show would be were out of the way, he asked why on earth "the Academy people" had gone to a world that had to be dead.

"Looking for life isn't the only thing they're doing," she said. "A lot of it has to do with just trying to find out how the universe works." The account of the inexplicable lights was out in the open and had, for several days, been receiving heavy media coverage.

"Sure. But the aliens are the only thing people are really interested in."

"You know, Cal," she said, "when people hear what I do for a living, they always ask the same question: Do I hope to meet some aliens? I wonder what it is about that subject that fascinates us so much."

"I don't know," said Cal. "But you're right. I think what we'd really like is to find somebody out there that we could talk to, and maybe have some beer with. That's really what it's all about, isn't it?"

"I suppose so. But I don't think we'll be drinking any beer with whatever it is that's on Orfano."

"I guess not." He sat staring at her. "It's a really scary story. You're lucky they weren't unfriendly. Or hungry, or something."

"It got me thinking, Cal. We're probably better off not having aliens in the area. Think where we'd be if there was a civilization nearby with technology a million years ahead of ours."

They finished their meals and ordered a couple of drinks. "You know," he said, "not to change the subject or anything, but you're absolutely gorgeous. Most beautiful woman on the station."

She smiled. "How many of the women up here have you been involved with?"

He looked off to his right. "Well, there's another knockout over near the window." A tall brunette, stacked, with classic features. "Not in your league, though."

She wondered what had happened to the shy Cal she'd known earlier. Mark Klaybold, his stage character, had taken over.

The drinks arrived. She tried hers. Rum with a sprinkle of lemon. Cal lifted his glass and looked at her over its rim with those large brown eyes. "You're going to be a hard catch, aren't you, Priscilla?"

She looked back with as much puzzled innocence as she could manage. "What do you mean?"

His voice softened: "I'm not sure I'm going to have much of a chance with you. There's too much distance. And I suspect I'm in the way of what you want to do with your life. Am I right?"

"Let's just live for the day, Cal. It's not an easy situation. Right now, I'm still trying to get my career straightened out."

"Okay. You're being noncommittal again. But I understand that. I just want you to know that I've never known anyone quite like you." He lifted his glass. "To you, Priscilla. Thanks for the moment."

THEY STOPPED BY the Lookout Lounge, to have a drink and watch the Earth turn, or the Moon, or sometimes just sit in the starlight, while pop music played softly in the background. "You still plan to come back to Princeton occasionally, right, Priscilla?"

"Yes, Cal," she said. "Of course. My mom lives there."

"Can I get you to agree to let me know in advance when you're coming?"

"I'll try, Cal. But I tend to be forgetful sometimes."

He grinned. This guy was not going to be easy to discourage. "Maybe I need to pop in up here more often."

Shuttle tickets weren't cheap. Priscilla got them at a substantial discount. But Cal had a healthy income. It probably didn't matter much to him. "Look," she said, "now that you're here, why don't you plan on staying the night? You still have time to change your reservation."

"I'd love to, Priscilla." Those brown eyes lit up. "Did you mean, with you?"

"I have a sofa."

SHE LED HIM back to her apartment, unsure whether she'd done the right thing. The truth was, she'd have liked to give herself to him. The guy looked good, he loved her, and she liked him. That should be enough. But she wasn't sure that she should encourage him. It was hard to see how any permanent relationship could evolve out of their circumstances. And she didn't want to hurt him for the sake of her own sexual pleasure.

So, when they arrived in the apartment, she immediately arranged pillows on the sofa so there'd be no misunderstanding. But, a few minutes later, she took him into her bedroom.

THE SECOND ORFANO mission was getting itself together. They were down working every day prepping the *Venture*, storing supplies, loading gear that, when assembled, would constitute the shelter. She couldn't help feeling jealous. The sense of being left out was intensified by the fact that the *Venture* was the ship she'd used to retrieve Monika Wolf from Selika. It was a Kosmik vehicle, of course, but they had no immediate need of it, and Broderick was undoubtedly happy to lease it to the Academy for a few weeks.

She'd have enjoyed taking her tour groups inside it, but the bombing of the *Gremlin*, even though it had been the act of one of their own people, had changed all that. Tourists were no longer permitted access to the ships. So the experience wasn't what it had been, but she took them close enough that they could see the *Venture* and watch supplies being loaded. She even saw Jake on two occasions, but he appeared not to notice her.

There were rumors that he was coming back permanently, that he'd signed on with Interstellar Transport, but she heard nothing official.

She didn't get a chance to talk to him, and it seemed best not to call. So she simply took her tour groups down and showed them the *Venture* and the *Baumbachner* and the *Sydney Thompson*, which was in port for several days.

Then, one morning, the *Venture* was gone.

NEWSDESK

MCGRUDER CAUGHT ON LIVE MIKE: ENJOYS MAHLER
Gaffe May Undercut Him with Base

ANTITERRAFORM GROUP SEIZED IN OKLAHOMA
Planned to Bomb Space Station
Infiltrated by FBI: "Never a Danger"

TORNADO HITS OTTAWA
Two Dead; 23 Injured
Power Loss Restored within Hours

MEYER'S PROSTITUTE WAS POLITICAL ACTIVIST
Withdraws from Missouri Race

ATTACK ADS GET PERSONAL AS CAMPAIGN INTENSIFIES
"Idiot" vs "Blockhead"
Editorial: Campaign on Issues
Were Politics Really Less Nasty in the Old Days?

INDUSTRIAL AVERAGE PASSES 100,000
Wall Street Celebrates

Bickley: "Affirmation of the President's Economic Policies"

MY FAIR LADY REVIVAL GOES INTO FOURTH YEAR
Twentieth-Century Musical Boffo at Box Office

RAKOVIC FACES WORLD COURT
Ex-Dictator Charged with Crimes Against Humanity
Demonstrators Demand Death Penalty

MORE TORNADOES HIT MIDWEST
Wind Speed in Three Kansas Storms Reaches 170 mph

BREAKTHROUGH IN EDUCATION
Parental Involvement Critical Factor

THE WASHINGTON POST COLUMN

by Anika Avery

We had a report a few days ago that invisible aliens have been found on a sunless world. The expedition that discovered them returned last week to the space station. The first question that comes to mind is: How can we be sure the expedition came back alone . . . ?

Chapter 46

JAKE BOARDED THE *Venture* a half hour before the scheduled departure time and got a surprise. Samantha Campbell, the Academy Project director, was seated in the passenger cabin. "Dr. Campbell," he said, "it's good of you to come see us off."

"Not at all, Jake. I'm going with you."

"You are? Well, welcome aboard."

"Thank you." She looked genuinely pleased to see him. "Since we're going to be together for a while, you probably should call me *Samantha*." She started to drift off the chair, grabbed a restraint, laughed, and hauled herself back. "No way I'd miss this one."

"I'm not sure I'd get my hopes up."

"We'll see how it plays out."

Jake smiled. "Maybe we'll get lucky." He went onto the bridge, said hello to Lily, and began his routine check. It included ensuring they had a pallet to retrieve Otto's body.

The rest of the team trooped in a few minutes later. He could hear them talking, laughing, saying how this was the mission they'd all waited for. Mission of a lifetime. When he'd finished, Jake went back into the cabin, and Samantha introduced them. Tony and Mary Carpenter, she explained, had been with several high-stakes Academy expeditions before. They'd penetrated a library on Nok and made off with as much reading material as they could carry. "One of them— one of the Noks—saw us as we were heading for the lander," said Tony, smiling at his blond wife. "I guess we scared the devil out of it."

"He's not kidding," said Mary. "It screeched and ran into a wall."

"They don't look so good themselves," said Tony, who realized halfway through what he was saying. "Not that *you* don't look good, hon."

Mary had nothing to worry about. But the Noks, of course, were long, spindly creatures, all eyes and husk and clutching jaws, and the color of dried grass. Not exactly showstoppers. At least not in a positive sense.

Brandon Eliot was the Academy's hi-tech guy. He'd be responsible for getting the shelter put together when they decided on a site for it. Brandon was chunky, a little less than average height, about fifty years old. Usually, when Jake saw him in the Cockpit or the Pilots' Club, he had a looker on his arm. And it seemed never to be the same one twice.

Denise Peifer was a specialist in extraterrestrial biology. Denise was gorgeous, with light brown hair, a captivating smile, and penetrating brown eyes. She sat down beside Jake. "Drake asked me to say hello," she said.

"Drake?" He had to think about it. Oh, Drake Peifer. "You're his wife?"

"His sister." Denise was momentarily amused. Then it was on to the serious stuff: "I hope you got everything right, Jake. It sounds as if there's something really weird going on out there. But I'll tell you"—she was talking to Samantha now—"if we find something alive on a world that hasn't had sunlight for millions of years, I will be shocked. In fact—"

"I get your point," said Samantha. "But you've seen the report. And if you have any questions, the guy who wrote it is right here."

They all looked at him, and Jake avoided their eyes. He didn't want to be responsible for taking anybody on a long wild-goose chase. If that was the way it turned out. "It *was* strange," he said. "But the report is as accurate as we could make it."

* * *

WITHIN A FEW minutes after clearing the station, Samantha joined him on the bridge. "Jake," she said, "I was looking at the pictures you got of the landscape."

"You mean the artwork?"

"Yes. That's what it looks like, doesn't it?"

He nodded. "It's hard to see how those curving hills and domed peaks and the rest of it could have happened naturally."

"You have any theories?"

"None."

"Tell me about the rain. Was it falling everywhere across the area?"

"No. It only extended a few meters out from Priscilla and me."

"Your own private shower?"

"Something like that."

PRISCILLA HAD BEEN good company during that long qualification flight. But as amiable and easygoing as she was, Jake knew that having several people on board constituted a vast improvement in social atmosphere. Given a group, you almost always got a conversational flow, and the content was much less predictable. In addition, Tony was an accomplished violinist.

Within an hour after they'd submerged and were on their way to Orfano, they'd gotten into several debates. Samantha thought that some of the more radical physicists might well be right in claiming that the universe was an illusion. Tony, a mathematician with a conservative taste in politics, found himself in a duel with Denise, who had a liberal mind-set. Mary, at one point, asked him to shut up. Tony commented that he was only upset that he was being cut off from the presidential campaign as it was heating up. "I'm just saying the timing for all this could have been better."

"We could have gotten someone else to come," Samantha told him.

"No, no," he said. "Don't misunderstand me. I wouldn't miss this for anything. But the economy's been losing ground for years. I'll be surprised if McGruder doesn't walk away with the election."

"McGruder doesn't have a prayer," said Mary. Once a reporter for *The New York Times*, she was now a freelance writer, the author of several books on popular science, including the bestseller *Clockwork*.

Denise looked around at her colleagues. "I wonder if there's any possibility we could discover something out there that would impact the presidential race."

And so it went.

MARY SPENT A lot of time taking notes, and Jake got the impression that, if they were successful, everything they said would show up in an autobiography, or a bestseller.

Denise was so excited by the mission, she had trouble sleeping. She was full of theories about the prospects on Orfano. "It's possible," she said, "that the world was home to a hypercivilization when it was ripped out of orbit. If you have enough technology, you can survive pretty much anything. They'd have had to go underground, though."

Mary was skeptical. "If they were a hyper, couldn't they have prevented it? Kept their world in orbit?"

"How," asked Tony, "would an underground civilization have stepped in to prevent the lander from going down?"

"I didn't say they'd have been *limited* to being underground. That's just where they'd live. But for all we know, they're wandering around out here themselves."

"If they could do that, wouldn't they have moved to a sunnier world?" asked Mary. "Someplace warm?"

"Maybe," said Denise, "some wanted to stay home. Like people who won't leave town when a hurricane's coming." She looked at Jake. "You were there. What do you think?"

Jake had no clue. "It looked to me like nothing but ice and rock. I couldn't imagine anything living there. Still, we *did* see lights."

"None of it makes any sense," said Tony. "A hypercivilization would have moved the world elsewhere, or encased it, or done something that we'd be able to see."

"Well," said Samantha, "there *is* the artwork."

"You think that's really what it is?" asked Tony.

"I've talked to a number of specialists. Nobody can account for it as a natural occurrence."

"Whatever they might be," said Mary, "they didn't attack Priscilla and Jake. That suggests they might be pretty advanced."

Denise smiled. "Maybe they saw no need to attack anybody. Maybe they concluded we're not very bright and pose no threat." She realized what she'd said and looked at Jake. "I guess I didn't phrase that very well, Jake. That's not quite what I meant."

He laughed. "It's all right, Denise. I've been called worse."

Her smile widened. "I guess we can all see who's the dummy around here. But seriously, there are other possibilities. They've had millions of years. At least. They may have been initially underground, but eventually they could have transformed into something else entirely. They may have adapted to the cold. They may have gotten control of the climate. We tend to assume you have to have sunlight and water to have life. That's not necessarily true."

"Can you offer any examples, Denise?" asked Samantha.

"We have life-forms in the oceans that have never seen the sun. Though I'll confess you probably have to have it, along with water, to get started. But life is tenacious. Once it gets rolling, it's very good at adapting."

"Maybe," said Tony, "intelligent life *is* there, but on a very small scale. So small we wouldn't be able to see their cities."

Denise's eyes sparkled. "Tony, that may be pushing it a bit."

THE OFFICIAL PURPOSE of the mission was to recover Otto's body. That was a relatively prosaic, if requisite, matter, but Samantha explained they didn't want to get everyone excited about aliens, then look foolish if they came home with no answers. But the actual intention was to determine what precisely had happened to the *Vincenti* lander. How had it gotten almost intact to the ground? "What we'll do," she said, "is just try to get some indication whether the business with the lander could have been, in any way, the result of natural causes. Or whether something else is happening."

* * *

DENISE WAS A fitness nut. The interstellars all had a workout room, and it was usually cramped and boring. This one was no exception. Priscilla had ignored the one on the *Copperhead*. Jake was inclined not to bother either when he didn't have company. So he'd gained a few pounds on that certification flight.

The *Venture* had a treadmill and a stationary bike. And Denise produced an elastic cord two feet long. "It functions as a bungee."

"In what way?" asked Jake.

"Come on. I'll show you." She demonstrated, using it to stretch arms and legs. Jake tried it.

"The best way to do it," she said, "is for us to play tug-of-war."

"In zero gravity?" asked Jake.

"Try it."

Each took one end of the bungee and grabbed hold of a handrail. Then they began to pull. The cable tightened, and Jake got surprised when Denise, who wasn't much more than half his size, yanked him off his feet. He quickly discovered that hanging on to both the cord and the handrail was tricky. It didn't help that he began to laugh. Finally, he released his hold on the rail and, as he was dragged through the air, lapsed into hysterics.

Odd things happen in zero gee.

Tony and Mary came in to see what the commotion was. "Don't worry about it, Jake," Tony said. "She does that to everybody."

AT THE BEGINNING of his career, Jake had thought of the pleasures of starflight as being contained in the arrival at whatever far-flung destination, with its alien sunlight and its family of planets, with the vast oceans sometimes found on Goldilocks worlds, with rings and moons and comets, with the potential for other life-forms and always, especially, the possibility of a new civilization. That was what it had been about.

But he'd quickly discovered that there was an interior pleasure to be had as well, derived from sharing the experience with others driven by similar passions. Even to the extent of simply taking advantage of the sense of being together in a place so distant from the rest of humanity. It reminded him of how fortunate he was. And that he had no way to explain any of this to Alicia. He realized that he'd blundered. He should have found a way weeks ago to take her on a flight. When he got home, he'd do it. No way she could decline.

LIBRARY ENTRY

The more we study art, the less we care for nature. What art really reveals to us is nature's lack of design, her curious crudities, her extraordinary monotony, her absolutely unfinished erudition.

—Oscar Wilde, *The Decay of Lying*, 1889

Chapter 47

THE BLEU-CHEESE SALAD was delicious. Priscilla was wearing a soft, silky blouse to which she'd just treated herself. It was midnight blue and intended as compensation for missing the Orfano flight. Drake Peifer, seated across the table, was frowning at his sandwich.

"Not good?" she asked.

"It's okay. A bit flat."

Behind him, through the room-length window, a comet was gliding past, its tail of incandescent gas disappearing behind the curtains near the host's desk. She could also see moving lights at Moonbase.

Drake was scheduled to leave in an hour on a flight to Quraqua. He saw that she was focused on the window and turned to look. "The view is spectacular enough," he said. "I don't think they need the comet."

She smiled. "Maybe not. But the tourists love it." It was, of course, a projection. But that didn't matter. Everyone in the Skyview, forty or fifty people, stared at it with their mouths open. Even the people in the silver-and-blue uniforms.

"But it's outward-bound, Priscilla."

"So what?"

"The tail should be in front of it."

Priscilla tried to remember what she knew about comets. She was more into ship operations and couldn't recall ever having seen a comet up close. "I thought the tail was always in the rear. Isn't that why they call it a tail?"

Drake shook his head. "Not really. I mean, if they do this stuff, they should get the science right."

Priscilla waved it away and went back to her salad. Drake was amiable enough, but he tended to be a perfectionist. Anyone mispronouncing a word in his presence would get a tolerant smile. Some poor woman would pay a price for that one day. "I prefer my tails in the rear," she said. But he was looking over her shoulder now, not paying attention. "What's going on back there, Drake?" she asked.

"Oh," he said, "I was just watching the kids." There were about a dozen of them who'd left their tables and were lined up along the window, pointing and laughing at the comet. "An experience like that, for a child, is probably a life-changer. The world will never look the same." Frank was also back there, sitting alone at a table, engrossed in his notebook. And a thin guy with blond hair who looked lost. Priscilla sipped her tea. "It's too bad we can't get everybody on the planet up here for a couple of hours. Maybe there'd be a lot less parochialism."

Drake shrugged. "Ah, you think it would give us world peace. Good luck on that one. It's what they said after the first photos of Earth were taken from space." The bill arrived. Priscilla reached for it, but he waved her off. "I've got it," he said. "Can't allow a beautiful woman to buy her own salad."

THEY CAME OUT of the restaurant into the concourse. Music, laughter, and the sounds of lasers in a gaming room. Priscilla accompanied Drake as far as the connecting tube, which would take him down to the boarding platform. He was about to start down when the public address system activated: "Everyone please stay in your quarters until otherwise notified. There is no reason for alarm. But in the interests of caution—"

"No reason for alarm," said Priscilla. She couldn't think of a better way to induce panic.

The message kept running. ". . . keep everyone informed as the situation develops . . ."

A burst of noise erupted behind them, frightened shouts, raised voices, people all talking at once, one child in tears. "I think the commotion's coming from the Skyview," said Drake.

Priscilla stopped one of the women. "What's going on?" she asked.

The woman was so rattled she could barely speak. She looked at Priscilla with bleak eyes. "A bomb," she said. "There's a guy in there with a bomb."

The Skyview also had long windows that fronted on the concourse. She and Drake hurried back to look. Most people in the restaurant were out of their chairs, backing up against the bulkheads. All were focused on the blond young man who'd looked lost minutes ago. He was about twenty-five, wearing gray slacks and a white pullover. Average size, with blue eyes. There was something in his hand. He was speaking but she couldn't hear anything through the Plexiglas. The diners had gotten as far from him as they could.

Other than Frank, who hadn't moved except to activate his link so security would be able to overhear everything.

Priscilla called her office. The AI responded. *"Yes,"* she said. *"There is a threat at the Skyview. The subject is talking with Security now. We're getting it here. Do you want the feed?"*

"Please."

"—calm. If any of you get in the way, everybody's going to be dead." He lifted his right hand, the one that held the device. It looked like a phone. The voice was cold and angry, and loud enough that everyone in the restaurant could undoubtedly hear whatever he decided to say. They were in tears, begging the bomber not to hurt the children, asking what they'd ever done to him. They were holding up hands, standing in front of children, hoping to shield them.

"All right, sir." One of the security people on the link. His voice would have been coming into the restaurant through loudspeakers. *"Don't get upset. We don't want anyone getting hurt here. What is it that you need?"*

"Just so you know," said the blond man, *"it's a dead man's switch."* He waved the thing that looked like a phone. *"If I let go of it, it'll go off."*

That caused a fresh wave of hysteria in the Skyview, more

screams, kids bursting into tears, people falling down. A couple of them got out the door.

"Hey," he said, *"you guys told me you'd locked the doors. Do it now. Anybody else goes out, I'm blowing this thing. Now do it."*

"Sorry," said the other voice. *"We couldn't locate the code. We've got it now."*

"You're funny," said the bomber.

"My name's Abel, sir. We're trying to do everything you ask."

"Yeah. Try to be a little quicker about it. And keep the security guys outside."

And, finally, Frank got to his feet. *"What's your name, sir?"* he asked.

"What's it matter? Who are you?"

"My name's Frank. I work here. And I'll help you if I can. We just don't want anybody getting hurt."

The blond man stared at him. *"I'm James Addison."*

"Is it okay if I call you James?"

"Maybe you better get over near the wall, Frank. With the rest of these people."

Someone yelled, *"Get over here!"*

Frank smiled. *"James, would it be all right with you if we let these people leave? I'll stay with you, and we can talk this—"*

"No! Nobody goes anywhere."

"All right. What can we do for you? What do you need?"

James was waving the device. *"Just back off, okay?"*

"We're doing that. No problem. What else?"

James began talking into his link again. But Priscilla wasn't getting the transmission. *"He switched channels,"* said the AI. *"Security says he's talking to somebody off station."*

One of the women, with a child in tow, was edging toward the door.

Then James was back: *"Don't do it,"* he said. *"Nobody moves. If anybody tries to go out, I'll set it off."*

"Sure, pal," said Frank. *"We're going to close up, to make sure no one gets out, okay?"*

"That's what I told you to do—"

Emergency doors slid into place, sealing off all entrances. If he set off the bomb, the effects, hopefully, would be contained.

"Okay," said Frank. *"It's all right. I'm sure we can reach an understanding."* Security guards moved into position outside the doors. *"Now, what's the problem? And what can we do to make it right?"*

"I want some airtime." James's voice was crisp, sharp. *"I want HV coverage. I have something to say to the country."*

"HV coverage?" More security people were arriving, fanning out. *"We can't do that, James. We don't have the connections."*

"Don't try to play me. You can do whatever you want. Get me the media people."

"We can't manage that, sir. You have to be reasonable."

He smiled pleasantly. *"No, I don't. I don't have to be reasonable at all. And it would be a good idea if you didn't lie to me. I know you can make it happen. If I'm wrong about that, if you really can't, everybody in here is dead."*

That drew more gasps and pleas. *"Don't."*

"My kids."

"Please don't do this."

Somebody in the concourse began screaming that her daughter was inside.

"You have three minutes," James said, *"to make it happen. I have friends on the ground who will let me know when it does."*

"Okay," Frank said. *"We're trying. We're working on it. But you have to give us some time. You have to—"*

"No, I don't," he said. *"I don't have to do anything. Just get it done."*

"All right. We're doing everything we can. May I ask what this is about?"

"I'll tell you in a minute. As soon as the hookup is complete."

"Okay. Listen, can we make an arrangement?"

"What did you have in mind, Frank?"

"I'd appreciate it if you'd allow the people to leave the restaurant. There's no need for them—"

"Forget it. I don't want to hurt anybody. But I'll get a lot more attention if things stay as they are."

Drake moved in close to her. "If he sets the bomb off in there, Priscilla, none of them will survive. What happened to security? How'd he get a bomb up here?"

"I have no idea."

The guards were signaling for them to move. "Drake," she said, "I have to get to the command center. I'll see you later."

"Why?"

"It's where I'm supposed to report in case of emergency."

More hatches were closing. That entire section of the concourse was being sealed off. Frank let James see he was listening to his link. Then he said, *"You're a graduate student at Western Indiana University."*

"You guys are pretty good."

"James Addison. You're working on a master's in literature." He sounded surprised.

"I'm not much interested in delaying tactics, Frank."

"I'm not trying to delay anything. I'm just wondering why you ended up here threatening strangers."

Patricia came out of an elevator and jogged through the door leading to the command center. Priscilla followed her into the room, where Abel Parker, wearing an earpod, sat at the comm panel. The restaurant scene was on a wide display.

James looked painfully casual. *"So what are you going to do, Frank? Do I get my airtime?"*

Abel reacted to something that had just come in on his earpod, gave Patricia a thumbs-up, and leaned over to speak into the mike. "Frank, tell him he's on. We've got a feed through Worldwide. Tell him to look at the imager. It's over the main door."

Frank passed the message on, and James looked directly out of the display. The nervous look was gone. *"What about it, Monk?"* he said.

Abel listened and then nodded. "He said yes. They've got it."

"Okay," said James. *"Just so you know, Frank, when this is over, my buddy's going to let me know how things went. If I don't hear from him, or if I hear anything I don't like, you can say good-bye to everybody. You understand?"*

"Yes. I understand." Frank pointed toward the entrance. "Look that way. The imager's over the doors."

"Okay. Good." James turned and smiled. Everybody's best friend. *"Hello,"* he said. The good humor didn't come through. *"My name's James Addison. In case anybody out there's wondering, I'm an American. Originally from Aurora, Kansas.*

*We are currently in the process of killing off an entire world,
every living thing on it. Most of you are probably not aware of
this, but the World Space Authority, which is financed by us,
by the citizens of this country, and by the citizens of a lot of
other countries, is aiding and abetting this vicious genocide.*

"*That world has as many animals, as many life-forms, as
we have on Earth. And we are massacring them. Killing
every last one. I wish I had pictures to show you. I mean,
many of these are very much like the cats and dogs and par-
rots and rabbits we keep as pets.*

"*They call it terraforming, and the world I'm talking
about has been code-named Selika.*

"*If you're wondering how and why we are going to kill
these helpless creatures, it's because we want their world for
colonization. We want to take it over. But before we can do
that, we have to change the environment. We have to change
the mixture of gases in the atmosphere. We have to make it
warmer. We have to produce more rain. And those actions
may sound harmless, but they are lethal to creatures that
have been living there for several billion years.*

"*And this is only the beginning. We're initiating the same
process on another world. God knows when, if ever, we'll stop.*

"*That brings us to the question of what we can do. You
and me. There is currently a bill before the Congress—*"

Patricia rolled her eyes. "Full-scale nut job."

"*This bill,*" James continued, "*is HR210. It provides for a
halt on terraforming until a further examination of the consequences can be made. It's not as strong as what we need,
which is a total ban, period, with no further debate. But it's
a—*" He stopped, lifted a link to his ear, and listened for a
moment. Then his face hardened, and he turned toward
Frank. "*I don't know whether you're aware or not, Frank, but
they've blocked the broadcast.*"

"*That can't be right.*" Frank, for the first time, lost his cool
demeanor. "*Give us a minute. Something like this, it takes
time to set up. You didn't give us enough time.*"

James shook his head. No. "*You don't allow me to communicate in a rational way—*" He lifted the device, stared at it,
and showed it to the imager. "*You're not giving me any choice.*"

There were gasps and cries from the people in the room.

"Please don't." "For God's sake—" "You can't do this." "The kids."

"Please, Mr. Addison."

Abel was talking into the mike, nodding, looking back at Patricia. "Frank," he said, "they're telling us the broadcast is going out."

Frank took a couple of steps forward. Stopped when James held out a cautionary palm. *"Whoever that is on your link,"* he said, *"they're giving you bad information. You're still on."*

James stared back at him. *"You'd have no qualms about lying, would you?"*

"For God's sake, I'm not interested in putting all these lives at risk. You're getting the coverage you asked for."

James poked at his link. Looked up. Nodded. *"Okay."* He took a deep breath. *"He's telling me I'm back on. But don't try that again."* He returned to speech mode: *"There are a lot of us who are not going to stand by while these people destroy entire worlds. It's just starting, and God knows where it will lead. Nobody will benefit from it except outfits like Kosmik. I am warning the people who are behind this: Shut it down, or we will shut it down for you. And shut you down as well."* He drew his right index finger across his throat, signaling that he was finished.

"That's it?" asked Frank, who was taking no chances.

"Yes."

"Okay."

James looked around the room. *"Everybody may leave now. But go slowly, and don't anybody get close to me."*

The diners cautiously got up from their tables and started for the doors, where they piled up, waiting for them to open. When finally they did, they hurried out until there remained only Frank, James, and a couple of security people.

"Time to go," said James.

"What are you going to do now?"

"I'm going to extract a price from you people, something to remind you about what we've been talking about."

"What do you mean?"

"Get out of here and seal the doors."

"Don't do it, James."

"Get out, Frank. Or you'll go with me."

Frank hesitated, took a step toward the exit, and stopped. He signaled the guards to leave and close the doors. Then he turned back to James. *"If you kill us, nobody will ever take you seriously."*

"Get out." The guards stared at them from outside the window. *"Frank,"* said James, *"you've got two minutes."*

Patricia looked around the small room, eyes desperate. "We need a distraction."

"The outside projector," said Priscilla. "Why don't we throw a comet at him?"

Patricia leaned over the mike. "Frank, we're going to try to distract him."

Abel was reaching for a tab. But Patricia pulled his hand away. "No," she said. "Scare him and he'll probably loosen his grip. We need something to make him tighten up." That steady gaze fell on Priscilla. "Abel, do we have an imager?"

He started searching through a cabinet while James repeated his warning. "Here," he said, producing one from a drawer filled with cable, tools, and instruments.

Patricia took it, pointed it at Priscilla, and tied it into the console. "I need you to do something that'll catch his attention."

"What are we talking about?"

"Use your imagination, Priscilla. Distract him."

"Oh." She hesitated.

"But that's all right. Take your time. Why don't you wait until the bomb goes off?"

Priscilla took a deep breath. She undid the top three or four buttons of her blouse.

"Okay, Abel," said Patricia. "Let's do it."

"Listen, please," said Frank. *"Think about what you're doing here."*

James stared back at him. *"Are you serious, you idiot? You think I'd come here like this without having thought about it long and hard?"* He raised both hands over his head, still holding the trigger down. *"Get out. Last chance, Frank."*

PRISCILLA HAD NEVER thought of herself as having pouty lips and smoky eyes. But on that occasion she went all out. She smiled provocatively for the imager and saw her projection appear outside the long window, where usually diners and tourists saw only asteroids and interstellars. Unfortunately, James had his back turned.

But he must have noticed Frank suddenly staring over his shoulder. He turned toward the window and his eyes went wide. Priscilla looked straight into the lens, wishing she could see him from outside the portal so she could look directly into those eyes. She formed the word *hello*, and inhaled.

And she watched, hoping Frank would make his move, listening for the explosion that seemed inevitable. But her boss only stood quietly until James turned back to him. *"Who's she?"* he asked.

"One of our pilots. She thinks I'm crazy for staying in here with you. She was hoping I'd take advantage of the distraction and try to grab the bomb."

"Why didn't you do it?"

"It wouldn't have worked. No way I could hold your hand down on the trigger until help got in here. But more important, you've been in here talking about the value of life. Okay, I'm betting I have a better chance if I just leave you to do the rational thing."

"The rational thing is to blow this place to hell."

"James, you haven't hurt anyone yet. Moreover, you've become a celebrity. You'll be able to do more damage to the terraformers by staying alive. And if you kill me, and yourself, and maybe some of these other people, the message you just delivered becomes a joke."

James turned back to the image beyond the window. And he laughed. *"There's an element to all this I hadn't considered."*

"What's that?"

He looked at the bomb. *"If I change my mind, how do I get rid of this thing?"*

THE ART MAJESKI SHOW
(Frank Irasco, guest)

MAJESKI: All right, Frank. Did you know what was coming?

IRASCO: I knew they were going to try to distract him. But I had no idea how (*laughs*). I thought they might try having someone in a clown suit show up in the concourse and start jumping up and down.

MAJESKI: You *are* kidding, right?

IRASCO: To be honest, Art, I couldn't think of anything that seemed as if it would have a chance of working. The person you *should* be interviewing is Priscilla Hutchins.

MAJESKI: The woman who was floating outside the window, right?

IRASCO: Yes. She's the one. And Patricia McCoy. The director.

MAJESKI: Well, good for them. But tell me, Frank, what about the terraforming? Are we really killing off whole worlds? Is that true?

IRASCO: I'm not an expert, Art, but my understanding is that there *is* a risk. We just don't know enough yet. We might wipe out some critical part of the food chain. If that were to happen, yes, I suppose they could lose everything. Though it would take a while.

MAJESKI: One other question, Frank. I was watching the broadcast. It did *not* get interrupted. So what really happened?

IRASCO: My understanding is that individual stations have control over what they show. Sometimes they use the network feed, sometimes they don't. The station where his accomplice was reporting from apparently went to something local. Though I can't imagine a more riveting show.

Chapter 48

PRISCILLA'S ATTITUDE TOWARD Frank had completely changed. When he called her into his office that afternoon, she felt awed in his presence. *Who are you? What have you done with Frank Irasco?* "That was a pretty gutsy performance out there today," she said, trying not to sound obsequious.

"Part of the job, Priscilla." A box of jelly donuts was secured to a side table. "But yes, I'll admit that was a scary few minutes." He picked up the box and offered it to her.

She took one. And also got some coffee.

"We have another mission for you," he said. "I don't know whether you were aware of this or not, but McGruder's bringing his campaign here. To the station."

"I saw that," she said. "You're not going to ask me to go shake his hand again, are you?"

"No," he said.

"Good."

"I'm going to ask you to be his pilot. But it's okay. No long flight. He's only going to Iapetus."

"You're kidding."

"He wants to see the monument."

"Why? I can't believe it would help him politically."

Frank couldn't restrain a laugh. "You're terribly cynical for one so young, Priscilla. I hate to think what you'll be like after you put on a few more miles. Anyhow, three or four members of his team will be going with him. They'll get out, take some pictures, get back in the ship, and come home. That's all there is to it."

"Why on earth does he want to go out there in the middle of the campaign? What's he expect to gain?"

"I don't know whether you've been following the news, Priscilla, but his campaign isn't going well. He's perceived as not very exciting. As stuck with old ideas and unable to adapt to a rapidly changing world. He probably *will* get the Gold Party nomination, but he's going up against a sitting president. We both know Norman's not very popular; but, nevertheless, incumbents are hard to beat. The only reason McGruder's leading the nomination fight is because nobody else of any substance really wanted into the ring. They're all waiting for 2200. He needs to shake things up. And I guess this seemed to be a way to do it. It won't hurt him, by the way, to be seen traveling with the hero who brought the schoolkids home."

"That's a little over the top," she said.

"I calls 'em the way I sees 'em."

"You're saying he asked for me?"

Frank's jaw twitched. "Yes. He did."

"I'm not excited about hauling politicians around."

"I thought he was very nice to you when he was here."

"He was. But I'm not inclined to become part of his campaign. That's what he did last time."

"You're a pilot, Priscilla. It's what you do. Haul people who need hauling." He closed his eyes for a moment. Then: "We need you to do this. Look, he may become the next president. If that happens, we need to do everything we can to get him on our side."

"Even if he thinks we should be shut down?"

"We'd have a better chance of dissuading him if we treat him well now. Anyhow, he can't be any worse for us than Norman."

"Frank, even if the voters were dumb enough to put him in, he wouldn't be able to shut us down. There are a few other countries involved in the Authority."

"Come on, Priscilla. I'm asking you to take one for the team." He picked up one of the donuts and took a bite. "You're always talking about how you want to sit on the bridge instead of in your office. Okay. Do it. And don't screw it up."

"I assume we won't be using the *Starhawk*?"

He looked momentarily puzzled. "Oh, you mean the *Bomb*? Priscilla, you do tend to be a trifle sarcastic. But no, we'll want something a little more classy. Fortunately, the *Thompson*'s available."

THE *SYDNEY THOMPSON* was bigger, more spacious, and considerably more elegant than the *Baumbachner*. Of course, the *Baumbachner* paled in significance to some of the fishing boats along the Jersey shore. Priscilla was seated on the ship's bridge running status checks while her passengers' luggage was being placed in their cabins by the handlers when Yoshie Blakeslee called. *"The governor's arrived,"* she said. *"They're ready to board."*

"Okay, Yoshie. The air lock is open. Send them up the tunnel."

"They want you to be waiting at the hatch, Priscilla."

"I'm a little busy at the moment."

"Frank says do it."

"Okay." She got up, straightened her cap, went back through the cabin, and assumed a position outside the air lock. There were voices in the tunnel. Then laughter. And finally, the passengers themselves. The governor was flanked by a woman and three guys. He was looking back over his shoulder, waving at a group of trailing reporters. Then he turned, saw her, and broke into the broad smile that had been enchanting millions during the campaign. That, despite her dislike for politicians, had impressed her during their first meeting.

He came forward and shook her hand while one of the males took pictures. "Priscilla," he said, "it's so good to see you again. I'm glad they were able to fit you into the schedule."

The guy with the imager took more pictures. He was older than the others, with an extended belly and a ridge of gray hair circling his skull. "That's Al Devlin," said McGruder.

"He's one of my staff." The reporters were taking pictures, too, and he shook her hand some more. "I read about your flight out to that place in the middle of nowhere. You lead an exciting life, Priscilla." He pointed at the woman. "This is Vesta D'Ambrosia, my campaign manager." She was tall, middle-aged, with bored eyes. She did not give the impression she was anxious to see Iapetus.

"Hello, Priscilla," she said, extending her hand.

McGruder glanced at the other two guys. "These gentlemen are my official protection, Michael and Cornelius."

They both nodded. Priscilla welcomed them to the *Thompson*, answered a few questions, and posed for some more pictures. The reporters wanted to follow them through the air lock, but Priscilla, because of the security issue, kept them outside and, after apologizing, closed the hatch. She showed her passengers to their quarters. Within minutes, everyone was back in the passenger cabin.

Vesta was conservatively dressed in dark slacks and a white blouse. She stood looking down at Priscilla. "Is this flight really going to take three or four *days*?" She emphasized the last word, as though a reasonable flight time would have been measured in hours.

Michael, probably in his late forties, was easily the older of the two agents. He asked Priscilla how long she'd been on board, whether she knew of anyone else's having been on the ship that morning, what security measures were in place to ensure that no one could have boarded the *Thompson* surreptitiously, and so on. In the meantime, his partner, Cornelius, wandered through the ship, armed with what must have been a bomb detector.

Priscilla answered the questions and excused herself. "Time to get moving," she said. "We'll be heading out in a few minutes. I'll let you know when we're ready to go." She went up onto the bridge and was surprised when Vesta followed.

"I was anxious to meet you, Priscilla," Vesta said. "The governor thinks very highly of you."

"Thanks, Ms. D'Ambrosia. I'm happy to hear it."

"Vesta, please. We're going to be in here for a while. Might as well go to first names."

"Yes, ma'am. Umm, Vesta."

"One thing, Priscilla. The governor has a tendency sometimes to take risks. While we're on this trip, I don't want anything to happen to him. If he wants to do anything that seems at all to you to constitute hazardous behavior, do not allow it. Understood?"

"Of course." Priscilla felt more intimidated than she had been by the governor. "We wouldn't want to lose him."

"No, we certainly would not."

The bridge link sounded. "Excuse me." Priscilla leaned over the mike. "Go ahead, Yoshie."

"You're clear to go, Priscilla."

"Roger that." She opened the allcom. "Attention, everybody. We're five minutes from launch. If you've anything that needs to be taken care of, please do it now. When you're ready, take a seat, secure the harness, and do not release it until I advise you that it is safe to do so. That will be approximately forty minutes into the flight. If anyone has a problem, push the red button at the lower right of your display."

Vesta looked down at the right-hand seat. "Mind if I sit up here?"

"Sure. If you like." One by one, the safety lamps turned green, indicating everyone was belted in.

"All right, gentlemen, Vesta, we are on our way." Priscilla released the ship from its magnetic clamps and let the AI, Louie, guide the *Thompson* out past two docked vehicles and through the launch doors. Then she turned slowly in the direction of Saturn and began to accelerate.

AS THEY APPROACHED the jump point, Priscilla explained to her passengers what they were about to do. None of them had been in Barber space before or, for that matter, any farther out than the space station. "The passage is simple enough," she said. "You probably won't even notice the jump. The only thing you're likely to be aware of is that, if you're looking outside, the stars will seem to go out." She said nothing about the possibility of an upset stomach, which was not an uncommon feature of the experience, especially for people going through it for the first time. But Jake had told her he knew no better way to ensure passengers would throw up than to warn them that it might happen. A bag was available at each seat if needed.

"Nice view," Vesta said. Earth and Moon glowed in the sunlight.

"I doubt I'll ever get used to it," said Priscilla.

They indulged in small talk for a few minutes. Vesta had grown up in Oregon, graduated from the University of California Business School, got into politics because of President Goulart, twenty years earlier. "He was trying to control everything," she said. "Progress stopped dead while he was in office. Everything was run by the bureaucracy. So eventually—"

"You went into politics yourself."

"Damn right," she said. "You're probably not aware of it, but the best thing that could happen for the space program would be for the governor to win."

THEY MADE THE jump into Barber space with no visible ill effects. "Everybody stay belted," Priscilla said, speaking over the allcom.

"Why?" asked Vesta. "There are a few things I need to talk over with the governor."

"Just hold on a few seconds."

The sound of the engines shifted a notch higher as the Hazeltine unit cut in. Suddenly, they were floating in the gray mist, with little indication of forward movement. But Vesta was holding her stomach. "What was that?" she asked.

"A transdimensional jump."

She laughed. "Okay. I know what you're talking about. We're on our way to Saturn. How long—?"

"Hang on," said Priscilla. "Transition complete. Everybody prep for another jump." She was enjoying herself. The drone of the engines changed again, and the mist was gone, replaced by a vast globe and a series of rings. "Okay," she said, "we're *there*."

Vesta's jaw dropped. An enormous yellow-brown globe filled the sky. And a set of rings. "That's Saturn, right? How could we be here already?"

The rings spread across the sky, dazzling in their brilliance and perfection. Priscilla stared at them, thinking that if a convincing argument for the existence of God could be found, this was it.

"Incredible," said the governor.

Priscilla wasn't sure whether he was referring to the planet or the rapidity of the flight. It was her first visit also to Saturn, and she was probably as impressed as anyone at how quickly they'd arrived even though she'd known what to expect. But she was careful not to show it.

"I don't understand," Vesta said. "Why were we talking about three or four days for this?"

"We just did the easy part," said Priscilla. She went back to the mike. "Everybody stay belted in, please. We'll be making a course correction in the next few minutes. Then you can get up and wander around or whatever. By the way, be careful when you do. We are in a zero-gee environment. It'll take some getting used to."

"WHERE IS IT?" asked Vesta.

Priscilla put Iapetus on the display. "We did pretty well. We'll be there in about twenty-seven hours."

"Good," she said. "I'm glad to hear it. Can you by any chance make it quicker? There's a presidential campaign on, and whatever time we save—"

"I can, if you want. But if we do that kind of acceleration, we won't be able to get out of our chairs, and nobody will be very comfortable."

Those expressionless eyes came to life and targeted Priscilla as if she were responsible for any inconvenience. Then the animation faded. "Okay," she said. "I guess we can live with that."

Priscilla wondered how she'd have responded if they'd needed three days or so. That would not have been unusual. "So," she said, "what's the point?"

Vesta frowned. "What's *what* point?"

"Well, as you said, you're running a presidential campaign. What are you doing out here?"

She took her time responding, finally nodding toward the view, the giant planet, the rings, stars probably more brilliant than she'd ever seen them before this day. "The governor has a passion for history. He's always wanted to visit the monument."

Later, she had a chance to ask the same question of McGruder. He smiled. "Are you serious, Priscilla? We're talking about something that was put here by aliens thousands of years ago. Nobody knows who they were or what happened to them afterward. But it changed our whole perspective about the universe. We found out we were not alone. Why would anyone *not* want to come out here?"

"But you're in the middle of a campaign."

He nodded. Looked amused. "It's an opportunity to remind everyone of the glories around us. And why we need spaceflight. And don't look so surprised, Priscilla. It's what presidents do."

It's what presidents do. "A month or two ago, Governor, you were opposed to all this. You were saying we were wasting resources out here. What happened?"

He smiled and shook his head. "I was wrong," he said. "The country *does* have some fiscal problems, and I went for the easy solution. The obvious one. But I was wrong. I've said as much. The problem is that sometimes it's difficult to change your mind. At least for a politician. You do that, and they call you a flip-flopper."

"They will," she said.

"They already have. Within an hour after we made the announcement about coming here." He was staring at the rings. "Politics is the only career I know of where you're not allowed to profit from experience. Not allowed to learn anything."

"Well," she said, "I hope it works for you." She thought about adding that she'd vote for him. She expected to do that, but saying it would seem too much like groveling.

SHE SLEPT ON the bridge. Had to, because McGruder and his team showed no sign of retiring. It wouldn't look right if she went back to her cabin while the passengers worked all night. She couldn't make out what they were saying without turning on the commlink, but she wasn't going to do that. They didn't invite her to join the discussion. In the morning, when she woke, the passenger cabin was empty. By then, Iapetus was visible as a small disk. She went back to her quarters, showered, and changed clothes.

When they were still a few hours out, she got on the mike: "We'll start braking in thirty minutes. Everybody up, please. You'll need to be in your seats and belted in when we begin." It was midafternoon of the second day.

She heard doors opening and closing. And voices. But no footsteps, of course. You never hear footsteps in zero gee. She got up and went back into the passenger cabin. Devlin, the governor, and Vesta were talking about his three Gold Party rivals, how to get rid of them without alienating anybody. Michael and Cornelius were missing. She wondered why they were along at all. Did someone think there might be an alien attack? "Everybody doing okay?" Priscilla asked. "Does anybody need anything?"

"Some gravity would be nice," said Devlin.

McGruder laughed. "They're working on it. Artificial gravity's just a couple of years away."

"We still have a few minutes," said Priscilla, "before we start reducing speed. Once we do, we'll continue for two hours, and you won't be able to leave your seat. After two hours, we'll take a twenty-minute time-out, and you'll be able to wander around again, eat, drink, whatever you like. Then we'll brake for another two hours. That'll put us in orbit around Iapetus. In the meantime, if anybody *needs* to get to the washroom or something, let me know and we can go to cruise. One other thing. Iapetus is not visible from the windows here, but you can put the forward view on your display. Any questions?"

Devlin raised a hand: "Priscilla," he said, "could you explain again how the shower works?"

VESTA D'AMBROSIA'S DIARY

Andy insisted on getting Hutchins to be the pilot for this misbegotten flight, on the grounds that she had received some recent publicity and people would recognize her name. Unfortunately, what they're also going to recognize is that she's a kid. This trip is going to draw a lot of mockery as it is. I can see the comedians and the cartoonists now, showing Andy standing next to that concrete two-legged lizard on Iapetus talking about having a meeting of minds. They'll kill us. At least, if we had a grizzled tough-looking captain, we might be able to sell this thing. But no, instead we get a high-school kid.

—March 4, 2196

ON THE NET

So the guy who doesn't believe in space travel goes to Saturn and develops an appreciation for alien art. Does he really think that's going to bring in the swing voters?   —CatMan

CatMan, are there any voters at all out there, other than the loonies, who will be impressed by McGruder's going out to Saturn? Maybe he could do us all a favor and stay out there.   —Big Joe

I wish I could go.   —Marcia43

Kosmik has two days to issue a statement terminating its terraforming program on Selika unless and until it finds a way to continue without harming local life. If it fails to do so, I will terminate the Wheel.

—Adam11

Chapter 49

JAKE, SAMANTHA, AND Tony rode the lander down through clear skies, tracking the transmission from the radio Jake had left with the wreckage. They were at about a thousand meters when Samantha caught her breath. "Look!" she said.

Jake looked, but saw only the opaque, snow-covered landscape.

"No question," said Tony. "They have to be artificial. No way that could happen naturally."

They were talking about the symmetries. They were hard to make out in the darkness, but they were there, surface features that were almost but not quite polygons, ovoids, cones, and cubes. A thousand assorted shapes. Lost in the blowing snow, they were easy to miss. Literally *buried* in snow. But they were there, arranged in grids and circles and abstract dispositions that might have been chaotic yet nevertheless suggested a kind of order.

Mountains might have been oddly shaped bubbles. A canyon cut through snowfields like a lightning bolt. Then it all went away, and they were over an area in which nothing unusual could be distinguished. "They're incredible," said Samantha. "Seeing them like this is a little different from just looking at the record—" She took a deep breath. "That settles it for me. *Somebody's* been here. Or still is."

There was more. Directly ahead, they could make out a cluster of parabolic hills.

"WHERE DO YOU plan to put the base?" asked Jake.

"Originally," Samantha said, "I thought locating it near the downed lander would be as good a spot as any."

"But—?"

"It probably wouldn't hurt to set it up near one of those grids." She took a deep breath. "Jake, you know what we're dealing with here, right?"

That took him by surprise. "I'm not sure what you mean."

"Whenever you referred to the presence, you always used plural pronouns. As if it were a species of some sort."

"What else could it be, Samantha?"

"I think we're about to give new meaning to the term *living world*."

Jake grunted. "That's crazy. You're saying the planet's *alive*?"

"Not exactly. I doubt that's possible. But I think there's something alive in the atmosphere. More or less the atmosphere itself, maybe. It takes a lot of air to support a falling lander. If we were looking at an ordinary world, with sunlight and oceans, I doubt I'd even consider the possibility. But out here—" She shook her head.

"That's hard to believe."

"Jake, we're just beginning to look around outside the solar system. Before we're finished, I'd be surprised if we don't discover that a lot of what used to be basic dogma is really pretty narrow. So yes, let's recover Otto first. Then we try to send a message to the occupant any way we can. Meantime, we can talk about where to locate the base."

"What do you think the grids *are*?"

"An art form. It's hard to see what else they could be." Jake couldn't hide his skepticism. "Look," she continued, "if there *is* something here, it's been here a long time. What else would it have to do other than carve designs?"

"Using *what*?"

"The wind. Snow, dust—"

THE NIGHT WAS absolutely still.

Jake followed the signals, a steady beep-beep-beep, through the darkness. They were at about three hundred meters when Samantha tapped on her display. "There it is."

"Okay," said Jake. "So what's the plan?"

"Let's see if we can find that missing wing. The scanners can penetrate a couple of hundred feet of snow and ice. So even if it's buried, we should be able to see it."

"Why do we care?"

"I don't want any loose ends."

"All right," said Jake. *Waste of time, though.* He activated the scanners, turned on the searchlights, dropped lower, and began to circle the area. They saw nothing they hadn't seen before.

"All right," Samantha said finally, "let's go pick up Otto."

JAKE STILL DIDN'T like the landing area, but it was all they had. He bounced down and rolled toward the rocks. His passengers were clinging to their seats, and he heard a few gasps. But they stopped where they needed to, and he tried to act as if it were routine. "Thank God," said Denise.

"Actually," said Jake, "I'm getting better with practice. That's the best one I've done."

"Glad I wasn't here for any of the others," said Tony.

He turned the spacecraft around and assured them that the departure would be less exciting.

They pulled on air tanks and activated their Flickinger units. Jake liked the slight tingle that always accompanied the process. It reminded him that this was what he lived for. The sensation was a built-in characteristic of the field to alert the user that it had turned on. Jake recalled the story of Alan Jarvais, who would probably be featured in every pilot-training program for years to come. Jarvais had not been aware of a defect in his unit. When he pressed the activator, the field had not formed. He hadn't noticed and went into an air lock and started to depressurize. When he discovered that breathing was becoming a problem, he could have reversed the process, but he apparently hadn't known how, or he had simply panicked. In any case, it was exit Jarvais.

He trained the spotlights at the top of what he had come to think of as Vincenti Hill, and the lander came into view. "We'll leave them on for now," he said, "and shut them down when we're coming back, so they don't blind everybody. It'll be slippery out there, so be careful."

The air lock opened, and Jake stepped down onto the ice. The others followed, and they pulled the pallet out of storage. Tony insisted on carrying it.

Samantha wore a blue jumpsuit. She was rotating her shoulders. "I see what you mean about the gravity," she said.

Mary's voice broke in from the *Venture*: *"Be careful, guys."*

"We will," said Samantha.

Jake switched on a wrist light and took the lead. The darkness was oppressive. Midnight World. Priscilla had it right. "This way," he said, starting the uphill trek. A mild breeze sprang up behind them and pushed him gently, as if urging him forward.

THE LANDER GLOWED in the spotlights. Samantha circled it, looking for damage. She didn't find much they didn't already know about. Then she opened the hatch and, followed by Tony, went inside. Jake heard Tony react when he saw Otto. Jake preferred the wind to the grisly interior, so he waited where he was.

Lights moved around inside. After a few minutes, Samantha came back out. She stood looking at the lander, then lifted her eyes to the sky.

Jake went in. He and Tony picked up the body and carried it out. Tony lost his footing coming through the air lock, staggered against the hull, and almost went down. Samantha, fortunately, grabbed his shoulder and steadied him. "Careful," she said.

They laid the body on the pallet.

"Pity," said Samantha. "He was a likable kid. With a bright future. Now all he gets is his name on a wall."

Jake's footprints from the earlier mission were still visible. "Doesn't snow much here, does it?" said Samantha.

"I guess not. At least not in this area."

"What's really odd," said Denise, "is that, if nothing else, the wind would have filled them in. We've got some wind now, and it's moving the snow around. Does it only blow when somebody's here?"

"The snow has a crust," said Samantha. "That might have been enough to keep it in place. When you got here before, Jake, did you see any prints of any kind? Anything to indicate anybody else, *anything* else, might have been here?"

"No," he said. "I didn't see anything unusual."

"Okay." She looked down at Otto. "I guess that's all we can do here. You guys ready to roll?"

The spotlights atop the lander were in their eyes now. Jake turned them off. He and Tony picked up the pallet, and they started back down the slope. The cabin lights looked warm and comfortable.

JAKE HAD A hard time keeping his balance while he helped carry Otto. Moreover, a sudden wind that blew up behind them didn't make things easier. "Maybe," he said, "your buddy is trying to help."

Samantha let the remark pass without comment.

The steepest part of the descent came during the first ten minutes. Samantha led the way, testing the ground as she went, warning Tony and Jake where the going was especially slippery. About halfway down, Tony's feet went out from under him. Denise grabbed hold of him and the pallet but only became part of the general spill. All three plus the body went tumbling.

"What happened?" asked Mary, speaking from the *Venture*. *"You guys okay?"*

"Just a minor accident," said Samantha. "We're fine."

They put Otto's body back on the pallet and started again. And they got a break: The wind eased off.

* * *

FOR THE LOCATION of the shelter, Samantha picked a strip of flat land along the edge of a grid on the opposite side of the planet, not far from the south pole. "Denise," she said, "you stay with the ship."

The grids themselves did not seem to be laid out in any discernible pattern. There were hundreds of them, scattered randomly around the globe. The one Samantha chose was not special in any way. It was about average size, a square block of ground approximately ten kilometers on a side. She'd based her decision on two factors: It was an easy place to bring the lander down. And they had visibility in all directions.

Moving the shelter down required three flights. The first two carried the exterior shells and interior necessities for four cubicles. Brandon Eliot took over, with Samantha to assist, and the four structures were assembled and connected when Jake got back with the final load. "How'd you get it done so quickly?" he asked.

Brandon shrugged. "All you have to do is attach a generator to the packages. Turn it on and the modules assemble themselves." Two would provide sleeping quarters, and the third one gave them a pair of washrooms. All three connected to the fourth—the largest—which functioned as an operations center/common room/dining area.

The third shipment brought chairs, tables, cots, and general supplies, much of it packed in plastic containers. Brandon, assisted by Jake, connected air and water tanks, an AI, and installed the mechanicals. Tony filled the water tanks. They placed a radio antenna on a nearby hilltop and an imager on the roof of the operations center. And they added some outside lights, so the base would be visible. "We want to be sure nobody gets lost," Samantha told Jake.

When they finished, they staggered inside, closed the hatches, pumped air into the structure, turned off their Flickinger fields, stacked a few empty containers, and collapsed into the chairs and cots. The ops center had two large windows. The grid outside glittered in the starlight. It was just after 8:00 P.M. ship time, and Brandon's automated kitchen provided a round of meals.

They congratulated Brandon on the quality of the food. But Jake suspected that what really fueled a generally happy mood was being sheltered from the cold, dismal climate. "All we need," said Tony, "is a fireplace."

"What's next?" asked Mary, as they finished eating.

Samantha could barely contain her excitement. "We have the same pattern of signals that Jake thinks got a reply from whatever's out there. We're going to try to take that a step further."

"In what way?" asked Brandon.

"Let's talk about it tomorrow when we're awake. But I think right now it would be a good idea to crash—"

JAKE HAD TROUBLE sleeping. He kept waiting for something to happen. When nothing did, he got up and wandered into the ops center. Light snow was falling. Someone was seated in the dark. He wasn't sure who it was. "Awake?" he whispered.

"Hi, Jake." It was Samantha.

He sat down beside her. "I wonder how much snow we'll get?"

She smiled. "We don't care now. The shelter's up and running."

He watched the flakes drifting against the Plexiglas. "I've been thinking about your theory."

"That the atmosphere is alive?"

"That it's a global creature of some sort. Is that really what you meant?"

"I think that's a possible outcome."

"Just one of its kind?"

"Yes. Probably."

"How does it reproduce? Like an amoeba?"

"My guess would be that it doesn't."

"It would have to, wouldn't it?"

"Not really. The thing might not age."

"That can't be right."

"Why not?"

"That would mean it's been out here alone for millions of years."

"Maybe hundreds of millions."

"My God, Samantha. If that were true, it would be deranged. This thing actually seems pretty friendly."

"Jake, if we're right, it's probably always been alone. Even when it had a sun. It's not hard to understand why it might appreciate some company."

HE WOKE IN absolute darkness. There was a window, but he couldn't see it. Where the hell were the stars? He got up and turned on a light. The window was covered with snow.

Samantha was gone. He checked the time. Four hours had passed.

He sat back down and stared at the window.

What the hell was going on?

He pulled on the Flickinger gear, let himself into the lock, and closed it. The lights came on. He activated the field, and, when decompression was complete, pushed on the outer hatch. It moved slightly. But there was resistance on the other side.

He let go and stood staring at it.

He couldn't resist laughing. The life-form that Samantha had talked about was standing out there holding the hatch shut. *Hello, World Sentience. How are* you?

All right. What had happened, of course, was that they'd had more snow than anticipated. It was up over the windows and now it was blocking the exit. He pushed on the hatch again, this time with a more determined effort. It moved, and some flakes fell into the air lock. Another shove produced still more flakes.

He tried to pull the hatch shut, but the snow blocked it. It was a bad moment: Until he could close up, he couldn't retreat back into the shelter.

He heard a woman's voice. It was muffled. Then his link activated. *"Who's in the air lock?"* It was Mary.

"I am," he said.

"Jake, what are you doing in there?"

"I'm stuck."

"Stuck? What happened?"

"Take a look at the windows."

He scuffed more snow out of the way, kicked it into the

chamber, and pulled on the hatch again. After a moment and some more tugging and kicking, it closed. *"Holy cats,"* said Mary. *"Are we buried?"*

Jake began decompression. "I'd say so, yes."

"Can you get out of there?"

"I'll be out in a minute."

"TRAPPED IN AN air lock," said Tony as Jake came through the hatch. "Never heard of that happening to anyone before." The comment created a painful echo.

"Okay," said Samantha, "we have to get a sense of where we are. The snow is above every window in the place. Let's hope it was just a storm and not some sort of avalanche."

"Couldn't very well be an avalanche," said Brandon. "We're on flat ground."

"We need a shovel," Jake said.

Brandon shook his head. "We don't have one."

"Sure we do." Jake picked up a couple of the lids that had come with the plastic containers. "We'll go into the air lock, open the hatch as much as we can, and start dragging the snow inside until we clear some space. But there's only room for one person." He glanced over at Brandon. "Can we decompress the entire cubicle so we can open both hatches together? That would make it a lot easier."

"We can do that," he said.

"Okay." Samantha sounded exasperated. "Let's get to it."

THEY TOOK TURNS digging with the lids, dumped the snow into the containers, and hauled it to one of the showers. Eventually they got outside the cubicle, but they were still buried. When finally they broke through and saw stars again, everyone breathed a sigh of relief. "Thank God," Mary said.

But it was Samantha, climbing out of the hole and in the effort pulling more snow in on top of them, who stopped dead when she got clear. "I don't believe this," she said. Her voice shook.

They were standing on a mound of snow that covered the four cubicles but nothing else. The ground beyond it was as bare as it had been when they'd arrived. The grid was still clear. The lander, parked only meters away, showed only a light dusting of snow.

"What the hell's going on?" said Brandon.

Somebody was breathing hard.

"Not possible," said Mary.

Jake slid down and went over to look at the lander. "Is it okay?" asked Brandon. "Any damage?"

"No," Jake said. "At least nothing I can see."

Tony was looking up at the sky. It was clear. No clouds. No sign of a storm. "Somebody doesn't like us," he said.

Mary climbed down off the mound. "You were right, Samantha. There really *is* some sort of global force here."

"You wanted to find a way to communicate," Jake said. "I think we did."

"What do we do now?" asked Mary.

Samantha delivered a sad smile. "Anybody here who didn't get the message?"

Chapter 50

EVEN IF ONE excludes the monument, Iapetus easily qualifies as the strangest moon in the solar system. One side of it is dark, the other light. It has a crunched appearance, as if something had squeezed it. It is the only one of Saturn's satellites that, because of its distance and the angle of its orbit, actually provides a decent view of the rings. But these elements shrink in contrast to its oddest feature: a ridge rising from the equator that almost completely circles the moon. It's fourteen hundred kilometers long and twenty wide. At its highest, it reaches an altitude of eleven and a half kilometers, making it the tallest mountain range in the solar system.

Even stranger, three parallel ridges run beside it.

"How did that happen?" asked Devlin.

"It's a bit much for me," Priscilla said. She brought the explanation up on the display, but it was complicated, connected with a more rapid rotation millions of years ago.

Devlin looked at it and shook his head. "Incredible."

As they drew closer, McGruder came onto the bridge and took the right-hand seat. He wore a pullover and shorts, dressed for a day on the boardwalk. "You know, Priscilla," he said, "if I had my life to live over, I think I'd apply for pilot training. For interstellars."

"As opposed," she said, "to being president of the NAU?"

"Ah, yes," he said. "I think so. In fact, to start with, I'm not sure any sane person would want to be president. I understand what you're saying. But the truth is I'd rather have *your* job. You run around, you get to see places like this, and you go where no one's ever been before." He sat for a few seconds, simply breathing. "I envy you," he said.

She thought of herself primarily as a staff assistant who checked maintenance records and conducted guided tours, but she let it go. Maybe she *should* stop feeling sorry for herself. If nothing else, she was on the Wheel, and she was getting some flight opportunities. "You know," she said, "you may be right, Governor."

He looked out at the approaching moon. At the dark-tinted surface. It would have been easy to conclude that the sunlight was being blocked by a black cloud. Except, of course, there was no cloud. "You know where it is?" he asked.

"You mean the monument?"

"Yes."

"It's in a flat plain near the Persechetti Crater."

"The Persechetti Crater?"

"It's named for the person who did the bulk of the theoretical work about the moon. She more or less locked down why it has the two color tones and why it has an angled orbit."

"You're pretty knowledgeable, Priscilla."

She smiled. "Actually, I've been reading about it all morning."

"And you're honest, besides. May I suggest you not seek a career in politics."

DEVLIN AND THE Secret Service guys had worn Flickinger units before. (That, obviously, was why Cornelius and Michael had gotten the assignment.) Priscilla ran over the basics with Vesta and McGruder. When she was satisfied they wouldn't kill themselves, they got into the lander and waited for the optimum launch time. Vesta appeared uncomfortable. She denied having a problem but finally admitted that the lander seemed very small. "Is it really reliable?" she asked.

"It's fine, Vesta," said Priscilla. "We never have problems with landers."

The campaign manager looked skeptical. Pale. "Wasn't that the problem at Teegarden?" she asked. "Their lander wouldn't start?"

Priscilla managed a smile. "Well, almost never. But we're close to home, just in case."

"It's all right," said the governor. "We wouldn't be doing this if there were any danger. But, if you want, Vesta, you can stay with the ship."

"No." She was pulling herself together. "I wouldn't want to miss this. Anyhow, if something happens to you, the rest of us better not even think about going home."

Devlin climbed back outside the vehicle and began taking shots of the lander and of Priscilla at the controls and of the governor seated beside her. As launch time approached, he got back in, and she started to depressurize the cargo bay.

When the process was complete, the launch doors opened, and the lander slipped out into the night. Vesta breathed a long *ohhhhh*, then held her breath as Priscilla took them down.

IAPETUS LIVES IN perpetual twilight. The distant sun is little more than an extremely bright star. The moon is riddled with crags and mountains and impact craters. Pole to pole, the terrain is rugged. There's not much flat ground anywhere, but whoever created the monument found some by the Persechetti Crater. The monument is set in the exact center of a plain bordered by clusters of broken ridges. Nearby, Priscilla could see one of the landers from the Steinitz expedition, a century and a half earlier.

It lay about two hundred meters from the monument. It was a gray, clumsy vehicle. An old US flag imprint was still visible near an open cargo door. She circled the area once, descending slowly, and finally touched down. "Okay," she said. "Get your air tanks and activate your suit. Let me know when you're ready, and we'll depressurize the cabin."

She didn't trust them to do everything correctly, so she maintained a watchful eye. When the tanks were in place and they'd all gone slightly out of focus because of the energy fields, she conducted a brief inspection. Then she removed the air from the cabin and opened the air lock. "You'll find ramps in a few places," she said. "Wherever there is one, please use it. They're trying to preserve the marks from the original mission."

Devlin was first outside. He turned immediately to get pictures of McGruder coming through the air lock. Michael preceded Priscilla and Vesta. Cornelius remained inside.

Priscilla called him: "You okay?"

"I'm fine," he said. "We figure there's nobody here to create a problem and the biggest danger would be that the air lock jams or something, and we get locked out of the lander."

"I left the hatches open, Cornelius."

"That's no guarantee it wouldn't close on its own. Look, no sweat, Priscilla. I know nothing like that is very likely, but we have to take into account all the possibilities."

MCGRUDER APPROACHED THE monument and stood looking up at it.

Carved from rock and ice, it stood serenely on that bleak plain, an unsettling figure of curving claws, alien eyes, and lean power. The lips were parted, rounded, almost sexual. Priscilla wasn't sure why it was so disquieting. It was more than simply the talons, or the disproportionately long lower limbs. It was more even than the suggestion of philosophical ferocity stamped on those crystalline features. There was something—terrifying—bound up in the tension between its suggestive geometry and the wide plain on which it stood. It was scratched and clawed by micrometeors, the driving dust between the moons, but no serious damage had resulted. Its wings were half-folded, and its blind eyes stared at Saturn, frozen low in the hostile sky by its own relentless gravity just as it had been eons ago, when Iapetus received its visitors.

Most striking, the creature was female.

There was no obvious evidence to support that notion. Certainly, no anatomical clues were apparent through the plain garment covering the body. It was, perhaps, some delicacy of line or subtlety of expression. It reminded her vaguely of a stalking cat, and yet was somehow erotic.

"It *is* creepy, isn't it?" said Devlin.

Vesta agreed. "Wouldn't want to meet one of those in my backyard."

It stood on a block of ice about as high as Priscilla's shoulders. There was an inscription. Three lines of sharp white symbols, characterized by loops and crescents and curves, were stenciled in the ice, possessing an Arabic delicacy and elegance. And, as the tiny sun moved across the sky, the symbols embraced the light and came alive. No one knew what the inscription meant.

The ramp was designed to allow visitors to get close enough to touch the artifact without disturbing anything. McGruder stood close and gazed at the figure while Devlin took pictures. Despite the show business aspect, the governor looked as if the experience was having a genuine impact. "How old is it, Priscilla?"

"The estimates run from twenty-three thousand to twenty-eight thousand years."

"We were still sitting around campfires."

"Of course," said Vesta, "we're still active. Looks as if these things are gone."

McGruder reached out and *touched* it. Pressed his fingertips against one of the legs. "You know," he said, "if not for this, we probably would never have had a serious manned space program."

He might have been right. At another time, when support for NASA had dried up, and the space industry was effectively closing down, a robot vehicle had detected the monument. The hard reality had been that interest in spaceflight had faded when Mars was ruled out as a potential home for life. Unfortunately, there was nowhere else to go. The United States had put men on the Moon to make a political point. Without the Cold War, there would probably not even have been an Apollo XI.

"I'm not sure we do have one," said Priscilla. "A space program."

McGruder could not take his eyes off the monument. "Economies go through ups and downs. This is the first dip since the development of the Hazeltine drive. We haven't discovered anything out here except ruins. So we're back where the public is bored and doesn't want to pay the bills. What we need, Priscilla, is a major discovery."

"You mean first contact."

"That would be good."

Maybe, she thought, *we should give Talios some publicity.* But she resisted the temptation to ask him if he knew about the missed opportunity. *Maybe if he becomes president—* "We've already had one of those. A couple, really, if you count the ruins."

"Voters don't get excited by ruins," he said. "And the Noks are so dumb, nobody cares." He chuckled. "That might be *our* future if we don't get seriously off-world. No, what we need is somebody who can set an example for us. Show us what we might become. Inspire us."

Well, what the hell? She didn't want to be overheard, so she signaled him to switch to a private channel. Then: "It's already happened, Governor."

"How do you mean, Priscilla? What's already happened?"

"They don't want it released. But there was an encounter years ago at Talios. I'd appreciate it if it went no further. Or at least if you wouldn't mention your source."

She told him about Dave Simmons and the lander, and the *Forscher.* And about the message she and Jake had found.

He listened. Initial surprise morphed into disbelief. "That can't be right, Priscilla."

"I wouldn't lie to you, Governor."

"No," he said. "I don't guess you would." He was silent for a moment. "Thank you. I appreciate your telling me."

"I'd be grateful if you said nothing about it."

"I won't," he said. "Unless I see a need. In any case, you'll be protected. I'll see to that."

SO FAR, FOURTEEN monuments had been found. This one was unique because it was the only one that was arguably a self-portrait. The creature's hands, each with six digits, reached for Saturn. That this was what the sculptor had looked like was established when the Steinitz expedition matched the prints on the ground with the statue's feet.

"Governor," said Devlin, "if you can move over a bit more and look up at the head, I'd like to get some more shots."

McGruder waved him off. "We have plenty of time to take pictures, Al. Let it go for now." He turned back to the monument. "It's magnificent," he said.

Priscilla looked away from the figure, out across the plain, frozen and white and scarred with a few small craters. The landscape ascended gradually toward a series of ridges, outlined in the pale light of the giant world. Saturn's rings were tilted forward, a brilliant panorama of greens and blues, sliced off sharply by the planetary shadow.

Saturn was just above the hills. It would still be there when another twenty thousand years had passed, and Priscilla's distant descendants were standing out here. She wondered where mankind would be then. Spread across the stars? Or would everybody instead be hanging out back on the home world watching talk shows? And maybe laughing at people who claimed we'd once walked on the Moon.

THEY WERE STILL taking pictures when Michael pressed a hand to his ear, listening to something. He nodded a couple of times. Then she heard his voice: "Governor, we're being ordered home. Immediately."

McGruder turned and stared at the agent. "Why?" he demanded.

"There's a threat."

"How the hell can anybody threaten us out here?"

"Not here, sir. Apparently there's a credible threat to destroy the Wheel. They want us to start back without delay. To go directly to Reagan. They're evacuating the space station."

"Okay," said Vesta, "let's move."

McGruder laughed. "Hold on. We come all the way out to Saturn, and we get ten minutes? Let's just relax. I'm not finished yet."

Priscilla's link chimed. Yoshie's voice: *"Priscilla, we're evacuating the Wheel. Bomb threat. We need the* Thompson *to help. Please get back here as quickly as you can. But take*

your passengers to Reagan first. Make all possible haste."
The message was, of course, already well over an hour old.

She acknowledged, then switched back to Michael. "You have any details?"

"Negative, Priscilla."

"Okay," she said. "Governor, I guess we're ready when you are."

THE MILES CONOVER SHOW
(The Science Channel—Guest: Howard Broderick)

MILES: Howard, what is your response to this latest threat?

HOWARD: I don't see that we have a reasonable option, Miles. You're not suggesting, I hope, that we should give in to these lunatics?

MILES: Bear with me, but I don't see what's so important about a terraforming operation light-years away that we should be willing to risk so much for it. Marcus Barnes was on the show yesterday, and he maintains that we're only a few years away from developing the technology to do this without harming anything.

HOWARD: You're suggesting we just shut everything down? That we cave in to these nut jobs? Do you have any idea what that will do to the colonists who are already planning to move out and claim these worlds for humanity? Or what it would cost? And if we were to do that, and the next time somebody got upset about some corporate or government policy, do they just threaten to blow up the Wheel to get their way? Is that the kind of precedent you want to set?

IVY: Mr. Broderick, I can't help noticing you're not on the Wheel today.

HOWARD: That's correct, Ivy. I'm attending a Seattle convention, where I am the guest of honor. Consequently, as much as I would have liked to remain

up there, I had no choice. I do not think, in any
case, there's any real danger. Security on the
space station is solid. I'm not worried, and I expect to be returning as soon as the convention is
over. If you'd like, Kosmik would be happy to have
you come up and join us for a few days. At our
expense.

Chapter 51

EMOTIONS WERE MIXED as the *Venture* left Orfano. Samantha sat with Jake on the bridge, watching the fading image of the dark planet on the auxiliary screen. A sad smile played on her lips. "Can't believe it," she said. "An intelligent life-form unlike anything we've seen. And we're leaving it behind."

"It's the right call," said Jake.

"I know. Thing like that: We don't know how much patience it has. I didn't want to push it. And when we get home, nobody's going to buy the story."

"Will you come back again at some point?"

"I'd like to say no. But I don't see how we can avoid it in the long run. Eventually, there'll have to be another mission. I'm just not comfortable with the idea."

"You know what makes no sense?" said Jake. "Something alone like that for possibly millions of years. You'd think it would welcome some company."

"I suppose," she said. "Though I guess we shouldn't expect much in the way of social skills."

When Jake announced they were five minutes from entering Barber space, he heard Denise whisper a soft good-bye.

Tony broke out his violin and played a few mournful notes. Everyone laughed, but the laughter was artificial.

Then the stars were gone.

THE MOOD DURING the flight home was different from what it had been on the way out. The casual conversations about politics and science went away; the general lightheartedness was not to be found. They had succeeded, at least in their own minds, in establishing the existence of a sentient being. Or beings. And they'd even made contact, after a fashion. But, as Mary put it, "Who would have thought we could have done all that and still failed?"

The presence on that world became the sole topic of conversation. Where does it get its energy? What would it have done if we'd stayed? Obviously, it was empathetic, but did it have any curiosity at all about us? Was it there when Orfano was torn away from its sun? Was the superdense object a remnant of that event?

"We've always assumed," said Denise, "that if a living world got expelled from the planetary system, everything would die. But here's a possible exception. And if it *was* there at the time, what must it have been like watching the sun grow smaller and dimmer every day?"

"It probably doesn't have eyes," said Tony. "Maybe it just felt the cold coming on."

That led to a discussion of senses.

And so it went.

BY MORNING, THE shock of the experience had, to a degree, worn off. They still talked about nothing else, but the conversation took a lighter tone. Since the presence had responded to Jake's projections, Samantha argued, communication seemed possible. "Maybe we could get it to say hello. And eventually get answers to some of these questions."

"Like how long it had been there?" asked Jake.

"Or," said Tony, "how it brought the lander down."

"That would be easy enough to explain," said Mary, "if we really are talking about a sentient atmosphere. A thing like that could lift pretty much anything it wanted."

Denise smiled. "Do you think it could tell us how long it had been there?"

"Sure," said Samantha. "Why not?"

"I don't know. How would it measure time?"

Tony had an answer for that one: "Maybe by counting Orfano's rotations."

"You think," said Mary, "it's been counting?"

"I'm kidding. But it might be aware of changes in the positions of stars."

"Whatever," said Jake. "It doesn't seem as if it would have much else to do."

"Except reshape mountains." Denise frowned. "I feel sorry for it." Nobody responded, so she continued: "We should give it a name."

"The Omnivore," said Brandon.

Samantha shook her head. "I don't think we should use anything that has 'the' in front of it. That makes it sound like a monster."

Tony laughed. "How about Herman?"

"Is it a male?" asked Mary.

"That's a point," said Samantha. "We need something sexually neutral."

Brandon grinned. "Windy."

THEY'D BE MAKING their jump into the solar system a couple hours before midnight.

As the time approached, Samantha came onto the bridge and looked down at the right-hand seat. "Mind?"

"No. Of course not."

"Jake, I just wanted to say thanks. This has been an odd mission, the goofiest I've ever been on. We've got some major questions remaining. But we wouldn't have gotten anywhere without you."

"I was glad to help," he said. "Truth is, I wouldn't have missed it. Orfano's been a whole new experience for me."

The others were in the passenger cabin, belting down.

"Two minutes," said Lily.

"Are you going back to Virginia?" Samantha asked.

"I don't know."

"We'd like to have you at the Academy. This discovery will bring in some extra funding. I expect we'll be expanding our operations. If that happens, we're going to be looking for another pilot."

"I appreciate the offer, Samantha. Let me know if it develops, okay? And let's see how it goes."

The engines began to pick up, signaling that the transition to normal space was beginning. Gradually, the mist swirling around the ship faded, and stars broke through. And the Moon and Earth.

"JAKE," SAID LILY, "we are approximately six hundred thousand kilometers out. Estimated time to Union: twenty-two hours."

Jake switched on the allcom. "Okay, guys, we're approaching the station at about twenty thousand kilometers per hour. We're going to increase that a bit, but before we start, you have ten minutes to wander around. Then I'll need you belted down again." He opened a channel to the Wheel. "Ops," he said, "this is *Venture*. We are insystem and on our way."

There was laughter in the passenger cabin. And Tony started with his violin.

"*Venture.*" The response from the Wheel. "*This is Ops. We have you logged in. Wait one. The chief of the watch wants to speak with you. Hold, please.*"

Jake frowned, wondering what that was about.

Another voice took over, a baritone that he recognized. "*Jake, this is Morgan. Do not approach the station. We want you to use your lander to take your passengers directly to the Reagan terminal. Stay away from the Wheel. When they're safely down, come back to us. We're under what the FBI is calling a viable threat. Someone is saying they're going to destroy the station, and we're taking it seriously. The Feds aren't giving us many details. When your passengers are on the ground, we want you to come back and help with the evacuation. Over.*"

"Roger that," said Jake. "Terraforming again?"

He waited while the signal traveled to the station, and

Morgan's response came back. About fifteen seconds in all. *"That's what we're hearing. They're demanding Kosmik promise to stop."*

JAKE INFORMED HIS passengers, adjusted course, and began to accelerate. He talked to Reagan and set his arrival time, which would now be about thirteen hours. It would burn a lot of fuel, but that had become a minor consideration. Eventually, he was able to slip back into cruise. "You guys can go in and sack out now if you want," he said. "See you in the morning."

All but Samantha retired to their cabins. She was working on a project, or just reading. Jake wasn't sure, but he stayed on the bridge. Everything remained quiet. He kept a feeder circuit open to the station, so he would know if something happened. Two hours after midnight, Yoshie called. *"We're still here,"* she said, with a smile in her voice. *"The people in charge are beginning to think it's a false alarm. I hope they're right."*

"So do I, Yoshie."

Eventually, Jake fell asleep. Lily's blinker woke him. "Incoming message," she said. "It's from Alicia Conner. Addressed to *you*. Do you know her?"

"Yes," he said. His spirits rose. "I believe I've heard the name somewhere."

He heard the click as Lily switched to the transmission. Then Alicia's voice: *"Jake. Glad you're back. When you get a chance, let's talk. Okay?"*

Yes. By all means, Alicia. He closed his eyes and was still wearing a silly smile when Lily broke in again. "Got another one, Jake. From Lyda Bergen. Sounds as if the women are all very happy to have you back in town."

"From *who*?"

"Lyda Bergen."

"Who's it addressed to, Lily?"

"Actually, just to *Venture*."

He sighed. She was probably a reporter. "Okay. Let's hear what Lyda has to say."

Lily paused. Then, a scrambled voice, actually a series of

voices, said, *"Welcome, home,* Venture. *We, are, really, happy, to have you back, again."*

"That's it," said Lily.

It was unsettling: There were a lot of pauses, and the words were spoken by several different voices, both male and female. "Anything else?"

"That's it."

"Okay, Lily. Thanks."

Crank transmission. He called Samantha. "Hate to bother you."

"It's okay, Jake. What is it?"

"Does the name Lyda Bergen ring any bells with you?"

"No," she said. *"I don't know her. Why do you ask?"*

"Captain," said Lily.

"Yes?"

"Something strange is occurring."

"How do you mean, *strange*?" He became suddenly aware that the ship was changing course. It was a gradual shift, barely noticeable. But it was happening nonetheless.

"I no longer have access to some circuits. I am most concerned over those that control navigation."

Jake opened the allcom. "Everybody wake up and belt down. Let me know when you've complied."

Samantha again: *"Jake, what's going on?"*

"Not sure," he said. "The AI is experiencing a minor problem. Give me a minute." They were beginning to accelerate. He heard a couple of yelps from the passenger cabin, and somebody crashed against a bulkhead. But they all checked in. He turned back to Lily: "You have any idea what's going on?"

"No, Captain. But I think there is a connection with the message from Lyda. It may have contained a code of some sort."

"Somebody screwed around with you, Lily."

"Yes. I think that is exactly what happened. Somebody got into the software. A virus has been introduced, and I retain only partial control."

"Where are we going?" The acceleration was increasing. He was pinned in his chair, barely able to move.

"I'm not sure. We have also executed a modest course change."

"If present conditions hold, where would we go?"

"We would be headed for Pluto."

Pluto was shorthand for leaving the Earth-Moon system. "Lily, get me Ops."

He sat staring out at the distant Earth. And finally Ops responded. *"Go ahead, Venture."*

"Is Morgan available?"

Tony's voice from the passenger cabin: *"What's going on, Jake?"*

"Give me a couple of minutes, Tony. I'll get back to you."

Then Ops: *"Morgan's stepped away, Jake. This is Yoshie. What's wrong?"*

"The threat to destroy the station: Did you guys get any details?" When the answer came back, there was nothing that Jake hadn't already heard. "Yoshie," he said, "is there any information on the specific nature of the threat? Is it supposed to be a bomb?"

Another long wait. He could hear the voices in the passenger lounge. They were all unhappy.

Then Yoshie was back. *"We don't have anything specific, Jake. As far as I know, nobody actually mentioned a bomb."*

"Okay, Yoshie, thanks." He went back to the allcom: "We don't know yet precisely what's happened. Still trying to find out."

"I might be able to help," said Lily.

"Go ahead."

"We are back on a course that could take us to the station. Although we would run out of fuel well before an arrival."

"We're talking about a collision."

"Yes, if we keep moving at our present pace, we will be just past 220,000 kph when we exhaust our fuel. The appropriate way to control an impact would be to shut down the engines while some fuel remains, and have that available for any final course adjustment."

Damn. Had he still been aboard the *Baumbachner*, he could dump the fuel. But the newer ships, like the *Venture*, had no such provision.

He stared out at the stars. "Lily," he said, "we're the bomb."

THE MILES CONOVER SHOW
(The Science Channel—Guest: Biologist Janice Edward)

IVY: Janice, did you see the lost world story we now have from Samantha Campbell?

JANICE: Yes, I did. This is one that simply blows me away.

MILES: Why is that, Janice? I mean, even if they're right, and there *is* something alive out there on— what is it?—Orfano, it's not as if it's the first time we've found life outside the solar system.

JANICE: Miles, this one, if it turns out to be true, flies in the face of everything we thought we knew about life. I mean, the place is brutally cold. There's no sunlight and no water. If we weren't hearing this from Samantha Campbell, I wouldn't believe any part of it. And, of course, she admits the evidence they have will probably be seen by many as less than persuasive.

IVY: So what does it mean if they've got it right?

JANICE: I would say it means that life can take on more wildly different forms than we have ever thought possible. It looks as if there's an open door for anything. Now we know there could be living things swimming on Jupiter. Maybe an entire *galaxy* can be alive. I just don't know where the possibilities would stop.

Chapter 52

FOR THE SECOND time in a few days, Priscilla was forced to change her mind about someone she hadn't liked. Her respect for Governor McGruder had soared during the mission. He'd seemed genuinely interested in the monument, had been unable to take his eyes off Saturn, had reacted with dismay when the news from the station arrived. Moreover, he'd expressed his concern for *her* when he learned she'd be returning to Union after taking them to Reagan. "I wouldn't want to see us lose you," he said. "Can't they send someone else?"

"I'll be fine, Governor," she said. "But I appreciate your concern."

The transdimensional portion of the flight had taken little more time than the blink of an eye, and they'd surfaced only a few hours out. The Earth, Europe, Africa, and a substantial piece of Asia, filled the sky ahead. Immediately after she'd informed her passengers they were free to move around, McGruder appeared on the bridge and took the right-hand seat. "Priscilla," he said, keeping his voice low, "I have a suggestion."

"What's that, Governor?"

"It's going to take time for you to deliver us to Reagan,

then go back to Union. Why not go directly to the station, pick up as many people as we can accommodate, *then* head home?"

"Governor, that would put Vesta and Al and the Secret Service guys at risk."

"We've already talked. They have no problem."

"Cornelius and Michael are okay with it?"

He hesitated. "They don't want *me* doing it. But you know how it is."

"I'd have to run it by Frank."

McGruder frowned. "Who's Frank?"

"My boss."

"Okay. Ask him."

"Louie," she said, "get me a channel to Ops."

Yoshie responded: *"Go ahead,* Thompson.*"*

"Yoshie, can you patch me through to Frank?"

"Wait one, Priscilla."

It took a couple of minutes. In the meantime, McGruder thanked her for what she was doing. She was impressed that he was willing to take an unnecessary risk to get a handful of strangers off the Wheel early. It wasn't the sort of behavior she routinely expected from a politician. Then it occurred to her that, if he'd bypassed the station and gone home, had thought only of himself, it would almost certainly have been used against him in the campaign. Especially if a few people died because the bomb went off before they'd completed the evacuation. It might even destroy his chances.

Frank's voice broke through: *"Yes, Priscilla, go ahead."*

"The governor wants to go to the station first to pick up more evacuees."

"You mean before he leaves the ship?"

"Yes."

"You can't do that."

"You want to explain that to him?"

CORNELIUS WAS NOT happy. Priscilla heard raised voices as she made a course adjustment and headed for Union. His objections were logged and forwarded to the appropriate authority. Vesta and Devlin seemed somewhat nervous, but they raised no objection. And a few hours later, as they approached Union, McGruder dropped another bomb.

"Priscilla, we've been talking, and we're going to stay on the station until the evacuation has been completed."

"Governor," she said, "no. Absolutely not."

"Notify whoever needs to know."

"What are your Secret Service people saying?"

He smiled. "I think Cornelius is going to have a stroke. But they're going to stay, too. How many people can this thing carry?"

"Normally about ten. We can add a couple more in an emergency for a short flight."

"Good. Set it up for me, okay?"

"What about Vesta and Al?"

"They'll stay, too."

CORNELIUS WASN'T THE only person riding into stroke country. *"What the hell is going on out there?"* demanded Frank. *"We can't allow that."*

McGruder was still on the bridge. He signaled for the mike. "Frank," he said. "This is Andy McGruder. How's the evacuation going?"

"Slowly, Governor. We don't have the resources that we need."

"I'm beginning to realize that. Well, maybe if I can make it into the Oval Office, we can change things. Meantime, we *are* going to stay on at the station until the evacuation is complete. Priscilla informs me we can put between ten and twelve people into this ship. I'd appreciate it if you have them ready to go when we arrive."

"Governor, you can't—"

"Frank, I'm sure you have more important things to do than waste time arguing with me. Everyone here is on board with the idea. So please just make it happen." He smiled. *"Thompson,* over and out."

THEY DOCKED AT the station and began refueling. Priscilla said good-bye to the governor, to Vesta, who was beaming when she wasn't looking scared half to death, and to Devlin, who was first through the air lock and turned immediately to get pictures of McGruder coming out. They would, she realized, be all over the networks within ten minutes. She wished Michael and Cornelius luck, and they just shook their heads.

The governor took a long look at Priscilla. "I appreciate everything you've done. If I can ever return the favor, Hutch, please let me know."

She smiled at the name change. "Thanks, Governor," she said. "I hope everything works out for you."

"So do I."

"I have a question before you go."

"Go ahead."

"Would you have done this if you weren't running for president?"

He hesitated. "I don't know. I like to think I would have. I hope so."

Then they were gone, the governor, his aides, and the security guys. Moments later, a group of ten people carrying luggage arrived, with a tech. "Your passengers, Priscilla," the tech said.

SEVERAL OTHER PEOPLE showed up and also tried to board. But more guards appeared and kept them out of the tube. Priscilla returned to the ship, took her new passengers on board, closed the air lock, and invited everyone to spread out through the spacecraft. "Find a seat somewhere and belt down. We'll be leaving in a few minutes."

She took her own position on the bridge and ran through her check-off. Yoshie informed her that she was refueled and ready to go. She released the magnetics and began to move away from the dock. The launch doors opened. The last thing she saw before pulling away was a young woman out on the concourse watching the *Thompson*. She looked to be in tears.

"*Thompson, this is Yoshie. Your destination is the Brandenburg Terminal, in Berlin.*"

"Roger that," she said. "Do the passengers know?"

"*Negative. The decision's just been made. Berlin will probably not be the terminal of choice for them. But it gets you back here quickly, which is what we need right now. You are expected there, and arrangements are being made to move your passengers as necessary. There'll be no additional cost to them. Union out."*

THE PASSENGERS SPOKE several different languages. Priscilla relayed the destination by putting a map on the displays throughout the ship and marking Berlin. They understood it was a make-do operation, so they were not surprised they weren't going back to their home terminal. One of the men, a father with two kids at his side, told her in Spanish that it didn't matter, as long as they were off the station. Priscilla had no grasp of Spanish, but it would have been impossible to miss the message.

Two hours later she delivered her passengers to Brandenburg. Everybody thanked her and pretended they'd enjoyed the ride, but they were obviously relieved to get back onto solid ground. They refueled the lander, and within minutes she'd lifted off and was on her way back to the Wheel.

The call came in before she got clear of the atmosphere. *"Priscilla?"*

"I read you, Frank. I'm on my way."

"We need you to do something else first. The Venture's *back, but Jake is reporting a problem. We're not sure yet what it is, but he's lost control of the ship. He's accelerating, and he can't shut it down. We've already fed you his course information. We want you to get within range of him and stand by."*

"Okay. You think he might need an evacuation?"

"I'm not sure yet what we're looking at, Priscilla. By the way, you may not be able to do much in any case. He's moving too fast, coming in at two hundred thousand klicks at last count and still accelerating. Just get close, okay? If you can."

"Two hundred thousand?" she said. "That's crazy."

"Like I said, he's lost control."

"Okay." She didn't see what she could possibly do. But—"Louie, open a channel to the *Venture*."

JAKE DIDN'T SOUND happy. *"Acceleration's constant, Priscilla. It's taken over."*

"Frank says you're at two hundred thousand klicks."

"We're at two ten. And climbing."

"That's not good," she said. "I'm on my way."

"I don't see what you can do, Priscilla."

"I don't either. How much fuel do you have left?"

"At this rate, maybe twenty minutes. We expect the acceleration to shut down momentarily. We're almost out of fuel. Whatever's controlling the ship will want some left for last-minute adjustments."

"Last-minute adjustments to do *what*?"

"We think we're aimed at the station."

"What?"

"You heard me."

"Jake," she said, "how about putting everybody on the lander? Get out of the ship, and I can pick you up."

"Can't do it, Priscilla."

"Why not?"

"The acceleration's too much. Nobody can move. We're sucking a couple of gees. We'll have to wait until the acceleration stops."

"Okay. Then that's what we'll do. Just hang on. I'm headed your way. When the engines shut down, I'll catch up and take you off."

"If I'm right about this, the engines will shut down in about ten minutes. If they don't, there's no chance we'll ram the station, and we can stop worrying. But I don't expect that to happen."

"If they shut down, Jake, how long will we have before the *Venture* gets to the station?"

"A little over an hour."

A chill rippled through Priscilla's breast. "Okay," she said. "One problem at a time. First, you need to get off the *Venture*."

Louie was putting the tracking on the navigation display. The *Venture* and the *Thompson* were running on intersecting trajectories. But the *Venture* would go past her like the proverbial bat out of hell. "Jake, once you launch the lander, I'm going to need a couple of hours to catch up."

"Okay."

"Have you told Frank?"

"Of course."

"What's he saying?"

"You know how he is, Priscilla. Don't worry. Everything's under control. But he can't give me any answers. The only other ships they have available are the Baumbachner *and the* Copperhead. *The* Copperhead *left the station a half hour ago with a bunch of evacuees. The* Bomb *just unloaded some people in Toronto. It's on its way back, but it's not in a position to do anything either."*

"Jake, how could this happen?"

"Somebody screwed around with the AI. I have no way of knowing how they managed it. But they set up the system and made it vulnerable to a code. We got an odd message a little while after we surfaced. I'm pretty sure that's what triggered it. Welcome home. Glad to have you back. *Something like that. Signed* Lyda. *You know anybody named Lyda?"*

"Not anybody who'd be likely to commit mass murder, no." She had to fight down a growing sense of panic.

"As soon as I can move around, I'm going to see if I can disable something. Shut us down. If I can do that, we should be able to head off any collision."

The mechanical aspects of AIs and engine drives were a mystery to Priscilla. "You think you can?"

"I hope—"

A FEW MINUTES later, Frank was back. *"Priscilla,"* he said, *"set up for a conference with Jake."*

"Okay, Frank. Hold one, please."

Louie's comm lights blinked. "Got him, Priscilla," he said.

"All right," said Frank. *"We have three-hundred-plus people on the Wheel right now. So there are a lot of lives hanging on this. Jake, when your drive shuts down and you can move around again, I want you to get everyone off the* Venture. *Everybody goes into the lander. Then launch the thing. Do it as soon as you can."*

"Okay, Frank."

"Priscilla, you're going to have to intercept the Venture. *If we're lucky, and it runs past the point where it no longer presents a threat to the station, we'll let you know and you can forget it and go after the lander. Okay?*

"But if it shuts down at the wrong time, where we're still a potential target, I'm going to need you to take it out. We'll let you know if that becomes necessary. In the meantime, assume that it will. We've fed the information to your AI. It'll put you on the right trajectory."

Take out the *Venture*? She didn't have a cannon on board.

He's talking about ramming it.

"Louie," she said, "can we manage a collision? With the *Venture*?"

"Priscilla, it will be traveling at an extreme velocity when we intersect with it, approximately 220,000 kilometers. It will require precision."

"Then we can do it?"

"Yes. But I will have to make immediate course adjustments, and set for acceleration. You should go down and get into the lander while you can."

"Okay," she said. "I'll let you know as soon as I'm set, Louie."

She went through the hatch into the passenger cabin, got her gear, took a last look around, and went down the tube to the cargo bay. Frank came back: *"The* Baumbachner *has been given responsibility for picking up Jake's lander. So all you have to worry about, Priscilla, is the* Venture.*"*

"Who's in the Baumbachner?*"* asked Jake.

"Drake Peifer."

"Good," he said. *"You got the right guy. Priscilla, are you in your lander yet?"*

"I'm on my way."

"Priscilla," said Frank, *"if you have to launch, you should be able to make it into the Wheel on your own."*

Provided the Wheel is still there.

"We're coming up on fifteen minutes," said Jake. *"If they're actually targeting Union, this is the prime spot for a shutdown."*

"Okay," said Frank. *"Good luck, Jake."*

Priscilla was just arriving on the cargo deck. She climbed into the lander and shut the hatch. "Okay, Louie," she said, pulling the harness over her shoulders, "whenever you're ready."

"Very good, Priscilla. Course correction commencing." She was pushed back into the seat.

"Frank," said Jake, *"once the engines are off and I can move around, it might be possible to disable them. If the virus can't bring them back up, it won't be able to make the final adjustment. That should solve the problem."*

"Do it my way, Jake: When the engines cut off, just get everybody out of there. Okay? And leave the rest to Priscilla."

"Will do."

"All right. I'll see you both back here in a while. I hope. Priscilla, you are *in the lander, right?"*

"Yes, Frank," she said. *I figured out it might not be a good idea to stay on board.*

"By the way," said Frank, *"you might be interested in knowing that Kosmik has issued a statement agreeing to stop the terraforming and wait for the development of a less invasive methodology."*

Jake laughed. *"I always knew their hearts were in the right place."*

Priscilla had enjoyed being on the bridge of the *Sydney Thompson*. It was quieter than the other ships she'd ridden. And somehow smoother. This would have been the perfect vehicle for a casual flight with friends to Epsilon Eridani. It had been ideal for transporting the presidential candidate out to the Iapetus monument.

Now she would lose it.

"Priscilla." Jake again. *"Frank, our engines just shut down."*

LOUIE'S VOICE: "NINETEEN minutes to impact with the *Venture*."

Priscilla started to decompress the launch bay.

Jake would need about five minutes to get everyone inside the lander, another four minutes to get it launched.

The station was now visible through the *Thompson*'s scopes. At least, its lights were. It was just coming around the planetary rim. If this thing played out, next time around it would be in the crosshairs.

The blinkers representing the *Venture* and the *Thompson* on her navigation screen were gradually drawing together at about a sixty-degree angle. "Jake—?" she said.

"Should be out of here in just a couple more minutes."

She sat in the darkness. Louie announced that decompression was complete. "Open launch doors?" he asked.

"Yes."

Jake came back: *"Okay, Priscilla. They're gone."*

That brought another chill. *"They're* gone. What do you mean *they*? Jake, are you still on the *Venture*?"

"Priscilla, I don't know how this thing is programmed. It could do evasive action. Who knows? There are too many lives at stake. I have to try to shut the engines down so they can't be brought online."

"It might not matter, Jake. You could hit the station anyhow." She was close to screaming. "We're ten minutes away from the collision."

"I know."

"How the hell am I supposed to do this with you on board?"

"Don't worry about it. If I can shut it down, I'll know pretty quickly. If I can do that, I can get control of the ship again, we'll get out of your way, and the problem's solved."

"Jake—"

"Priscilla, I don't have time to argue. I backed off once. I'm not doing it again."

"Is that what this is about? You and Joshua Miller?"

SHE COULD HAVE ripped her seat from its moorings and thrown it against the bulkhead. Outside, the launch doors were open. "Louie," she said, "good-bye."

"Good-bye, Priscilla."

Jake's voice again. *"You out of there yet?"*

"Heading out now. How are you doing?"

"Probably not going to have enough time."

She thought about trying to talk him into getting some air tanks and leaving the ship. She could try to pick him up in the lander. But that wouldn't work. They were both moving too quickly, and in different directions. She'd never get to him before he ran out of air.

"Jake, this is crazy."

"Quiet, Priscilla. Please."

She was out of time. She took the lander out and turned

hard to starboard, watched the *Thompson* race ahead and dwindle quickly to a handful of lights.

She stayed off the radio. Did not want to distract Jake.

"We are safe," said the lander AI. "It is extremely unlikely we will be hit by any debris."

With a minute or so remaining, Jake's voice interrupted the silence. *"It wouldn't matter now if I did shut it down."*

"Jake—"

"Sorry, Priscilla," he said. *"I hope you're clear."*

"I'm clear."

"Good. Tell Alicia I got her message. Tell her I love her."

SHE NEVER REALLY *did* see the *Venture*. She was watching the *Thompson*'s lights fading into the night when, suddenly, there was a fiery eruption.

"Jake," she said, "are you there? Please?"

She listened. Then tried Louie.

Finally, Frank was on the circuit. *"Are you okay, Priscilla?"*

"I'm fine," she said.

PRISCILLA'S JOURNAL

(No entry this date)

Chapter 53

"HELLO." IT WAS a female voice. Priscilla, fighting back tears, couldn't place it. *"What happened? Is Jake okay?"*

"Who is this?"

"I'm Samantha Campbell. We're in the lander. What happened to Jake?"

"We lost him." Her voice broke up. The idiot. Dead to prove a point. Goddam it. At the other end, she heard screams.

"I told him not to do it," said Samantha. *"I told him. I told him."*

Priscilla was still trying to breathe.

"Priscilla, you there?"

"Yes," she said. "Are you guys okay?"

"We're okay. We even have some extra air tanks."

"Good." She was getting her voice under control. "Drake's on his way. He should be alongside in a few hours. Tell the AI you want to brake, but make sure everybody's locked in before you do."

"We got all that from Jake."

"Okay. You guys know how to use the Flickinger units, right?"

"Yes." She had to stop to blow her nose. *"It's no problem, Priscilla."*

"All right, Samantha. I'll see you back at Union."

"Where are you*?"*

"Pretty much the same place you are: in the middle of nowhere."

A CROWD WAS waiting when she arrived back at the Wheel. Mostly, they were WSA people, technicians and construction specialists, who knew what it would have meant had the *Venture* blasted into the space station at a quarter million kilometers per hour. There was applause when she climbed out of the lander. They lined up and shook her hand, said they were grateful she'd been out there, that they were sorry about Jake, that they'd never forget her. One young woman, whom she hadn't known and could never have identified later, simply said, "Thanks, Hutch."

A few others, assuming that was her name, picked it up. *"Incredible, Hutch."*

"Bravo zulu, Hutch." It was the old naval code for *well done*.

"Welcome back, Hutch. Thank God."

Frank and Patricia appeared from nowhere. They wore sad smiles. Patricia embraced her, the first time Priscilla could remember a show of affection from the director. "You all right?" she asked.

"More or less."

And then McGruder, with his aides and his Secret Service guys, showed up. "I can guess what you've been through," the candidate said, "but we owe you. We *all* do."

Eventually, she was able to ask Frank about Drake's effort to overtake the *Venture* lander.

"He's still in pursuit," Frank said. "But he's closing. Should reach them in a few hours."

THEY WATCHED FROM Patricia's office, munching cheese sticks and drinking coffee, as the *Baumbachner* closed on the hurtling lander, which had done as much braking as it could, but to little effect. It was still traveling at an outrageous velocity. "I didn't want to ask before," said Priscilla, "but how's

Drake going to get turned around again? He can't possibly have enough fuel left." Even a ship with a full tank couldn't accelerate for an hour and a half, then execute a U-turn and come back.

"We were worrying about that, too," said Patricia. "This was strictly a one-step-at-a-time operation. But Drake said it would be no problem."

"Oh," said Priscilla, as the lights came on. "He'll do a couple of *jumps*."

"Exactly," said Frank.

"That's clever." He wouldn't even have to leave the solar system. A jump out in any direction would reduce his speed to a standard 20,000 kph. Then he could turn around without using a ton of fuel and jump back in.

"Drake tells us that's standard operating procedure."

That was embarrassing. "We were about to do an exercise with runaway engines, but we got distracted. We never got back to it. But I should have known—"

"Don't worry about it, *Hutch*," said Patricia. "You're the hero of the hour." She got another squeeze from the boss.

"Do we have any idea who did this?" Priscilla asked.

"We're working on it. But no, so far, we haven't a clue. If the FBI has anything, they're keeping it to themselves."

"I assume Jake told you about the transmission from Lyda Bergen?"

"Yes," said Patricia.

"I'd think it would be easy enough to track down the source." Off-world transmissions carried a charge. "How was it paid for?"

"According to the record," said Patricia, "the caller *was* Lyda Bergen. The call was made from the Starbright. But the hotel has no record of anybody named Bergen staying there."

"That's no surprise. So who paid for it?"

"The hotel."

"Somebody rigged their AI."

Patricia nodded. "They don't have anyone at their service desk between midnight and 0700 hours. You check in with the AI."

"And," said Priscilla, "if you know what you're doing—"

"—You can go behind the counter and download a virus.

They'd never had a problem, so they seem to have dismissed any notion of a risk."

"All it would have taken," said Frank, "was a call to the *Venture* to trigger the virus."

Patricia nodded. "It looks as if it's another one of our techs. Somebody who had access to the *Venture*. We might have been wrong in assuming that Carlson was a loner." She looked tired. "The immediate question now is whether we can trust the crazies to accept Kosmik's promise that they'll quit."

"How many techs do we have who could manage something like this?" she asked.

The director exhaled. "Listen, Priscilla, why don't you let us handle this? You've been through enough."

"Okay." It didn't matter. She knew who it had been.

PRISCILLA'S JOURNAL

Impossible to believe he's gone. Have I really only known him a few months?

—March 7, 2196

Chapter 54

PRISCILLA LOOKED UP the Baxter Intelligence address. The general retreat from Union had slowed, but there would still have been no space for her on the shuttles for two days. She got a reluctant clearance from Frank to use the lander after telling him she needed some family time and agreeing to take some passengers with her. She delivered them to Heathrow Terminal, then traveled across the Atlantic to Chicago's O'Hare.

She rented a car and, by midmorning, having discarded six time zones from the Wheel, she was approaching De Kalb, a quiet university town of about one hundred thousand. Baxter Intelligence was located on the north side in an area of lush trees and oversized hedges. She pulled into the parking lot in front of a flat, gray, two-story building that would have housed maybe a dozen employees at most.

A chill wind was coming from the west as she got out of the car, crossed the lot, climbed two stone steps, and went inside. A guy probably in his midtwenties was seated behind a desk. He looked up at her and smiled. "Yes," he said. "What can I do for you?"

"I'd like to see Dr. Wolf, please."

He glanced at a pair of doors that opened into a passageway. "Do you have an appointment?"

"No. But I think she'll see me. My name's Hutchins."

He nodded. "One minute, please."

The walls were decorated with award certificates and advertising extracts testifying to the value of Baxter AIs. There were also photos of homes, trains, and large buildings presumably under their reliable care. "She'll be right down," he said. He glanced at the divan and chairs scattered around the room, but she indicated she was fine and remained on her feet.

Within a minute one of the twin doors opened, revealing a smiling Monika. The smile was tight, though. Almost pained. "Priscilla," she said, "how good to see you." She held the door open. "Come on in."

Priscilla followed her down a corridor. The woman had aged. Not that any gray streaks had appeared in that pristine black hair. Or lines in her near-classic features. But she had hardened somehow.

"How are you, Monika?" Priscilla asked.

Monika picked up the pace a bit. They passed several doors and stopped at an elevator. "I'm sure you can guess," she said. The elevator opened, and they got in and rode up to the second floor. "Are *you* okay?"

"Not really."

Monika nodded and led the way into her office. "I've looked forward to seeing you again, Priscilla." She turned and leaned back against a worktable, waiting for Priscilla to sit.

Again, she remained standing. "Why did you do it?"

"Do what?"

"You know what I mean."

She tried to look puzzled. "What are we talking about?"

"When we were coming back, in the *Venture*, you were angry."

"Well, sure. Of course I was. I'd just been through all that nonsense with Chappell."

"And—what was it?—Project Rainbow."

"Yes. It *was* frustrating."

"You were going to come back and raise hell about it. At least that's what you told me."

"I know."

"I never heard anything from you. Not a word."

She shrugged. "I guess I cooled down a bit."

"I guess. Then there was that morning in the *Venture*. When I got up early and walked in on you on the bridge. That was when you set it up, right? That's when you put the bug in the system."

Desperation was creeping into her eyes. "This is ridiculous. You can't prove any of this. The FBI's already talked to me."

"Really? Why?"

"They talked to everybody who had access to the *Venture*."

"They haven't talked to *me*."

"That's because they probably don't feel you have enough of a technical background to have rigged the AI."

"But *you* do."

"Of course I do. But that doesn't mean I did it."

"You know Jake Loomis died."

"Yes," she said. "I know." She lowered herself into one of the two armchairs. "I know. I was sorry to hear about Jake." She wiped her eyes. "I knew him."

"I killed him," said Priscilla.

"I heard how it happened. You did what you had to. But you didn't—"

"You have any idea what I'm living through right now? What I'm going to live with for the rest of my life?"

Her voice broke. "I'm sorry, Priscilla. I really am." Her eyes closed. "I'd thought—I thought those idiots at Kosmik would back off when I sent the original ultimatum to the FBI. How could they not have? Ignorant sons of bitches. There was no way they could not have realized it was a serious threat. I gave them too much information. I thought they'd concede, and it would never go as far as it did." She looked at Priscilla with horror. "You must hate me."

Priscilla stared back in silence.

"It was a trade, Priscilla. I wish I had it to do over. I'm sorry for Jake. And for you."

"Well, you're really being hard on yourself, aren't you? I'm happy to tell you, Monika, that it was a near thing for a lot of people."

"Ultimately," said Monika, "they were going to kill *everything* on Selika." Her fists were clenched, and she was beating the arms on the chair in a slow synchronicity. "But they've *stopped*. I didn't know any other way to force their hand."

"Monika, let me make one thing clear: Right now, I don't give a damn about the cause. You don't get to endanger innocent people no matter what your cause is. Worse, you and I killed a close friend. So if you're looking for sympathy—"

"I'm sorry to hear you say that, Priscilla. I'd thought you were better than that. But I understand. It's your fault, too, you know."

"I know."

"That's not what I mean. How can you believe I'd actually put several hundred people at risk? If you'd stayed out of it— If you'd just left things alone, the *Venture* would have veered off at the last minute. There's no way I would have done the things you're accusing me of." She began to sob. "There's no way."

A sense of rage and guilt swept through Priscilla.

"Turn me in if you want," Monika said. "You call it. But keep in mind who's really guilty here."

Priscilla got up, walked to the door, and opened it. "If I'd known who you were, I'd have left you on Selika."

Monika nodded. "I wish you had."

"Yeah. You can explain your feelings to the FBI."

Chapter 55

DRAKE PEIFER, IN the *Baumbachner*, needed another two days to get back to the Wheel. Priscilla had just finished conducting a tour and was on her way to her office when she received a call from Morgan White. *"They'll be here in about thirty minutes,"* he said. *"We thought you might like to come down and be the comm op who brings them in."*

She needed a boost. "Yes. Absolutely, Morgan. Should I dress for the occasion?"

"Just come as you are, beautiful. We'll have champagne for the occasion."

She called Frank's office and left a message letting him know where she was going. But he and Patricia were already at the operations center when she arrived. And, as usually happens when a ship comes in, a crowd of sightseers had shown up. Appropriately enough, Yoshie was the op on duty, but she got up and gave her seat to Priscilla. "Live mike," she said.

"*Starhawk*," she said. "Get ready to turn control over to us."

Drake laughed. *"Hi, Priscilla. Ready when you are."*

"How'd you know it was me?"

"Who else calls this happy wreck Starhawk?"

"I'll drink to that," said Morgan, looking at the champagne.

She pushed a white pad, and the launch doors began to open. The *Baumbachner* was visible on one of her screens, silhouetted against a full moon. She relayed the ship's ID information. "Okay, Drake," she said, "we'll take it."

"All yours, Ops," said Drake.

An amber lamp blinked on. He'd relinquished control. She transferred it over to the AI. And they watched as the ship made its final approach, slowed, and eased into the bay. All engines shut down, and it floated directly to delta dock, where the magnets took hold and locked it in place. An access tube reached out to it and connected with the air lock. Then, after a few seconds, the hatch opened, and they came out, Denise and Mary, Tony, Brandon, Samantha, and, finally, Drake.

They exited the tube, and everybody applauded. There were smiles, embraces, and laughter all around. Drake came over to Priscilla. "Good show, Hutch," he said. "I think you have a new career, if you want one." He saw people headed for the champagne and joined them.

"You know," said Denise, "you enjoy referring to *that*"— she indicated the *Baumbachner*—"as the *Starhawk*. But *you're* the starhawk. You and Drake and Preacher and Easy and the rest of them. And Jake—"

Morgan popped the cork.

Epilogue

ALICIA TOOK THE pass and flipped it to Dani, who drove for the basket. The defense closed on her, and she went for the jump. Somebody hit her arm, the ball popped into the air, and a whistle blew. "Personal foul, number eleven," said the referee. "Two shots."

The crowd began waving and clapping to encourage Dani as she stepped to the foul line. It was still early, only a few minutes into the second quarter with the Hawks down one.

Alicia took her position behind the circle, where it would be her job to make sure that if the Explorers got the ball, they wouldn't be able to charge down court and make an easy basket.

Dani made the first toss. Tie score, and the crowd applauded. The referee handed it back to Dani. Then the Explorers' coach called time-out. His team strolled back to the bench and huddled.

While she waited, Alicia looked around at the spectators. She hadn't realized how much it had meant to her when Jake was sitting up there with them, usually near midcourt. He always came early and usually got one of the seats behind the Hawks' bench. That had been a good time. She hadn't realized how much it had meant to her until suddenly he wasn't there anymore.

She didn't even know whether he'd received her last message, the one she'd sent when she saw that the *Venture* had returned from that Orfano place. *"When you get a chance, let's talk."* Marvelous.

She'd gotten in the habit, when they played at home, of surveying the stands. Of pretending that he might show up. That they might get one more evening together. *We never really appreciate what we have until it gets lost.*

Then the Explorers were jogging back to their positions. When they were in place, the referee blew his whistle and handed the ball to Dani. In that moment, just before Alicia's attention went back to the game, she saw a familiar face.

Not Jake's, of course.

She wasn't sure until, as she backed up on defense after a Hawks' field goal, she had time to look again. Six rows down from the top, near the center of the stands. An attractive woman with black hair. It was Priscilla Hutchins.

Their eyes met. Priscilla smiled and raised a hand. Alicia responded.

AT HALFTIME, PRISCILLA descended to court level. "It's really nice of you to come by, Priscilla," she said. "You don't live in this area, do you?"

"No." She laughed. "I'm from Jersey." They stood facing each other for a few moments. "I wanted to tell you how sorry I am about what happened to Jake."

"Thank you," she said. "I miss him."

"I have a message for you."

WHEN THE GAME was over, Alicia and Hutch went to the Roundhouse. Hutch didn't really care about the outcome of the game, and Alicia had already forgotten it.

NEWSDESK

November 6, 2196

MCGRUDER SWEEPS TO VICTORY
Wins 52 States

THE WASHINGTON POST EDITORIAL

Norman's campaign went underwater after his effort to paint McGruder's leaving the *Thompson* during the space-station incident as "a political stunt."

—November 7, 2196

Now available from
Jack McDevitt

COMING HOME

AN ALEX BENEDICT NOVEL

Thousands of years ago, artifacts of the early space age were lost to rising oceans and widespread turmoil. Antiquities dealer Alex Benedict and his pilot, Chase Kolpath, have gone to Earth to track them down. When the trail goes cold, they head back home to rescue the *Capella*, the interstellar transport that vanished eleven years earlier in a space/time warp.

Alex now finds his attention divided between finding the artifacts and anticipating the rescue of the *Capella*. As the deadline for the *Capella*'s reappearance draws near, Alex fears that the secret of the artifacts will be lost yet again. But Alex Benedict never forgets and never gives up—and another day will soon come around...

PRAISE FOR JACK MCDEVITT
AND THE ALEX BENEDICT NOVELS

"The logical heir to Isaac Asimov and Arthur C. Clarke."
—Stephen King, #1 *New York Times* bestselling author

"Jack McDevitt is a master of describing
otherworldly grandeur."
—*The Denver Post*

jackmcdevitt.com
facebook.com/AceRocBooks
penguin.com